Love on the Rebound

Aries Skye

WWW.BLACKODYSSEY.NET

Published by
BLACK ODYSSEY MEDIA

www.blackodyssey.net
Email: info@blackodyssey.net

This book is a work of fiction. Any references to events, real people, or real places are used fictitiously. Other names, characters, places, and events are products of the author's imagination, and any resemblance to actual events or places or persons, living or dead, is entirely coincidental.

LOVE ON THE REBOUND. Copyright © 2024 by ARIES SKYE

Library of Congress Control Number: 2023919164

First Trade Paperback Printing: December 2024
ISBN: 978-1-957950-20-4
ISBN: 978-1-957950-21-1 (e-book)

Cover Design by BlackEncryption Designs
To the extent that the image or images on the cover of this book depict a person or persons, such person or persons are merely models and are not intended to portray any character in the book.

All rights reserved. Black Odyssey Media, LLC | Dallas, TX.

This book or parts thereof may not be reproduced in any form, stored in a retrieval system, or transmitted in any form by any means—electronic, mechanical, photocopy, recording, or otherwise—without prior written permission of the publisher, excepting brief quotes or tags used in reviews, interviews, or complimentary promotion, and as permissible by United States of America copyright law.

10 9 8 7 6 5 4 3 2 1

Manufactured in the United States of America

Distributed by Kensington Publishing Corp.

Dear Reader,

I want to thank you immensely for supporting Black Odyssey Media and our ongoing efforts to spotlight the diverse narratives of blossoming and seasoned storytellers. With every manuscript we acquire, we believe that it took talent, discipline, and remarkable courage to construct that story, flesh out those characters, and prepare it for the world. Debut or seasoned, our authors are the real heroes and heroines in *OUR* story. For them, we are eternally grateful.

Whether you are new to Aries Skye or Black Odyssey Media, we hope that you are here to stay. Our goal is to make a lasting impact in the publishing landscape, one step at a time and one book at a time. We also welcome your feedback and kindly ask that you leave a review. For upcoming releases, announcements, submission guidelines, etc., please be sure to visit our website at www.blackodyssey.net or scan the QR code below. And remember, no matter where you are in your journey, the best of both worlds begins now!

Joyfully,

Shawanda Williams

Shawanda "N'Tyse" Williams
CEO & Founder, Black Odyssey Media, LLC

NAME GLOSSARY

This is how I pronounce the characters' names. It's meant to be lighthearted, fun, and entertaining, but feel free to skip past them and dive straight into the story.

ANGELA: *Like Davis. Like Bassett. Like Simmons.*

KINSTON: *It's KEN-ston. Not Kingston. The "G" is not silent. It is nonexistent.*

NIGEL: *It's NIGH-gel.*

NISSI: *It's KNEE-see. Like Jehovah Nissi. If church isn't your thing, like Niecy.*

KANNON: *It's KAY-none. Not CANNON. This pronunciation and spelling is also my prerogative. Nickname: Kann like Cane.*

AQUILA: *It's Ah-KEY-lah. Like Akeelah and the Bee. Not Ah-QUILL-lah. Nickname: Qui – Pronounced as "Key."*

JOEL: *It's JOE-EL. One word, one syllable.*

ROMAN: *It's Roman. Like the Empire.*

NIA: *It's KNEE-ah. Like Long.*

NISANTE: *It's KNEE-sun-tay. And probably the one that you needed most, lol.*

ABIGAIL: *It's Abigail.*

CIARA: *Like Russell Wilson's wife and Future's ex.*

ZACH: *It's short for Zachary.*

JAH: *Like Ja Rule without the Rule.*

LILAH: *LIE-lah. It's Lila with an "h."*

FAWN: *It's just how it's spelled, like Von with an F.*

JOVAN: *It's JOE-vaughn. Like Von. Not Van.*

KAIN: *Like Cain and Abel. Or a walking CANE. Just with a K.*

MERCEDES TOPAZ: *Mercedes like the luxury vehicle. Topaz like the jewel.*

ALYSSA: *Like Milano. And if you don't know her from Who's the Boss or Charmed, get it together.*

TYROD: *Like Taylor, if you're not into football, it's TIE-ROD.*

GIANNA: *It's GEE-Unna, like the famous chef.*

JOB: *JOE-OB from the Bible, not job like a workplace or Steve.*

TRIGGER WARNING:

This book is an emotional and spicy romance story that includes the following:
- Sex
- Cursing
- Violence
- Depression
- Bullying
- Weight Loss/Weight Gain
- Verbal Abuse
- Mentions of Miscarriage
- Coparenting Struggles
- and Real Life in General

If you are eighteen years and older and are sensitive to the subjects being explored in their rawest form, this may not be the book for you. If it is, please be sure to practice self-care because self-love is the first and best love. Be safe, sweethearts.

Prologue

ANGELA

*O*NE TIME FOR *the birthday chick! Two times for the birthday chick! Three times for the birthday chick! Fuck it up if it's your birthday, chick! Ayyyyeeee!"* My friends and I screamed the lyrics as I dropped down into a twerk move with money raining down on me.

It was a rare occasion for us to turn up like we were in college, but my thirtieth birthday was more than worth the reminiscent party days. I may not have been as agile on my feet as I was back then due to a few extra pounds of sexiness, but these wide hips, thick thighs, and curvy backside held all that extra lusciousness to sheer perfection tonight. All of my BBW beauty was on full display in this fitted one-strap jumpsuit, and I knew I looked amazing as I felt my rump spinning with the beat of the song. I may not have always been secure in my body—although many women often told me they'd kill for my body type—but tonight, my confidence was on a hundred thousand.

By now, we were at club number three, and I was two sheets to the wind as liquor sloshed around in my belly. My sister, Aquila, tapped out on me after the first club, claiming she had to get home to her boys. I understood that as the mother to a four-year-old and a two-year-old little boy, her mommy duties superseded everything, especially with a husband like hers. Joel

1

Oliver, restaurateur to the stars, always found a reason to be missing in action. Even knowing that his wife had planned to spend time with her sister on her birthday, he still didn't approve or change from his selfish antics. I loathed that man with every fiber of my soul. Hell, our entire family did. Truth be told, I believed Aquila did too, but until she faced the reality of her failing marriage head-on, there was nothing anyone could do about it but accept it. So, although I was perturbed, I hugged her tightly and gracefully allowed her to go about her merry way. At least I still had my other sister—my ride-or-die bish—our baby sister, Nissi.

That was . . . until the end of club number two.

She'd broken the news that she'd promised her fiancé, Kannon, she wouldn't be out too late. Since she'd been with me from seven that evening, and it was a little after midnight, she explained that she needed to get home to her man. If I didn't love those two together, I'd be highly upset, but they were so stinking cute as a couple, and I adored Kannon. They'd recently purchased a brand-new home and were living together. Although our parents weren't too excited about them shacking up, the fact that they were only three months away from exchanging nuptials soothed their concerns. I knew Nissi was caught up in all of her premarital bliss, so I overlooked the fact that she was also abandoning me to get home to her soon-to-be husband. I couldn't blame her. I knew she was about to do something that I only wished I could do—blow her back out. Because that Kannon Jordan was fine, and from the kissing and telling my sister provided us with, he was a certified Gold Medal Champion in bedroom sports. I gave her my blessing to leave as long as she promised to get some for me too. And you better know she made that promise!

Now, it was my best friend, Nia, me, and a few of our girls from our old college days holding down the party on this last stop . . . before we crashed and regretted everything the next day.

"Here's one more drink for you, my girl! Happy thirtieth birthday, babe!" Nia shouted over the blaring music, handing me a small fishbowl as our other girls cheered.

"Yassss, sis!" I screamed, taking the concoction. "What's in it?"

She shrugged. "The bartender said it's his specialty and to make sure you don't drive anywhere after you drink it."

Challenge accepted. I sipped, and the flavors that touched my palate were fruity and delicious. Reclaiming the straw with my lips, I gulped that beverage down, thinking that the bartender seriously needed to learn how to make stronger drinks. While it was the best-tasting mixed concoction I'd had, it lacked the powerful punch of alcohol.

"Girl, did you drink that entire fishbowl in one swig?" Nia asked as we danced while she looked on in amazement at my empty bowl.

"That drink was weak. You should get your money back."

She grabbed the glass and placed it on the bar as I turned back to the crowd to dance some more. The music turned up at least ten notches in the middle of slow grinding on one of my friends. I could've sworn everyone swarmed around me, and as another twerk song came on, I dropped down, busting it wide open on the dance floor. All kinds of men were slinging bills at me as I scooped them up and clipped them to the remaining cash pinned to my birthday button. When I finished putting on my performance, I saw a face staring and grinning at me that I hadn't seen in two years.

Nigel.

As much as I hated the sight of his face, he looked good. I'm lying. He was fine as hell. His rippling muscles bulged through the silk button-down, and he'd grown a goatee, making his deep chocolate tone appear even more godlike. I wouldn't dare look farther down than his chest, and shit, I didn't have to. Whether desired or undesired, his effect on me was potent from the current visual alone. If I could describe Nigel in one word, it'd simply be . . . *divine*. His mesmerizing eyes drew me in like a snake charmer, and as I sexily walked toward him, he seemed to move my way simultaneously, the laws of attraction connecting us like an invisible magnetic force field. When we met in front of each other, I fell into him, placing my hands on his sexy pecs.

"Hey, you," I cooed.

"*An—ge—la Richards.*" He stretched out my name, his sexy African accent on full display as he stood there looking like M'Baku, instantly making me want to indoctrinate myself into the Jabari tribe. #WakandaForever and ever. "It's good to see you, baby. Happy birthday."

My hands patted the rippling muscles of his broad chest before I walked my fingertips up to the base of his neck. "Aww, you remembered little me's birthday?"

His thousand-watt smile was on full display as he nodded. "How could I ever forget? I've only been knowing it now for nearly twenty years. Even if I didn't, I think the birthday button and birthday queen sash would be a dead giveaway."

I giggled, and my forehead dropped onto his chest. "You're so funny, Nigel. I've always loved that about you."

"And you're drunk."

Pouting, I wagged my finger. "Not drunk. Tipsy. Just *un poquito*," I said, squeezing my index and thumb together before I stumbled in my clear block heels, causing us to fall against the wall.

"Yeah, it's time for you to go home. Listen, I'll take you."

"Aww, you're so sweet. I came with my friends, though." When I tried to swing around to look for them, I almost lost my balance again.

"Yeah, you're done here," he said as he slowly guided me back toward Nia. Once we reached her, he whispered something to her.

Nia gazed at me in protest. "I don't think so, Nigel. We came together. We leave together."

Nigel's face contorted. "I'm perfectly capable of escorting Angela to her house."

Nia rolled her neck and her eyes. "And I don't trust you. It's not like you did a great job protecting my girl in the past. By the way, how's Leticia?"

"Go screw yourself, Nia," Nigel spat.

"Nah, that's what you were doing with Leticia. I got my girl." She tried to muscle me from Nigel's grip.

Too tipsy at this point to care, I shrugged at her. "It's okay, girl. He can take me home. I'll be fine."

"Angela!" she shrieked.

"I wanna go with Nigel," I whined.

Nia eyed me for the briefest of moments before her facial expression showed her forced concession. Her attitude was on full display as she pointed her finger into his face. "You better call me as soon as you drop her off, and that's *all* you better do. I'm not playing with you."

"Whatever, Nia," Nigel said, securing me in his embrace. "I'll call you."

"Bye." I wiggled my fingers at Nia, who shook her head at me for a reason my foggy brain couldn't comprehend.

As I left the club with Nigel, I waltzed and sang all the way to his G-Wagon. Inside, I sank into the comfortable leather seats as he got in on the driver's side and pulled off. The music pumping through the speakers had me completely enthralled as I sang and swayed to my heart's desire. That was . . . until I felt Nigel trying to get me out of his truck.

"Wait. What happened?" I asked groggily and confused.

"Two lyrics into a City Girls' song and you passed out in my truck. I know it's your birthday, but you should know not to get this plastered, Angela," he fussed as he helped me down.

"But it's my birthday," I sang as he helped me to the front door of my townhome.

Ignoring me, he slipped the wristlet off my arm and fished around for my keys as I stood on my front stoop, still dancing and singing as if I were in the club.

"You hoes be trippin' like I won't bat you in yo' shit!" The lyrics in my head boomed out of my mouth with extra loud emphasis. Nigel opened the door and spun around quickly to clasp his hand over my mouth, simultaneously catching me before I fell over in my heels.

"Let's get you inside before your neighbors call the cops. It's three in the morning."

His strong embrace engulfed me as he lifted me over the threshold and inside my place. Nigel secured me in his arms before kicking my door closed and locking it. All I could do was hang on for the ride as he carried me upstairs and placed me on the bed in my master bedroom. Nigel carefully removed my heels as I fell back in a fit of giggles for reasons unknown even to me.

"Nigel, I feel like I'm flying," I wailed, spreading my arms out and making pretend snow angel wings on top of my comforter.

"I'll bet, as high as you are off that fishbowl," he said, picking up my cell phone and scrolling to Nia's number. "She's home," he said after a few seconds. I heard Nia yelling something, but I couldn't understand what she said.

I sat up as Nigel said something back to her and ended the call. He stood there rubbing his temples, looking as sexy as ever. Just watching the defined physique of his back, his masculine thighs in those fitted slacks, and his corded biceps lit an inferno in my puss, reminding me just how long it'd been since she'd had a milk bath. My mind battled my body, competing to stop me from what I yearned for, but as I lifted from my seated position, it was clearly my body that won. Nissi wouldn't be the only one participating in the athletic competition tonight. I was about to Simone Biles in this bedroom. Before Nigel could turn to face me, I was on him, planting kisses against his back.

"Aaang." A strangled moan escaped as he stretched my nickname before turning to face me. "What are you doing?"

I lifted his shirt, planting soft kisses against his washboard abs before my lips parted and whispered, "Trying to have a little birthday sex." Before he could interrupt my mission, I glided my tongue to circle his nipples and licked.

"We can't—"

His words were muted when I gripped his growing erection. As I eyed him, massaging him through his slacks, he swallowed roughly, and his head fell backward—face to the ceiling in ecstasy. No words came from my mouth as I turned him, backed him to the bed, and pushed him onto it.

"Angela, we shouldn't do this." The words barely croaked out.

Ignoring him, I straddled him before bending to kiss him. There was no subtlety in my movements. Everything was urgent, as urgent as the need to douse the inferno blazing between my thighs. Our tongues danced as I hungrily lapped at his lips. He still tasted so good. By the time I lifted my lips from his lips, his resolve had dissipated. With excited enthusiasm, he unzipped my jumpsuit as we continued exploring the depths of each other's mouths. Moaning and groaning in familiar and excited anticipation, he took control, flipping me over on the bed and peeling the jumpsuit off me. Pantyless and braless, I lay before him as there had been no room for either in the painted-on outfit.

He sucked his teeth as he stared at me longingly. "Shit, Angela."

I scooted back on the bed, and my head was spinning, but I didn't care. I wanted Nigel. He leered before pulling his shirt over his head and pushing down his slacks and boxers. Once he'd kicked out of them, he reached to the nightstand and opened the bottom drawer, retrieving a condom.

"Still in the same place, I see," Nigel noted as he sheathed himself.

I bit my lip and nodded slightly before lying on my back. When Nigel climbed on top of me, he bent down and ravished my neck. He still knew exactly what ignited me. My legs opened as if they were on an automatic timer, and I could feel his thickness at the apex of my sex. It'd been so long since I'd been pleasured, and Nigel felt just right to me. Without warning, he flipped me on all fours.

"This is what you want?" he asked gruffly, pulling my hair until my head came back, and he smacked my round derriere. "Still got a luscious ass, I see."

"Yes, Nigel. I want you."

Those words from my lips crumbled the barrier between us. His thickness pushed into me with force and took my breath away. The pain that ripped through me was quickly replaced with pleasure as he rocked into me with skilled determination. Nigel felt so good, better than I remembered. Our sex sounds and grunts took me on a euphoric high, and I was floating. Floating so high, I could've sworn I'd ascended. My mind began to fog as I felt my climax nearing.

"Nigel," I whimpered, struggling to stay in this moment that felt too good to let go but yet too good to hold on.

"Mm-hmm. That's it," he growled, relentlessly pounding my core.

My only recourse was to tighten my hold on the sheets and hope I survived this merciless lashing. With his hands gripped about my waist, he slammed into me with a death stroke, and I shot off to the moon like a rocket. As I faded in and out of the abyss, I didn't remember anything except vague memories of some of the nastiest and most tantalizing sex I'd ever had in my life.

The light from the curtains filtered inside and beat against my eyelids so disrespectfully. In my sleepy haze, I slapped my hand against my face to stop the brightness. Not only was it intrusive, but it also was making my head feel as though it were splitting. That's what made me turn my face into my pillow, but I felt a warm body beside me and nearly jumped for dear life. Peering out through slitted eyes, I noticed the one man I swore off for the rest of my life lying stark-naked beside me.

"Nigel?" I mumbled to myself as I scooted away from him. Lifting the comforter, I saw that I was also naked, and that's when I realized that my six-hundred-dollar salon hairstyle was a hot mess on top of my head. "What did I do?" I asked softly. *Clearly, that drink from the bartender was some type of island specialty. Never again.*

Nigel stirred, and I had to admit that he was still as sexy as ever. Although I'd sworn this man to the pits of Hades, considering what obviously happened last night and how my emotions were churning right now, I guess I had decided to take up residence in the fiery cave with him. My mind began to flash back over last night with everything we had done, and I had to admit that despite my previous feelings, I wanted this man right here and now. We had to have worked some things out before working each other out. That's the only way I could assess him being in my bed. It's the only way I would've ever let him back in my bed.

Nigel—in my bed. Again. Wow. That was a turn of events I never expected, but how could I be surprised? We'd been lovers for years. He was my first love. He took my virginity. He was my fiancé. Ex-fiancé. A familiar giddiness came over me as I lay there watching the rise and fall of his chest and listening to his light snores. Nigel was back in my bed. Perhaps we could make things work this time and call me a simp, but I low-key wanted to work on us. I hated to admit it, but I'd missed him so much over the past two years. If he were down to give us another chance, I'd try. I'd try for him.

I snuggled up against him with a smile and lay my head on his chest. I couldn't believe he was back in my arms. Deep down, I always knew that Leticia was just a fun time. Nigel and I had a history. I was the one in his heart for the long term. I knew he couldn't stay away from me. I knew it.

"Shit, I fell asleep." I heard his deep tenor say as he attempted to clear his voice.

"It's okay, babe. You can rest, and I can make us some breakfast when we get up," I said as I snuggled against him.

"Rest? Breakfast?" He exhaled. "Angela, get up, please."

I sat up on my elbow and gazed at him. "What's wrong, Nigel?"

He sat up straight and looked at me as he beat his balled fist against his forehead. "I wasn't supposed to stay. I was supposed to drop you off and leave. I got caught up because you were kissing me, and the shit felt good—"

"And I can make you feel good again," I said teasingly.

He tossed the comforter from over him and stood up in all his naked glory. "No, you can't. I should've been stronger than this," he fussed at himself as he moved to put on his clothes.

"Wait, Nigel. I'm a little muddled from last night, but I'm sure we talked about this or had some sort of discussion ... didn't we?"

He whipped around, eying me with astonishment. "Talk? Outside of nasty talk? No." He scoffed, placing his hands on his waistline. "Do you even *remember* what happened?"

Shrugging, I sat up completely. "Not really."

He shook his head in angst. "Of course you don't." He turned to me, now fully clothed. "You were at the club last night. I popped up there because I was blowing off steam, and we ran into each other. You were extremely drunk, so I volunteered to bring you home against Nia's wishes, but you insisted. I was only going to make sure you were in the house and safe, but you started kissing me. My head wasn't in the right space, so I gave in, and we had sex, I mean, incredible sex, until the wee hours of the morning. I was supposed to leave, but I was exhausted, and I guess I passed out." He hit his head with an open palm. "Fuck."

I stared at him a moment. This wasn't the ideal situation for either of us. There was much that we needed to iron out, but the universe didn't make mistakes. For us to end up here on my birthday, after all we'd been through, made me feel as if what we had was worth the chance again.

"Well, Nigel, maybe it was a sign that we can start over. We've known each other for years, since the sixth grade. We were in love at one time. I was supposed to be your wife. Perhaps this is a sign that we can get it right this time."

He stared at me incredulously. And then laughed. Outright laughed in my face. "Angela, are you all right?" I eyed him in disbelief before he continued, "No, seriously. Because you know damn well I'm not trying to get back with you. I can't even believe I allowed myself to sleep with you."

His reaction stirred up deep-seated hurt I'd momentarily forgotten because of my genuine love for this man. The intensity of his words caused me to grip the comforter over my body. For years, even after our breakup, I kept trying to convince myself that the Nigel I knew growing up and loving most of my life was still there, just a bit misguided. I still held on to that belief—a belief that I had denied to others and was utterly ashamed to admit that I still held.

"Then why did you?" I spewed angrily.

"Because I was angry, horny, and you wanted it so damned bad!"

"Apparently, you wanted it too!"

He threw his hands up. "I'm still a man, Angela. Any man would take the opportunity for free and available sex, especially from someone he's had before."

My head cocked back at his sheer audacity. How *dare* he say that to me. We became best friends in the sixth grade after I beat up a boy for bullying him about his weight. He'd always been overweight until a few years ago. Back then, I'd befriended him and fell in love with him, even when he was at his highest weight of three hundred pounds at six feet tall, and I loved him unconditionally. He was my chocolate teddy bear. I accepted him when society rejected him because of his weight, and now, he stood there speaking to me as if I were the scum underneath the bottom of his Ferragamo slipper.

Before I could speak, he did. "Don't act surprised, Angela. You know how I feel. I made that known when I left. I can't be with a woman who doesn't take her health and body seriously. And from the looks of it, you've gained a few extra pounds since our breakup."

Tears threatened to well in my eyes, and I closed them to keep them from falling and to keep me from lunging out of the bed and choking the life out of him. He'd made the decision to lose weight and live a healthier lifestyle, and his way of encouraging me to take the journey with him was to insult my weight and eating habits. It pushed me further and further away from something that we could've embraced as a couple. As he soared, conquering his lifetime battle with weight gain, I sank further into depression at our crumbling relationship. I was losing not only my first love and lover but also my fiancé and my very best friend. Nigel became a man I didn't know right before my eyes.

"Yet, your self-righteous ass had no problem swimming in my guts last night to the point that all this BBW sexiness put you in a sleep coma!" My eyes flickered with flames at his insults. I put up with it in our relationship, but I wasn't tied down to him now and would not tolerate the disrespect. "Seems like you missed who could've been your wife!"

"No, I was angry with the wife I have!" His voice boomed in a roar.

The classic line is that time stood still. I'd always assumed it was a metaphor until those words spewed from his mouth. Nothing moved. Not even the air in my lungs. Literally, I was frozen until my system overloaded, and my body quaked at his words. My lips trembled, and this time, my voice shook at his revelation.

"Wi . . . wife?"

The expression in his eyes softened for the first time since he woke up beside me. He released a sigh and rubbed the nape of his neck nervously. "Leticia and I got married three months ago. Last night, we had a lovers' spat. I went out to get up under her skin, not to sleep with you. But it just . . . happened."

Wife. Married. Leticia. Nigel. Married. Leticia. The words swam in my head as I grasped to hold on to the little bit of sanity left. I couldn't formulate a word. Not a single solitary word. I knew if I did, the waterworks would follow, and I refused to allow him to see that. He'd taken so much from me. He wouldn't take that.

Rubbing his temples, he explained, "I know you didn't know, so I didn't say that to throw it in your face, but the facts are the facts."

The facts. *The facts?* Yeah, *now* I had my voice.

"Facts? I have some facts for you." I jumped out of the bed and flew in his face. "How about the fact that I always had your back since we were kids? I fought Tristan—"

"Because he picked on me because of my obesity, and you were my girlfriend when nobody wanted me, and you loved me even when I was physically at my worst. Yada. Yada. Yada. I've heard it all, Angela. It's a broken record that you repeated to guilt me into staying where I was not happy. *You don't turn me on!* Last night was just as much about me giving Leticia the middle finger as you being a horny drunk. But as I look at you with a cooler and regretful head, there's nothing there. I'm forever grateful for what you did back then, but it's in the past. We're in the present. And my future is with Leticia and *not* you. She's my wife, for Christ's sake. You gotta let that old crap go. The excuses are useless and tiring, and I'm over it. Been over it. Been over *you*."

The slap to his face was quick, fierce, and thunderous. It was my first time putting my hands on him, and I realized it was long overdue. As he straightened up and rubbed his jaw, he glared at me.

"Happy now?" he asked smugly.

"Get the hell out of my house! And I hope she stays with you and makes your life miserable for all the days of your doggish life!"

Grabbing his keys, he smirked and shook his head. "Better misery with her than to be seen with you."

"Get out!" I screamed.

"Gladly." He turned to leave and stopped at the threshold of my bedroom door. "Happy birthday, *big girl*." And with that, he slammed the door.

Those two words jolted me more than the slam of the door. *Big girl.* After all I'd done, even gifting him *my* treasure on *my* special day, he would insult me with words he knew would cut me to the core.

I slid to the carpeted floor in my naked glory at those words as I heard my front door slam as well. The tears I'd been withholding slid down my face, and I snatched the comforter off my bed, wrapping it around me. The dark hole I'd struggled to climb out of slowly sucked me back inside. My goal for my birthday had been accomplished in the wrong and worst way. I expected to wake up with regret from party-hopping and alcohol-binging. Only I woke up this morning filled with regret because the first day of my thirtieth year began just as the first day of my twenty-eighth, with Nigel walking out on me to be with his firm and fit sidepiece-now-turned-wife, Leticia.

Chapter One

ANGELA

*B*REATHE. JUST BREATHE. Internally, I coached myself. A shrill of laughter caused me to jump as it momentarily brought me back into the present. My eyes closed again as I leaned my forehead against the door, practicing the breathing techniques I'd learned years ago from my bestie, Nia, who was a registered nurse. Panic attacks had been my frequent visitor when my relationship with Nigel began to deteriorate. Since I refused to get counseling, Nia assisted me with information to help control what she'd deemed as panic attacks. They increased after Nigel and I had broken up, but I hadn't had one for the past year. Until today. My sister's wedding day.

Go figure. I didn't even have an attack the day that Nigel reopened the stab wound he'd placed in my heart and gutted me again. I spent the day having a pity party and then did what I did best and tossed myself into work. When Nissi approached me a couple of weeks later, asking me to help her with the last-minute preparations for the wedding, I jumped at the chance. Anything to keep my mind off Nigel and that last night of embarrassment. It worked. I'd been more efficient than the wedding planner, so much so that the planner asked me to assist her as well. They all viewed it as me being the greatest big sister in the history of weddings.

There was no doubt in my mind that I would've done the same things if I hadn't had that fiasco with Nigel. Still, I was positive that my immediate availability and over-extravagantness were spurred by my need to drown out the memories of that "one-night stupidity." Yes, stupidity. He'd have to have left money on the nightstand to be considered a "one-night stand." The way he left me, I'd rather have had him pay for the goodies instead of giving them up to him freely in a drunken haze. At least I could have gotten some kind of compensation out of the ordeal. Instead, all I was left with were broken memories of yesteryear and a wet, fat ass.

The sound of my name being called forced me to try to hurry and center myself. Inhaling and exhaling with my eyes closed, I found my center as my heart rate began to slow, the anxiety dissipated, and my labored breaths gradually returned to normal. Just as I heard a chorus of "Where's Angelas," I exhaled deeply and relaxed my shoulders before opening the restroom stall, washing my hands, and heading out the door.

As I walked into the dressing area, I saw a couple of people scurrying off to go in search of me and the panicked expression on Nissi's face, so I plastered the biggest smile and forged forward.

"Pull your skirts down. I'm right here." I fanned my hand in the air.

A flood of "thank Gods" and "where were yous" floated through the air as I approached Nissi and Aquila.

"Can't a woman go to the little girls' room? Geez."

The wedding planner and the two other bridesmaids, a couple of Kannon's cousins whom Nissi had met and fallen in love with during their courtship, stopped their search and finished beginning to prepare for the start of the ceremony. Ciara, Nissi's bestie, had just finished with makeup and was double-checking her appearance in the mirror.

I stood beaming in admiration of all the fodder happening for my baby sister, frabjous about her big moment. The day she married her king, Kannon Jordan. But we will forever know him as Mr. Fire and Rescue. Their love story was one for the ages. The two of them met when he'd rescued my sister from a faulty elevator at her job, and Nissi became smitten with him at first sight. With all the hustle and bustle surrounding the incident, she lost contact with Kannon, so our other sister, Aquila (and please let me be sure I give her all the credit for that idea), convinced her to put out a TikTok video asking others to help find him. See, my baby sis is a bit of a viral sensation originally due to the dances and skits her dental office would perform on the company TikTok page. However, Kannon's and her pages went ultraviral once the TikTok video went out to the masses and ultimately linked them back together. They had a rough patch for a while, simply trying to get it right to even be together. Admittedly, I loathed him at first when they were trying to figure it out, but once Kannon finally got his clutches on my baby sis, she was his, and he proved that he was hers. And now, she'd be his for life. I was overjoyed for them.

When I turned around, Nissi was eyeing me through the mirror, Aquila had her arms crossed, and our mother sat glaring at me.

"Whoa. Did I do something wrong?" I asked, eyebrows furrowed.

"Where were you?" Aquila asked in her most Aquila-esque tone.

"Using the restroom. I said that."

Tightening her folded arms, she rolled her neck. An obvious indicator that she did not believe me. "Are you *sure* you're all right? I've been asking you all day because you seem off. You better not be lying," Aquila pressured.

I was, in fact, lying, but now was not the time. This day was about Nissi and Kannon. Not me. "Girl, if you don't leave me alone. I've already told you I had to pee. Now, do you want to inspect the toilet for urine particles or not?"

Our mother audibly gasped and stood as the hairstylist tried to stifle a giggle while pinning the lace veil to Nissi's bridal headpiece. Our mother scornfully walked in between Aquila and me, shooting daggers that could've slayed us on the spot. It was enough to snap both of our over-thirty-year-old mouths closed.

"Aquila, don't harass your sister. Today is not the day for your bratty big-sister tirades." With a head nod, Aquila gracefully bowed out and went to sit on one of the sofas out of the way. Then my mother turned to me. "And you, such language, young lady. We are in the house of the Lord. Stop feeding into your sister, and allowing her to get up under your skin. Especially not today. Nissi is already trying to hold it together as is."

Complying, I lifted my hands in the air. "My bad, Mama. Aquila just grates me sometimes, but you're right. Today is not the day."

My mother eyed me for a moment, reading through my soul. That's one thing about her. We could lie to anybody else, but there was no lying to her.

She gripped my hand inside hers. "Are you *sure* you're all right?" she pleaded with her eyes for me to tell the truth.

"I'm fine." My voice echoed; however, the expression on my mother's face told me that my eyes told her a different story.

She straightened her posture, and her gaze pierced into me. She said reassuringly, "You know it's okay *not* to be okay. Even though it's your sister's day, it doesn't diminish the painful memories of this type of occasion." Her hand lightly caressed my cheek, and she finished, "You are *both* my daughters, and my responsibility is to make sure that you both make it through today."

Water pooled in my lids, threatening to fall, and I tried desperately to withhold them. If I released these droplets, an endless puddle would cascade from my aching heart. I couldn't afford that right now. As much as I needed the release, I had to do what my mother was attempting to do for me ... bear my own pain to see my baby sis through this day. Although I knew my mother meant well, I also knew that Nissi required her devotion more than me. I could not, and I would not be selfish about that fact.

With a sorrowful spirit, I bit back my true feelings and said, "I know, Mom, and I am good. We're here to celebrate Nissi and Kannon. Let's do that. She needs us."

My mom held my gaze for a beat before conceding by pulling me into her arms. Her embrace nearly shredded my façade, but I held out and simply relished in the brief moment I had to soothe the sting of the day—a day I never got a chance to experience. A day that Nigel and Leticia robbed me of—the day that deemed me the bridesmaid but never the bride.

The wedding planner called for everyone to take their places, and as everyone scurried to the exit to line up, I felt someone gently grasp my hand. When I turned around, it was Nissi. Our mother gazed back at us, but Nissi nodded her head, and our mother smiled before taking her exit with the rest of the ladies.

"Nissi—"

"Sis, let me say this," she interrupted me. When my eyes fell, she lifted my chin, and the warmest and most loving pair of eyes reflected back at me. "Thank you."

"You know you don't—"

"Not just for helping to plan my day, but for doing so unselfishly as I neglected how it could affect you. Thank you for burying your hurt feelings, your disappointments, and your regrets to stand in the gap for me. I know that you would've done this because you're my sister, but I'm not speaking to Angela, my bestie big sis. I'm speaking to Angela, the woman suffering in silence over the heartbreak of a bum-ass man."

I waved her remarks away with my hand. "That was years ago, Nissi."

"Nia told me what happened on your birthday."

An audible gasp escaped my lips before I could suck it back down my airway. I'd only confided in Nia about what happened with Nigel, and that was only because she'd come over to my house to check on me because of my drunken stupor when I left the club. Rather than ring my doorbell like a normal person, she used my hidden spare key. She stated she wanted to make sure I hadn't died of alcohol poisoning only to find me ready to meet my maker over my stupid decision. One look at me, and she knew without a doubt that Nigel had come in and messed up my world again. In order for her not to go run and blab my business to my sisters, I confessed my transgressions to her and thus began another round of healing to pull me out of the black hole that Nigel had thrust me back into. A hole that I was still desperately trying to climb out of. If I didn't know for sure that Nia always had my best interests at heart, I would John Wick her ass right out of my life—excommunicado. At the very least, I was going to strangle her just enough to make her pass out and then wake her up to continue being my best friend. Damn snitch.

"And don't be upset with her. She only told me a few days ago so I could ensure you were good leading up to today. We've all seen flashes of your pain, sis. I just want you to know that I appreciate all you do and that you don't have to suffer alone. We want to be here for you, just like you're there for everyone else."

That did it.

The tears I'd been withholding flooded my eyes, and a cascade of droplets slid down my face. She should be glad this makeup was waterproof; otherwise, she'd be late for her own nuptials. Nissi hurriedly reached to the vanity and grabbed a handkerchief so that I could blot my face before lovingly running her hand up and down my back in consolation.

"I'm so angry with myself, sis. I can't believe I was so dumb."

"No, Nigel is the dumb ass. You let him in because you have history and a huge heart; there's nothing wrong with that. You just gotta learn how to open it to the right person."

My eyes shot up to her because I knew exactly who she was referring to. I'd already suffered enough at the hands of Nigel; I'd be damned if I opened myself up to new heartbreak. At least Nigel's brand of BS was familiar. To travel that lane with a new guy, especially one that I was an hour away from being indefinitely connected to, was not an option.

"One Jordan man in our family is good enough, and speaking of it, I have to get you to the lineup before he and the entire venue think you've reneged on this marriage."

Nissi rolled her eyes before recapturing my hands. "Fine. I just want you to heal and, whenever you're ready with whomever that may be, to be open to the possibility of love again."

My eyebrows dipped in warm thanks as I gripped my sister's hands. I was so grateful for her. Out of the three of us, Nissi and I always had a special bond. She understood me without me having to explain myself, and I so loved her for that. Just like I appreciated her thanks and apology for today. Although I was a professional at shielding my emotions most times, her words were just the soothing balm I didn't know I needed.

Wrapping her in a gentle embrace, I whispered in her ear, "Thank you, Nissi. I love you ."

"Love you, roundtrip," she whispered back with our favorite ending.

"Am I walking you down the aisle today or not?" Our dad's voice boomed as he opened the door where we were still huddled. "The wedding planner was too scared to come to check, and Kannon looks as if he's going to pass out."

We giggled at our dad's antics. When I turned toward him, Nissi came into full view for our dad, and he audibly gasped, bouncing his eyes between the two of us before placing his hand over his heart. Tears gathered at his lids.

"I have the most beautiful daughters in the world," he quipped, making us giddy.

I nudged Nissi forward, and she met my dad as he placed his hands on her shoulders and peered at her. "Simply breathtaking. I don't know if I can let you go."

Nissi dabbed his eyes with a handkerchief and kissed his cheek. "You never have to. You're gaining a son, not losing a daughter."

"And he's gaining an ER bill if said son passes out. Now, let's go," I playfully broke up the sentimental banter.

My dad's boisterous laughter filled the room as Nissi headed out the door, and my dad wrapped his arm around my shoulder. "At least that Nigel bailed before I could kick his ass."

"You still can."

We cackled as we waltzed out the doors together to swap my sister from being Dr. Ms. Richards to Dr. Mrs. Jordan.

Chapter Two

ANGELA

"Now, who set me up to catch this thing?" I tossed an accusatory question to Nia and the group of women who'd participated in the bouquet toss.

I'd only stood and participated because it was protocol. I'd perched myself in the back of the crowded floor to ensure I didn't get anywhere near that bad luck charm. All those husband-hungry women were in the front, and somehow, my short little sister managed to hurl that bed of flowers over all their heads for it to land right in my face and fall into my hands. I even tried to toss it down but leave it to Nia and Aquila to yell out that I had it and couldn't give it away. When I looked at Nissi, she stood there with a Cheshire grin plastered on her face. Today was just filled with Benedict Arnolds, I see.

"It was fate." Nia shrugged.

"About as much fate as you telling my sister my business." Her dazzling light brown eyes bucked at my admission, and I smacked my lips at her. "Mm-hmm, ol' snitch."

She recoiled with her hands raised as if to say she was out of it. Nah, she was all *in* it. All up and through my good business. Between the snitching and this possible setup, that best friend contract was about to be up for cancellation.

"No one set you up for the bouquet toss. Honestly, it was fate," Sheena added, trying to help rescue Nia from the sinking sand.

My lips pursed, considering her words. Perhaps. But I knew our friends and family. It may not have been a complete setup, but they weren't pulling out the stops to circumvent it, either. Whatever. It was just a stupid tradition that meant absolutely nothing. The thunderous roar of men howling brought my attention back to the present, where the garter toss had just happened. When I turned to look, I saw Kinston standing there, victoriously holding the garter in his hand as the other men patted him on the shoulder. Immediately, my eyes darted to Nissi and back to Nia, who both suddenly pretended to be paying attention elsewhere—the treachery. When I returned my attention to the men, my eyes fell on Kinston, who was staring directly at me.

My God in heaven. Harold is his name. Kinston Jordan. That man was the reason sin was created. All six feet and more of him stood there dressed to the gods in his tailor-made, all-cream Bespoke tuxedo, looking like a bucket of decadence. His body seemed sculpted for the suit he wore. He was chiseled to utter perfection. His deep, dark, auburn eyes bore into me so intensely that my body threatened to combust. Everything about that man was a ten out of ten, from his shoulder-length, golden-brown dreadlocks, which were neatly pinned into a stylish man bun atop his head, to his lusciously thick but neatly trimmed mustache and beard, his radiant smile, and down to his custom LOLU cream and lavender suede loafers. He appeared as if he'd stepped right off the cover of *GQ* magazine. The man wasn't fine; he was whatever word that hadn't yet been created to describe the word fine.

I broke my torturous stare when the DJ shouted, "Okay, maid of honor and best man who caught the bouquet and garter, report to the dance floor. Any special requests?"

These hoes ain't loyal, my mind thought as I glanced over at Nissi, Aquila, and Nia huddled together like the get-fresh crew.

As I made my way to the dance floor, I cursed under my breath the entire time. I'd avoided Kinston this whole day except for the two times I had to interact with him: walking out of the church and our reception speech. Aside from that, I'd successfully managed to stay out of his clutches . . . only to be forced into interacting with him for this ridiculous dance.

"Anything in particular?" the DJ asked Kinston and me as we met at his booth.

Unable to remove my focus from my feet, I remained mute.

"Surprise us," Kinston's baritone voice sounded, causing me to shift my focus. When I chanced a glance in his direction, his orbs were peering intently at me. He held his massive hand out to me. "Shall we?"

I reluctantly placed my hand into his as he led me to the middle of the dance floor. I was prepared to do the middle school two-step to keep my distance away from this man, but he quickly rid my plans when he captured my waist and pulled me close to him, leaving no choice but for me to brace my hands against his broad chest. *Emmanuel.* I mentally called out the earthly birth name because ain't no way my Lord and Savior Jesus Christ would subject me to such punishment. I didn't realize I was holding my breath until Kinston called out to me. Then I made the mistake of inhaling his masculine scent. *Father, take me now.*

I shot a fiery glare at the DJ as he began to play "Beauty" by Dru Hill. It was at that moment that I knew either the universe had a vendetta against me or my family and friends were some master manipulators because there was no way that I was stuck in this alternate reality.

"Now that we have a moment, why have you been avoiding me?" Kinston asked in a hushed tone.

"I haven't been avoiding you. I've been celebrating our siblings' big day."

He chuckled, and a slight smirk graced his face. "You've definitely been avoiding me, Angela. For over a year."

That was true, but I'd never admit it. Kinston has been interested in me for nearly as long as his brother and my sister were interested in each other. As luck would have it, he was the one-half owner of KinRo Fitness and Aquila's personal trainer. It wasn't until Nissi and I showed up at the gym with her one day that we found out that Kinston and Kannon were brothers. He'd recognized Nissi from TikTok and, within the same session, had expressed his desire to get to know me. I ran from his advances that day, and I've been running ever since.

"Kinston, I'm not looking for a relationship."

"So, that means you can't eat dinner or go to see a movie or have a friendly conversation?"

"That sounds a lot like relationship-type activities." My gaze fell away from him as I tried to gauge how soon this song was ending.

I felt the crook of his forefinger turning my chin so that we were facing each other. He tilted my chin upward, capturing me with his mesmerizing eyes. He was kryptonite.

"Beautiful, if you were in a relationship with me, there are other *activities* that we would be doing that would easily keep you preoccupied and superbly satisfied."

Lump meet throat. I tried my best to moisten the dryness that invaded my mouth by swallowing deeply before I shriveled up in this man's arms. He sighed, realizing my discomfort, and pulled me close to him without uttering another word. My head rested against him as he caressed and cocooned me from the outside world and my unspoken feelings. Emotions that I'd never felt before swirled between us at our closeness. I could hear the rapid and constant thump of his heart, and it seemed to mimic my own after a while. If I were being honest, I began to feel comfortable and relaxed, wrapped in his embrace; dare I say . . . safe? It left me feeling utterly befuddled because there was no way this man could make me feel these feelings of this magnitude simply from a dance. Yet, here I was feeling that shit.

As the song neared the end, it felt as if Kinston and I were the only ones there. An unfamiliar air of curiosity, possibilities, and lust simmered between us as I slowly eased my head upward to meet his stormy stare. It was as if the song crashed like a cymbal reverberating in our ears as Dru Hill sang, "*Cause you are wonderful. You're wonderful. I'm just dying to make you see. Anything you want inside your heart. You can find right here inside of me.*"

"Right here," Kinston affirmed with assertive assuredness.

We were lost in that moment when the applause of all the wedding guests forced me back into the current reality. It took a second for him to relinquish me from his hold, but when he did, I bolted away from the floor and him as if I were on the U.S. Olympic Track Team. Sensory overload had punched me in the gut, and it was all I could do to get away from that man.

"Angela." I heard him yell after me, but I refused to turn around.

Nia and Aquila found me in the ladies' restroom, and I only had one request.

"Please, get me out of here."

Chapter Three

KINSTON

THE BLARING OF my alarm startled me out of one of the most sensational wet dreams I'd ever had in my life. It was so vividly real that I had to lie there for a moment to fully understand that it was indeed a figment of my imagination. So intoxicating was the memory that I had to sit in reverie at my wanton thoughts.

I'd been in my gym after hours working out when the most beautiful and sexy woman strolled through the door, walking seductively toward me as she peeled off her workout clothing piece by piece. First, her towel. Toss. Next, her shoes. Toss. Then, her sports bra. Last, her gym shorts. Until all that stood before me was her bodacious naked body, leaving me completely captivated. Her glossy lips parted, asking me if I wanted her. I was so enamored with the lovely sight before me that my voice was stolen, and I could not formulate a sound. The bob of my head was my only recourse as I sat on the workout bench, paralyzed by the vision in front of me. My man below was on brick and ready to explore the curvaceous depths that gingerly approached me.

I quickly pulled down my compression tights before she straddled me and eased off my fitted tee. The intensity and heat radiating between us were reaching a fever pitch as our tongues lashed and tasted each other with hurried exploration. I wanted to beast out and feast on every morsel of her being, but she placed a manicured-tipped finger on my bruised lips and eased upward. My attention traveled southward as I watched with excited anticipation when she gripped my girth in her hand to align against her opening. My chest heaved up and down, awaiting the expectation of her warmth. Just as she was about to slide her creamy goodness on me, the Apple ringtone blared, forcing me out of my dream state into the real state. In this reality, there was no gym, no woman, and no sex. It was just me, alone in my Texas king-sized bed with a morning wood so taut that it could choke a horse. But even worse than waking up in this state was the realization that I couldn't seal the deal with the woman, even in my dreams. The woman? None other than Ms. Angela fucking Richards.

At least the dream was consistent, if nothing else. I'd been chasing behind Angela for over a year and hadn't even moved past first base. Scratch that. I'd have to be up to bat to *get* to first base. My black ass was still in the dugout screaming, "*Put me in, Coach.*" If it weren't for the endless amount of female attention I received at my gym and on social media, I'd think something was wrong with me because Angela dodged me like I was that annoying OG that popped up in those young girls' DMs talking about, "How you doing, Beautiful?" You'd think that I'd catch the hint and move on the way she continually swerved me, but she tugged at something down in the pit of my soul, and that made me press up every single damn time.

It'd been two weeks since the wedding when my baby brother married Angela's baby sister. Not even the magic of wedding bliss could win her over. When I saw that she'd caught the bouquet, I was determined to be the man to grab the garter. Otherwise, I would've been like the rest of the men beside me and moved as far away from that piece of garment as I possibly could. I knew the symbolic significance of catching it, but that aside, I needed to create a space to have some alone time with Angela. Because God knows she'd avoided me like I was a COVID variant throughout the entire wedding weekend madness.

When we shared the couple's dance after the bouquet and garter toss, I just knew that I'd finally won my chance to shoot my shot. We were both caught up in the moment, and I knew she felt the same electric energy that I felt. The intense staredown we held during the song when I confirmed Dru Hill's lyrics as the answer to Angela's burning question about us couldn't be mistaken. Before I could open my mouth to pull the trigger, she bolted like a rocket, leaving me calling after her backside. I figured she needed a minute, so I let her run off to gather herself, but Angela proved that Black girl magic was real because she straight disappeared on me after that. And I haven't seen her or talked to her since. My brother was only just now getting back from his honeymoon a few days ago, so I didn't bother him to give him some time to recuperate from jet lag and sex lag because, knowing my brother, he had Nissi pent up from the second they sat in the limo leaving the venue through the plane ride *back* to the States. If my dad was an example of how to love a woman, then Kannon was the carbon copy. He worshipped Nissi. But no cap, li'l sis deserved it because she loved my brother with her whole heart, and I loved them together. If they could just sprinkle a tad of whatever love potion they'd tapped into on me and Angela, then maybe I could join in on that feeling. I desired Angela so badly it literally pained me.

"Broooo," my baby brother whined when he answered the phone.

"That tone tells me you not meeting me at the gym this morning."

I heard a scoff on the other end and then a huff of air. "Nah, man. I gotta take a rain check on that. It's my last day off before I return to the station, and I need rest."

I couldn't help the chuckle that I released. "Then your ass should've been resting instead of blowing out your back."

"Fuck you, bro," he chortled. "I'ma stay in it every chance I get, believe that."

His banter was interrupted by what sounded like a light thud. Clearly, Nissi had overheard our brotherly teasing. I had to remember he was now a married man.

"Ouch, my bad, baby. It's just my brother," he said to my sister-in-love. "See, bro, you 'bout to get me in trouble. I'll holler at you later."

"My bad. Tell sis I said hello."

"A'ight. Love."

"Love."

The day at the gym had been hectic. I was already slightly drained between sanitizing, restocking supplies, processing paperwork, and my early-morning aerobics classes. My business partner and best friend, Roman Patterson, and I were working on constructing our second location of KinRo Fitness, which he was tending to while I held down the fort at our primary location. We were short-staffed because one of our receptionists was out on maternity leave, and the other one called in sick. Between me and another one of our trainers, we were manning the floor, the classes, and the front desk.

I'd just wrapped up the paperwork in time for one of my personal training sessions. This is one I'd been waiting for all day. My session with Aquila Oliver, Angela's older sister. It's wild how the universe brings situations full circle. Aquila Oliver had been my client for a year, and during that time, our siblings had met and had an interesting kindling over a TikTok that had gone viral. The entire time, neither of us knew that we were related for obvious reasons. Aquila was married, so she didn't share the same last name as Nissi, and they only vaguely resembled each other. Aquila had only seen one video of my brother and barely knew his name. It was insane how that entire fiasco was happening around us without knowing how closely the other was involved. The truth came out when Aquila invited her sisters to one of our sessions, and I recognized Nissi from the TikTok videos. Talk about awkward. During the time, Nissi and my brother were on the "outs," so it was a tad uncomfortable, to say the least. However, Kannon and Nissi's issues aside, my focus had landed on their middle sister, Angela. She was a sight to behold.

Li'l mama stood about five feet five inches tall and was stacked like a brick house. Many men couldn't appreciate a woman with extra inches in the middle, thick thighs, and ample ass. Well, maybe the ample ass they could appreciate, but by society's standards, Angela wasn't the modelesque type. Being a fitness instructor, most people assumed my ideal woman would be bone thin and muscular. But that simply wasn't true. Hell, I had enough muscles for both of us. I loved a woman with meat on her bones, soft and cuddly with baby-making curves and childbearing hips. A little fupa ain't never hurt nobody.

I'd always advocate for good health, but having those attributes didn't always equate to unhealthiness. Women, just like men, varied. There were plenty of women who outwardly appeared healthy because of their physique but exposed their bodies to all kinds of unhealthy toxins, foods, and drinks. On the other hand, a woman who carried a bit of weight because of genetics or stature could be one of the healthiest women in the world. Therefore, health had nothing to do with my preference. My degree in sports science and experience with nutrition and physical fitness qualified me to help anyone obtain and maintain a healthier lifestyle. Still, my primal urges wanted what I wanted . . . and that was Angela and all of her voluptuous lusciousness.

"Hey, hey, hey, almost brother-in-law! Go easy on your girl today. I have been trying to recoup since the wedding, so my regimen has been off," Aquila announced as she waltzed into the small fitness room where I was to prepare for our warm-ups.

"Man, go 'head on with that," I cackled at her playful nickname for me.

It was her way of teasing me for never being able to secure a date with Angela while my baby brother was able to land and marry Nissi. *Almost brother-in-law*. If the shit weren't so funny, I'd feel slighted because it was straight facts.

"My bad. Let me not get you riled up." She tossed her hands up in surrender. "You'll have me having to call an ambulance just to transport my weary body out of this place."

"Too late!" I queued the calming music so that we could begin.

She finished unrolling her mat and put her hands in the prayer pose. "What can I do to change your mind?"

Her playful inquiry made a lightbulb go off in my head as I placed my hands on my waist. She rolled her eyes when she saw the small simper grace my lips.

"Anything but that," she declared with a point of her finger.

"You don't even know what I was about to say," I pleaded my case.

"Not specifically, but I know it has something to do with Angela, and I refuse to get involved. Absolutely not. I don't care for my sisters to be all up in my business, so that's a 'no' for me, dawg," she said, mimicking Randy Jackson.

I tossed my hands up with frustration. "Come on, Aquila. I promise I don't want you to do anything that will cause a rift in your relationship with your sister. Just hear me out, please."

She pouted and kicked her foot. "If I don't, you're gonna work the hell out of me, aren't you?"

Laughing, I lightly tapped her shoulder. "You can handle a hundred planks."

Her face contorted as she waved her hands. "Eff that. What do you need me to do?"

Balling my fist in celebration, I said, "Just tell Angela that we have an unfinished conversation from our dance, and I'd like to continue it over a cup of coffee at Starbucks."

A sly smile spread across Aquila's face. "Okay, Mr. Jordan. Subtle yet incorporating her favorite place on earth. I like that." She pointed. "And pray tell, how did you know she loves Starbucks?"

Shrugging, I quipped, "I've been preparing for this day for over a year. At this point, the question should be what *don't* I know about Angela."

She high-fived me in excited exuberance. "I see you, almost brother-in-law!" I gave her the side-eye about the name, and she hurriedly apologized. "I'm sorry. Last time, I swear."

"Let's start before I change my mind about those planks," I joked, and we began our warm-up routine.

Chapter Four

ANGELA

ONE GLANCE AT my watch, and I knew my sisters would have my head. I was running thirty minutes late. I wished I had an acceptable reason for my tardiness, except I didn't. Nissi planned a lunch outing with Aquila and me so we could hear all about her honeymoon and catch up on each other's lives. It's not that I was opposed to hearing all the delicious details and watching the picturesque memories they'd made. But I hadn't spoken to Nissi since I ditched out of her reception, leaving Aquila and Nia to play defense. I assumed my sister was still upset with me since Aquila explained that she literally cursed about my premature exit in three different languages. Hell, I didn't even know the girl was bilingual. Aside from a group chat text informing us that she was back in the States, I hadn't spoken with her. So low-key, I was hiding. Scratch that. High-key.

After the dance with Kinston, the last iota of strength I had was zapped away. Between my botched reunion with Nigel and Kinston's incessant pressure, my emotions were in overdrive, and I needed a beat to breathe. Nia had taken me home and then returned to be my fill-in assistant as maid of honor, instantly causing me to forgive her previous snitching transgression. It was wrong to leave the reception and not see my sister and new brother-in-law off, but I could no longer place my needs on the back burner. I'd seen her through the wedding and all of the fanfare of the reception, so I'd hoped my early departure wasn't seen as a slight but rather a self-care necessity.

Closing the mirror on my sun visor after checking my makeup, I mused to myself, *Woman up, chick.*

Exiting my BMW X5, I smoothed out my creamsicle-colored fitted sundress and straightened the cropped jean jacket on my shoulders. Pulling my Versace shades over my eyes, I placed my clutch under my arm and strode to the restaurant with my head held high and a small fib on my tongue. Once inside, I spotted my sisters and made my way over to them.

"Hey, sissies!" I greeted gleefully as I bent down to hug Aquila first, then walked around to hug Nissi.

Immediately, Nissi tossed up her hand to block me. "Back up. I know this hug better come attached with an apology since I haven't seen you since you ditched my reception, and then you have the audacity to be late."

With a sad pout, I plopped in the chair between my sisters, placed my clutch on the hook underneath the table, and then turned my attention to Nissi. "I know. I know. It's just—"

Waving her hand to signal she didn't want to hear it, she halted my impending fib. "I smell the BS oozing off you before you even try to fake it to make it."

It took me thirty minutes to think of that good lie. That meant I had to switch up my antics because she knew me too well. My gaze roamed to Aquila, looking for an ally, but the smirk on her face as she sipped her water from the bottle (and never tap) told me I had none in her. Figures. Aquila might not run me over with the bus, but she wasn't above handing the driver the bus keys.

I released a harsh gust of air and admitted the truth. "I was late because I knew you were mad at me about the reception, and I was scared to face you."

Nissi rolled her eyes at me. "Mm-hmm."

Gently, I clasped her hands, pleading with her. "I'm sorry, sis. I let my emotions get the better of me, and I did the only thing I knew to do and bolted. You know I love you and Kannon with my whole heart. Please, forgive me."

She scoffed and sat back. "I'm such a wuss for you."

A smile crept on my lips. "So, does that mean you forgive me?"

"My drinks and this lunch are on you." She chastised me with a stern point of her finger.

"Done." I lifted my hands in acceptance.

"And I totally want that new Telfar bag we saw online three weeks ago."

I stretched my neck to ease the tension creeping at the base because she was going for the damn gusto, but I deserved this. "Okay, done."

"And—"

"Nissi," I shrieked.

She'd gotten an apology, a free lunch with drinks, and a designer bag. What more did she want—a blood oath? My goodness.

She relented grudgingly. "Fine. I guess that's enough."

"So, you forgive me?" I asked giddily.

With her lips pursed, she folded her arms and said with a roll of her neck, "I guess so."

"Ayyee," I bellowed, outstretching my arms. *"Come on. Bring it in. Come on. Twinkle, twinkle, baby. Twinkle, twinkle. Stop hating. Start participating,"* I giggled, quoting lines from our favorite Vince Vaughn movie.

Nissi's stoic expression turned into a crimson blush as she burst into gelastic cackles over my hilarity. "I can't stand you," she said as we embraced tightly.

"You still my bish?"

"Your best one," she playfully bantered back with me.

Aquila fanned off our silliness. "All right, the Rock and Kevin Hart. Now that y'all are best sisters again, can we order some food and get on with the honeymoon details?" Aquila interjected, side-eyeing us.

Leaning over, I patted her hand and giggled. "Do you need a Snickers?"

Nissi tried to stifle her own titters as Aquila shot us both a death stare. It'd always been this way. Aquila always played the Mother Hen role between my partner in crime, Nissi, and me. Yet, we loved one another immensely.

"No, but apparently, you wanted the Snickers bar that is attached to Kinston," Aquila quipped, taking another sip from her water. "*Boom.*"

My mouth fell agape as Nissi gasped and high-fived Aquila. Traitor. This might've been the first time in the history of my aliveness that Aquila had come for my jugular so harshly and swiftly that it left me speechless. Usually, I was the queen of clapbacks amongst our sister circle, but Aquila chop-sueyed my ass so fiercely that she proved why she wore the oldest sister's crown. I couldn't do anything but bow out. She added some jewels to her crown for that one.

My senses were replenished when I felt Nissi's hand lifting my chin. "Close your mouth, Ang. You deserved that one."

Shaking my head in amusement, I bowed my head to Aquila. "To-the fuck-uché, sis."

Just then, the waiter appeared and rescued me from an embarrassing conversation because I was sure that "Kinston" comment was about to launch an entire diatribe about my unexplored attraction for that man. Was I attracted to Kinston despite my hang-ups over Nigel? Yes. Hell yes. I was hurt and healing, *not* blind. If Nigel was divine, then Kinston was the entire Holy Trinity. He was the type of man who invented slow motion because whenever he entered a room, time stood still. A man that fine was dangerous to a woman's mental health. And don't let the sex be phenomenal. They might as well lock my nutty self up in the psych ward because I would be batshit crazy and proud. I was a "put-three-dollars-on-a-Powerball-quick-pick" type of person, not an "all-chips-on-red 37-bet-it-all" type. And that was Kinston. Someone you'd risk it all for just to keep the high of his presence. No, I was all good over in my quick-pick lottery lane.

We devoured our delicious lunch of oysters and crab dip with our selection of Prosecco while watching videos and pictures of Nissi and Kannon's honeymoon. In between, she had us teary-eyed at the stories she told about their adventures in and outside of the bedroom. If they weren't ready to procreate, then they both needed to be on birth control. With the way they were humping, Nissi would be having a basketball team full of baby Jordans.

"Well, sis, I can see why you needed the extra few days after the honeymoon," I teased before clasping her hand in mine. "But I'm so glad you all had a nice time. I absolutely adore you two."

Before Nissi could respond to me, Aquila offered similar sentiments. "Yes, you two are meant for each other." Exhaling, she sat back with a far-off glance in her eyes. "You give me such hope," she croaked, tossing back her glass of Prosecco in one gulp and then clearing her throat. "Anyway, that was a breathtaking destination."

Nissi and I glanced at each other knowingly. Joel. We hated that she was stuck in a dead-end marriage to that man, but Aquila was not the talkative type about her personal business, even with us. She preferred to share what she wanted us to know, and heaven forbid we pry. She would lock down tighter than airport security searching for contraband. Aquila and I loved each other with the same veracity as we fought with each other. All I wanted was for her happiness and positive mental health: her and my nephews. Joel was a disruptor of peace, and it was beyond time for peace to be still in that household. Either he needed to get his life together, or he could get his shit and go. If it were up to me, he'd be sliding his no-good tail right down memory lane, but since my sister was grown and it was her marriage, all any of us could do was bear it and pray she'd become just as tired of taking his load of crap as we were of seeing her take it.

Nissi was the first to address the elephant in the restaurant. Looking at Aquila with soft and sympathetic eyes, she touched her shoulder gently. "You know you can always talk to us about it—"

"Talk about what?" She shrugged nonchalantly with a nervous chortle dancing off her lips. "I promise I'm good."

Nissi leaned back, straightening the white linen napkin on her lap and eyeing me to intervene. Honestly, I didn't want to, not because I didn't care but because I knew the outcome. Nissi was Switzerland between the two of us. If she couldn't get Aquila to open up, I knew I wouldn't be successful. And selfishly, I was trying to dodge my own conversations about Nigel and Kinston, so I was trying to avoid diving into their personal business unless invited. After Nissi kicked my leg under the table, I decided to try because if she kicked me one more time, I would air this restaurant out and be on the hook for more Telfar bags to make up for it.

"Lah," I called out, using my childhood sobriquet for her because I couldn't pronounce her first name back then. "If you can't be real with your sisters, who can you be real with? We're here for one another. Tell us what's going on."

She scoffed and whipped her head around at me so fast I thought *I* had whiplash. "That's laughable coming from you. Like you told us about your little birthday tryst with Nigel, right?"

See what happens when I try to be Switzerland for once? I swiftly delivered a kick right back to Nissi because it was *her* fault that my business was getting laid bare. Despite my testiness with Aquila, I remained sangfroid about that guttersnipe because I knew she was only deflecting. Besides, I would not take the bait and have these two digging up my bones today.

With a hunch of my shoulders, I raised my hands and waved the white flag instead of retaliating. "You've got it, Aquila. We don't mean to intrude. Just know we're here."

The storm that had been brewing in her eyes at the anticipation of my tongue-lashing drifted into confusion and then pooled into regret as the realization sparked that I hadn't given her the response she'd expected. Her eyes closed, and a remorseful sigh emitted from her lips. "Ang, I was wrong, and I'm sorry."

Well, look at God. If I had known all these years that a little faux humbleness could get her to retreat and offer up an apology, I would've subscribed to this form of fuckery a long time ago. Still, I didn't gloat. I simply accepted it because I wouldn't dare press my luck. This win was worth basking in.

I embraced her in a side hug. "It's okay. I understand."

Pushing away from me, she quipped, "Who are you, and what have you done with my sister?"

I sucked my teeth. I knew my win wouldn't last.

"Amen!" Nissi bellowed, throwing up unholy hands. "Because I was about to ask the question if you didn't!"

"Whatever. I have a right to mature and understand when you two redirect to get a rise out of me."

Aquila snapped her fingers before wagging her pointer at me. "That's it. Right there. One redirection deserves another. You don't mind me deflecting because it, in turn, helps *you* to deflect. You're not slick, Angela."

Nissi's wide-eyed expression revealed she'd just caught on to Aquila's analogy. She bobbed her in agreement. "Mm-hmm. You don't want to talk about Kinston."

"Girl, please. I just don't want to discuss Nigel," I lied.

"Don't nobody care about Nigel—not even you. Because Nigel ain't the one who had you running up out of my wedding reception," Nissi assessed. "You know what I think?"

"What do you think, sis?" Aquila chimed in, just like the assistant bus driver she was.

"I think she wants to hide under the guise of her old feelings for Nigel so she doesn't have to speak about her repressed feelings for Kinston."

"I was with Nigel—"

"If it hadn't been for one drunken night, Nigel wouldn't have been on your radar. Sure, the whole married-to-Leticia situation was a low blow, but forget that dude. If you're honest with yourself, your decision to hide from us that dreadful night had more to do with your illogical choice to give that man your cookie after two years than it was that he had moved on. I mean because, truthfully, he moved on two years ago," Nissi explained, calling me out on my unspoken bluff.

For the most part, she was correct. However, finding out he had married his sidepiece on the anniversary date of our breakup and my birthday had been difficult to swallow. The side chicks weren't supposed to win. He was supposed to miss me and realize he made a mistake, and I was supposed to send him back to his horrid decision. Only my drunk and dumb soul wound up dicmatized, only to find out that *I* had now been the "side chick." The one who didn't win. The reverse wizardry left me dumbfounded and honestly . . . embarrassed. How do you lose as the fiancée *and* the sidepiece? And who'd willingly admit that? Not me. Not ever. The whole fiasco reinjured old wounds that took me a year to recover from, so, no, I didn't want ever to recant that ill-fated decision again.

"Regardless of why I ran out of there, the catastrophe with Nigel still weighs on me. That is why I had to get away from Kinston. I'm still battered and now, reinjured, from the foolishness with Nigel. I'm not ready to trudge that path with another man, especially not Kinston."

"Why the focus on Kinston?" Nissi probed.

"Because she wants that Snickers attached to him and a boatload of other perks that I'm *sure* he has," Aquila chimed in. "Just admit you're afraid so we can address it and hook you both up."

I fanned them both off, trying desperately to get off this subject. "Please. That man probably only wants one thing—"

"He does," Aquila intercepted my comment. "A date. And you should go."

"A *date*?" I repeated.

"Good. You heard me the first time I said it," Aquila said smartly. "Yes, a date."

"And how do you know this?" I asked, my curiosity piqued more than I wanted to share.

"Because he asked me to tell you," Aquila admitted. "I wasn't going to at first because I wanted to mind mine, but it's so obvious that you want to go out with this man. You're just running scared."

"And I agree," Nissi added. "That man has been after you since damn near the entire time Kannon and I met. A man who hasn't even made it to first base and keeps trying wants more than a little rumble in the jungle." She leaned over and squeezed my hands. "Give him a chance, sis."

"If I say I'll think about it, will you all change the channel because this day isn't even about me?"

They eyeballed each other briefly before offering, "Deal."

"Fine. I'll think about giving him a chance."

Nissi clapped her hands together once and switched the subject back to the original reason for our gathering: her honeymoon recap. It would be astonishing how quickly they moved on if I didn't know why. Once my stance changed from a permanent no to a possibility, they would be relentless until I moved that possibility to a yes. Yep, I have just been played. That was the true punishment for my dashing out of the wedding. Slick asses.

Chapter Five

ANGELA

"It's not *that* funny, Nia." I rolled my eyes at my best friend, who was in near stitches, as I reminisced about my lunch date with my sisters two weeks ago.

She wagged a finger at me before sipping her Passion Mule. "Actually, it is. They straight-up played you, and I love it."

"Every day, you get a little bit closer to me canceling this friendship contract," I snipped at her playfully behind an exaggerated eye roll.

Nia and I had been so busy these past couple of weeks that we hadn't seen each other and rarely spoke to each other. Therefore, I was game when she contacted me yesterday with the idea of a girls' day out. Her plan was to shop, head to the spa for some much-needed relaxation, and then round it out with a late-afternoon lunch. We'd scorched through our favorite stores and indulged in a glorious best friends' spa package treatment, where we enjoyed facial masques and an aromatherapy body massage. We rounded it out with a foot soak with foot Shiatsu. The combination of retail therapy mixed with the after-effects of the mellifluous music and the rejuvenating healing hands from my favorite masseuse left me in a beatific mood. The natural euphoria continued as we sat on the back patio with an oceanfront view at one of our favorite restaurants, replenishing our system with scrumptious appetizers of burrata caprese toast with avocado while sipping on our favorite spirits—Passion Mule and Luxury Paradise Martini. Such an elated mood had me feeling all chatty with my bestie.

My loose lips ran free with the recap, including the portion about Kinston, which had her doubled over in hysterics and threatening me to enforce the termination of a twenty-plus-year friendship. Normally, I wouldn't have dared to reiterate that portion of the conversation because, just like my sisters, Nia felt I should also give Kinston a chance. And what I *didn't* need was yet another amen choir selection on his behalf.

Finally calming her giggle box, Nia took a deep breath before saying, "Girl, listen. You know how I feel about you trying to move on. It's been time. Hell, half past time. And all I'm saying is getting over the hump with a man as fine Kinston Jordan is a problem I wish I had." She threw up her hands in surrender. "I'm just saying. There could be far worse options. At least his option comes with manners, muscles, and money."

"Ooh, facts," I said, tapping my chin with my finger in deep contemplation because I hadn't thought of it that way.

"Mm-hmm." She winked. "So, did you or he ever reach out since you claimed you'd think about giving him a chance? I'm sure Aquila sprinted to class to hand deliver *that* message."

Realization swept over me, and my eyes lowered because I knew she wouldn't believe my answer, but it was the gospel truth. "Well, you already know I did not," I informed her. "He did call about six days ago, but I was working late that day, so I missed the call." I placed my hand up to stop her interruption. "And before you chastise me, I didn't return his call because he didn't leave a message, and I honestly forgot about it until you just asked."

As suspected, Nia met my confession with a swift and firm side-eye, but I held my ground, never diverting my contact, so she knew I was serious.

She released a sigh before relenting. "I'll give you that because I know you have been working your tail off these past few weeks, but today is a new day. When you get home, return the phone call. The man isn't asking for love, marriage, and a baby in a baby carriage all in one day or even at all. You may go out and find that you're better off as friends. Or at least friends with an excellent benefits package. Either way, it's a win-win for you."

"You're right. Ugh. All three of y'all. Fine."

Nia squealed in delight, clapping her hands with a cheesy grin. "Does this free psychotherapy session I just dropped warrant a free meal because I kind of feel like I earned that?"

"For an *unsolicited* session, not on your life or mine," I joked as the waiter approached us. "One tab, please," I said, kissing my teeth as Nia steepled her hands in thanks.

After I paid the bill, we sat and chatted for a while longer before deciding to leave. As we made our way through the inside of the restaurant from the outside patio, my eyes grew wide as it became evident that we were about to cross paths with two men. With nowhere to run or hide, I braced myself for impact in three . . . two . . .

"Angela Richards," a low, sultry, baritone called out to me as our footsteps approached each other.

Impact.

"Kinston Jordan," I breathed out as my eyes fluttered upward to him, meeting his excited gaze.

Whatever else I was about to say vanished from memory as I drank him in. His Miami runway fashion was on full display today. The multicolored silk, short-sleeved, collared button-down clung to his upper body, showcasing his undeniable muscle mass. It was tucked into tan-colored, cropped chino pants that hugged his massive thighs. The look was topped off by leather Ferragamo slippers. One Cuban link chain dangled at the base of his neck, drawing attention to the tattoo playing peek-a-boo underneath while his wrist was adorned with a big-faced gold watch. His luscious beard was groomed to utter perfection, and his dreadlocks were pulled to the top of his head in a tight and neat man bun. My God. He took his sweet and precious time crafting this mighty specimen of a man.

Instinctively, my bottom lip curved into my mouth as I gnawed on the corner of my lip from his stunning presence. When my eyes finally rounded back to meet his, he held a seductive smirk on his face and a sexy glint in his deep, auburn orbs before he purposefully allowed them to roam over my body. Though I wore a simple, flowy sundress with bedazzled flip-flop sandals, my skin ignited under his gaze as if I wore a hundred layers of clothing. My throat ran dry, and I desperately wanted to scramble out of that restaurant before I took this man on somebody's table.

"Nia, good running into you again," a voice broke our trance.

It was Roman Patterson, Kinston's business partner. Apparently, when Kinston and I were coupled in our own universe, Roman and Nia exchanged pleasantries. We'd all met through Nissi and Kannon's wedding rehearsals, as Roman was also a groom's man.

Nia offered her hand to Roman with a gentle smile. "Hey, Roman. Nice to see you again as well."

From there, we all exchanged pleasantries before moving to the side and out of the pathway of other patrons.

"I tried to reach out to you," Kinston said, not even giving room for the nonessential small talk.

Smoothing my hand down the nape of my neck, I sighed. "I know. I meant to return your call, but work has been working these past few weeks. It's why Nia and I are out today, winding down from the stress."

His mouth formed the "O" as he ran his thumb and forefinger around his goatee and beard. "Well, look at fate." He winked at me and bit his bottom lip. "And opportunity."

I almost fainted.

Nia smirked slyly. "Yes, look at it." She softly nudged me.

My jaw twitched slightly as I held back the scathing glare I wanted to toss at my bestie. I was already drooling out of my mouth. *Could she make this lustful interaction any more obvious?* As soon as the thought entered my mind, I immediately scratched the musing because if anyone could make anything more apparent, it would be my bestie. I could only be grateful my sisters weren't here to multiply the shenanigans and cause me complete embarrassment.

Kinston's slight chortle drew my attention back to him as he swiped his thumb across his bottom lip.

Clearing my throat, I asked, "So, what brings you guys here today?" I scolded myself as soon as the question came out. *What kind of silly question is that?*

Kinston's eyebrow lifted, and Roman's snicker confirmed that I was seriously tanking on my attempt to stall the real conversation that Kinston wanted to have.

"Besides lunch, we had a business meeting," Kinston answered.

"Right." I pointed a finger at him. "I mean, we *are* in a restaurant, so you probably ate."

Take me now, Jesus. I slid my hand nervously down the nape of my neck again. I was a dual-degreed, independent, thirty-year-old woman wholly capable of fielding merger and acquisitions talks with the most powerful and elite businessmen nationwide. But in the presence of Kinston Jordan, I couldn't string together two words that didn't make me sound like a Fee-Fi-Fo-Fum blubbering idiot.

Moving closer to me, Kinston reached his hand out and brushed it down my arm. "Angela, we can make this easier for both of us and just—"

If this day couldn't get any more awkward, Nigel entered the restaurant with whom I'd come to know as Leticia, draped on his arm. As my horrendous fate would have it, the waitress led them straight toward us so it would be impossible for us to avoid seeing each other. Desperation kicked in, and just before our trains were set to collide, I thrust myself forward into Kinston, wrapping my arm around his waist.

"So where are we going next, baby?" I asked, peering up at Kinston just as Nigel and Leticia's approach landed directly in front of us.

"Angela?" Nigel queried as if he was trying to remember who I was.

I'll bet your dick knows me, I sneered internally. Two could play that game.

"Um, Nigel?" I returned his faux remembrance.

Nigel's glance bounced between Kinston and me. Whatever shock that Kinston must've had at my actions did not appear. This man's poker face was strong. Without a flinch, he gripped my waist, pressing me deeper into his side as if we were a couple.

"Heyyy," he drew out with a bit of uncertainty and curiosity lacing his tone. "I'm sorry, and you are?" Nigel extended his hand toward Kinston.

Intercepting, I hurriedly said, "Kinston, this is Nigel. Nigel, this is Kinston, my—"

"Boyfriend," Kinston interrupted. "I'm Angela's boyfriend." His tone was definitive as he shook Nigel's hand.

"Hey," Leticia intervened. "And I'm Leticia. Nigel's *wife*," she said poignantly with a death stare in my direction as she visibly gripped Nigel's upper arm closer.

Nigel patted her hand on his arm. "Ease up, babe."

It was evident she thought he was referring to the clutch she held on his bicep, but I knew Nigel like the curl pattern of the hairs on his chest. He was really trying to stop her from getting into a titty-fighting contest with me because he and I held the same shared secret. Her *husband* had been balls deep inside of me a mere two months ago. While I would never let that slip at this moment to protect my dignity and indiscretions, Nigel didn't know that. I was a spitfire, and if Kinston wasn't here, I would've lit a flame and burned that bish's entire world down ... just as she had done to me because turnabout was such fair play.

Instead, I politely smiled and did the second pettiest thing—snuggled against Kinston.

"Yes, we're here on a double date," I said, verbally cueing Nia and Roman that they'd better play along.

My girl. Like clockwork, Nia smiled at Roman easing close to him, and he followed suit by wrapping his arm around Nia's shoulder as if they were the perfect couple. Friendship contract extended.

Nigel's expression was stuck between perplexed and ... was that a hint of jealousy? A smirk grew on my face as I realized it was. He'd tried to keep it low-key, but I could still read the depths of that man's soul. He couldn't hide it from me. Not that I was trying to make him envious, but I would be a liar if I didn't say it felt good to knock him down a notch. Just because he didn't want all of this luscious sexiness didn't mean that others didn't. And having a man like Kinston Jordan be interested in me was enough to show Nigel that what he failed to appreciate was worshipped elsewhere.

Leticia's face scrunched as she pointed a finger between Kinston and Roman. "Don't I know you guys?" she asked as Nigel looked back at her. Then his eyebrows furrowed. She snapped her fingers and continued before either of them could answer. "That's right. You guys own KinRo Fitness. I used to attend Cami's spin class with my girlfriends until our schedules got crazy."

Roman bounced his head up and down. "That's right. I do remember you now. It was about ten of y'all."

"Right!" Leticia gushed and focused on Kinston. "You remember us, right?"

With the straightest and plainest expression on his face, Kinston shook his head. "Nah, can't say that I recall."

Slightly embarrassed, Leticia quipped, "Well, I'm sure it'll come back to you."

Kinston shrugged. "Maybe. We have a lot of clients, so . . ."

His voice trailed as if he was completely disinterested, and my insides were doing the Milly Rock in celebration. Her incessant pressure to be "remembered" by Kinston further proved how this attention-seeking, needy sidepiece could swoop in and finesse Nigel. It also proved that Nigel was the only dumb ass who fell for it because it was also abundantly clear that sis sought that attention from any attractive fitness head willing to pay attention. Good luck with that marriage when she got bored with him. But if he liked it, I loved it for him. It would serve Nigel precisely what he deserved.

"Is Angela one of your clients?" Nigel asked.

I bit my lip to quell the string of expletives that were about to spew from my mouth. To the untrained ear, his question may have seemed innocent enough, but because I knew him, I understood his question to be the backhanded insinuation I needed to lose weight. He didn't realize I had. The best weight I'd ever lost was all two hundred pounds of him. *How's that for my weight loss journey?*

"Heh," Kinston smoothed his beard. "Only if she wants to be." He pulled back, and pure seduction caressed my body from his piercing gaze. "There is absolutely nothing wrong with this physique—at all."

He licked his lips as his stare fell back into my eyes, causing a slight shiver to course through my entire being. It took all the energy I had to rip myself out of his trance and refocus on Nigel and Leticia, who both held the same mouth-gaping expression on their faces. My soul was satisfied by that alone.

Refocusing my gaze on Kinston briefly, I cooed, "Aww, babe."

In return, he ran the tip of his forefinger along my jawline and tenderly caressed my chin, staring at me with such adoration. "Time to go, baby."

As if I were a child obeying my parent, I turned to Nigel and Leticia without an ounce of hesitation and said, "Well, it was good seeing you two. We gotta run." Not even waiting for a formal goodbye, I lazily bid them ado, and we began walking out of the restaurant, arms interlaced at each other's waist while our friends fell in step behind us.

As soon as we reached the parking lot, out of the visibility of Nigel and Leticia, Kinston bent down and whispered in my ear, "I'm going to walk you to your car, and you're going to fill me in."

I didn't even argue. After what he'd done for me in that restaurant, I'd be Lucy and explain everything. Our friends didn't even need to be clued in. Nia and Roman hung back at Roman's truck as we proceeded to my car, which was only a few rows over.

As soon as we arrived at my vehicle, I leaned against the door, and Kinston stood in front of me, ready for this discussion.

"Talk to me," was his simple direction.

Taking a deep breath, I exhaled and folded my arms across my chest. "He's my ex."

"I gathered that much by your reaction." He nodded, folding his hands in front of him. "What is it about him being your ex that you don't want to tell me?"

I glanced away, suddenly embarrassed as I thought of the full story. How could I reveal the damning truth? It was already awkward enough that I thrust him into a fake relationship to save face. Tears of shame welled in my lids as I closed my eyes, trying to will them not to fall.

I felt my face being turned back toward Kinston when I realized he held my chin in the crook of his hand. Hurriedly, I swiped at the tears as my reddened orbs gazed into his. "Don't ever let a motherfucker tilt your tiara, baby. You were *born* a queen. Remember that."

Be still my heart. Kinston could ask me for anything at this moment, and I would give it to him. You want a date? Yes. You want some sex? Yes. Hell, you want a baby? A boy or a girl, I got you. Because he had me.

"Tell me."

"He ... ah ... he used to be grossly overweight, but then he started getting into the gym. When he became this fit and trim man, he decided I wasn't a good fit for him anymore, so he left me—for her."

"I see," Kinston said as he squinted his eyes. "So I was correct in assuming he has an issue with your body."

I could only nod my answer.

He winked at me and toyed with my fingers after he captured my hand. "Good thing I don't." He smiled, causing a blush to fill my cheeks. "That explains your hesitancy to go out with me. But real talk, Angela. Fuck him. I meant what I said to him in that restaurant. You're perfect, just as you are. To be honest, I ain't mad at him. His ignorance made space for me. I just need you to do the same."

My sister had been right back when Kannon was pursuing her. There was something about them Jordan boys. I didn't know if Kinston was about games, but tag me in player one.

Playfully, I rolled my eyes. "So you really meant what you said in the restaurant, huh?"

Slowly, he closed the gap between us. "Everything. About fate. About opportunity. About your physique. And," he leaned forward, placing his lips to my ear, "about being your boyfriend." He stood erect and gazed at me again with those intense orbs. "Go out with me so I can prove to you I'm a man of my word."

My breath was taken away, so all I could do was bob my head in agreement. But I'd be damned if Kinston wouldn't let this moment bypass us without my verbal assurance.

"Tell me."

"Yes," I crooned, the same way my pearl was crooning below. This man had my body and my mind in sensory overload.

He licked those gorgeous lips, chock full of excitement. "Finally," he mused. "When I hit your line, answer."

"Okay," was all I could muster.

Bending down, he planted the softest kiss on my forehead and lingered there. I gripped his forearms and willingly basked in the sentiment with him. My eyes closed as I relished in the feel, the touch, and the essence of him.

When we heard Roman clear his throat, we leisurely lifted out of our moment. The glint in his eyes nearly pummeled me. "We have to get out of here, but you take care, and I'll be in touch ... *soon.*"

When he turned to walk away, Roman tossed a knowing smirk and waved in my direction. I waved back just before Nia stepped into my view, cheesing at me with a goofy grin.

"I hate you." I rolled my eyes at her as I turned to get in my car.

"Hate and talk, bish," she cackled and slid into my passenger seat.

Chapter Six

KINSTON

I SLIPPED ON MY silk, all-black, button-down shirt as I ran down my mental checklist. Everything had to be perfect. My pops taught me that the first impression was the lasting one, but for Angela Richards, my first impression might also be the *last* one if I didn't get it right. Therefore, I ran through every check and balance to ensure that tonight's date would go off without a hitch or glitch.

After the restaurant incident, I tested the waters and called her to check on her that night. If I'm being honest, it was also to see if she'd actually answer. To my surprise, she did just as I'd requested. The next shock was that we fell into an easy conversation of random thoughts as time passed. There was no flirting and no expectations, just the casual comfort of enjoying each other's company. We debated, joked, and laughed well into the wee hours of the morning until I heard the faint sounds of her lulled breathing, indicating that she was dozing off. After that night, we spoke a couple of other times during the week, and the final time was when I called her to confirm our date. That's what made me nervous. Everything with Angela just flowed. There was no awkward phase. It felt too natural to be real. But my pops and Kannon had told me that when the right one came along, it just felt right. That's how it felt with Angela. And it'd felt like that since the moment I first laid eyes on her.

As I slipped on my classic Panerai watch, I smirked at how I'd eventually gotten here. Many men would've given up the chase of her by now, and I won't lie, I was pretty much nearing the end of my pursuit when the perfect coincidence fell into my lap. From my short interaction, I sensed that Nigel was every bit of the arrogant chump that Angela professed him to be, whom I could bet every dollar in my bank account deserved to be dragged. However, I appreciated the man. His mess-up was my come-up. Without him, I'd probably never have secured this precious time, so while it was middle fingers high to him, I meant it in the most grateful way.

My phone went off, and I chuckled as I swiped to answer the FaceTime call. "What's up, bro?"

"Just calling to check on you for your big night tonight. And to calm your overprepared ass down. Everything will go fine," Kannon assured, around a soft chuckle.

"Ain't nobody over here obsessing over details. I'm just . . ."

"Obsessing over the details," he finished.

I slid my hands down my face. I hated that he knew me so well.

"Listen, bro, Angela is easygoing. Just be you, and show her a nice time. Everyone can see that you guys are into each other, so all you have to do is not mess this up."

My eyes bulged as I shot a stern glare at him. "Bro, you not helping."

He burst out laughing, bobbing his head. "I'm just messing with you. You got this, bro, for real. Throw that Jordan charm on her. Gets them every time."

A smile crept onto my face. "Thanks, bro."

"Now, step back and let me see your fresh."

I placed my phone on my dresser and stepped back with my arms outstretched. Since I wanted to give Angela a different facet of me, I decided on a fitted dark grey polyester suit and Ferragamo slippers with my signature Cuban link and classic Panerai watch to polish the look. My dreads were freshly retouched and twisted down into one long ponytail. All I needed was a few splashes of my cologne, and I'd be all set.

"A'ight, bro, I see you. Outchea serving the Jordan legacy proud."

"'Preciate you, bro." I bowed my head, bringing steepled hands to my lips. "But listen, I have to get out of here so we're not late. Wish me luck."

"You're Kinston effin' Jordan. You don't need luck." He winked with a chuckle, causing the first confident smile to grace my lips.

"Now *that* helps. Love."

"Love," he repeated as we disconnected the call.

After I added a few sprays of Sauvage, I grabbed my car keys and wallet, gave myself the once-over, and headed to the door for my date with the lovely Angela Richards.

Aching. That's all I felt in my chest, and I couldn't understand why. Until I realized I'd stopped breathing. The sight of her had captivated my mind and stolen every ounce of air in my body. She was . . . Ravishing. Radiant. Regal. A goddess. The dress that adorned her gave empress vibes, showing off just enough to leave me salivating. Her short hair was in big curls that stopped just below her ears—a sort of modern Marilyn Monroe style. What I loved most about Angela was that she didn't need a whole face of makeup. She was simplistic in that way, allowing more of her natural beauty to shine through. Hell, she didn't need it. Women paid life savings to have the long lashes she'd been born with and the pouty lips that didn't require a single dose of Botox.

And that ass that protruded through the fabric of her dress was BBL-worthy without the BBL. She was already bestowed with everything that women desired, and I had the distinct pleasure of having her on my arm tonight. I owed God a few good tithes and offerings for this blessing.

"Do I look that bad?" she asked coyly, brushing a loose curl behind her ear.

That's when it dawned on me that I'd been standing there staring at her and not inhaling air. Breath finally found its way into my lungs, and I exhaled before fiercely shaking my head.

"No, no, no. You're ... you're ... *breathtaking*."

Her cheeks flushed at the compliment, and a shy smile formed on her face. "Thank you." Her eyes roamed me from head to toe, and then she stated, "And you look very dapper yourself."

"I appreciate that." I captured her hand in mine and brought it to my lips for a kiss. "Shall we?"

After she'd locked up her place, I escorted her to my Range Rover and tucked her inside before climbing into the driver's seat. I couldn't wait to show her the time that was in store for her tonight. The mere thought brought a sly grin to my face.

"So, where are you taking me?" she asked as if reading my mind.

"I can't tell you that, and you promised me you were cool with the mystery of it all."

She scoffed. "And I was, but I thought that was up until now. I kept my promise. I haven't pried the entire week." Slightly leaning over, she coaxed, "Come on. You can tell me the secret now."

I licked my lips and interlaced my free hand with her fingers. "So you want to be my diary?" I turned my face to her as we stopped at the red light. "I'll trust you with my secrets if you trust me with yours."

The way she blushed with embarrassment and quickly retreated caused a small chortle to escape. I knew she wasn't ready for that, but it was cute to see her squirm.

I patted her hand. "I'm just teasing you. But seriously, I never said it was a secret. I said it was a surprise. What kind of surprise would it be if I ruined it now?"

Playfully, she rolled her eyes, tossing her index and middle fingers in the air. "Touché, Mr. Jordan. Touché."

The remainder of our ride was relatively quiet, only filled with small talk about our work week, but when I pulled up to The Deck at Island Gardens, her eyes lit up like fireworks over the bay on the Fourth of July. It was the exact reaction I'd hoped for.

"Oh my gosh, Kinston! Island Gardens!" She placed her hands over her heart. "You did *not* have to do all of this."

"Actually, I did." I smiled at her before bringing her fingers to my lips for another kiss, never taking my eyes off hers. "Shall we?"

Lost in a trance, she listlessly nodded her head. As I savored the taste of her skin on my lips, I licked them slowly before exiting the car to retrieve her from the passenger side. I won't lie. The patio dinner overlooking the waterfront at sunset created the perfect ambiance, and I had to admit I'd done the damn thing with this date.

As we sipped our Sauvignon Blanc and waited on our seafood tower, Angela's eyes danced around like a child visiting Disney World for the first time. Though it was big enough for an entire dinner party, I rented a private cabana because I wanted the space for us to be comfortable and not be grouped at tables around others. It was also right next to the marina, giving us an impeccably pristine view as we dined. The lights of the nightlife, combined with the sensual, secluded atmosphere, were the perfect backdrop for what I prayed would be the start of a beautiful night of many nights. She was captivated, and for that, I was elated to be the man who put that excitement in her eyes.

"I know you said it was a surprise, but you outdid yourself, Kinston. Truly."

"You only get one shot to make a lasting first impression. It took me forever and fate to get a chance to make mine, so I was determined not to miss. I ain't trying to be amongst the stars. I need to be with the moon."

She blushed and shook her head. "You already have me on the date. You don't have to butter me up."

Her reaction caused me to point my finger. "That right there. Why do you think you're not deserving of my best?"

My words stung her for a second as she blinked twice before swallowing the invisible lump. She cleared her throat and asked, "Why do you feel I am so deserving?"

I leaned back and rubbed my hand down my beard. "Answering a question with a question. But no worries, I'll bite." I sighed. "Angela, since the moment I met you, something about you has tugged at me. Getting to know you a bit more since our siblings have dated and married, I see you. The way you stand for your sisters. The way you support them: your charm, quick wit, and fiery attitude. I've gotten an opportunity to witness it. And I like everything about it. So much so that I want to explore more of it and all the facets that I don't know about you. That's why you deserve my best, so I can get to know *all* the parts of you. Can I do that?"

Chapter Seven

ANGELA

Baby, you can have whatever you like, I sang internally, in my T.I. voice. Kinston was going to be trouble. Good trouble. *Too good.* What stirred me was that for any other man, I'd call his words as game, but I'd been around Kinston . . . and his brother . . . long enough to know that this was just who he was—a Jordan man. Smooth, suave, and salacious. I didn't know how to handle that, and even if I could, because he was a man I could lose myself with, I refused. I'd done that with Nigel. He'd seemed harmless for years, but then he gradually grew from sunshine to a category-five hurricane that blew in and disrupted my entire world. However, I'd somewhat prepared for him—put up my storm gates, put down my sandbags, and weathered it. Yes, there was some devastation, but I'd been able to tear down his damage and rebuild. But Kinston was no Nigel. Where Nigel was a hurricane, Kinston was a gawd-damn tsunami, guaranteed to fuck shit up. He had the power to not only damage but also to destroy me. If things didn't work out with him, I'd never be fit for another man. Never. I'd be displaced forever.

Picking up my wineglass, I sipped my Sauvignon Blanc before answering, "We'll see if you can unlock all the parts that are me, but I know you certainly bring out the best of them so far."

"I'll take that." He leaned back and unbuttoned his suit jacket. "So, tell me more about those parts, and I'll work my way to the rest."

For a moment, I was silent because the way the all-black shirt fit over his broad, muscular chest nearly had me drooling. *Good Lord in heaven. Did you have to make this man this fine?*

"Angela?"

"Hmmm?"

His eyes shone mischievously when I noticed the tinge of a smirk on his face. "See something you like over here?"

"I . . . umm, I . . ." I cleared my throat before leaning forward to eye his face. "Oh my goodness. You have dimples."

The sound of laughter roared so deeply from him that his masculine belly bounced with each reverberation. "Yes, I do. All my life. Courtesy of Marie Jordan. Kannon may be our pops's twin, but I'm our mama's."

"I can't believe I just noticed."

He lifted his shoulders insouciantly. "In all honesty, you typically divert your attention from me if you're not running altogether, so that doesn't surprise me."

I wanted to say it was because my attention *was* diverted to other parts of his anatomy, but, of course, I wouldn't divulge that tidbit of information. Instead, I decided to offer another piece of honesty.

"My bad. It's not you. After dealing with my ex, it has left me guarded."

"Hmm, the slick-mouthed motherfucker from last Saturday?"

I pointed at him. "That would be the one."

A slight moue formed on his face before he fanned his hand at the answer. "I'm not surprised." He sipped his wine. "Let's move around."

Confusion etched my brows. "It's that simple for you?"

"Indeed."

"So, you don't want to dig into what happened with us and what made me this way?" I asked, twirling my hands around with a shrug, honestly baffled by his disinterest.

Kinston released a soft chortle. "Oh no, I do, and eventually, I will. But tonight is not the night for that. I think it's safe to say that clown has wasted enough of your time, so I'm not about to waste any of ours on him. Tonight is about us."

Well, damn. And just like that, Nigel was forgotten. Between glasses of wine, cocktails, and our delicious seafood tower, we exchanged childhood stories about our families. It was hilarious to hear about young Kannon and Kinston growing up with Papa Kain and his mother, Marie—may she continue to rest in paradise. Although I didn't have the pleasure of meeting his mother, I feel as though, between his stories and his father's, I would have loved her. I met Papa Kain throughout Kannon and Nissi's engagement and subsequent marriage. He was a riot but a good-spirited older man who was still a down-home country boy. I could sit beside him for hours just to get lost in his wise tales. He had lived in Miami most of his adult life but never lost that "Georgia boy swag," as he called it, mimicking us millennials.

Of course, that conversation led me to share stories about my sisters and me growing up with my parents. Between speaking about our sibling rivalry to our mother enrolling us in every activity imaginable to my interest in debate and numerous wins on the debate teams in high school and college, he hung on to my every word as if trying to encapsulate each one into memory. Admittedly, it felt good to simply be seen and heard when it dawned on me that I hadn't spoken so freely and comfortably with a man in a very long time—if ever. With Nigel growing up with me, he bore witness to much of what I'd revealed to Kinston, so rarely did I have the chance to bear my soul without him already knowing and formulating his warped opinion before I could express my feelings. Having a man to talk to and, more importantly, to listen was a welcomed experience.

"Debate. That explains it," Kinston said as he wiped his hands on the white linen napkin.

By now, Kinston and I were sitting side by side on the plush sofa after sharing a decadent dessert, so we'd turned our space into a more intimate setting with the closeness of our proximities.

Feigning offense, I slightly jerked back and scoffed, playfully hitting him on the shoulder. "*Excuse* you?" I giggled.

As if my connection packed a punch, he flumped over and then bounced back, chuckling. "I didn't mean any harm. I'm just saying your profession . . . a paralegal."

"Oooh, right. *That*," I gasped, scrunching my face.

He gently shook his head. "But as my pops says, a hit hound will holler. Going all Mayweather on me, knowing full well that you're the queen of snaps."

"As long as you know," I clapped back.

He raised his hands. "It's all good. I can handle it."

I bet you can. I drank the last drops of my wine.

"Ooh yeah, I can handle anything you throw at me, Angela. Willingly."

The wine I'd just drunk went down the wrong pipe, causing a coughing fit as I realized that I'd vocalized what I'd internally thought. I lightly patted my chest to clear it when Kinston brought his hand to my back to help relieve my coughing spell. Our eyes met, and I knew if I didn't tear my gaze away, he'd be the death of me. Or at least the death of my kitty because her horny self was purring like a cougar at this point.

I was barely over my embarrassment when Kinston wrapped an arm around my shoulders and leaned in closely, his lips next to my earlobe with the hairs of his luscious beard tickling my skin. "Are you good?" he asked, his breath caressing me.

If I had words, I doubt I'd have been able to formulate them. Instead, I nodded while still fake clearing my windpipe.

He touched my cheek and gently stroked it with the back of his fingers, ceasing all movement.

"You're right," I blurted. "About debating. I wanted to be a trial lawyer."

Was I deflecting? Hell yes. It *was* the initial topic before my blunder, so I felt this was the perfect time to bring it back to the origin of my faux pas.

Taking the hint, Kinston leaned back, crossing his ankle over his knee, and I followed suit, loosely snuggled in his arms, still a safe enough distance away from him to be all clear of his danger zone. Hopefully. *Prayerfully.*

"So, why didn't you become one?"

Exhaling with a shrug, I answered, "Honestly, when I interned, I found a love in the research and preparation of cases. Sure, I loved to argue a case, but the purpose of that was to win. The first time a client lost a case was devastating, and I realized I couldn't live with that in my heart. To have someone's livelihood hinging on your ability to successfully argue a case was too much of a burden that I didn't want to shoulder. I couldn't live with that if I lost."

"That's understandable."

A frown formed on my face. "Really? You don't think I copped out?"

His expression was one mixed with confusion and query. "Nah. You still followed your path. Just because the dream changed directions doesn't mean the goal did. You're still a valuable asset to the firm and the people you serve. To that end, I gather that's what mattered most to you. So, I'd say you're fulfilling your purpose." He nodded his head toward me. "Why does that surprise you?"

"Aquila has sworn that I got scared and gave up. Low-key, I think she convinced my parents and Nissi of the same thing. Hell, I think, at times, she convinced *me* that was my reasoning."

"As long as that isn't true, then stand on what you believe. Have you ever asked yourself if it is true?"

"Sure, but I've always been satisfied with my career and have no desire to pursue it any further. I believe it was my dream to be an attorney for so long that it isn't believable to others that I changed course. But, honestly, Kinston, I'm... happy."

"Then don't let anyone distract you from your happiness. Not even yourself. Most people don't even know what makes them happy, let alone find a way to attain it. It's your life, and you're the only one who has to live it. If you don't, when it's all said and done, you'll detest every decision that wasn't yours. Life is too short to live with even one regret."

He caressed my shoulders inadvertently, causing me to furrow closer into his embrace as our orbs never left each other. His words were a soothing balm to my soul that I hadn't fathomed that I needed. For so long, I felt less than by the indication that I'd somehow sold myself out that I often shrank at my profession. Besides, it wasn't as if being a paralegal was the worst occupation I could aspire for. I mean, I wasn't out here peddling street pharmaceuticals. Kinston's confident reminder restored something in me that had been lost. It also explained the essence of him... What made him tick. Why he'd continued pursuing me for much longer than any man should, or that was even necessary. It explained his confidence in pursuing what he felt made him happy and his choice to live regret-free. And for the first time, I saw him in a new light. Admiration. Not only was his physicality all man, but his inner workings were also. One hundred percent thoroughbred. If I hadn't been attracted to him before, I would be totally smitten now.

I was cocooned in his arms. Our lips moved closer as the night winds stirred around us. Amidst the ambient lights and dulcet tunes serenading us under the glow of the obsidian ocean, our mouths found each other and feasted tenderly. Dare I say... lovingly. There was no rush, no hunger, no lust. Just fated magnetism. As if we'd been longtime lovers basking in the familiarity of our kindled union.

The interruption of the waiter clearing his throat pulled us from our private bliss. Though our eyes fluttered open with my attempt to back away, Kinston was unhurried, bringing my chin back to meet his lips with three more saccharine pecks before slowly dragging his tongue across his bottom lip and bringing his attention to the now-blushing server. But I was still caught up in the trance of Kinston, never letting my gaze fall from him.

"I have your check, sir."

Kinston retrieved the guest check holder and held up his hand, indicating that the waiter should stay while giving him a moment. Quickly, he scanned the bill before pulling out his wallet, placing a credit card in the holder, and handing it back to the young man. As soon as the waiter left, Kinston's attentiveness returned to me. No words were exchanged, only tender miens and supple caresses as we continued to immerse ourselves in our contented enjoyment.

It wasn't until the waiter returned with Kinston's credit card that he completely uncoupled with me to sign the tab and slipped two one-hundred-dollar bills from his wallet as the tip. After he thanked Kinston profusely for his generosity and left, Kinston stood and turned to me.

"Shall we?" he asked, extending his hand to mine.

With a sigh, I placed my hand in his and stood. This marked the end of our date, and I was saddened because I didn't want this magical night to end.

"The tip. That was very thoughtful," I complimented him.

"Nah, it was warranted. He did an excellent job. Kept the wine and cocktails flowing, the food was hot and timed perfectly with its delivery, and he ensured our needs were met yet left us enough space not to be intrusive. He earned that."

My head swayed. "You are such a man's man."

"Just the way my daddy raised me." He smiled as we made our exit from the restaurant, hand-in-hand.

Once he tucked me inside his vehicle and climbed in the driver's side, my head lolled backward, wishing for a delay. "Well, I had a wonderful time."

"I'm glad you did, but unless you're ready to go home, I still have one more surprise."

My head bounced up, and I turned my entire body toward him, giddiness pulsing through my core. "Another surprise? What? Wait. No. I mean, sure, I'd love to continue our date."

Kinston winked at me before biting his bottom lip, and I swore I was two seconds from attacking this man if he didn't stop.

"Glad to hear it. Sit back. We'll be there soon."

He turned up the smooth R&B music that cascaded the interior from the surround sound speakers. I took that as my cue not to ask questions and sat there as enthusiastically as a kid on the way to their favorite theme park. When we parked at what seemed to be a secluded parking area, I was curious, but I withheld my questions until a pilot met us. By now, my curiosity was tapping double time. When Kinston and the pilot greeted each other, my lips parted to start my inquisition, but the pilot beat me to the punch as he explained that we'd be going on a private helicopter tour of the city.

"Helicopter tour?" I asked, completely astonished.

"I asked if you were afraid of heights, but I guess I should've asked about helicopters. You aren't, are you?" Kinston asked, worry lines plastered across his features.

"No!" I yelped excitedly. "Kinston, this is so . . . wow. I've never done anything like this—never even thought of it. I'm just . . . in awe."

The pilot clapped his hands. "Well, that's great. Your excursion tonight will last an hour and include a guided tour with views of South Beach, Coconut Grove, Fisher Island, Key Biscayne, South Miami, Surfside, Bal Harbour, Sunny Isles beaches, the Venetian

Islands, Vizcaya Museum & Gardens, Brickell, and the Port of Miami. And the most important part, champagne, is included. For you two, not for me," he finished with a laugh as we joined in. "We'll get the releases signed, go over protocol and safety precautions, and then we'll be on our way." With that, he clapped Kinston on the shoulder with a knowing glance.

Kinston turned to me. "I want to make sure you're good—"

Hopping like a spry teenager, I bounced into his arms with a gentle hug. "Thank you. I'm so *ready* for this." Pulling back, I clasped his hands in mine. "This is perfect. Really."

Kinston brought a hand to my cheek and caressed it. "Perfect."

Soon, we went through all the particulars, and with our pilot headsets and champagne flutes in hand, we were whisked off on our grand tour of Miami. I'd flown a few times for clients' cases and vacations, but I'd never appreciated the aerial view. Moreover, it never dawned on me how breathtaking my own backyard was. I'd grown up here my entire life, and it was as if I was only just now, for the first time, seeing the city I'd been residing in. The luminous glow of lights, lush greenery, pristine waters, and grandeur of flowers and sculptures were awe-inspiring and made me understand why Miami was one of the most popular tourist attractions in the world. And I got to call it home.

"Having a good time?" Kinston asked, his voice barely above a whisper.

"The best," I answered truthfully as I interlaced our fingers.

By now, the bubbly mixed with my natural high from the most thoughtful and elaborate date I'd ever encountered had my lids hanging low and my heart thumping fast. I knew that I'd probably be slightly tipsy once I polished off the glass I held.

"If I forget to tell you when we get back, this is the best date ever," I said in a singsongy fashion, positive that the effects of the wine, cocktails, and champagne shone in my demeanor.

"And *you* are the best date ever," he added.

"My man," the pilot chimed in and quickly apologized. "I'm sorry. Not my business."

We both chuckled at his Freudian slip before I agreed. "But you're absolutely correct. He is most definitely *the man*."

Kinston's brow rose, and the sexiest glint danced in his eyes. "Careful, Ms. Richards. I might get the idea that you actually like me and start thinking of the possibility of a second date in our future."

I raised my flute to clink to his. It was my turn to tease. "In the words of a man's man, you earned that."

For the first time, a blush crossed his face as I finished off the last of my bubbly. The liquid courage had me brazen and equipped for all things Kinston Jordan. His massive frame moved closer, and I tilted forward, meeting him halfway. We were so close that his liquor-flavored breath caressed my earlobe when he spoke.

"Second date, next Saturday. Be ready at seven p.m."

Lazily, I dragged one finger down his chest as my head tilted backward and peered into his eyes. "Just one question."

"Ask me."

"What should I wear?"

The pilot cleared his throat. "Our tour will be ending in five minutes, folks. I hope that you had an unforgettable time." His voice was laden with a not-so-subtle hint of amusement.

Kinston and I continued our lustful observation of each other, our eyes probing the depths of our beings. Wonderment and exploration danced in my belly as I completely gave into the fact that I wanted . . . hell, *needed* . . . to discover more about this glorious man. For the first time, I allowed myself to accept the fact that he desired the same from me. And that created a craving that I could no longer withstand. There was no denying it. Kinston Jordan had me.

Chapter Eight

KINSTON

"I DON'T UNDERSTAND WHY y'all insist on bothering me. Can't have no peace in my own home," Kain fussed as he sat in his La-Z-Boy. Although his attention was diverted from us, his attitude was clearly aimed like a bull's-eye straight at the three of us standing in his living room.

Kannon, Roman, and I shared glances, our non-verbal cue that we would be in for yet another trying time with my pops.

"And don't be giving each other the eye about me. Y'all in *my* house, aggravating *my* damn nerves, and bringin' Roman out here." He shot a look at him. "I'm sorry my sons dragging you all the way over here."

Roman held up his hands. "It's no problem, Mr. Jordan. I'm here for you."

A huff of air expelled from my lips when I crisscrossed my forearms across my chest. "The only thing aggravating is the nerve you pinched in your back working on this house when I told you to wait on me." I pointed a stern finger at him. "And you know the only reason we're over here is because you refuse to go to PT at the doctor's office, and since Roman is certified, we're bringing the PT to you. Doctor's orders."

Our pops grimaced and waved off my comments before returning his attention to his television as if he hadn't already watched every episode of *Gunsmoke* that aired. He was stubborn and tough as nails, all qualities we loved about him and also qualities that exasperated us. He could be as ornery as he wanted. This was one of those times of annoyance we couldn't let slide. Not when it came to his health. Good thing for me that he raised me to be just like him. Bad thing for him, though, and I was sure I'd hear all about it later, or now since our pops wasn't the one to mince words.

"Pops, you know Kin is right. Besides, you're the one who agreed to it."

"I know what I agreed to—" Kain yelled, interrupting Kannon.

"So then, be the man of your word that you taught us to be," I interrupted his tirade.

Pops scoffed and reared back in his chair. This time, he did angle his head to glare at me with disbelief and an authoritative warning piercing my soul. "I know you ain't getting flip at the lip with me. Your ass ain't too grown to wrap my belt across your backside, son."

I damn near chuckled at the thought as my sidelong stare equally challenged him. "Not only am I too grown for that, but you also can't even do it because your nerve is pinched, and you refuse to do what you need to do to get better." It was a risky smart-aleck remark I knew was effective enough to get the job done.

Pops tried to scurry out of the seat and hollered in pain, and Roman rushed to his side. "Easy, Mr. Jordan. Easy."

"Ugh!" he cried out in agony, instantly reaching for his back. "Ooh, you wait until Roman makes my back better. I'ma whip your ass for that and all the other ass whoopings I promised you when you was a kid."

Overlooking his idle threat, Kannon and I eased over to help Roman lift him out of the recliner and over to the table so they could begin physical therapy.

"Okay, Pops. I'll give you that. As long as you're better."

With a grunt and a wince of pain, our pops hobbled over to the adjoined patio where the PT equipment was set up so Roman could start on the rehab orders for him. Once he was on the table, Kannon and I glanced at each other again, shaking our heads at how impossible that man could be at times. Our mother was the only one who could tame him. It was the reason I knew he was in an extreme amount of discomfort because if he could've gotten out of that recliner to beat me, he surely would've, and Roman would've wasted a trip. The fact that he was about to allow this physical therapy session to happen meant that even he knew he needed it.

Kannon clapped my shoulder, bringing my attention back to him. "While they are working, you need to fill me in on your date with my sister-in-law."

The mere mention of Angela ignited happiness to explode like a bomb and course like a virus through my entire body. I couldn't help the Kool-Aid grin that spread across my face.

"That good, huh?" Kannon smirked. "Yep, I'm ready for these details." He slapped his hands together and rubbed them as if I were about to deliver some TMZ-worthy gossip.

When I motioned for him to follow me inside, our pops' voice rang out. "Oh, hell nah. You ain't about to leave me out here in the torture chamber and think you about to go up in *my* house and leave *me* out of this news. All them times you done whined to me about how to get her to give you a chance, and you think you gon' leave me out? Sit yo' ass down and talk."

Everyone seemed to think that was hilarious. I gave Roman the side-eye and pointed at my pops. "Can you tell this man he needs to focus on his therapy?"

Roman shrugged. "Nah, fam. I'm calling BS too. Talking helps clients relax during therapy, and you know that. Besides,

I'm with your dad. I seem to remember a certain Saturday where I had to pretend to be boo-loving with Nia for you and Angela, so I wanna hear about this date too. Besides, we're boys. How you gonna leave me out?"

Our pops nodded and touched knuckles with Roman. "I knew'ed I liked you. You welcome back here anytime besides to press on my backside."

"Bruh, just spill it." Kannon sat down on a nearby bench.

My eyes scanned all three of them as they waited excitedly as if we were all some preteens about to discuss our first kiss. But I couldn't blame them. Each of them had counseled and supported my pursuit of Angela, so I owed them the courtesy of the outcome.

That wasn't my hang-up, though. Since I knew I'd deliver the news of how well this first date went, they'd naturally expect my excitement about a second date. And I was excited, but there was also a sense of apprehension. My hang-up was worrying if Angela and I would have the same chemistry the second time around. Was the first date just a magical fluke, or was it the beginning of something of substance? A real relationship? I wanted it to be, but I wasn't sure of Angela's stance, and the uncertainty low-key shook my confidence. Admittedly, I'd never had to vie for a woman's attention and time so intensely. Women usually vied for *my* attention, or if I made the first move, they willingly gave of themselves to keep me interested. No cap and no cockiness intended. But not Angela. Ms. Richards made me work like a Hebrew slave. For her, I didn't mind at all, but with that came a level of insecurity that I wasn't accustomed to. And that was a scary feeling because I was so sure about Angela. But was *she* sure about *me*?

Despite my anxiety, the brightest smile formed across my lips that I couldn't stop if I tried. My brother sprang from his seated position, slapping my shoulders and arms as all three of them let out a boisterous series of catcalls. After a few minutes of their playful teasing, I pumped my hands to calm the banter.

"I ain't trying to brag or nothing, but ya boy did his thing, ya feel me?" I said playfully, clapping my hands together for emphasis. "Real talk. I almost lost my breath when I first laid eyes on her, though. Man, the way she bodied that dress. I mean, the fit was fitting, dawg." I slapped hands with Kannon.

"I assume she looked fine as aged wine," Pops added. He was so old-fashioned that it was comical.

I agreed with a nod. "Yeah, Pops. She was fine."

"Man, that girl could wear a paper bag, and you'd still say she was fine," Roman joked. But he wasn't lying. "Where did you take her?"

"First, we had a sunset dinner in a private cabana at The Deck at Island Gardens."

"First?" Roman stressed with a raised eyebrow. "Damn, bro. That move right there carries weight by itself. You mean to tell me you did something else that *topped* that?"

I bit my lip, recalling the night in my mind. "Yeah, man. A private champagne helicopter flight over the city."

Their mouths dropped, and Kannon was the first to respond as he pounced up and hopped up and down on his toes. "That's my effin' brother!" he roared, pointing his finger.

Roman even stopped therapy long enough to ease over and clap his hand on my shoulder. "My man," he cheered, bringing me in for a one-armed hug. "That's top tier right there. You did your thing."

Pops even stared at me with admiration dancing in his eyes. "I have done some things in my day, but that's a new one on me, son. Marie would be impressed. You done good."

The mention of our mother brought a somber moment. We all quieted it down. I'm sure my pops and brother were just as lost in their own recollected memories as I was. Hearing that my mom would've been impressed was fuel to my soul. That was all the encouragement that I needed for date number two. Yet, the fact that she wasn't here to witness it was like a double-edged sword. I'd never get to hear her tell me those words for herself, and she'd never get the chance to say them.

Sensing the shift, Roman cleared his throat and asked, "So you gotta tell us what she thought about this elaborate first date."

"Well, she was shocked, of course, but it wasn't so much about what I'd done, but rather she didn't feel she deserved it. I don't know the full story about what ol' dude did to her, but that motherfucker tore down her self-worth."

Kannon gritted his teeth. "Who? Her ex?"

"That lame we ran into at the restaurant?" Roman chimed in.

I acknowledged they were both correct before continuing. "On the one hand, I'm glad he fumbled the bag. On the other hand, I don't know how many broken pieces are inside the bag that needs to be repaired for me to have a real chance."

"Well, son, the question ain't about how much needs to be repaired, but whether you're willing to stick with her through it. We all damaged. You just have to be honest about how much damage you're willing to help rebuild." Pops winced. "Ease up there, Roman. Talking was supposed to take my mind off it, and you bringing me right back to it."

We all chuckled at that, and Roman lifted his hands in surrender. "My bad, Mr. Jordan."

While we all took a beat after Pops clowned on Roman, what he'd said weighed on me. He was right. I didn't mind the broken pieces. It's not like we were teenagers experiencing our first taste of new puppy love. I was old enough and wise enough to realize that, at my age, any woman I chose would come with some dirty laundry and possible necessary repairs. Honestly, I had my own basket tucked in a corner. However, everyone wasn't worth a trip to the laundromat, let alone having to be on some Lowe's home improvement mission. But Angela? After our one date, I hated to admit it, but for her, I was willing to go through the thick of it because, somehow, I just knew she was worth it. I was ready to buy up every laundromat and Lowe's store if it meant making her whole again and ready for me ... Ready for us.

A calm resolve passed over me as I shrugged and leaned against the wall, marveled yet absolute in my admission. "Honestly, Pops, Angela makes me want to go through the fire as long as we come out together on the other side. For her, I don't mind."

While Pops and Kannon cast knowing looks at me, Roman glared at me as if I'd suddenly turned into a three-headed Medusa. "Seriously, bro?" His unsure expression caused his brows to furrow into a deep scowl. "I'm happy you finally got the girl you've been hunting, but you barely know her to declare those deep emotions. You sure it ain't the thrill of the chase speaking? The conquest and the conquering are two different things. It's a bit soon to overcommit. I mean, hell, you ain't even tasted the goods yet. Unless ..."

Kannon tossed his hands up. "Wait. Hold on, bruh. I ain't trying to get a play-by-play on my sister-in-law's goodies. So save that part of the conversation for my absence. For real," he groaned.

"And I don't have one to give," I admitted. "I hear you, Roman, and I know you're only looking out, but you can add that to the list of reasons why I know in my gut that Angela is it for me. I haven't tasted the rainbow, and as much as I desire to, our connection isn't solely based on those carnal urges. For me, her *goods* are only a bonus. *She's* the prize."

Roman's head shook in disbelief as he released a sharp hiss. "I hear you, bro, but I don't subscribe. You do you, though. That shit there ain't it for me. Never will be."

Shared recognition passed between Kannon, our pops, and me. In unpracticed unison, we chorused, *"When you know, you know."*

"Man, I don't know what kind of witchcraft those Richards sisters got over y'all, but I don't want no parts, bro," Roman tittered.

I don't know what kind of power those Richards sisters held, either. But I knew Roman had better be happy that Aquila was married and off-limits, or his forever bachelor life head ass may have been sucked up in the same Richards abyss hanging around us and those sisters. Consider himself saved by the ring. Whether it was Marie Jordan or the Richards sisters, Roman couldn't fathom it because he hadn't felt it. It wasn't explainable. You couldn't witness it. It was only a feeling that you received from the experience. Until or unless he walked a mile in my shoes, he'd never fully understand what I felt, what all three of us felt.

In my opinion, people misused the meaning of the term YOLO. They assumed you should try things because you only live once. No, we only *die* once. We lived every day, and with the right person, each one of those days gave us something beautiful and hopeful to look forward to. So, yeah, for Angela Richards, I'd YOLO like a motherfucker for the rest of my days and die happy at the end of them. Of that, I was positive.

Chapter Nine

ANGELA

TWO MONTHS LATER

THE CHATTER AROUND the massive dinner table became calm as Kannon stood, tapping his wine goblet with his silverware. All of us gave him our undivided attention.

"For our first official couples' dinner, I wanted to thank you all for joining my wife and me and allowing us to host you all. It feels good to be surrounded by family and friends we love and support and to know that it is reciprocated." He raised his glass. "So, a toast to forever love and lifelong friendships."

Nia placed her hand in the air, ceasing the ceremonial greeting momentarily. "That's sweet and all, but two of us are only here to support said couple friends," she joked, setting off a barrage of laughs.

Kannon patted Roman's shoulder, who sat to his left. "You hear that, bro? You may want to do something about that."

All the fellas joined in, teasing Roman, who took the badgering like a champ, but his face reeked of embarrassment. Noticing his discomfort, Nia raised her hand in a surrender pose, an apology spreading across the lines of her face.

"My bad, Roman. I wasn't trying to insinuate anything by that. I was only making an observation," Nia chimed in, trying to save face.

"And so was I," Kannon teased, making Nia blush as Nissi swatted at him.

"Leave those two alone, babe," Nissi playfully scolded.

Jumping in to save my bestie, I added, "Well, technically, Nia is right. Not everyone here is officially a couple."

As soon as the words left my mouth, I felt laser beams on the side of my face. I didn't need to turn to acknowledge it to know that Kinston was boring a hole into the side of my head. To add to the insult of my apparent injury, the banter at the table turned awkwardly silent, punctuating the wound.

"Well, not for long. For a couple of us, anyway," Kinston added much to the appreciated smiles and coos to everyone at the table as I sat like a bump on a log, not knowing exactly how to react to his declaration.

Thankfully, I didn't have time for my discomfiture to take root as Kannon took Kinston's remark as his cue to lift his glass again. "On that note, let's toast to lifetime friendships and endless possibilities."

"Here, here," we all uttered, lifting our goblets and taking sips. On the other hand, I gulped my wine as the weightiness of the hot seat fell on my shoulders.

Once Kannon took his seat, Nissi led us in prayer, and then we all quickly passed around the saucers and filled our plates with the delectably appealing food. This had to be Kannon's handiwork because my sister boasted a knack for several skills, but a cook was not one of them. She wasn't terrible, but she was not a dinner party chef extraordinaire. She was more like a soccer mom of five kids, tossing a precooked-casserole-in-the-oven-type of person. You'd get fed and filled, but she'd never beat Bobby Flay or even Joel Oliver.

"Mmm," Ciara hummed at the first morsel that landed on her palate. "This is really good. Joel, did you come over here and whip this up? I'm not sure if I believe Kannon prepared this meal, and I know for sure my good sis did not."

"My meals are five-star rated," Joel scoffed arrogantly before Aquila bumped his shoulder in irritation. Uneasy glances passed around the table before he tossed his hand up apologetically. "I simply mean that I wouldn't have the time to do this given the time I need for my clients."

Ciara placed her hand on her heart. "My apologies, Kannon and Joel. I was only joking. I didn't mean to offend anyone."

"No offense taken," Kannon murmured behind the sip of his wine.

Nissi shot a scathing glare at Joel and added, "We understood what you meant, Ciara, and so did Joel. Sometimes, he's just as pretentious as his five-star clients."

I choked at her comeback as the wine slid down the wrong pipe, and I felt Kinston's broad hand patting my back. Ever since Nissi met Kannon, she'd been in rare form. Usually, it'd be me with the smart-aleck clapbacks, but apparently, I'd trained my baby sister very well. Served Joel right.

Aquila's exhale was an instant indicator of her disapproval of Nissi's snap toward her husband. However, if Joel practiced common courtesy and human decency to anyone other than his clients, then he wouldn't be subjected to our snarky attitudes. He'd better be glad that was all he received because our entire family had been waiting for the day to light him up.

"He's already explained what he meant, so can we not go there?" Aquila asked snidely.

"I was just going wherever he went with it." Nissi hunched her shoulders nonchalantly.

Aquila opened her mouth to rebut Nissi when Joel placed a cautionary finger in the air, silencing her. "I didn't ask for a mediator, darling. It's all good."

I had no clue what anybody else's response was because my heated eyes darted at Joel, and my head cocked to the side so swiftly that I almost caught a crick in my neck. Before I could part my lips, I felt the same firm hand grip my thigh underneath the table, quelling my reaction. Chancing a glance at Nissi, Kannon must've put the same death grip on her because she also held a bewildered gaze in her eyes with her lips pressed together in a tight line.

"I wasn't butting in, I was just—"

The same cautionary finger from a moment before rose again sternly, interrupting Aquila. I swore to the Holy Trinity that I was two seconds away from snatching his digits clean off his hand if he didn't put that dusty finger down out of my sister's face. Suddenly, a massive hand was pressing atop Joel's forearm. Everyone's focus turned to find Roman gently lowering Joel's arm to the table.

"Hey, man, let's be cool. Obviously, she was being your wife. We get it. No harm, no foul. Right?" Roman asked with the calm and collectedness of a trained caretaker.

Joel's expression twitched for a millisecond, but one sweep of Roman's physique quickly reminded Joel that Roman was not one he needed to challenge. Testing him would be like throwing a grape at a concrete wall. Useless. With that recognition in place, Joel placed one of his award-winning, kiss-ass smiles on his face and surrendered to Roman's pleasant but serious request to let it go and get his hand out of his wife's personal space.

"You're right, buddy," Joel laughed, nervous energy spreading throughout his body. He then turned his focus to Nia. "You better snatch this one up, Nia. Seems like he'll make great husband material."

Both Kinston and Kannon got trapped in a fit of coughs at that statement. We didn't have to ponder why that was as Roman quickly tossed up his hands, waving the "no" motion emphatically.

"Geesh! Tell me how you *really* feel, Mr. Patterson," Nia smarted, folding her arms.

With a sheepish grin, Roman wiped his mouth with the linen napkin before placing it back on the table beside his plate and leaning forward. "Trust me, Nia. It's nothing against you at all." His smoldering eyes salaciously roamed over Nia's frame, causing a blush to settle on her warming cheeks. "But rather my stance on marriage. Is that a bad thing? At least you know what I'm *not* about. In a world of men who'd rather sell you the dream, I would hope you'd appreciate my free honest reality."

If it were possible, I believe Nia would've melted into a puddle right there in the seat, and to be honest, the rest of us women wouldn't be far behind her. To me, Roman had always been a quiet and unassuming man. A bit of a mystery. He proved that all it took was the right one to bring a person out of that shell. It was now even more apparent how he was friends with these Jordan men because he fit right in. Nope. You could not sleep on Roman Patterson, and Nia should not either.

"Damn, that was smooth," Zach, Ciara's husband, whispered with a snicker, causing the playful banter to turn up a few notches around the dining room table. This time, it was Nia's turn to be slightly embarrassed as the men slapped fives with Roman for the suave line.

From that moment on, the conversations were light and comical. Even uppity Joel relaxed and was able to have fun. Filled with a delicious meal and never-ending libations, everyone easily flowed from one topic to the next as if we all had known each other for our entire lifetimes.

When we finished stuffing our faces, the men moved into the entertainment room while we women helped Nissi clear the dishes away. It was their compromise. Kannon cooked, and she cleaned. I loved the partnership in their relationship and the fact that my baby sister was sneakily intelligent. Of course, she'd agree to clean because she knew she'd have assistance. On the other hand, my poor brother-in-love was the only one who slaved over the hot range to provide said feast for ten. As much as I cared for him, I wouldn't point it out because sisters before misters, and that was on life.

As I loaded the dishwasher with Nia, I teased, "I don't know what Mr. Patterson is selling, but you should for damn sure be buying."

Nissi and Ciara playfully slapped hands with me in agreement among a barrage of cackles.

Wagging an accusatory finger, Aquila quickly spouted, "Don't be praising her for that comment. She's telling poor Nia what she should be doing, knowing good and well she hasn't even secured her own man."

To that, Nia bumped fists with Aquila. "That part!" she hooted.

Ciara and Nissi diverted their eyes away from me, signifying that a valid point had been made. It was further emphasized by the imaginary string of pearls Ciara clutched in her palms and Nissi's outburst of "and I oop," putting the period on the fact that Aquila had successfully come for my jugular.

"*Really*, Aquila?" was the only comeback I could muster.

"Yeah, *really*," she poked, the curt smize on her face making me suck my teeth. "If you want to discuss missing chances, start with yourself first."

"I haven't missed any chances." The irritation in my voice was palpable as I tossed my hand on my hip.

"Well, you sure haven't taken advantage of any either," Nia added her two cents, no doubt continuing to steer herself off the topic of conversation.

Usually, I could take the heat, especially since I often dished it out, but something about Nia and Aquila ganging up on me was getting under my skin. Who was I kidding? I knew exactly why. If my earlier slip was any indicator, my defensive mood had Kinston Jordan written all over it. It was true that Kinston and

I were still not official, but it's not like we hadn't dated steadily and regularly over the past two months. We'd had plenty of fun since that first spectacular date. Our second date was a day on the beach, frolicking in the water, and we challenged each other to explore a water sport that we both feared. For him, it was snorkeling. For me, it was parasailing. We ended the day with our favorite water sport: jet skiing. We even teased how he didn't like being under the water, and I didn't like being above the water, but being *on* the water was our neutral ground. Following that date, we'd been on several others: the movies, the museum, a concert, and even a picnic in the park. We talked on the phone often, and he was generally the last person I spoke to before retiring for the night. These days, I talked to and hung out with Kinston more than I did with my bestie and my sisters. So, it wasn't that I wasn't giving the man a chance because I was. We were simply taking matters slowly. There wasn't any harm in that.

"Listen, my point was that it wouldn't hurt if Nia went on a date with Roman. He seems interested, and from what I know of him, he's a good guy. Marriage might not be his thing, but dating is. So, why not?" I sneered with a shrug. "Besides, I am going on dates with Kinston, so you can't argue with that."

The quiet murmurs of agreement filled the air as I finished loading the dishwasher while brooding from being placed on the hot seat. I couldn't understand why I was the only one consistently being put on blast. Nia hadn't had a man in so long that her lady parts were probably applying for retirement, Aquila and Joel's marriage was on the cusp of disaster, and well, I couldn't speak negatively about Ciara and Zach or Nissi and Kannon because their marriages were couple goals. Still, out of the other two bosom buddies, my situationship with Kinston was a far cry better than their nonexistent and damn near extinct relationships.

Sensing my irritation, we finished cleaning up in near silence. We were just wrapping everything up when Kinston waltzed inside.

"Hey, ladies." His voice oozed out in a pleasant singsong fashion. However, the tension in the room must've alerted him that everything was not copasetic in our area of the Jordan home. He paused his steps, his eyes brimming with concern as he swiped a hand down his beard. "My bad. Are y'all good in here?"

Nissi broke the silence first. "Ahh, yeah. We're good. We're just finishing. What's up, bro? You need something?"

"Nah, sis. You know my baby brother can't live two seconds without his wife. He sent me here to check on you ladies to see if you needed any help."

"Oh, so he sent *you*. So *he* didn't have to pitch in," Nissi cackled, wagging her finger. "I see how he does. But no, we're heading into the entertainment room now."

Kinston nodded at Nissi, but his attention immediately returned to me. Kinston gently clasped my hand as the ladies filed out of the kitchen and headed toward the men, prompting me to stay behind. He stood beside me, his tall masculine frame leaning over so that his lips were directly next to my earlobe.

"Are you good?"

"I'm fine."

My answer came out short and not as convincing as I intended for it to sound. When I chanced a glance up at Kinston, his furrowed brow and questioning gaze reaffirmed that he didn't believe the words I'd spoken. Before he could call me out, I straightened my facial expression and demeanor before placing a smile on my face.

"I'm serious. Everything is fine. I'm good." I hoped that this time, my words would seem more confident.

Kinston walked in front of me, and for a few brief moments, skepticism clouded his deep auburn orbs as he gauged me. No doubt he was trying to decipher if I was being truthful. After a minute, he conceded with a slight nod and took my hand. I was positive he didn't fully buy into my answer, but I was also positive that he'd dropped the subject for now.

"If you say so. Let's go out here and join the crew." His response confirmed my thoughts.

Grateful for the reprieve, I followed him, hand-in-hand, into the entertainment room, where the remainder of our family and friends assembled. That feeling was short-lived because no sooner had Kinston and I taken our places on the love seat did Joel, in all his tone-deaf glory, **disrupt** my peace.

"So, Kinston, we were just **talking** about it. You've been dating Ang here for a while. When do you plan on making it official?"

Could they be any more obvious? All eyes peered at us, and I was too afraid to chance a glance in Kinston's direction. Honestly, I couldn't do much of anything, given that my body felt as if it were about to lose all its faculties. Electrical charges set off my nerves in a fury of tingles, setting my internal temper ablaze. A stark contrast to the balminess of my hands. I swallowed roughly to open my constricted airway, even as each breath felt as if hot coals were scorching down my throat. If this fake friends' dinner was a ploy to dig into Kinston's and my business, I wish they would've just saved us the trouble of showing up and simply asked. We could've had this discussion over group chat. Kinston's hand on my back felt like an additional jolt, causing me to jerk forward from the contact.

"I'd love to, but we're taking it slow." I turned toward him at what felt like a snail's pace, and his intense stare crashed into me. "And that's okay because I'm a patient man."

Love on the Rebound

The deep longing embedded in his eyes told our, my, untold secrets. This union was on me. Truth. Kin asked me several times to move our situation to a relationship status. The first time, I found a way to evade the conversation, or perhaps he allowed me to avoid it because he may have been a bit afraid himself. Kinston's confidence grew with each date, so when he asked me the second time, he wanted an answer. I'd asked if we could take it slow, blaming my career and enjoying the dating aspect of our connection as my reasons why I didn't want to take the plunge. Grudgingly, he accepted my excuses. Regardless of whether he believed me, he agreed, and since then, he hasn't pressured me, and we continue to go on beautiful dates all around the city.

Truth. I wanted Kinston in that way. Very much so. However, I couldn't bring myself to invest in a relationship with him. Things were going well between us. Better than well. We learned more about each other every single day. I could immerse myself with him, having the time of my life, whether we were out on the town or just sitting quietly in stillness. Without strings. Without attachments. Without commitments. This way, when he decided he no longer wanted to be involved, there wouldn't be any hurt feelings or broken hearts. We could both walk away unscathed. There would be nothing to resolve or restore. I'd dedicated years to Nigel, only for him to depart without a speck of remorse. I promised myself I'd never go through that again, and I wouldn't. The best way to ensure that promise was not to make any fool-hearted decisions that would land me in the same predicament. Hence, my situationship sans relationship with Kinston. It was better this way . . . for both of us.

Fanning my hands out with a shrug, I finished. "See, we've got this. At our pace." I placed my hand on Kinston's knee, giving it a soft squeeze. "Rather get it right than be stuck getting it wrong." My heated gaze shot toward Aquila and Joel.

"More drinks?" Nissi asked, quickly intervening.

Aquila sat forward with her finger raised. "Hold on, sis," she said to Nissi, but with her focus fixated on me. "I feel like you have something to say, *Ang*, so let's hear it." She finished emphasizing the sobriquet in a way that she knew made my skin crawl.

With a chuckle and a shake of my head, I pursed my lips. "I've said it plenty of times before. The entire family has, actually." Waving my hand to dismiss my snippy remark, I settled my resolve and continued. "That's neither here nor there tonight. Let's leave it with the fact that we are all content with our lot in life until we decide to make a change, and we can all respect that, right, *Lah*?"

She knew whenever I called her Lah, it was my peace treaty. She may not have wanted to stop the train wreck of an argument, but she knew that in terms of our "relationships," hers was far worse and that I would have an immediate reinforcement in Nissi. Rather than fan the flames, she quelled her own ire and agreed to the conciliatory terms.

With raised hands, she bowed her head in consent. "Sure, Angie." By then, Nissi had retrieved wine coolers and handed Aquila her favorite, Jamaica Me Happy. "Besides, we both want what's best for each other."

"Right." After taking a sip of my Peach Bellini, I plastered on a contented mien.

To others, her comment seemed harmless enough. For me, I knew it was her last-ditch attempt to scrutinize my decision not to pursue more with Kinston. From the despondent expression on Kinston's face throughout the remainder of the evening, her message had been duly noted and well received. I wondered how much longer I could hide in my protective bubble.

Chapter Ten

KINSTON

ANGELA RICHARDS WAS a mystery that I couldn't solve. As intrigued as I was with putting the puzzle pieces of her heart together, it annoyed me. It was clear as the sunny blue skies over Miami Bay that this woman did not want anything more than a companion to share a few outings. The two times I pushed for more, she retreated. Rather than have her completely recoil, I decided to go at her speed with her flow. But that flow wasn't flowing, no matter how hard I tried.

When I received the invitation from Angela, instead of my brother, for dinner at my brother's house, I thought we'd made a turn. My sister-in-love had already told me that she and Kannon were planning a couples' dinner with friends when I stopped by to drop off Kannon's protein drinks that were exclusively sold at my gym. She hadn't invited me; she just mentioned it in our casual conversation. I assumed she meant with their other married friends, so I didn't even think twice about it until Angela extended the invitation during one of our late-night phone calls. It was the first time she'd made an effort to spend time with me without my prompting, and it was with other couples. My swag was a hundred thousand, and I accepted it so quickly that I'm not sure if she'd even finished asking. However, the exuberance I felt for this opportunity was short-lived when I arrived at the dinner.

Mix in a few poorly timed questions, and Angela reaffirmed to me and all our family and friends that this was not only not moving to the next phase, but it also had possibly stalled completely out. I sat there throughout the night, embarrassed and feeling somewhat played. During that disastrous evening, I'd decided to back away from Angela. She knew how I felt. She knew what I wanted. If she wanted something of substance with me, she knew where to find me.

After dinner, as I drove to take Angela home, I tried to tuck my feelings inside, but I guess I had been a tad more transparent than I wanted.

"Your brother can really burn in the kitchen. Nissi always bragged about it, but I didn't realize he was a real-life Chef-Boy-R-Negro," she joked.

With my thoughts on the other aspects of that dinner, my one-word reply was, "Yeah."

I could feel the air deflate in my truck. Angela was never one to mince words except the ones that united us as a couple, so I knew the interrogation was about to be underway.

"Kinston, are you okay?"

"Yep."

After that second one-word response, I felt the cold and curious stare of her eyes on me. But I refused to give into this charade. We'd been getting to know each other for two months. She might not have known me completely, but she knew enough to know that I was not okay, and I'd bet every dime in my bank account that she knew why I wasn't talkative tonight.

"Are you sure?"

Am I sure? Is she serious? Yeah, she is. I felt stuck between a rock and a boulder because answering her question honestly wouldn't garner the real conversation I wanted to have. Me and her together. As a couple. Not on some companion-for-dates type shit. Quite frankly, *her feigned ignorance of it was starting to truly piss me off, so rather than utter a word, I gave her a nod because if I said anything, all of my efforts to woo this woman would be in vain.*

We sat awkwardly for a few more moments before she attempted conversation again.

"And my sister is not slick. I peeped game with them, inviting Nia and Roman over. But I think they'd be cute together, don't you?"

At that point, I was livid. Angela was intelligent. One of the brightest minds I'd ever met. And I knew she wasn't as arrogant or tone-deaf as her dumbass brother-in-law, Joel. The fact that she'd had the audacity to ask me if my boy and her girl would make a cute couple when our own—whatever the hell we were doing—was in disarray set off an inferno inside of me. My hands gripped the steering wheel so tightly that I thought I'd break the steering column. Thank God I was pulling up to her townhome because I needed to be away from her and alone by myself.

"We're here, Angela. Good night," I said with a slight scoff, my focus remaining ahead.

"Kinston," she said, her voice dragging the last syllable of my name out in a slow drawl.

"Angela, don't. Good night."

"Listen, I'm sorry about Joel and my sister. They can be so—"

Finally turning to face her, my words came out like a rush of roaring floodwater. "Joel and your sister?" I asked incredulously. "Angela, if you think this is about Joel, Aquila, or hell, Nissi and Kannon, and especially Roman and Nia, then you're as ignorant as you sound, and I know neither of those things to be true," I huffed, pinching the bridge of my nose. "Please do us both a favor. Go inside, and let's call it a night."

"Kinston!" she bellowed. "I don't appreciate that, but I'll give you that because tonight was tough. But you shouldn't let outside people impact your mood when we both decided on the course of our situation."

If anybody is impacting my mood, it's you. Those are the words that longed to fall from my lips. I wanted to speak the desires of my heart, but more than anything, I ached for those desires to be acknowledged and met. That was the real problem. Regardless, if I laid my soul bare, it wouldn't change the fact that Angela had to be willing to grant my wishes. And she wasn't. So, why waste breath on a never-ending circle of denial?

Silence ripped through the stillness of the night and cocooned us in a test of wills. My disengaged and unrelenting stare met her determined and dominating glare. We sat there in a battle royale, our internal emotions warring with sentiments and arguments our lips refused to formulate. This was the side of me that she hadn't gotten familiar with. Intro to Kinston 101 was in full effect. The same relentlessness I used to pursue her replicated in all things, even anger and stubbornness. There was no fold in my heart. Sure, I'd bend when necessary, but fold—never. This was the part of me that Kannon called Dade County. While I cared for Angela, she wasn't about to play with me either. She hadn't been the only person to suffer heartache and loss. I'd suffered in the past too. Trust and relationships didn't come easy for me either. But for her, I was willing to try. Wanted to. Yearned to. But I had limits. That night, at that dinner, I'd reached mine.

With a resounding sigh, Angela's eyes softened along with her entire demeanor. Shoulders slacked, and eyes lowered, she reached one hand out to caress my hand, now draped on the center console, while her other clasped the door handle.

"Listen, I'm sorry for what I said. I'm also sorry if my sister and her husband slighted you and, most of all, that our private matters were the center of discussion." She dipped her head, urging me to return my eyes to hers. "I'll talk with you later, okay?"

Although I appreciated the apologies, they didn't change our stagnant situation, so again, my only response was the bob of my head. Without another word, she exited my vehicle, and I watched until she *safely made it into the house before releasing my own weighted breath and pulling away.*

That had been two weeks ago. She'd kept her promise and called me that night, but I never answered. As a courtesy, I did send a text to let her know that I'd made it home. Other than that, I'd purposefully cooled communication with Angela. Surprisingly, she'd initiate several more phone calls to me that had gone unanswered. I wasn't running or pushing her away. I needed a beat, and I needed her to take what was transpiring between the two of us seriously. That's why when I listened to her voicemail that she'd left last night, I knew she was ready to talk openly and honestly, and I was more than prepared to listen.

As I drove, I replayed those words that had my over six-foot-tall burly frame giddy and blushing.

"Hey, Kinston. I hope your day was well. I was thinking of you, and I . . . Kinston . . . I miss you. I miss speaking to you daily. I haven't slept well in two weeks because I haven't heard your voice at night. I miss us hanging out. I miss our stupid debates and corny jokes. I miss just being around you. I know we need to talk. I need to talk. And whenever you're ready, if you'd like to, I am too. I can't believe I'm leaving an Usher Raymond message on this phone. Please call me."

Exiting my Range, I grabbed the bouquet and approached Pearson, Paulson, Price, and Associates. Triple P, as the professional community referred to them. This firm was one of the top in the country and boasted a client list of Fortune 500 companies that ensured they would be in business for years to come. The mirrored, ten-story modern building reeked of every bit of the money they collected and earned. The doorman greeted me and allowed me inside, which led me to the state-of-the-art security desk.

"What can I do you for today, sir?" the husky older gentleman pleasantly asked.

Throwing on my Mr. Miami Smile, I held up the flowers. "I'd like to surprise my friend. She's a paralegal for Attorney Pearson."

His smile deepened as recognition seemed to splay on his face. "Ms. Richards?"

"You know her then."

He nodded. "Indeed. Pearson couldn't tie his shoes without her. A beautiful and sweet young woman she is. She's beloved by us all."

If he'd been younger, his raving remarks might have lit a bit of a jealous streak in me, but since he was older, it came off as more of a fatherly compliment. But then again, old cats liked young women too. When I didn't readily respond, he continued.

"It's good to see a young man coming to visit her. She deserves someone in her life that will treat her right."

My guard dissolved at that, and I noticed the gold band on his left finger. My first assumption was correct. Good, because I didn't want to have to lay hands on this old man over Angela. I knew I had no right to be jealous or lay claims on her, but Pops and any other man needed to tread lightly regarding her. She wasn't officially mine, but she was mine. On Gawd.

"That she has, sir."

His brows lifted pleasantly at my words before he stood and grabbed his wand. "Just need to scan you, log your identification, and then I'll give you a visitor's badge to the tenth floor. Stop at the receptionist's desk, and Molly will call Angela out for you."

Stepping off the elevator, I glided my way over to the glass door bearing the name Attorney Daniel Pearson Esq. engraved in it and opened it. Sitting at a mammoth cherry oak desk was a petite and dark-haired white woman who met me with the same booming smile as the security guard had.

"Welcome to Attorney Pearson's office. How may I assist you?"

"I'm here to see Angela Richards, please."

"Is Ms. Richards expecting you?"

I lifted the flowers so she could see my intent. "No, she isn't. I just wanted to surprise her if that's all right."

Excitement lit up her face as she slightly bounced in place. "Oh, how sweet. I'll let her know she has a guest. You can have a seat right over there."

I went to the softest leather couch I'd ever sat on. Cloaking their clients in comfort had to be one way they secured them because I was ready to doze off within seconds. When I'm tired, I'd agree to just about anything to get some shut-eye. If this sofa was a tactic, I can guarantee it worked. Thankfully, I heard Angela's voice before I could be lulled to sleep by the comfy couch and feng shui atmosphere.

"Kinston?" she queried, her face marred with surprise.

I could barely speak. The feathery feel of cotton invaded my mouth. *Damn, she is a vision.* I'd seen this woman dressed to the nines and dressed down, but her business attire added another level of attraction to her sexy physique. The short-sleeved blouse with the small peephole sitting perfectly above her cleavage and the form-fitted, knee-length skirt with those sky-high Stella Hues screamed, "Come fuck me," and I wanted to take her right here on this comfy couch and put both of us to sleep—Molly, Pearson, and whoever else in this office be damned.

"Yes, it's me. I received your message last night, so I figured I'd stop by," I said, extending my hand with the flowers. "Show you how much I appreciate your sentiments and hope you'll forgive me as well. If you're ready to talk, then I'm ready to listen."

Curiosity danced in her eyes as she slowly reached for the bouquet. She brought the flowers to her nose and gently inhaled the wafting scent before softly fingering the petals.

"Interesting flower choice, but you know if you're offering an apology, pink carnations or orchids would be the go-to," she said with a playful note on her tone.

"Perhaps," I said, pocketing my hands in my pants with a slight shrug. "But the amaryllis flower represents splendid beauty, both external and internal. That's what I see every time I'm in your presence. A woman who radiates beauty from the inside out."

A coy smile spread across her lips. "Humph." She placed one hand on her hip. "It's also my favorite flower, so I guess Nissi told you that?"

"No," I chuckled at her flippant assumption. "You did." Her eyes and body flinched, and then she blinked rapidly, obviously trying to recall when she told me that tidbit of information. So, I decided to put her out of her misery. "It's the screensaver on your cell phone."

A faint gasp escaped her as she stared demurely at the bouquet again. Her round orifices pooled with water when she lifted her gaze back to me. "You paid attention to that?"

Keeping my eyes locked with hers, I closed the space between us and gently took her hand, caressing my thumb across her knuckles. "I pay attention to *you*."

Warmth flooded her face as she released her hand from mine and swiped at the lone tear threatening to streak down her face. I extended my hand and trapped hers underneath mine, caressing her soft cheek with the gentle brush of my thumb. She leaned into the touch of our connected hands with closed eyelids, savoring the intimacy. After a few seconds, her eyes fluttered open, and she stepped back, clearing her throat. The guards were falling back into place, so I had to stop them before she closed me out again.

"Bless me with your thoughts."

She flashed a wry smile at me. "It's just that ... I keep that as my screensaver to remind myself of that exact message. I'm a beautiful person, inside and out."

Clasping my fingers around the back of her neck, I brought her close again and kissed her forehead. "Good to see you keeping your tiara polished because that's exactly how I see you. Exactly who you are. All day. Every day."

Resolve washed over her, and she touched my arm above my elbow. "I'm ready to talk."

"And I'm ready to listen. Go out on a date with me."

"I'm not sure if you noticed, but I'm at work right now," she teased.

Flipping my wrist to examine the time, I shook my head. "Actually, it's just turning five, so you're off the clock."

Just then, a white man a little shorter than me with a slim build and a slight tan walked out in a crisp, expensive, tailor-made suit, toting a briefcase.

"Molly, I'm gone for the evening," he said until Angela and I caught his attention. "There you are. I went to your office to tell you I was heading out." He approached us and outstretched his hand for mine. I accepted his handshake. "Hello, I'm Attorney Daniel Pearson."

"This is Kinston Jordan, Attorney Pearson. A friend of mine," Angela introduced.

He gave me that dazzling lawyer grin that all attorneys use and said, "Well, any friend of Angela's is a friend of ours." He turned his attention to Angela. "I'm heading out. Becca will have my head if I'm not on time for tonight's godforsaken art auction."

"Turnabout is fair play. She has to attend all your benefit functions."

He cackled. "Christ, you sound just like my wife. How much is she paying you to advocate for her?"

"Oh my goodness," Angela shrieked around our hearty laughter. "Although, that's not a bad idea. But you better get out of here if you don't want to be late."

"In your famous words, touché." He held up two fingers. "Besides, I better leave before you find a way to get an additional paycheck out of me." He turned his focus to me. "Kinston Jordan, it was a pleasure to meet you. Be sure to get her out of this office, please."

"That's the plan," I agreed, both of us ignoring Angela's pursed lips. "And likewise, it was a pleasure."

He patted me on the arm and tossed a hand to the ladies before waltzing out of the office.

Angela turned to the side to view the clock on the office wall, reflecting that it was indeed now after five o'clock in the afternoon. Molly's knowing smirk greeted both of us. I'd forgotten all about her until Attorney Pearson came out. I'm sure she received the ear hustle of her life today. Angela's embarrassed blush attested to the same fact.

"Hmm, Molly—"

"There are no messages and nothing outstanding on Attorney Pearson's calendar. I do believe that we are both free to go on time for once on a Friday," she interjected. "And I didn't hear a peep."

"And let's keep it that way." The two ladies nodded their agreement before Angela returned her attention to me. "Wait for me?"

"I wouldn't dream of leaving."

Chapter Eleven

KINSTON

After leaving the law offices, I followed Angela to her house so she could park her car, and then she hopped into my ride with me. The depth of our conversation required our whole and undivided attention, which neither of us could commit to on an empty stomach, so we decided to grab a bite to eat first. Throughout our meal, we both exchanged office stories, and she explained how she came to work for Daniel Pearson and her experience with one of the nation's largest firms as a Black woman. I cringed at the tales of her other counterparts, underestimating her intelligence, work ethic, dedication, and comprehension. However, I was thrilled that Pearson and the partners shut down the antics with swift punishments or severed ties. Having true allies was a rarity, so it was refreshing to know she worked in an environment that kept her covered.

By the time we finished eating, I had just wrapped up some of the details about my company's upcoming expansion and our plans for the new facility and showed her our event coordinator's plans for the grand opening celebration.

"You know, I don't think we ever chatted about how you became a gym owner. I mean, given your athleticism and collegiate background, it's not a farfetched idea, but we've never talked about it."

Mulling it over, she was right. We hadn't. Most of our time was dedicated to my getting to know her and breaking down her barriers that I willingly put myself aside. However, I stayed away from my profession with Angela because it was hard to gauge her emotions regarding health and fitness, given what little I knew of her situation with that Nigel clown. I didn't want to trigger some deep-seated wounds mistakenly, so I never opened the door on that subject. Tonight was probably the closest I'd come to sharing about my business with her out of the sheer excitement of the grand opening and the elation with being done with the renovations.

"Well, Roman and I met in college. That's how we became best friends. We were a part of the same undergrad program, with different degree focuses. We were also roommates."

"Oh, so he played college ball as well?"

"Yeah, for the first two years. A knee injury pretty much deaded his college sports career. Still, Roman is super intelligent, so he was there on an academic scholarship and made the team as a walk-on. Since he had an internship with the sports trainers, they allowed him to continue to stay in the dorms dedicated to the athletes."

"Ouch!" She winced. "I hope that didn't ruin any professional chances he had."

I chuckled, considering what she'd just said. "Nah, Roman was good, but the NFL wasn't in his sights. He loved the sport. I mean, you have to with the physical and mental wear and tear it puts on your body. But he always said that football was just a hobby and a way to get the ladies for him. He's doing exactly what he aimed to do. Granted, I'm sure he wishes he didn't have that injury because rehab was a bitch, but careerwise, he's right where he wants to be."

"Well, that's good," she said, flailing her hands. "I mean, not him getting hurt. That it didn't impact his aspirations."

I caressed her hand softly, slightly amused that I still flustered her during our conversations. "I knew what you meant, Angela. No offense taken at all. Trust me, he surely wouldn't have gotten offended, either. Roman is the type who'd rather own the team not play for it. Exactly why he's my business partner."

Angela's demure blush pinged in my chest. Jesus, this woman lit me up with the slightest gestures. Keeping my hands and my dick away from her was getting more challenging with every passing day. Our brief absence from each other did absolutely nothing to quell my yearning for her. In fact, I believe it heightened it.

"So, when you graduated, you and Roman decided to open a gym?"

Her question caused me to tense a little bit. Life had been going so well for so long that I rarely reflected on that dark period. It was a piece of my past that I rarely wanted to discuss. Though time had healed the wounds, that didn't mean the scars weren't equally painful. There was so much associated with that stretch of my life that went wrong that I didn't believe that the blows I'd been delivered would ever cease. Discussing the gym with Angela was a safe space I'd readily reveal. In my years before the gym, not so much. My apprehension had nothing to do with her but the pressure of reliving a hell I'd fought tooth and nail to climb out of. That was the reason I never pressed too much about Nigel. I understood exactly how it felt to want to bury some demons so far into the past that they would never resurface. Except here it was resurfacing.

Angela's brows furrowed as she held my hand a bit tighter when she noticed the change in my demeanor. "What's wrong? Did I say something?"

Heaving a sigh, I pinched my brows with my fingertips and shook my head. "No, it's not you at all. It's just—"

The words failed me. I didn't even know how to begin with this story, and though we were secluded in the restaurant, it wasn't a subject that I wanted to unpack in public, either. If I could change the topic altogether, that would be perfect.

Her eyes caught my downcast ones as she squeezed my hand reassuringly. "Remember what you told me about my tiara? Talk to me. Let me polish your crown."

Damn. Never had a woman used my words on me. And the beauty was that they weren't spewed against me but rather *for* me. At that moment, my chest cracked with something unfamiliar to me, and my carnal feelings were replaced with something of greater substance, magnifying the emotions I'd felt for her. Sure, I'd been in love, or so I thought before. Even that paled compared to what I felt for Angela at this very moment. No rhyme or reason could explain it. Angela just hit different.

At this point, she could have whatever she wanted out of me, just not here. This was a conversation that I would only endure in the comfort of my own home.

Swiping my hand down my beard, I eyed her with sheer admiration. "Okay. I'll tell you, but let's not discuss it here. Do you mind if we leave and head to my place? I'll go into detail about how I opened my business, and then we can have our talk."

She hesitated for the briefest second before nodding and saying, "Of course."

Chapter Twelve

KINSTON

"Welcome to my humble abode," I welcomed Angela inside as I turned on the lights.

Angela glanced around as we made our way into the living room. "Impressive for a bachelor pad."

A grin danced on my lips at her insinuation. "You didn't think I knew how to decorate?"

"No, I didn't think it would interest you to do so. Most single men don't bother with such details." She shrugged before giving me the once-over. "It's apparent you know how to put *things* together."

It was clear that the wine had taken effect. A tipsy Angela made for a flirty Angela, and I think I liked it. My eyebrow lifted. "You like what you see, huh?"

My question must've pulled her from her lustful reverie because she shook her head and then massaged her throat as she cleared it. "Hmm . . . just taking notice."

She wasn't getting off that easily. I smirked, closing the gap between us. "I'm glad I'm not the only one taking notice then." My eyes bore into hers. She attempted to shift her focus, but I dipped my head, forcing her to hold my gaze. "Don't run from me. Lean into me."

Her lids fluttered softly as she quipped, "Mr. Jordan."

She searched my face with curious eyes as if trying to determine whether to run or lean. When she released a relaxing breath, slipped out of her heels, and headed to my sofa, I knew she'd opted not to run. I didn't know if it was the liquid courage or if I'd finally cracked the Da Vinci code of heart, but I hoped this newfound space would lead us to explore more.

When she sat with one foot tucked underneath her, I turned, wondering what my next move should be because I didn't want to scare her off. For the first time, she honestly seemed to open up, and I didn't want to ruin the moment.

She patted the cushion next to her. "Let's not run together."

My heart thumped, and I had to calm down to keep from taking off like my feet were on fire. To buy myself some time, I asked if she'd like something to drink, and when she agreed, I made my way into my kitchen and returned with a bottle of Hennessey and two glass tumblers, each with a couple of ice cubes. After filling both glasses halfway, I unbuttoned my suit jacket and eased it off my shoulders, then laid it across the love seat before unbuttoning and rolling up my shirt sleeves. Sitting beside her, I turned sideways so we faced each other.

She reached for her tumbler and took a sip before she settled into her next statement. "You've spent an extensive amount of time getting to know me, Kinston. Let's finish our conversation at the restaurant. Let me get to know more of you."

I sat against the sofa and then tilted my head back as I slowly swiped my hands down my face. I needed a few seconds to gather my thoughts and stop the blush threatening my cheeks. I couldn't believe this woman had me giddy like a female.

Releasing a deep breath, I gave her my undivided attention. I hated to rehash this, but I couldn't be afraid to speak on my past when there had been so many times she'd had to speak on hers. For her to trust me, I had to show her I also trusted her.

"When we were at the restaurant, you asked me if Roman's injury thwarted his NFL prospects." She nodded, still none the wiser to the devastating news I was about to lay in her lap. "Well, it wasn't Roman whose NFL hopes were crushed. It was mine."

The news settled between us like a bombshell. In an instant, her entire face morphed into shock. Her mouth fell agape as she placed a soothing hand on my knee. "Oh no, Kinston," she drawled out with sadness. "I'm so sorry. Listen, if you don't want to discuss this, I totally understand—"

"No, it's all good. I don't mind." I caressed her hand, which was still on my knee. "I don't mind with you." We exchanged sentiments with our eyes that made me feel as though there was no other woman with whom I'd feel comfortable sharing the intricacies of my life.

Taking a sip of my drink, I continued, "There was another guy I considered a best friend of mine who was also on the team. We'd been friends since the ninth grade, playing high school and college ball together. During our senior year in college, we both entered the draft. It was a celebration. After the combine and all the other crap the scouts and NFL put us through to determine our stock value, I was prized to be a part of the first round of draft picks. He was prized to be in the second round. Regardless, it meant we could have been on an NFL team, playing on the first string if all went well with the draft, possible trades, and practices."

With a brief pause, I reached for my liquid stress reliever. I took the remaining liquor to the head to give me the boost needed to finish the story. It wasn't until I felt the squeeze on my hand that I looked at Angela. Her encouragement was like healing water washing over my soul.

Swallowing deeply, I continued, "One day, some bullshit popped off, and he and I came to blows. Thirty-three-year-old me realizes how incredibly stupid it was to risk it all, but twenty-one-year-old me had been betrayed and didn't mind issuing out ass whoopings. During the fight, I slipped and fell awkwardly, completely shredding my knee. Just like that, I went from a first-round draft pick to a career-ending injury." I snapped my fingers for emphasis.

Angela's gasp made me realize I had been staring into space. Her eyes were watery when I brought my focus back to her, and she was lovingly gripping my hand tighter than before. I hadn't noticed the mistiness of my own eyes until I felt a streak of wetness on my cheek. Reaching over, she lightly thumbed away the singular tear.

"Best friends coming to blows," she whispered softly. "It was over a girl."

Her words were more of a statement than a question, indicating she'd already deduced the reason. Without uttering a word, I simply nodded my head as the answer.

"Did you all iron it out?"

"Nah," I hissed with a scoff. "It's like this. I ain't mad about the situation anymore. Dredging it up still hurts, I guess. But I'm not mad. Still, when a snake bites you, you kill it at the head because once a snake, always a snake. That's the one thing the devil isn't a liar about. In the same way that God is still God, Satan is gonna always be Satan: he and all his minions. My ex-best friend entered the NFL, and I did not. He can do him and be successful. I'm at peace with that. But he can never penetrate this or this with me," I answered, pointing to my head and heart.

Angela solemnly nodded. "That's fair." She caressed my face with her soft and dainty hands. "I'm proud of you. To have lost such a promising future at a young age at the hands of someone you considered a best friend, no less, and still come out as a successful and positive person is a beautiful testament to the amazing man you are. Most people would've lost their mind and their way. But look at you making a whole damn lemonade stand out of oranges."

If I hadn't known for sure before, I knew in this very instance that Angela Richards was mine. Not possessively, but infinitely. She was made for me, and I was made for her. In my thirty-three years, I'd dated numerous women and slept with my fair share of them. Not one of them penetrated my soul like Angela. Not one of them poured into me like Angela just had. Hell, I'd never shared that story with any woman. The only woman who even knew that story was the one who was involved in the mess of it . . . Lilah. She'd been the only woman I'd loved. Here I was . . . falling for another one. Angela. I'll admit I was scared shitless to fall in love with any woman after Lilah, especially Angela. Lilah might've folded me, but Angela Richards could break me, and she didn't even have a clue of the power she possessed.

"Thank you. Thank you for seeing me."

Clasping her wrist, I kissed the inside of her palm. Her breath hitched at the touch, so I did it again. Her other hand traced the outline of the base of her neck, and I could see her pulse thumping. Though she tried to hide it, I could tell she was becoming as turned on as I was. What I also noticed was that she didn't pull away. Cue activated. At this point, whatever conversation we would have was no longer needed. She was telling me everything that needed to be said through her actions. Gently, I kissed up the length of her forearm. The more kisses I placed, the more labored her breathing became. I leaned over, nuzzling my nose in the crevice of her neck and inhaling her scent.

"Angela." Her name on my lips came out low and gravelly. Animalistic.

She smelled like I would be drawing her a hot bath and making her breakfast in bed in the morning. Gawd, the way she smelled was my aphrodisiac and my kryptonite.

Lifting her, I sat back on the sofa and brought her to straddle me. She gasped when she felt the steeliness between my thighs. The heat I felt from her core let me know how much her body appreciated the feeling. Gripping the sides of her waist, I leaned forward, dragging my long and wet tongue along her clavicle to the sensitive place on her neck, causing her to release a deep moan. *That's the spot.* Yes, I was a researcher ... a fucking hunter, honestly. Now that I'd discovered one erogenous zone, I would cater to it on my quest to excavate all the others. I planted my lips on her neck, circling and sucking on it. Her moans hit a fever pitch as she completely engulfed me in her arms and pressed my face deeper on her tender flesh.

"Kinston," she breathed heavily.

"Mmm," I growled, my eyes closing as my head tilted back, savoring her soft pants.

The weighty tone of my name on her lips released a carnal urge inside of me that I'd only dreamed about, so at this point, I had to know. She had to be sure because anything beyond this was the point of no return.

"Angela." My voice drawled out in the deepest baritone as she gently ground her core into my throbbing member. "You gotta let me know you want this. *Now.*"

My eyes shot open to meet her lust-filled gaze, and she nodded.

"Tell me, Queen. Tell me."

Her eyes ballooned and then morphed into a pleasant mixture of appreciation and longing. "Ye ... yes, Kinston. I want ... you."

Her words were timid, but they weren't unsure. It was the exclusive pass that I had been waiting on, and I was going to use every bit of my granted access ... like a motherfucker.

Knowing that Angela was self-conscious, I had to make myself open and vulnerable to her first. I didn't mind wrapping her in my web, leaving her so spun there was no way she would weave her way out or desire to do so. Lifting her, I placed her on the sofa and stood facing her. Our lustful gazes collided with each other with an intensity that I'd never experienced. Slowly, I unfastened each button of my dress shirt one by one and watched as her chest rose and fell as her anticipation grew. When I lifted my tucked shirt from my waistline and eased it off my shoulders, I saw the disappointment in her eyes at the wife beater still covering my chest. But she didn't have to wait for what she desired to view. I lifted the undershirt off in one swoop, catching the intake of air as she swallowed deeply. A sinister smirk crossed my face as I pulled my bottom lip between my teeth. I was sure my dimples were on full display because she attempted to close her eyes.

Leaning over, I grabbed her hands and placed them on my chest while whispering, "Nah, Beautiful, open your eyes. Savor this. Enjoy this."

She damn near melted into the sofa cushions as her eyes flew open and fluttered from the touch of my chiseled pecs. Still holding her hand, I stood upright and moved her hands to explore the details of my body. I glided it over my nipples, down my core, to the V-cut at my waistline. Each touch seduced her as heat grew in her umber orbs and her core. I could smell the sweet scent of her essence rising, and I groaned with the urge to partake of my taste of her slice of heaven.

She wrapped her hands around my waist, unsure of her next move, so I helped her by placing her hands on my belt. "Take it off."

Oh, I saw she was a good girl in the bedroom, following my directions to the letter without hesitation. When the belt was undone, she slid it from the loops and discarded it on the sofa.

This time, I didn't have to instruct her. She eased my dress slacks from my waist and paused when they dropped to my ankles. Though restrained by my boxer briefs, she witnessed the full extent of my need for her. She was star-crossed and nervous as she scooted back against the sofa. I used the moment to step out of my loafers and pants. I opted to leave on my socks, especially for this first time. The heat from the socks was guaranteed to heighten my release. And I needed all that.

I lifted her from the sofa, and she wrapped her legs around my waist as our tongues met in a hot test of wills as our mouths dove into depths that we'd never explored. I walked us to my bedroom, placing her on my Texas-king bed. Her eyes roamed the expansive space.

"Massive bed," she whispered.

"Mammoth man," I whispered.

I wanted to rip her clothing to shreds, but I'd tuck away the lion for the lamb to ensure her comfort. There would be plenty of time for her to walk on my wild side. I beckoned her to me with my forefinger, and she scooted forward until she was on the edge of the bed. My eyes squinted with delight at how she obeyed my every beck and call. Taking her hands, I placed them over her blouse buttons and used my hands to cover hers to aid her in unclasping each one. I knew she'd be too nervous to complete the task alone and too self-conscious to allow me to take control, so I opted for us to do it together. With each release of a button, eagerness and hunger grew between us. By the time she slid the blouse off her shoulders and it cascaded to the floor, our mutual desire had synced into an undeniable synergy. When she sank back into my bed, it was understood that I'd been granted full permission to consume her body.

I planted one knee on the bed so that I could have the leverage I needed to lift her hips and remove her skirt. Easing the garment down her rotund ass and thick thighs had me ready to bust in my briefs. She was so damned sexy. I stood for a moment, studying and admiring her body as she lay before me in matching, sexy, black lace bra and panties. I tried to take in everything . . . the curve in her hips, the slight fupa that was tastefully hidden by her high-cut panties, the swell of her breasts, to the trim of her hair. Hell, I even noticed the small scar on her right knee.

"What . . . What's wrong?" she asked, and I could sense the hint of insecurity trying to consume her.

I shook my head, licking my lips. "Nothing, Beautiful. Just studying God's greatest creation and admiring his handiwork."

A demure smile graced her face, and the brief note of insecurity was replaced by bold confidence as she leaned forward, unlatching her bra. "Well, be sure to examine it all," she purred as her bra floated to the floor.

Chocolate gumdrops sat at attention against perky mocha breasts. They were the most glorious sights I'd seen, and my mouth watered for a taste. Easing on the bed, my massive hands circled her breasts as I ogled the distended beauties. I pinched her nipple before capturing it in my mouth and sucking. Angela's head fell back as ecstasy invaded her.

"Ooh, Kinston," she moaned at the feel of my mouth moving from the right to the left, getting my fill of each of her globular mounds.

I moved from her breasts, kissing down the center of her chest and caressing and kissing down her stomach until I reached the trim of her panties. Using my teeth, I pulled the flimsy material down until I had to use my hands to slip them from around that wonderous ass down her legs and off her feet.

"A fucking marvel," I groaned, eyeing the sweet spot between her thighs.

She let out a moan that killed every ounce of foreplay I had left. I stalked to the nightstand beside the bed and retrieved a covering. Lambskin. I always used these because, to me, it made the pussy feel better, but I never knew who had an allergy to latex, and for days like today, I damn sure didn't want that to be a deterrent. She gasped when I unsheathed myself from my briefs to secure the protection.

I stroked myself, priming to enter her and sinisterly chuckling at her reaction. "Well, a Queen deserves a King, Beautiful."

"Shitttt," she groaned at my wordplay. "Kinston, please." She reached for me, and I would not deny her any longer.

I'd wanted to tease her, touch her, and taste her, but neither of our primal urges could resist what we ultimately wanted: to be connected as one. I slid on top of her and eased inside of her. Halfway in, she started trying to back away from me.

"Nah, don't run. Let me guide you through it, Beautiful."

"Kinston, baby," she panted. "It's so much."

"Let me show you how to take it. Own this shit, Angela."

Her eyes rolled as she relaxed, gripping her hands around my neck. I anchored her body, slowly moving my hips into her. Her eyes fluttered closed.

"No, no, baby. Open your eyes. I want you to see what you're doing to me," I growled.

Her eyes popped open as she took in the sight of me over her, gliding in and out of her core. Wetness seeped down, moisturizing my dick with her juices, and I nearly lost my mind. Inside her felt so good. I knew she was a queen, sitting on this African diamond mine.

"Fuck!" I hissed as her pretty treasure sucked all of my girth inside of her.

I'd slipped inside the ocean of her depths. An oasis. A paradise. Destiny fulfilled. When she started meeting me thrust for thrust, there was no doubt about it. She. Was. Mine.

"Oh, gawd! Kinston," she crooned. "It feels so fucking good, baby!"

"Ahhh, Angela. Shit. Baby. Damn it. *This pussy.*"

Beast mode activated. The bed was too much of a constraint for me. I pulled out of her and stood, much to her dismay.

"Nooo, Kinston," she groaned, reaching for me.

My dimpled smile spread wide at her longing for me. "I'm coming back, Beautiful."

I lifted her from the bed, hoisting her up by her luscious thighs, and slipped inside of her again, going to work. She held my neck as her head fell back and let out a war cry scream from the reconnection. In and out, out and in, I jackhammered into her, bouncing her up and down my lengthy thickness.

"Mm-hmm, take it, Queen. Rule this motherfucker."

"Ooooh, gawd! Kinston. Babyyy."

The way she was contracting on my man below let me know she was close to her peak. Damn, if she wasn't about the squeeze the nut right out of me too. I couldn't even describe how glorious she was. She thought I was taking her on a ride, but it was she who had me on the roller coaster.

"Kinston, I'm com . . . I'm coming . . . so *hard*, baby."

And she did. She was a beautiful mess as her juices rained down on me, slicking me like an April shower. The power of her orgasm consumed her so much so that she went limp in my arms. I walked us to the wall, bracing her back against it for support as I continued my pursuit, thrusting and swimming into her depths. I fully expected her to run as she did initially, knowing how spent she was, but my queen reigned supreme when she gathered herself, pierced my gaze with soul-stirring determination, gripped my shoulders, and murmured, "Take it."

I bit my lip and growled, my own eyes closing. This woman was my undoing. I inched closer to her, burrowing my girth into her with terse and cavernous thrusts. My balls love tapped her pretty pussy.

"Beautiful," I ground out, my back muscles tense, arms aching, thighs and calves burning as I buried inside of her.

G-spot. Her fluids gushed down on me as a scream ripped through her throat that I was positive had set off every car alarm in the neighborhood. That did it.

"Fuckkk," I hissed through gritted teeth. "So *wet*. So *good*."

My release ripped through me like a tornado, and my seeds poured like a monsoon, filling the condom to the hilt.

The last bit of energy I could muster, I used to slip out of her and move us to the bed. I just barely had enough energy to remove the condom and sling it into the trash can. As we nestled in my bed, all I could feel was Angela's head on my chest as I wrapped my arms around her before slumber claimed both of us.

Chapter Thirteen

ANGELA

THE DELICIOUS SMELL of pancakes and bacon wafting in the air stirred me from my impenetrable slumber. My stomach gurgled in anticipation as my mind wondered who was at my house and cooking in my kitchen. Obviously, it wasn't me. That's when reality forced me out of my sleep-fogged and sex-drunk haze. Now alert, I peered around my surroundings. This was not my room or my house. Suddenly, the evening before danced into my memory. I'd come to Kinston's house with him, and he'd sexed me senseless, apparently. Definitely.

"What time is it?" I whispered aloud, holding my head from the slight hangover.

I lifted his watch off the nightstand and saw it was 7:43 in the morning. *The morning?* Did I really stay the entire night? It had only been going on eight p.m. last night when we'd arrived at his house. Yes, we talked for a while and sexed each other for a long time, but not me sleeping the whole night away in a strange house. I punched the air in frustration. I knew this man's sex game was dangerous. *I knew it.* One night and he had me holed up in his room as if he were "my man, my man, my man." *Fatha, help me.* I needed to gather myself and my belongings and escape this trap lair.

I promise I'll never drink again. That's a lie. I'd never drink around *him* again. Why? He already had me on the spend-the-night-bag tip. Next, he'd have me on a spare-key-move-in-ready tip. Nope. I would not be sexed to gullibility. No matter how luscious, glorious, and downright delectable the sex had been.

Just as I was about to make a mad dash for my clothing and try to locate my cell phone for an Uber, Kinston waltzed into the bedroom with a wooden tray filled with the savory-smelling meal that he'd been preparing. I quickly wrapped my body in the sheet before tucking my dry curls behind my ear. I slid upright against the headboard, offering him a guarded smile.

"Good morning, Beautiful," he bellowed, his rich baritone voice wrapping me in warmth.

"Hi," I offered softly under lowered lids as I toyed with my fingertips.

He paused, causing me to chance a glance in his direction. He stood there, eyeing me peculiarly. The awkward shift was felt between us. I could sense that a question was lingering on the tip of his tongue, but instead, he tapped the tray with his finger and continued toward the bed.

Placing it over my lap, he rattled off the prepared meal selection. "You have pancakes with fresh strawberries, and maple syrup is in this carafe. There's some turkey bacon, a bowl of raspberries and blueberries, and some freshly squeezed orange juice." He tapped my device on the side. "And I brought your cell phone from the living room."

To minimize the conversation and to further prevent an onslaught of questions from Kinston, I popped a strawberry into my mouth and mumbled, "Thank you."

His dimpled smile spread across his lips before he playfully tapped my foot and turned to walk out of the bedroom. The visual of his chiseled bare back in gym shorts that draped at his waistline sent my kitty into purrland. I had to clench my thighs together to stop it from singing. *See? Dangerous.* I couldn't even be in the vicinity of that man without turning into a sex-deprived fiend. The sight of his bare chest, abs, and pecs flexing with every moment didn't help when he reentered with a plate stacked high with pancakes and fruit in one hand and a tall glass of orange juice in the other. He placed his juice on the nightstand beside him and eased onto the bed beside me before saying a quick grace and placing a heaping mound of pancakes into his mouth.

"You didn't have to do this for me. I even have you cheating. Besides, I'm sure you have to be at the gym."

He placed a hand on my knee. "First of all, I *wanted* to feed you. What kind of man would I be if I didn't replenish what I diminished? Second, this is my actual cheat day. Lastly, the perk to being a gym owner is having employees so you don't have to go to work when you don't want to. Saturdays are my off days. The only thing I missed was my five a.m. workout, but I'd like to think I already made up for that." He jogged his eyebrows at me with a knowing grin on his face.

Rather than respond, I took a long drink of the orange juice and then dove back into my meal. Lawd, Marie Jordan taught these men right. Both Kinston and his brother could cook. These were the best-tasting pancakes of my life, and though I wasn't a fan of turkey anything, this bacon was good and didn't taste like rubber tires. Still, I ate just enough to kill my hunger pangs before moving the tray aside.

"Not hungry?" Kinston said, eyeing my half-eaten plate of food.

Embarrassment flushed over me. "All plus-sized women don't eat everything in sight." I stood with the sheet wrapped around me and picked up my phone. It was definitely time to make my exit.

Kinston flinched at my words before placing his plate on the nightstand. "Angela, you know I didn't mean it like that."

Rolling my eyes, I cast a stern glare in his direction. "Of course, you didn't," I quipped sarcastically before scrolling through my messages and missed calls.

He stood and met me on the other side of the bed. "Angela, I didn't. I just noticed you hadn't finished—"

"Because a big girl must always finish her food, right?"

He pulled my phone from my hands, tossed it on the bed, and gripped my shoulders, forcing me to look at him. "Stop doing that. Stop putting words in my mouth that you know I didn't say and would never mean. The question was purely to make sure that you were good."

My head reared back. "What makes you think I'm not?"

He scoffed, shaking his head. "We can get into that in a moment. But if you stopped eating because you had your fill, that's cool. However, if you stopped because you didn't want to eat in front of me, that's *not* cool. I'm not judging if you eat a tad bit or go back for seconds. I simply want you to eat and refuel, and you should be comfortable doing just that regardless of where you are or who is present."

I felt like an idiot. I knew he didn't mean it condescendingly. It's just that certain statements triggered me from my past hurts. Besides, I still couldn't fathom what this man saw in me. I wasn't the type of woman he was used to having around. Did I think I was a catch? Of course, but for a gymhead who made health and fitness a lifestyle and a career? Hell no.

I massaged my temples before sitting on the bed and giving him my attention. "I'm sorry. It's just me drudging up the past. Nigel—"

My words were snipped short by the stern freeze of his outstretched hand, signaling for me to halt what I was saying.

"And *that's* what you're *not* gonna do. Don't compare me to that motherfucker or any other. I am *not* Nigel. Never have been. Never will be. If I offended you, I apologize, but I won't apologize because of another man—ever."

Unlike Shereé from the *Real Housewives of Atlanta*, I no longer had to wonder who was gon' check me because Kinston proved it was him, hands down. There I sat, officially checkmated with my mouth sweeping the floor in astonishment. When I finally recovered, I tossed my hands up in surrender. "Understood."

His stare bored into me before he stood back, placing his hands into the pockets of his shorts and releasing a deep breath. "We're good?"

Nodding, I answered, "We're good." Because what else could I say to that?

The upset expression on his face dissipated. "Good. Now, I'm going to finish my meal. And if you so desire, you can finish yours. Judgment-free zone." With that, he sauntered back to his side of the bed, clicked on the TV with the remote, and began eating his meal again.

I bit my lip as I tried not to stare at this man. Never had I been told off and turned on at the same damn time. I wanted to climb his mountainous frame and fuck him until nightfall all over again. Instead, I chose the safe route and decided to eat more of the food I had remaining. It was still too much for me, but I could stand to consume a few more bites.

With a smirk, Kinston shook his head.

"What?" I quipped after swallowing the piece of bacon I'd been chewing.

"You, man," he answered with a chuckle. Leaning over and planting a kiss on my shoulder, he said, "I see that I'm going to need to put some 'act right' in your ass, Beautiful."

So help me, I wanted to resist entertaining him with any flirty talk, but I couldn't help myself. I giggled. "Didn't you do that last night?"

He let out a boisterous guffaw. "Nah, that was sweet. Beauty hasn't met the likes of the Beast yet." He winked, pulling his bottom lip between his teeth.

Not this man issuing out his own warning labels. Oh yeah. I was in trouble. I chose not to respond but rather to finish eating. Once I was truly content, I wiped my hands with a napkin and stood.

"Is your bathroom through that door?" I asked, pointing at the closed door across from him.

He nodded, and I made sure to wrap the sheet tightly around my body before making my way over to the bathroom to release myself and wash my hands. His bathroom was as well put together as his bedroom and living room. At this point, I shouldn't be surprised. Kinston was a man of refinement and displayed that in every facet of his life. Not to mention, everything about him was grand to accommodate his tall and muscular frame. His massive shower boasted multiple showerheads with clean and crisp double glass doors. An oversized garden tub sat in the center with the fresh scent of two Bergamot candles at either end. An expansive, single, oversized sink was surrounded by extra-long counter space on either side down the length of the wall. His grooming kit was neatly laid atop a hand towel on the sink. A toothbrush, toothpaste, floss, and mouthwash were encased in a mounted holder on the wall next to the sink. Hand soap and lotion sat neatly beside each other, and paper towels were placed inside a holder for easy access. How could I expect anything different? They say cleanliness was next to godliness, and Kinston was godlike in all things.

That was precisely why I couldn't be in a relationship with him. Last night, he officially affirmed that he held the power to claim me and own me. From the day I met him, well before I even gave him a taste, I'd known that he possessed that type of influence over me from the sheer dominance he exuded. If I gave into his whims, and he decided I wasn't good enough for him, I'd be utterly devastated. Truth be told, I felt that I should walk away completely, but I'd be a bald-faced liar to pretend I could. Kinston's friendship was a vibe, and his bedroom antics were an experience. That, I couldn't deny. Since I knew I probably wouldn't be able to resist him, at least sexually, I vowed to keep my emotions under lock and key. It may be challenging, but I could walk away from the sex, but I couldn't walk away from heartbreak. Therefore, as I stood there moisturizing my hands in lotion, I made a pact with myself: *guard your heart, girl.*

When I exited the bathroom, I planned to leave to prevent a Kinston overload because staying wrapped in his arms all day felt too easy of a preposition. Too intimate. So, I headed to grab my clothes so I could call for a ride when I felt him tug on the sheet, halting my steps.

"Why are you covering up?" His powerful arms pulled me into him as he sat on the side of the bed. "You don't have to hide from me. I've seen every sexy curve of this body." He gripped me about the waist. "And I for damn sure would like another taste."

Resist, resist, resist! "Umm, I was going to get dressed and call an Uber. I didn't want to tie up your day. Besides, I need to get home, shower, and get some things done around my house."

He released a gust of frustrated air and then pulled me closer between his masculine, gapped legs. "Stop planning my day for me. Today, I'm yours. And if all you have to do is clean up your house, then you're mine. When we're done, *I'll* be your Uber." That part he said with just enough bite that I knew I'd offended him with that Uber comment. As quickly as his annoyance with me came, it went. The hungry eyes of the wolf replaced it. A savage. The Beast. "Now, let me unwrap my gift."

Tugging at the sheet, he did exactly as he said. He unwrapped me. Slowly, he planted soft kisses on my belly and tongue-kissed my navel. Jesus. This man . . .

"Kinston," I whined, drawing out his name as my head fell back from those pleasurable kisses.

"Say my name just like that, Beautiful."

"I should—"

My words were lost from the feel of the rise of the steel between his legs mixed with his tongue lapping at my taut nipples. I gripped his head, pulling him closer to me. Fuck. He felt so good. My excuses were running out just like the juices between my thighs. There was no way I could deny him. He was a drug, and I was a user slowly getting addicted to him and "addickted" to his sex. My protective bubble had sprung a slow leak.

Before I could gather my bearings, my back was on his bed with my legs spread eagle in Kinston's grip. Lifting one leg, he licked from the inside of my ankle, up my calf, to my knee, and up my thighs, alternating between sweet pecks and sensual laps. His tongue was cool, but it heated my core. He nestled his nose in my thin-stripped mound and sniffed with a guttural moan.

"So sweet," he groaned.

He repeated the same action on my other leg, and by the time he brought his nose back to my yoni, I squirmed in anticipation. Couldn't he just devour me already?

Gripping his locs to hold his face near my soaking, sweet spot, I moaned, "Kinston, please."

This man had me begging. Begging and proud.

My eyes found his, and I knew he was about to unleash on me. I didn't have time to prepare before he gripped my ass and dove in. His tongue was on me, lashing at my pearl and sucking her tenderness between his thick lips. The length of his tongue explored the inner depths of my wetness, and I nearly lost it.

"Kinston," I whimpered, rolling my hips into his face.

"Mm-hmmm."

Kinston thrashed his tongue in and out of my core, slurping and sucking every drop he could consume. He feasted on me as if I were the seventh course of his meal. My hip rolls quickened, giving him full access as he hummed over his decadent dessert.

"Shit, Kinston! Oh, my fucking . . . shittt."

"Sweet, sweet pussy," he whispered as he continued to devour me.

My hands slipped deeper into his locs, and I gripped them. My legs locked tightly around his neck, and my stomach muscles stiffened. I was coming fiercely without a care who heard.

"Drown me," he ordered.

Instant downpour.

"Kinstonnn, babyyy!" The roar ripped through me, flooding him with my sticky goodness.

"That's it, Beautiful. *Drown. Me.*"

Tears leaked out of the corners of my eyes as I panted and held him so tightly that I thought I'd snap his neck. Huffing, I struggled to intake oxygen into my lungs. Kinston swiped my pearl, and I pushed against his head with my hands and locked my thighs to keep him away.

"No more. I can't take no more," I panted, my body still twitching with a flurry of tingles.

He lifted, licking his lips. His mustache and beard were drenched with my essence. My body collapsed against the bed as I peered at him through hazy eyes.

"The best," he declared, swiping a hand down his face and using my juices to stroke himself.

Heaviness fell over my lids, but I hadn't realized I'd drifted off to sleep until I felt gentle kisses on my cheeks and nose. A slow grin formed on my face as I fought against Kinston's attempt to pull me from the abyss of slumber, to which I was ready to succumb.

"Wake up, Beautiful," Kinston murmured softly behind a chuckle.

"You nearly lulled me to sleep with that tongue-lashing."

"If you're not already in dreamland, my job isn't done."

Giddiness replaced my tiredness as Kinston lifted me, securing me on all fours. Whatever ride I thought I'd been on before, I automatically knew was about to pale compared to the roller coaster he was about to take me on. With his girth already sheathed, he didn't even give me a chance to brace as he plowed into me with sheer power.

"Ugh!" I cried out, gripping the sheets. It pained so deliciously good.

"Shit, Beautiful," Kinston pelted. "I don't ever wanna come out. Pure magic gold."

Kinston thrust in and out steadily, digging trenches and reaching depths I hadn't known existed. I couldn't admit it. Hell, I wouldn't admit it, but deep down, I knew he was claiming ownership over my kitty. I'd lived with my yoni for thirty years, and she was ready to give herself to him in one sitting: signed, sealed, and delivered. Getting hammered by the beast was sending me into carnal bliss, but then he penetrated my second hole with his thumb, and I hit the stratosphere. Soul officially snatched. Utopia.

"Oooh gawdd, Kinstonn. Right there. Right fucking there!"

"Ooh, Beautiful," he sang out in pleasure. "That's right. Open up for your king. Just. Like. That."

Grabbing fistfuls of my hair with his other hand while still penetrating my second hole with the thumb of his other hand, my back arched into his movements. Kinston's stroke was breaking subterranean barriers, going berserk inside of me. He wasn't just tearing down my walls. He was discovering new lands. The sound of my cheeks clapping at a rhythmic pace was evidence of our uninhibited sex.

"Ooh, I feel it, Beautiful. The way your walls are gripping me. Give it to me."

Kinston's words rang true. My climax was imminent. I didn't think I could orgasm any harder than I had the first two times, but here, Mr. Jordan was introducing my body to heights previously unseen, unheard, and un-felt.

The grunt and wail that pierced out of me was unrecognizable, even though it was clearly my mouth and my voice that released it. "I'm coming, baby. *Fuck me.*"

I'd summoned the beast.

Kinston pulled my body upward, anchoring my back against him for a death stroke. His massive hand wrapped around my neck, slightly applying pressure. My hands flew to his thighs, trying to scramble away from the insurmountable amount of pleasure that he was inflicting on me. I could feel the intensity in his stroke and the contraction of his muscles as he pummeled my insides, throwing the gauntlet down as his official claim that my sex and my soul were his.

"Come," he snarled in my ear.

That one-word command was my undoing. My juices splashed on him, and I burst into tears full-on from the uncontrollable euphoric feeling washing over me in waves. At the same time, I felt the swell of his girth, and I knew he was peaking along with me.

"Ah, Queen. This is mine. *You* are mine. You hear me?" he thundered, gripping my waist flush to him as he released with a lion's roar. The King. Mufasa—*not* Simba.

For long moments, we stayed in that position with my head leaned back, his arms wrapped around my waist, and his head flush to the slickness of my back. When I went to move, he held me in place.

"No, no. Don't move," he panted.

Our erratic breathing was the only semblance of noise as our conjoined centers continued to pulsate the remnants of our pleasures. When Kinston's muscles began to feel weighted, he slowly lifted me off him, and I couldn't fathom the fact that even with that powerful release, he was still semihard—big dick energy at its finest. I was out like a light by the time my head touched his pillow, just as he'd proclaimed.

Chapter Fourteen

ANGELA

STILL IN A haze, I awoke to powerful arms wrapped around me. When I glanced down, I was partially lying on Kinston, both of us still stark naked from our earlier rendezvous. His soft breathing was so calm and soothing that it seemed he didn't have a care in the world. The television was off, our earlier plates removed, and I could tell he'd cleaned both of us. Wow. I slept through all of that. I'd spent all that time with Nigel to learn that I'd never been sexed properly until Kinston. And I could tell. He had me over here captive in his place, pushing aside my routine and responsibilities and sleeping like a log in a different location other than my cozy bed with my first taste.

"What's on your mind?" Kinston's low rumble startled me.

"Oh!" I shrieked, grabbing my chest. "I thought you were asleep."

"I'm aware," he said, finally opening and casting those sultry brown orbs on me. "I'm a lightweight sleeper. I don't require much to rejuvenate." He sat up, still giving me his undivided attention. "What's on your mind?"

I toiled with what to say. I was not about to tell this man that his stroke game was so good that it had me acting as if it was more than just sex. When I finally strung together what I felt was a safe zone, I uttered, "Honestly, you have me out of my element right now."

His brow lifted. "How so?"

Fanning my hand out, I answered, "This." I moved from propping on my elbow to sitting beside him in bed. "This is not my routine."

"Routine?" he quizzed. "Fill in the gaps for me."

I shrugged. "Just like I need to be taking care of my responsibilities, not laid up lazily with you."

My words were met with a slight chuckle that escalated to a bellow. Slightly taken aback, I stared at him blankly until he calmed down. The smile slightly eased from his face when he saw my expression.

"Oh, you're serious. Are you *serious* right now?" he said, then doubled back as a question of assurance as realization seemed to slap him in the face.

"Yes, Kinston. Don't get me wrong, I had plenty of fun. Loads. But it's the next day, and hell, I don't even know what time it is, and I'm loitering around with you as if I don't have a care in the world."

Kinston's facial expression turned into a ball of confusion as he scratched his temple. "*Loitering around?* It's called *spending time* together, Angela. What's so wrong with us . . ." he fanned between us, ". . . doing this?" He spread his arms outward, indicating our late-night and early-morning romps.

"Nothing," I spat with frustration because I didn't want to formulate my true thoughts. "I should be at my home."

Bringing the palms of his hands up to his face, he rubbed his eyes before interlacing his fingers on his lap. "Angela, there's nothing wrong with what we're doing or have done. You're acting as if I'm holding you hostage, and you're at risk of losing your job and putting your home in foreclosure. It hasn't even been a full twenty-four hours." He turned, lifting his cell phone from the nightstand. "Well, not yet. It's 2:27 p.m. since you needed to know," he said, slipping the phone back in its original place. "What am I missing here? Be real because this isn't making any sense to me."

Silence. I met his looming inquiries with nothing but silence. Fear had stolen my voice because I knew he wouldn't understand my position, not because he couldn't. He was an intelligent man, but rather, because he wouldn't. Before I could part my lips, his eyes flickered as if he had an inkling of knowing.

He turned his body to me, caressing my fingers and staring at me with concern etched in every crevice of his face. "Angela, Beautiful, please don't tell me you regret this."

"No, no." I hurriedly cleared the air. I didn't want him to feel as though, for one minute, I felt as though he had taken advantage of me or that I was ashamed about what we had done. That wasn't the case at all. Lifting my hand, I palmed his cheek. "I don't regret what happened between us last night and this morning at all. I enjoyed myself, really," I offered with a sexy smirk and glint.

The tension in his body released, and he leaned forward, nuzzling his cheek against mine before muttering in my ear, "I'm glad to hear it, and as my lady, you can take advantage of me any time you want."

Gently, he nipped at my lobe, and I almost lost my good sense again. The man was intoxicating. Then, his words landed on me, giving me pause. Kinston was a good man—scratch that—an *exceptional* man, and I'd gotten to know him well over the past months. I knew exactly what he wanted from me. That was what I was afraid of addressing. Not only had I heard him loud and clear throughout the months, but his expectation was also made crystal clear during both our sessions. I was too lost in his stroke sauce to care, but today, coming out of our sinful trysts, a clearer head prevailed. He must have noticed the shift in my demeanor because he pulled back cautiously, eyeing me with intent.

"What is it, Angela?" he asked flatly.

My nervous energy took over, causing me to fidget. I tucked a lock of curls behind my ear as I attempted to say what I had to without hurting his feelings.

"It's just that I enjoyed what we did, I honestly did, but . . ."

He sat with his back against the headboard and dropped his head back. Disappointment and aggravation clouded his features. "Please don't tell me you're having second thoughts about us being exclusive."

"With sex, no. With a relationship, yes." There. I'd said it as quickly and as painlessly as I could.

The deflated expression he tossed at me was filled with disbelief. He sprang from the bed as if it had been set ablaze, not caring that he was swinging and dangling like a pendulum surrounded by inch after glorious inch of muscle. Even in his perturbed nature, this man was divine. *Pull yourself together, girl. Now is not the time to thirst after him.*

With his arms crossed in front of his broad chest, he asked, "So, the talks we had and the sex we had, what was *that*, Angela? You've known what I wanted since day one. I've been straight up about that."

Climbing to my knees, I kneeled back on my haunches. Regret filled me. "The talks we had, I mean, we're friends, Kinston. Talking with you is natural and easy. And yes, you have made your desires known. I know it. And sex with you is great. I'm down for that. But I just don't think . . ." I dropped my head because staring into his eyes was gutting me. ". . . I don't think we should be together in a relationship."

My declaration was met with an eerie silence. I still hadn't returned my focus to him because I couldn't bear to see the hurt and disappointment that I was sure had started bubbling to the surface. But the silence was deafening. Whatever potential tension overcast that loomed in the room grew into full-blown storm clouds the moment I saw his face.

"*Friends?* The talk we had was because we're *friends?*" he repeated as if poison laced his tongue. "Angela, you've been around me long enough to know I don't lay my burdens down on a woman I'd only consider a friend. I opened up to you because you mean more. *We* are more—"

"But we're *not* more—"

"We could be if you'd allow it!" he boomed, his chest tight. Neither one of us said a word for what felt like an eternity. Finally, he inhaled and released a deep breath, pinching the bridge of his nose with his eyes squeezed tightly. "And you for damn sure didn't argue the point last night or this morning."

"Kinston—"

He placed up a hand, thwarting my rebuttal. "Angela, what is it that you exactly want from me . . . from this? Because you know where I'm at with it."

Timidness invaded my being. He was right. I knew where he was with it and what he wanted of us. I just couldn't hop over my own hurdles. I was scarred by love, and the fear of falling again held me in such a chokehold that I simply wouldn't allow Kinston into that space. Because the fact of the matter was I could fall in love with Kinston. And somewhere down in my innermost parts, I felt that I possibly already had. Kinston was not Nigel. A fact that I was emphatically aware of. It would be easier if he were because I could be resolute in what I was about to say. Since he wasn't, and I felt far greater for Kinston than I was willing to admit to him or anybody else, including myself, I had to protect myself. Protect my heart. Falling for Kinston was easy. It was the possible fallout that gave me pause. Kinston could demolish me, causing irreparable damage. I couldn't risk that. So, I had to do the only thing that I could . . . prevent it. Keep what we had on my terms. It was the only way to keep my emotions afloat without drowning because Kinston was the sea, and I'd swim freely in it without a life preserver if I didn't stop myself from going offshore. So, I hardened my stance and prepared to make it plain.

"We can be friends... with benefits."

The way his face fell immediately made me feel horrible, and I wanted to take it back. However, I'd already soured the mood and spoke it into the atmosphere. There was no coming back from what I'd said. So, I allowed my muteness to stand.

A lump formed in Kinston's throat, and I saw him visibly swallow it to clear away the emotion. Still, his voice cracked with pain when he asked, "After everything, *this* is how you're playing it?"

The offense in his question turned the air surrounding us stale and suffocating. I had to soothe him and make him understand this was best for us. Climbing out of the bed in all my naked glory, I walked to him and cradled his still-crossed arms.

Mustering all the sincerity that I could, I pleaded, "This isn't the end. It's just where I feel we'd be best. I hope you understand."

His mesmerizing auburn eyes glossed over with an intense dark glaze that felt cold and unwelcoming. A chill ran through my body because I'd never experienced anything like it. It wasn't frightful, but rather... distant. The endearment he'd always held for me was replaced with an arctic frigidness that clearly let me know he was over this conversation and possibly me. Even before, when we were on the outskirts, it didn't feel like this.

"Kin—"

He sniffed. "Nah, it's cool." He bent down and pulled on his basketball shorts. "Go ahead and get dressed so I can take you home."

He didn't even give me a chance to respond before he turned around so smoothly and glided into his walk-in closet. You would've thought we never had such a devastating conversation. I was still standing there like a lost puppy when he emerged fully clothed in a T-shirt, socks, and Adidas slides to accompany his basketball shorts. He walked to his nightstand and grabbed his wallet and cell phone.

"I'll be waiting in the living room." He breezed out of his bedroom without a second thought or backward glance.

"Wow," I mouthed softly.

The way he'd spoken wasn't rude, but it wasn't filled with the sugary tone I was accustomed to: no winks, shameless flirting, or even a sideways grin. He said it as if it were a business transaction, like he really was my Uber driver. And he walked out just the same. I'd never seen this side of him. But what could I expect? I'd made a mess of what was brewing between us, and nothing was left to say. Quickly, I dressed and grabbed my phone. Once I exited his bedroom, I joined him in the living room.

When he saw me, he stood from the sofa, turned off the television, and headed toward his garage door. With my lips sealed, I grabbed my purse off his coffee table, slid my phone inside, and followed suit. By the time I'd reached his SUV, he was already inside. A clear indicator that he was infuriated. Kinston always opened my car door. Always. Slowly, I eased the passenger door open and slid inside. As soon as my door closed, Kinston pressed the button to raise the garage door and pressed the remote start button. With his left arm propped on the driver's door windowsill and his right hand on the steering wheel, he pulled out and headed to my house without further conversation.

When he pulled in front of my house, I decided I couldn't leave us in limbo. I faced him, even though he didn't return the gesture.

"Kinston, I want to be clear that I love spending time with you, and I have no regrets about what transpired between us last night or this morning, which is why I'd love to continue. I'm not denying you, just structuring our arrangement. That's all." I placed a hand on his forearm, which still rested on his steering wheel. "You understand, right?"

Kinston's eyes fell to where my hand was on his forearm, and I felt compelled to remove it. So, I did. His attention returned ahead of him and not to me as he slowly stroked his beard with his left hand. It was as if he'd only just realized I'd stopped talking when he cast a taciturn mien on me.

"You need to get inside. I know you have shit to do today. Don't let me hold you."

"So, you're not going to address what I said?" I asked, my brows knitted.

His nose flared before he said, "Got you."

Yes, Angela. You've royally screwed this up. That was the only thought swirling through my mind as I eased out of his SUV with my skirt tucked in embarrassment and guilt. When I closed his door, I tried once more to pull the warm and gentle side of Kinston to the surface when I offered a tender smile and hand wave. His response? He hit me with a head nod and pulled away before I could head down my driveway.

"He didn't even ensure I made it inside safely," I whispered to myself as tears clouded my vision.

As I made a mad dash for the comfort and serenity of my home, I swiped at tears that poured from my heart and ripped through my soul. I couldn't be upset about this. I asked for this. Hell, I'd demanded it. He treated me exactly how I requested to be treated, like a jumpoff. And it hurt because that wasn't the version of Kinston that I desired, but it was the version that I'd requested. My mama used to tell me to be prepared for what I asked for. Sadly, I now finally understood the meaning of her words just as clearly as I understood Kinston's callous demeanor. He was done with me, and that was final. That's when I knew my mouth had written a check my heart couldn't cash.

Chapter Fifteen

KINSTON

"SHE ACTS AS if *I'm* the one that fumbled her heart," I vented, sipping my beer. "That fuckboy Nigel is the one who played her—*not* me."

My vent was met with my boys' chorus of "trues" and "yeahs" as we all sat in Roman's theater room watching the University of Miami football game. It was one of the rare occasions when we all had an off day together, so Roman, Kannon, Jovan, and I decided to kick back with a day of college football, food, and drinks.

"If it still bothers her that much, then she needs to confront him. Leave it all out there on the field with him. I shouldn't have to take the hit for his mistakes," I belted out again before chomping down on my turkey and Swiss slider. Again, I was met with the same barrage of answers.

"I'm just saying. It was foul how she handled it," I continued through a stuffed mouth full of meat, cheese, lettuce, and bread.

"Go, go, go!" My boys jumped up, yelling at the screen as a U of M wide receiver ran into the end zone for a touchdown. "Hell yeah," they shouted, slapping fives with one another.

I pointed to the screen. "See, that's what I'm talking about. I just wanted us to win together."

"Bruh," Roman dragged out, dropping back into his seat with his head slumping between his shoulders. "Are you going to watch the game or talk about Angela all day?"

Surprised, I scowled over at him before realizing they all shared the same annoyance on their faces.

"I'm not talking about Angela all day," I refuted. "It's just that she's—"

"Hurt over Nigel and taking it out on you." All three of them said in unison, interrupting my rant.

"How'd y'all know I was going to say that?"

"Bruh, because you been saying it all afternoon," Jovan spouted as the other two agreed.

Shaking my head, I snapped, "I'm not that bad."

Roman leered at me as if to say, *"Really, bro?"*

"If you get any worse, I'm going to slice off my own ears," Roman joked.

Jovan snickered as he and Roman fist-bumped, and I met his slick comment with my middle finger.

Kannon turned exasperated eyes to me. "Bro, I love you. You know I do. I want things to work out with you and Ang too, but you know how you get over her. On top of that, you've been correlating the incident with football terminology, so you can keep discussing it. Talking about fumbling her heart, taking hits, and leaving it out there on the field. You killin' us here." He fanned between them before dropping a supportive hand on my shoulder. "Bro, she's got you down bad."

At that, Jovan and Roman burst into laughter.

"He *was* over there spewing commentary like an episode of *First Take*," Roman joked as they burst into laughter.

"Club Shay Shay. The Relationship Edition," Jovan added, shoulder-bumping Roman.

I eyed Kannon, who was trying to hold his laughter inside by covering his mouth with a balled fist.

"You know what? Fuck all y'all. I'm trying to get brotherly advice, and y'all motherfuckers wanna clown. I see where y'all at with it."

Roman and Jovan piped down, and Kannon released a sympathetic sigh as he turned a remorseful gaze to me, leaning forward with his forearms resting on his knees. "Bro, look. I'm the last person to clown you about this. You know what I went through to get Nissi, so I feel you. You were there for me, so I'll be there for you. But if I give you this advice, you gotta press pause on the venting so we can enjoy these games."

I'd take any advice I could because I was desperate to find a resolution. Angela had hurt me to my core when she allowed me to pour out my past heartache and my current feelings, only to shut us back down to square one . . . with benefits. Let me not forget the "benefits" as if that mattered. Her sex was addictive, so I couldn't say I was mad about having access to it if that was what I wanted, but it wasn't. Having the goods without the substance made it too easy to stay in that routine. There were plenty of women I could call to fulfill my sexual urges. I didn't need Angela for that. What I needed, hell, what I longed for from her was a relationship. Something real. Something steady. Something of substance. Something just for us.

Though I'd left her house that day determined to hang up my Angela cleats, that was easier said than done. I missed her so much that it physically ached. The tug-of-war between what my head knew I should do and what my heart yearned for me to do was a battle I was exhausted from fighting. What I needed was a solution that prayerfully included Angela or at least the peace of mind to deal with not having her. And if my brother had a way to make that happen, I was all ears. So, I agreed to accept his advice and table any more Angela talk so I could stop being the buzzkill that I'd been and, hopefully, win over the woman who was created to be mine.

"I'll take any advice you have to offer, bro."

"Leave her alone," he said so swiftly I didn't think I heard him.

"Come again?"

"I *said* leave her alone." He stuffed some popcorn into his mouth.

"How is that supposed to help me? I attempted that once, remember? That's why I'm sitting here today because of that epic fail."

"Bruh," Roman chimed in, "that's because as soon as she gave you a glimmer of hope, you went running to her like she was on fire, and you were the water. You ain't never heard these females talk about absence making the heart grow fonder? That's what your brother is talking about. Stop chasing her and let *her* come to *you*."

I sat with that for a minute, but I still had some reservations. "What if she doesn't?"

"She will," they all said in a chorus.

"And if you want to make her move a little faster, get some new ass," Jovan added. "Don't nothing make a woman more jealous than when another kitty cat is sniffing around. Don't just let her come to you. Let her *chase* you."

Roman pointed at Jovan. "Facts!"

Kannon shook his head at our boys before returning his attention to me. "I ain't saying go *that* far with it, but giving Angela exactly what she asked for is probably your best chance at getting her to give you what you both want. I know my sister-in-love. She wants you too. She's just scared and stubborn."

Agreeing to allow the conversation to cease, I nodded despite being skeptical about her feelings and this reverse psychology plan. At this point, what other choice did I have? None. If this didn't work, I had to learn how to tuck my emotions away and get over Angela because we would be finished. I didn't mind putting in the work. I'd do that even after she was my lady. What I couldn't do anymore was continue to chase a woman who had no interest in being caught. If she wanted to let the past ruin her future, she'd have to do that without me, even as a friend with benefits, because I also deserved more. And I wouldn't continue to sell myself short for Angela or any woman.

"And I, for one, hope it works because y'all two are exhausting," Roman said, smarting off at the mouth.

I threw a throw pillow at him, hitting him on the head. "I'll remember that when you come to me for advice for Nia."

"That'll never happen," he quipped, sipping his beer.

All of us turned to him. Our faces frowned at the confidence in his revelation.

"I thought you all were kicking it," I said inquisitively.

He made a horn sign with his hand, waving it back and forth in Kannon's and my direction. "Nah, y'all wanted us to couple up. Unlike you, I'm perfectly fine with being a friend with benefits to her assets."

We all keeled over in laughter.

"But does *she* know that?"

"As sure as we know you're in love with Angela, and she's down with it," Roman answered nonchalantly. "Enough about this. Let me tell y'all about KinRo's grand opening party in two weeks..."

Roman explained to my brother and Jovan about our upcoming party for the grand opening of our new gym facility. Then they eased into more playful banter before eventually turning their attention back to the game. However, I sat quietly, reflecting on what Roman had surmised. I'd never let myself admit how deep my feelings ran for that woman, but having my best friend put it out there in the universe, I couldn't deny it. I was in love with Angela Richards. And I'd never felt so good yet hurt so badly in my entire life.

Chapter Sixteen

ANGELA

THE PAST WEEK and a half had been pure torture. There was no other way to describe it. Everything in my life had been going considerably well, except my—hell, I didn't even know what to call it—*situationship*, I guess, with Kinston. He refused to communicate with me for the first few days after he'd dropped me off from his house back to my house. He hadn't called or texted, so I did. My calls went unanswered, but he did send one text reply on the second day. It simply read: Hey. Been busy. When I tried to strike up a conversation, my messages were ignored. Since I was a glutton for punishment and a fiend addicted to the high of Kinston, I tried to call on the third day. Apparently, three times was the charm because he finally answered. My joy was short-lived when I gathered by his questioning tone that he only picked up because he hadn't screened my call.

"Are we good, Kinston?" I asked after I'd conversed with myself for about five minutes without any input or response from him.

"We're straight." His words weren't cold, but they lacked the warmth he typically extended to me. He also didn't offer any more than those two words.

"Then why are you so guarded and noncommunicative with me?"

"I don't have anything to say." He released a huff. "Listen, I've got to get to my class at the gym."

Fidgeting, I was instantly a ball of nerves. "Well, can I call you later? Or better yet, *see* you later?" I slapped my forehead, knowing full well I had plunged to the depths of desperation, and I felt foolish.

"Ahh, I'm pretty swamped, so I doubt it," he tsked. "Be easy, Ang."

Beep. Beep. Beep. The sound of his disconnected phone call was more than a symbol of his hanging up the line. It was also a symbol of him hanging it up with me. He couldn't make that plainer if he had just come out and said I don't want anything to do with you. And *Ang*? Since we'd been in a situationship, he'd never called me Ang. It'd always been Angela, Queen, or Beautiful. The informal use of "Ang" was another indicator that whatever I'd shared with Kinston was null and void. In my stupid attempt to keep him at bay, I'd cast my fish back into the sea. Since that apathetic exchange, we hadn't spoken, so I was perplexed about why my sisters were on FaceTime with me, asking me about attending KinRo's grand opening party.

"No, I'm not going. I'm sure he doesn't want me there."

"Did he rescind his invitation?" Aquila asked.

"No, not officially, but he has in all the ways that matter."

"Listen, sis, you two may not be gelling, but I'm pretty sure if you don't show up for his big event, it is a surefire way to ensure that whatever you all had brewing is completely fizzled out," Nissi deduced, popping a K-cup into her Keurig to make her favorite cup of joe. "If you want Kinston to pay you any time of day, you need to show up for him the same way you know he'd show up for you."

"Mm-hmm," Aquila chimed in, looking up from the vegetables she was chopping for her specialty, chicken stir-fry.

"Exactly. Besides, regardless of whether you two work it out, Kinston and Roman are like family. And Kinston is actually family to Nissi, so we all should be there to support them."

I see the tag team is back again. I hated it when they were right. Well, at least, when they were right when it went against me. But they had a point. I was so butthurt that I couldn't see past my own feelings and how I felt Kinston now perceived me to understand that. Regardless, this was important to him, and my presence may still be meaningful to him. Even if nothing ever matriculated between us again, I owed him that much as a friend.

"You know you two should really take this little act on the road," I quipped, rolling my eyes.

Nissi waved off my sneer. "Anyway, now that you're coming . . . and don't even try to argue how I know because the fact that you offered no rebuttal means you're coming . . . So, since you're coming, let's go shopping for white outfits tomorrow. I also set up a hair and spa appointment for the morning of the event."

Her declaration made me cock my head back at her audacity. "So, you just *knew* I was going to go, huh?" I giggled at the fact that she'd arranged these plans.

Aquila laughed, dumping the vegetables into the wok. "You know your sister. If she couldn't get you to agree for Kinston, she would've pled on her own behalf. To which you would've agreed because, contrary to popular belief, you're the one who spoiled our baby sister."

"Trust me, Lah. Not one person in the history of everness would accuse you of spoiling me or anybody else, for that matter," Nissi teased, much to my contentment and causing me to belt out a hearty laugh.

Aquila pointed a spatula into the camera. "Don't call me the next time you need me to help you out."

"Don't get mad because she's off your bandwagon. You already know her baby sis privileges allow her to jump on whatever wagon benefits her."

Nissi feigned surprise. "Ang, I thought *I* was your favorite baby sister," she whined.

"Bish, you're my only baby sister," I spat as we cackled like hens. "Cut the shenanigans. I'm going, and I'll see you tomorrow." I turned my focus to Aquila. "That means you and Joel are going too, right?"

Aquila briefly closed her eyes and released a deep breath. "Just me. Mom and Dad are going to keep the boys. Joel has another engagement."

Nissi and I gave each other the eye signal that we knew something was wrong, but we decided not to speak about our always MIA bozo-in-law. Not to mention that Joel's parents never seemed to step to the plate to help tend to their grandchildren. My dad had expressed wanting to attend the party, but again, he had to help our mother play super grandparents and fill-in father for Joel and his people. I wish to heaven that my sister would let us have one time to speak our pieces to the Olivers, and we'd shred their bad and bougie asses to smithereens.

"Okay, well, I'll see you both tomorrow. Love you," I said, ending the call on that note.

"Love you roundtrip," they both shouted together before we disconnected.

Chapter Seventeen

ANGELA

"Wow!" Nissi mouthed as she stepped out of the vehicle. Her mesmerized eyes roamed the marina as if she were a starstruck superfan in the vicinity of her favorite celebrity.

Once Aquila and I stepped out of her Audi, we understood exactly why she was entranced in a hypnotic state. The luxury yacht that hosted KinRo's grand opening all-white party was a sight to behold. The boat was abuzz with an array of people all donned and dripped out in all-white ensembles. From a distance, you could see deckhands ensuring the vessel remained pristine while the stewards floated around, catering to the guests' every need.

"This is exquisite," Aquila cooed in wonderment. "They have outdone themselves for this grand opening."

"Yes, indeed," I added as we stared around at the yacht illuminated in brilliantly golden lights with a banner displaying the KinRo Fitness logo that read, *Congratulations, Kinston and Roman!* ~ *KinRo Fitness 2 Grand Opening Celebration.* ~

"Let's head over. I'm ready to drink and dance nastily with my man," Nissi guffawed.

"In that outfit, your man is going to want to get nasty, not just dance it," I quipped with the snap of my fingers.

She pointed at me. "And *that's* the plan, good sis!" Our conjoined giggles spread between us. "But I will say the same for you. You came dressed to reclaim your man."

Waving my hands, I feigned denial. "No, I just wanted to look nice. I'm not trying to reclaim anyone. Besides, to reclaim something, you would first have to have a claim on it. I did not."

Both of my sisters shot me a glare as if to say, "Okay, you delusional, bish." This time, it was Aquila who spoke first. "Oh no, sissie. You *had* the claim. He filled out the paperwork for you and everything. *You're* the one who didn't cash it in."

"Ahaaaa!" Nissi snickered. "Facts!"

"How do you say 'fuck you' in all the languages you know?" I asked with an attitude.

Tapping her chin with her forefinger, Nissi gazed upward. "I don't know. Why don't you ask Kinston tonight after the party?" Nissi smarted slyly as she and Aquila slapped fives. "Because after the party—"

"*It's the afterparty!*" Aquila sang, finishing the song lyrics with Nissi.

At that, I couldn't help but be consumed by their mirth. That cute comeback was even enough for me to forego my snap about Joel and join in on their musings, albeit at my expense. Truth be told, we all were dressed to the gods tonight. Each outfit reflected our individual styles. Nissi donned a one-shoulder, bodycon jumpsuit with a short train, which added a sophisticated flair to her ensemble. Gold, strappy, red bottom heels showing off her white-painted manicured toes were the perfect addition to round out her look. I knew when she waltzed her cute self into this party that Kannon would be preoccupied with his wife all night long. Aquila, our ever so sexy yet conservative one, wore a fitted two-piece pantsuit. The asymmetrical blazer hugged her hips and showed off just enough cleavage to keep one guessing yet drooling simultaneously. Her nude-colored red bottom pumps were the stamp on her classic and elegant look. It was a shame that Joel preferred not to show off his vixen of a wife because she was stunning. Secretly, I hoped someone at this party would notice so she could let loose and have a little fun. Not adulterous fun, just "you must've forgotten I'm that bish" type of fun.

"Besides, that outfit is giving, and you would not have worn it if you weren't trying to hook that man," Nissi complimented, breaking my internal ponderings.

Though I rolled my eyes and pretended to be unbothered, somewhere deep down, I hoped that Kinston and I could hash out our differences. They had me pegged when they deduced that I missed him. My mouth might get away with the lie, but my heart couldn't. I absolutely missed that man. The way he made me laugh, encouraged me, talked to me for hours on end, made sure I received an early-morning FaceTime call just to check on me, wined and dined me, and, of course, the unnatural way he pleasured my body . . . The man was a beast and a damn superhero the way he ravaged my body but then swooped in to save me before I climaxed into the afterlife. All of it had me fiending for one Kinston Jordan.

So, I might have, kind of, sort of, a little bit of a micromorsel, dressed to impress him. The off-the-shoulder, asymmetrical, three-quarter-sleeved top flowed down to the top of my thigh, giving only a hint to the bodycon pants that fit the rotundness of my rear to perfection. My clear, four-inch block heels finished the ensemble. Thanks to Nissi's appointment at the hair salon and spa, not only was I refreshed for tonight's event, but also the manicure and pedicure with matching nude polish, along with the long, sleek, high ponytail, added the goddess flair that showed the King that this Queen still reigned supreme. And it was lengthy enough to tug a little act right into me.

"Ahoy, ladies! I am Captain Sorenson. Welcome abroad the *Majesty*. My chief steward, Alison, will assist you," the captain greeted us as he helped us each onto the yacht.

"Greetings, ladies," Alison stated. "May I have your ticket, please?"

We handed Alison our tickets, and she guided us into the vessel's interior, where all the partygoers were gathered. The sight very much resembled that of the Hollywood elite. In fact, some local celebrities had turned out. The layout was impressive. Champagne flowed from end to end with an open bar that seemed to have more distilled spirits than any retailer I'd ever patronaged. It was gorgeously decorated throughout the venue in the same gold, white, and black colors of the fitness center's logo. Subtle party music serenaded throughout the vessel. Platters of food were strategically placed all around, from veggie trays to fruit trays to meat and cheese trays, and an entire seafood buffet of shrimp, oysters, and clams was prepared in several different ways to accommodate and delight the palates of all the guests. People were mingling about, either enjoying themselves conversing in small groups or swaying to the soft beat of the music. If I ever wondered how the upper echelon partied, this had to be a spot-on representation of such life.

As we waltzed about admiring the yacht, it was as if Kannon's energy was drawn to Nissi and hers to his. Simultaneously, they turned to face each other, and slow, flirty smiles crept on both of their faces. *Yes, sis.* One gaze at how Kannon exhaled when he roamed Nissi's body from head to toe let me know they would be making an early exit tonight.

"There's my baby over there," she beamed brighter than the luminosities on the yacht.

Simultaneously, Kannon waved us over, yet his eyes never left Nissi. I recognized that wanton glint in his eyes because I'd been the recipient of the same sentiment from his older brother several times—those damn Jordan men. As we made our way in that direction, it seemed as if the crowd parted like the Red Sea. At the clearing, I could see Kannon standing next to Kinston, Roman, Nia, Jovan, Jasmine, Cami, and her husband, Travis, and a couple of other men I didn't recognize. Indeed, they were a good-looking group of people, but I nearly stumbled on my heels when my eyes landed on Kinston. His locs had been neatly braided and twisted into a man bun that was so intricately luxurious it could rival any sister's updo. The tailored white suit seemed to define every muscle in his body, from his broad shoulders, chiseled pecs, and pythonic biceps down to his herculean thighs. It was made even sexier by the fact that his bare chest shone through the opening of the blazer. The only covering was his gold chain that accented his collarbone. His Bvlgari timepiece and Ferragamo loafers finished his elegant style. My God today. The man wasn't just fine ... He was *gorgeous*. Exceptionally handsome.

"So damn sexy, baby," Kannon stated to Nissi, taking her outstretched hand and gazing at her in admiration before twirling her around and back into him for a tight embrace.

Nissi's giggle was reminiscent of a schoolgirl as she leaned into her husband. "Baby, let me greet the guests of honor, at least."

"Sis, we all know how you two get. It's cool," Kinston chuckled as Kannon begrudgingly unraveled himself from his wife, and Nissi and he embraced.

"Oh, whatever," Nissi fanned him off after they hugged. "Congratulations, bro-in-love, and you as well, Roman."

Roman nodded his head. "Preciate it," he acknowledged. "But I must agree," Roman said, looking around at us ladies. "We are surrounded by a group of the most stunning ladies at the party."

His remark was met by the agreement from the rest of the men to our combined coos of adoration. Once the banter settled down, we all made our rounds, giving out hugs and issuing our congratulations. Somehow, Kinston and I were in the last round of the group to speak to each other. Our hug landed awkwardly as I leaned in for a full embrace with my arms outstretched to wrap around his neck, but he turned his side to me, only offering a one-armed embrace.

"Umm, well, uh, congratulations, Kinston," I flubbed my words with a shrug, unsure how to bounce back from his slight.

Licking his luscious lips, he tilted his head in a short nod. "Thanks. I appreciate that."

Glancing around, I smiled in admiration. "And this party is fantastic. You guys outdid yourselves."

"Yeah, Elena was instrumental in executing the vision."

His lackluster tone and wandering eyes clearly indicated that he held zero interest in anything I said. Before I could gracefully bow out of the one-sided conversation, the chief steward appeared, requiring the attention of Kinston and Roman.

"Uh, excuse me," Kinston stated, patting me on the shoulder.

"Sure, of course," I agreed before politely stepping back out of his way.

Nia, Aquila, and I walked away, leaving Nissi, Kannon, Jovan, Jasmine, Cami, and Travis to their own devices. No sooner than we were away from them, Nia decided to bring up the iceberg that had formulated between Kinston and me.

"Girl, I know you said that your 'situationship' with Kinston was over, but I didn't realize he was over you too. That man treated you like a gnat at a barbecue."

"Thank you, Captain Obvious," I scowled, swiping a champagne flute from one of the stewards' drink trays and tossing it back in nearly one gulp.

Aquila sipped her drink with a slight chuckle. "Sis, relax. That man is not over you." When Nia and I gave her the side-eye, she scoffed. "That man is still bothered. If he's still bothered, he still cares. Now, if he were unbothered, you'd be screwed."

Leaning close to her, I whispered for only us three to hear. "So what do you suggest I do because I've tried everything besides throwing myself at his feet for mercy?" I asked, my impatience evident.

"Make him jealous," Aquila suggested. "You've already given your congratulations. Have fun and enjoy yourself. Stop snooping around him, waiting for him to pay you an ounce of attention."

Offended, I hissed, "I haven't been snooping around him."

Nia nodded as she sipped her drink. "Now, friennn, you were over there acting very *pick me-ish*."

I shot a stern glare at her. "Two words: friendship contract."

She raised one hand in surrender. "I'm just saying taking your sister's advice is not a bad move, especially when you're out of options."

I glanced toward Kinston, who was making his rounds schmoozing with their guests. For everyone else, he had all thirty-two teeth showing, but for me, it was the cold shoulder. Well, two could play this game. There were plenty of men without dates at this party, and I would take full advantage of the selections.

"Fine. Let's make our way to the dance floor," I said, turning in that direction.

"First, let's make our way to the buffet table. I haven't eaten a thing so that I wouldn't be bloated in this suit, and I need sustenance," Aquila said, halting us and making a beeline to the food table.

As she and Nia filled their plates with veggies and seafood, it gave me time to ponder my next moves. I desired Kinston and yearned for us to rekindle, even if only as friends sans the benefits. However, the more I contemplated the possible scenarios, the more I felt in my gut that playing that hand would push me further from my ultimate goal. In any other circumstance, toying with jealousy may have been warranted and enough ammunition to sway him if our disconnect were on him. But it was on me.

Seeing me entertaining another man when he had requested that I only be his was a recipe for permanent disaster in my book. Not only would it push Kinston further away from me, but it could also make it appear as if I'd only been tampering with his emotions. I couldn't afford that, especially when he felt, on some level, that's exactly what I had been doing . . . wasting his time. Tonight, I needed him to see that I was a woman worthy to be missed, not one that was for the streets.

Just as my sister and Nia finished their finger foods, the DJ flipped the switch from the casual soft greeting tunes to party anthems, starting with a throwback from Miami legend Uncle Luke, mixing samples better than any TikTok remix. When his "Birthday" song billowed through the speakers, the crowd turned up a notch, and throngs of partygoers headed to the dance floor. Grabbing both women's hands, I led them out to the floor, where we danced in a semicircle together.

Soon, Nissi and Kannon made their way to where we stood as she twerked on her husband, much to his booty-grinding delight. The mix changed between 1990s to 2000s classics from celebs like Uncle Al and Trina to the bass music from our bordering state of Georgia from Dem Franchize Boyz, Soulja Boy, and Lil' Jon and the Eastside Boyz.

Jovan, Jasmine, Cami, and Travis had joined us and even Roman at different times. Who I hadn't seen was Kinston. I was about eight songs deep, sloshing from wine and humming from the feel-good songs, when I turned to avoid being sandwiched between two men. That was when I spotted Kinston at the other end of the dance floor. His back was pressed against the wall as some chick sexily danced against him. It was so packed that I probably wouldn't have thought twice about it if I couldn't fully see them, but from my angle, I could see the full view. Though his back was against the wall, it seemed to be providing leverage for him as he tilted his pelvis to meet her salacious thrusts, with one of his massive hands roaming her waistline before lightly gripping her hips to brace her flush against him. With his bottom lip tucked between his teeth and his deep dimples protruding in delight, there was no denying this wasn't some random woman trying to maneuver past him with a little shimmy. No, this dance was intentional.

Time stood still as my eyes homed in on the details. His eyes glossed over her body with languid seduction, evidence of his potent mixture of lust and liquor. His hands meddled and roamed her nether regions: her waist, her hips . . . soft and subtle squeezes to her rear. My condemnatory stare traveled the length of the woman's body from the bodacious bubble that seemed permanently attached to Kinston's palms to her thin waist and generous breasts to her face double-dipped in so much makeup that she looked as fake as the BBL Kinston clutched and the inches upon inches of Brazilian weave that cascaded down her back.

Astonishment and incredulity coursed through every fiber of my being before settling on repulse and, finally . . . envy. By the time she lifted and turned to face him, wrapping her arms around his thick neck, I had become incensed by his audacious behavior. *How the fuck dare he?* Sure, I held no claim to him as he wasn't mine, and as a single and free-to-mingle man, he had every right to enjoy his party with whomever he chose, but I'd never suspect he'd do so in front of me. Was playing in each other's faces what we were doing now?

A hand on my forearm shifted my attention away from the dancing duo. When I followed the hand, I realized it was Nissi. "If looks could kill, we'd all be blown to hell right now. Stewing in rage and jealousy is *not* going to get your man back. You need to trot yourself over there and reclaim what's yours."

Irritated by being interrupted by my private bashing session, my attitude escalated into nonchalance and thrust me into a familiar fallback routine of denial. Shrugging, I turned to face her. "First of all, he was never mine. Second of all, he can do whatever he wants."

Nissi blessed me with the same expression I held, then jabbed one manicured nail directly into my arm. "And *that* is precisely why *you're* not the one being chosen tonight. Ray Charles can see that you're upset and that you want him. I love you, but for once, please do yourself and all of us a favor and stop these shenanigans. If you want him, go get him."

Nonchalance and denial melted into worry, quickly ushering in old feelings of fear and insecurity that began to spread from my psyche to the pit of my belly and festered like an open wound. "Ray Charles can also see that I was correct in my assessment. I'm not his type." I nodded toward the busty beauty encapsulated in his inviting arms.

Nissi deadpanned on Kinston and Ms. Irrelevant, pointing at them with her thumb. "Who? Ms. BBL over there? Sis, *please*. That woman is nothing more than an overinflated ass and no substance. I'm positive Kinston sees the same thing; however, he's still a man. But he's also a man who knows the difference between Mrs. Right and Ms. Right Now."

A nervous tick invaded my body as I fiddled with my fingers. I knew Nissi was right. And I wanted nothing more than to do what she demanded that I do, but I was also aware of how badly I'd wounded Kinston. His actions tonight proved my snub extended beyond a superficial scar. His was an underlying agony that permeated deep within the wells of his soul. The kind of heartache that wasn't easily repairable, and the possibility of rejection was both physically and emotionally stifling.

"I don't think I can make this right, Nissi." Sullenness befell me. The reality of what truly troubled my heart made its way from the innermost crevices of my heart to the opening of my mouth. "What if . . . what if I can't salvage . . . *us*?"

The crestfallen gaze in her eyes matched the one in my spirit. Just as quickly, Nissi fanned the emotion away and replaced it with hope. She lifted my trembling hands and patted them. "There's only one way to find out. Try. If you fail, walk away being content that you fought for the *us*."

Her words were gentle and fresh, renewing my mind, body, and spirit. For the first time, I was resolute in my feelings. Many times, I had told myself that Kinston wasn't Nigel. Still, I allowed Nigel's behavior, my past with him, and my insecurities to prevent Kinston and me from exploring the possibilities of us. I'd unjustly projected Nigel's shortcomings as a boyfriend onto Kinston when he had done everything he could to show me the essence of a man. Kinston Jordan had embedded himself into my life, invaded my continuous thoughts, and burrowed himself into the caverns of my heart. In fact, he'd done so since the day I met him at KinRo Fitness, and he'd never missed the mark.

Every ounce of my being knew without a doubt or debate that he was meant for me. The mere thought of that chick or any other woman having access to Kinston's conversation, time, and sexual appetite was enough to infuriate me. How trivial had I been to think it wouldn't? Thinking about it now, I had to be some kind of special stupid to throw away our budding relationship. It was my fault for handing him over on a silver dome-covered platter. But no more. Kinston Jordan was mine. And I was his. Tonight, I was going to seal the deal before that ratchet busty beauty could sink her BBL any further into his clutches.

A poised smile radiated on my face as I pulled my sister into a tight embrace, and she returned my hug in that sisterly way that only sisters could. As I withdrew from her, I planted a sweet kiss on her cheek and gripped her arms tenderly. "Thank you, sis. You always wanted to be the big sister." We snickered. "But sometimes, I need that."

Playfully, she pulled the tip of my ponytail. "I learned from the best. I love you."

"Love you, roundtrip." Straightening my stance, I squared my shoulders. "Now, go spend time with your man, and I'm going to go and grab mine."

Nissi's smile deepened as she gave me two thumbs-up and headed over to where Kannon and Roman were dancing among Nia and Aquila. When I turned to barge over and collect said man, though, neither he nor the blow up princess were anywhere in sight. I scanned the floor several times but couldn't find them. Not giving up on my mission to locate him, I headed off the floor toward the buffet, but still, I didn't see them. I made a beeline toward the open bar, where my eyes landed on the blow-up Barbie gently tugging on the front of Kinston's blazer. She was leading him to the lower deck where the private bedrooms were. As she backed her way down, he lazily followed, their libidinous stares guiding them on a mind of their own.

Mentally, I called out for Kinston, hoping and praying my mental telepathy would make him stop and back away. But when his loafers stepped down the stairs with only the view of the fake queen on his mind, I knew that it hadn't worked. I was too late. He gave me exactly what I asked for, except it was on *his* terms. No strings. No attachments. I'd officially been thrust into the pool of Ms. Right Nows as I watched him trek to give the other litter pick all the goodies he'd once withheld solely for me. Stinging pricked my eyes, and my heart cracked when their bodies disappeared below the deck. Swallowing the lump in my throat, I spun around, sifting manically through the crowd of people to the open bar to down the first tumbler of liquor I could get my hands on. Afterward, I'd deboard this yacht quickly to escape my harsh reality. Kinston Jordan. *My* Kinston Jordan had been taken.

Chapter Eighteen

KINSTON

"Ease up, baby," I said, barely placing the tumbler on the table before Mercedes pushed me down on the bed.

Hiking up her dress, she quickly straddled my lap so she could unfasten the buttons on my blazer. Her lips were on my neck, stroking her tongue up and down the base, alternating between sucks and pecks. Usually, I'd be into the aggressive come-on, but not tonight. Of course, I was attracted to her in that one-night-of-fun type of way, and when I initially descended the stairs, I had every intention of meeting both our insatiable needs, but now, it felt awkward and forced. But mostly, it felt wrong.

"I'm sorry, bae. I just want you so bad. I've been waiting on this day for a long time," she giggled, pouncing in on me again.

It was true. I wasn't lying about having a list of women to call to fulfill my sexual urges. Mercedes Topaz was one of them. Mercedes was a model and influencer in the Miami area and a former client of Roman's. We'd met when she was still a client, and Roman asked me to fill in for her personal trainer session. Her come-on was immediate, but we didn't date or have sex with our clients. Well, let's just say not anymore.

When we first started KinRo, the rule didn't exist. Yes, we were professional and would never jeopardize our business, but outside of business hours, everything was fair game. All it took was for one crazy chick to bring outside business through the doors of KinRo for us to implement the rule—no client fraternization. Roman had dated this woman named Alyssa, who'd been a client of his, and when he broke it off, she went batshit crazy. It literally took a restraining order and a threat to her government job to stop her antics. That ordeal resulted in a lifetime ban on Alyssa and the introduction of our new policy. Though I felt bad for my boy, I was grateful it hadn't been me. I'd dealt with my fair share of "crazy" already, and Roman kept his head on the swivel for a year afterward. That was no way to live.

But Mercedes was now fair play because she was no longer a client. She'd landed a contract as the spokesmodel for a Pilates fitness company. Therefore, she had to end her contract with KinRo due to a conflict of interest. Now, she worked out at the company she represented. It was an understandable move, and she still referred clientele our way who weren't interested in taking Pilates.

However, ever since she left, she made no qualms about her attraction to me. I'd never bitten because I knew she wasn't the type of woman that I'd want anything more with than a bedroom romp. Back in my younger days, I would've been all over her offer, but in my rolling thirties, I longed for wife material. The fact that she was willing and ready to sex me senseless on a yacht full of people she didn't know proved to me that she was the exact type that I had her pegged as . . . a "fun time, not a long time" woman. That thought gave me pause, but the thoughts of Angela being on this boat halted me. I loathed that she held that much control over my actions, but she did, and I couldn't do this until we cleared the air permanently on the state of our relationship. Except there wasn't one. She'd made that abundantly clear. And as I sat here with Mercedes in desperate heat for a piece of my time and body, I knew I had to put a stamp on this situation with

Angela for both our sakes. It was time to part ways with Angela so that I could clear my conscience for whomever I chose to date or sleep with. But I realized in these few brief minutes that the woman was not Mercedes Topaz and would never be.

"Yo, this ain't it." I slid my hand down my beard. "Get up, Mercedes."

"Come on, Kinston," she cooed, attempting to wrap her arms around my neck, but I blocked her, placing her arms to her sides.

"No knock to you, but I'm not feeling this right now. Let's head back upstairs."

"Nooo," she whined. "I can make you feel *so* good."

I glanced down at my lifeless member and gave her a side-eye. "Cedes, neither of us is rising to the occasion."

She stood up and slowly bent to her knees, gripping my pants by the waist. "That's because you don't know what this mouth can do. Let me show you. I'll get him right in no time."

Immediate turn-off. If there was one thing I couldn't stand, it was a woman who didn't understand the meaning of no. Not only was it bad for business, but I also refused to be trapped in some scam of a Me Too, Me Three, All of Us movement where one woman made a claim and then perpetuated a lie for others to join in. I'd never deny that some claims levied against other men were valid because I knew what these doggish men did to vulnerable women, but those types of claims have never and would never be valid for me. Forget Kain; Marie Jordan would descend from heaven to beat my grown ass with the right-hand wrath of God himself.

Gripping her hands more forcefully than I'd intended, I tossed a stern squint at her. "Mercedes, I said stop."

She hopped up with her attitude on full display. "What's your deal? We've been flirting for the past two days, and now that we have an opportunity, you're bailing on me?" She huffed, throwing her hands on her inflated hips. "If you have issues, then you should've taken the blue pill or not wasted my time."

Following the advice of the last two men that I shouldn't have ever taken advice from, Jovan and Roman, I'd run into Mercedes at the health food store, where I finally agreed to exchange numbers with her. We'd talked and flirted, she more nastily than me, over the phone. When she told me she would be at tonight's grand opening, I'd agreed to link up and spend time with her to make Angela jealous, as my boys suggested. I wasn't even sure if my plan had worked because Angela was parlaying on the dance floor with her sister and bestie by the time Mercedes came through. However, when Mercedes did arrive, I'd gotten entranced in a sexy dance with her and thought I'd show Angela what a friend with benefits truly was. And now I regretted even entertaining the thought of being with Mercedes.

Blue pill? Her words slapped my face with offense. Yeah, she'd lost her mind disrespecting me. On that note, I stood, irritated and ready to dismiss her from my presence. "Nah, ain't nothing wrong with my equipment. It's the operator."

She gasped at my dig as I moved around her to open the door. "Now, if you'll excuse me, Roman and I have to give a speech before we set sail."

Mercedes stomped her foot and began to storm out of the room. She spun on her heels just as she was about to pass me with her hand raised. Sensing the motion, I caught her arm in midswing before she could connect the smack on my cheek.

"That's what we're *not* going to do," I warned before releasing her hand and pointing down the hall. "And do you see that hallway camera? Before you get any ideas, please know surveillance is actively monitoring. So you'd do best to keep your hands and any allegations to yourself. Not only do I have a reputation to uphold, but you do as well. Remember that."

Her eyes narrowed to slits, and I could practically see the steam billowing from her skin she was so upset. "I knew I should've pursued Roman," she hissed. "Don't you ever dial my number again."

"That, my dear, is the one thing you never have to worry about."

"Go to hell, Kinston," she spewed before storming back up to the upper deck.

"I'm sure I'd meet you there," I grumbled once she was out of earshot.

Taking a soothing breath, I took a moment to compose myself before heading back to the top. Once there, it was exactly how I left it ten minutes ago . . . in full swing. The atmosphere was electric. Liquor was flowing. The music was pulsing. It was an all-around good time. But I couldn't focus on that. I had to find *her*.

My eyes scanned the vessel for Angela, but I couldn't readily locate her. I began to ease my way through the crowds of people when Roman met me with a worried expression on his face.

"Yo, what happened with Mercedes? She bumped into me muttering something about you being a time-wasting asshole and said she was leaving," he said as he tossed back more of the beer in his hands.

"She's just upset because I wasn't on the same type of time she was on," I answered nonchalantly as I continued to scan the yacht.

Roman tilted his head. "I *know* you didn't turn that down, bruh? That was an easy home run, my dude."

"And that's the issue. Anything that comes too easy comes with too many problems. Twenty-year-old me would've tapped it, but mature thirty-three-year-old me knew it was best to tap out. You're gonna learn one day."

Nodding his head, he touched knuckles with me. "I feel that." I felt him following my gaze and looked over at him. He held a knowing smirk on his face. "Besides, we all know the real reason you tapped out. No judgment. And no, I haven't seen her. Our speech is in ten minutes."

With that, he patted my shoulder and walked away. I continued toward the crowd and saw my brother, who seemed to be moving quickly to get to me. At first, I was perplexed by his rush until my eyes landed on his wife, who was on his heels behind him. One glance at me, and I knew she was ready to rip me a new one. For what, I didn't know.

"Bro, I was trying to catch you. What happened between you and Angela?" he whispered hurriedly.

Before I could answer, his wife was in front of us, asking the same question in a less subtle voice and a much-harsher tone.

"I don't know what you did to my sister, but you better start explaining right now," Nissi huffed, folding her arms across her chest.

Now, I was even more baffled. I hadn't seen Angela since earlier. "Nothing, Nissi. I swear it. I haven't seen or spoken to her since you guys first arrived."

Nissi eyed me skeptically. "The last I saw her, she was headed to speak to you, then the next thing I knew, she met me in tears, demanding my car keys so she could leave the marina."

A sinking feeling dropped in the pit of my stomach. "She was coming to speak to me? How long ago, Nissi?"

She shrugged. "I don't know. Maybe ten or fifteen minutes ago or so. When you were preoccupied with some BBL Barbie."

"Shit!" I cursed aloud.

I didn't have time to explain to Nissi. If her timing was right, Angela must've seen me and Mercedes heading to the lower deck. Without another word, I gave chase to find her, darting past people, heading toward the exit of the yacht. Once off, I frantically went up and down the plank, searching for Angela. I leaned on the railing overlooking the black ocean when I didn't see her. My heart plummeted. Everything inside of me wanted to hop in my ride and drive to her house to discuss all that had transpired. There was no way I wanted to leave this situation to gnaw on her heart and her mind, but I had no choice. I had to see this celebration through. Celebration. What a joke. This should've been one of my happiest and proudest memories. Instead, it was tainted by the possibility of losing Angela for good even though I'd planned to do precisely that. Still, I had to pull myself together and be the dutiful one-half owner of KinRo Fitness. As much as I cared for the fate of my *whatevership* with Angela, I owed my business partner this night, so I resolved to hold it together for Roman. As I turned to head back to the yacht, I bumped into a woman speeding quickly to leave.

"Angela?" I asked, catching her about her elbow.

"Excuse me," she spat, sniffles coming from her nose as she cast her head down.

"You're still here? I thought you'd left."

She tossed her head back at that, giving me a look of utter disgust. "Yeah, I'm still here. But no worries. I'm leaving so you can have as many boat romps as you want."

"Angela, nothing happened between me and Mercedes."

She backed up and attempted to walk around me. "Yeah, right. Now, my lying eyes are playing tricks on me."

Stepping back in front of her, I halted her exit again. "I'm telling you the truth. When have you ever known me to lie?"

Rather than speak, she tried to dart away from me. I almost let her run, but honestly, I had to get my own grievances off my chest so we could be done with these shenanigans.

"You know what? So what if I had?" I asked her retreating back. She paused midstride at my question. "You made it painfully yet precisely clear that you didn't want me. Friends with *benefits*, right? That's what *you* said. How are you upset with me for giving you exactly what you asked for?"

She whipped around so quickly the breeze could've blown me into the ocean. "Screw you, Kinston. You don't have to use my words to try to hurt me. If you wanna go pound the whole yacht of freaks, then do it."

In a nanosecond, I invaded her personal space. "Hurt you with your words? Besides the fact that you know I'd never try to hurt you, do you *hear* yourself? *You* spewed that shit at me without any regard for how it made me feel, but *I'm* hurting *you*? You don't want me, but you don't want me to want another woman. How is *that* fair?"

Angela stood frozen as water filled her eyes. When she finally spoke, her voice cracked with emotion. "You're right. It's not." She shifted her weight from one hip to the other and fidgeted with her clutch purse. "Do you *want* to be with her?"

My jaw tightened. "No. You don't get to do that." I pointed in her face. "You don't get to put this off on me so that I can give you a reason. Nah. Tonight, you're going to own exactly what you said."

I leaned down into her face, making her focus on me. "No relationship, right? Friends with benefits, right?"

"Yes!" she belted. "That's what I said. Damn."

"Then why are you here with tears in your eyes and wondering who I'm with and what I'm doing with them?"

"Because . . . because . . ."

The way she stuttered and stumbled over her words infuriated me. After all this, she still couldn't be honest with herself or me. This was madness, and I was finished with the circus. Shaking my head in disappointment, I turned to walk away, and this time, it would be forever.

She gripped my bicep and pulled me back. Tears dripped down her face as her shoulders slumped in defeat. "Because I want you, Kin. And I was so wrong about what I said and how I treated you. I let my past with Nigel interfere with what we have or had or whatever. And then I saw you with her, and I just knew . . . I lost you."

Staring at this woman, who ruled every fiber of my soul, shed uncontrollable tears over me, broke me. Gently, I pulled her into my arms, softly caressing her back as she planted her face into my chest.

"Shhh," I whispered with my chin settling gently atop her head as she released all her withheld tears. "You never lost me. I'm right here, Beautiful."

She raised wet eyes to me that ballooned with questions. "Are you sure?"

Before I answered her, I had to be positive about what this confession meant for us. I thumbed away her tears as I cupped her face in the palms of my hands. "I need to be sure we're on the same page. Are you asking if you lost me as a friend with benefits . . . or something more?"

Closing her eyes and swallowing the lump in her throat, she asked, "You're going to make me say it, aren't you?"

"Only if you mean it."

She bit her lip and gazed into my eyes. "I do miss your friendship, but I want that and all that we have to offer each other, with you as my man."

Those words made my heart soar as I folded her into my chest, cocooning her in a deep embrace. She squeezed me into her just as tightly. We stood there basking in each other and swaying softly to the sound of the soothing waters swooshing along the shoreline. All outside noise was blocked, and for a while, I nearly forgot we weren't alone. Then the sound of the DJ calling for Roman and me to make our way to the stage interrupted our private rekindling.

Pulling out of the embrace, I tilted her chin upward, a smile toying at the corners of my lips. "Was that so hard to admit?" We laughed in tandem, and she met my smart remark with a light swat on my arm. "Just gotta make it difficult."

She smiled up at me, wrapping her arms around my waist. "Not difficult, just challenging. I had to see what you were made of."

My eyes lowered half-mast as I licked my lips. "What did Pac say? *I don't want it if it's that easy,*" I sang playfully.

As we stood enveloped in the newness of our connection, our star-crossed gazes served as nonverbal cues to our innermost feelings. Our lips met for a tender kiss and ended with a sweet peck to seal the deal.

She pointed a finger in my chest. "That better go for Mercedes or any other chick."

"I'm a one-woman, man, Beautiful."

Resting her forearms around the back of my neck, she spoke words that made love to my eardrums. "And I, Mr. Jordan, am a one-man woman. *Your* woman."

I couldn't stop the dimpled smile on my face if I wanted. Backing up, I held her hand out and sucked my teeth. "That's right. Mine. All and only mine." I looked over my shoulder as I heard people asking for me. "But right now, your man has business to attend to, but we're definitely going to pick this conversation back up later tonight," I said, holding her hand and leading her back up to the yacht with me.

"There he is!" the DJ shouted from the booth, pointing toward Angela and me as we walked through the crowd.

Roman was already standing there holding the microphone and greeted me with a lighthearted smile and a one-armed hug.

"I see somebody finally got his wish," he said as a joke, but we both knew he was also serious.

"Indeed," I agreed as I took the microphone from him.

Facing the crowd, I was met with cheers. When I lifted the microphone to my mouth, everyone quieted. "You know, when I had the idea to start KinRo Fitness, I never imagined the growth we'd experience. I planned for this to be supplemental income, but with your support and patronage, it's become sustainable income, and it's my life's work to see individuals live their healthiest lives. KinRo is more than a place to work out. It's a place for transformation, not just for the body but also for the heart, the mind, and the spirit. It's become a second home to many; we've developed lifelong friends and even become a family. For that, I thank you all. Not just for tonight but for every day you come in and allow us to help you reshape your lives.

"This also would not be possible without my amazing best friend and business partner, Roman Patterson." We slapped fives. "And most of all, the Creator and the wonderful family he sent me that has had my back since before this idea was even a viable thought. My father, Kain, who, due to a pinched nerve, couldn't be here, my brother, Kannon." We pointed and patted our hearts in acknowledgment. "And my mother, Marie, may you continue to rest well, my sweet angel. With that, I won't delay the party from poppin' any further other than to say, with this new venture, I look forward to many successful years and the opportunity to share it with the people in my life who matter the most." My eyes found Angela, and she blushed as I winked at her. "Thank you all for coming, and let's keep the party going!"

Amid the handclaps, I returned the microphone to the DJ.

"Who's ready to set sail?" the DJ yelled to the cheers of everyone.

Roman and I walked out on the deck and popped a bottle of Cristal as we embarked on our journey. Our family and friends joined us, and I pulled Angela into me as all our people clapped, cheered, and catcalled their well wishes to us. All we could do was blush because they knew what this moment meant for us.

"I look forward to the future with you, too, Mr. Jordan," Angela whispered to me.

Rather than speak, I pecked her lips and then turned her to face the ocean as I held her from behind, nuzzling soft kisses into her neck. This celebration was precisely as it was supposed to be—the happiest and proudest night of my life.

Chapter Nineteen

ANGELA

Last night at the yacht party, we danced and drank with our family and friends as they roasted us for finally becoming a couple and expressing how we'd both driven them up a wall to get to this point. Being the woman I am, I shouldered the blame because it was my fault that it took us so long to establish our relationship. However, my bae didn't allow me to wallow in that too long, assuring me that all that mattered now was that we were a couple.

Whatever time I was on when I was pretending that I didn't want Kinston, I wish I could reverse and redo it. We hadn't even been a couple for a full twenty-four hours, and I already regretted the time we lost behind my foolish antics. That man was an experience no matter how I encountered him, but experiencing him as my man was on a whole new level. While the yacht party was lit, our private party at his house when we arrived here a little after one in the morning had me up now like I was Betty Crocker in the kitchen. The ways in which Kinston pleasured me last night had me clenching my thighs together to alleviate the pressure on my throbbing bud hours later, just thinking about it.

As I slipped the last plate on the wooden carrying tray, I glanced over the meal I had prepared: eggs, turkey sausage, cinnamon oatmeal, fresh fruit, and orange juice to wash it down. Satisfied with my preparation, I eased into his bedroom, leaning on the doorjamb for a second to commit this man . . . my man . . . to memory. As he lay there sleeping on his back, shirtless with one arm tucked behind his head, my eyes roamed his body. His rippling chest and ab muscles glistened with a slight sheen from our earlier morning session. I hated that the cotton sheet covered him from the waist down. I shuttered from the goose bumps just his sheer presence gave me.

"If you're going to ogle me, at least let me give you a sample," Kinston said, never moving a muscle or opening his eyes.

I gasped, lifting from the doorway to make my entrance as Kinston opened his eyes and smiled at me. By the time I reached the bed, he'd scooted up and leaned against the headboard.

He winked as I glided to him. "Come sit your sexy ass right here. I could get used to seeing you in my T-shirts."

"I could too," I said, matching his frisky energy. "But how do you do that? Do you ever sleep?" I placed the tray across his lap.

"Yes, I sleep, but remember, I'm a light sleeper. I've been up since I heard you in the kitchen. I've just been lying here resting my eyes." We leaned over and pecked each other before he turned to the tray. "Look at you. Chef'ing it up for your man. I could get used to this too."

Giggling, I picked up a berry and fed it to him. "Well, get used to all of it."

"Now, I just have to tell you which days are my cheat days."

My face fell. I'd been so wrapped up in doing something nice for him that I totally forgot his strict eating habits. "Ooh, baby. I'm sorry. You don't have to eat this."

He clasped my hands before I could remove the tray and eyed me lovingly. "Are you kidding me? I absolutely *am* going to eat what you prepared for me. I know what I need to do to compensate. But I would never disrespect such a thoughtful gift."

He moved the tray to his nightstand. "Come. Sit between my legs, and let's feed each other."

And I scooted my tail right over and tilted my head to look back at him. "Aww, baby." We pecked lips again as he wrapped his arms around me, and we snuggled into each other. Toying with his fingers, I said what was on my mind. "You're so sweet. I just keep wanting to pinch myself and see if it's real. Nigel would've gone off on me for messing up a cheat day."

Kinston reached for a turkey sausage link, bit it, and then fed the rest to me. "Well, it's a good thing I'm not him."

With that, he gently tossed me backward on the bed and turned on his side, slowly dragging his fingers up and down my exposed chocolate thighs. "Listen, I know you haven't really explained this entire Nigel situation to me, but I think it's important that you do. I don't want you to rehash anything that will be a setback, but I think talking about it can help you rid yourself of some of these past hurts and help us figure out how we move forward in our relationship."

My brows furrowed as I tilted my head forward to look at him. "Are you sure, baby? I don't want to keep bringing up Nigel when we should be getting to know each other, like when you have your cheat days."

Kinston grabbed the small ramekin of fruit and placed it between us. "Cheat days: Saturdays and Wednesdays. And any time you want to do something special for me. Now that we've covered that, let's cover this. When you tell me what's on your mind, what bothers you, how you feel, or anything, *is* me getting to know you. I don't give a damn if you want to present a dissertation on the glass being half empty or half full. I'm here to listen because I want to know *you*, Beautiful. The great, the good, the bad, the ugly, the unimaginable, and the extraordinary. I'm here for all of you."

Tears pricked my eyes as I placed one hand lovingly on his cheek. *Lord, I don't know what I did to be in the blessing business of Kinston Jordan, but, God, you are good, and I thank you.* Being with him felt natural, and it already felt like we'd been together for years instead of a mere day. "And I'm here for you."

His lips curled up in a boyish grin as he bent down and kissed the tip of my nose. "Good." He tossed a wild berry in his mouth. "I'll eat while you talk."

Sitting up and settling back on a pillow, I crossed my legs at the ankle. I didn't realize how difficult bringing up my past with Nigel would be, but Kinston sat beside me and placed an encouraging hand on my thigh as he continued eating his fruit while giving me his undivided attention.

"Nigel and I were classmates in grade school. Back then, he was short and stocky. Sadly, he already had people who picked on him because of his thick African accent, but adding his darker complexion, short height, and stubby physique made for a recipe for disaster. Back then, kids didn't understand that American Blacks and African Blacks were brothers who should band together. Most of them carried that slave-owner mentality. Anything different from them was beneath them. He was very timid back then, and it was hard for him to make friends, so he often took the abuse as if that would somehow one day cease the attacks. My mom and dad taught us to love not only our brown skin but also the brown skin of others just like us. So, one day, at recess, when I saw a well-known bully picking on Nigel, I stood up for him and beat up the bully."

Kinston coughed, causing me to pause my story because of his coughing spell. I patted his back as he grabbed his orange juice and drank to clear his throat.

"Bae, are you all right?"

He cleared his throat. "Yes, I got choked up at you beating up the bully for Nigel. A girl was bullying him in middle school?"

Chuckling, I shook my head. "No, his bully was a boy named Tristan. And your girl here tapped him up with a good ole two-piece." I made a muscle with my arm.

"Okay, look at you, little Ms. Floyd Mayweather."

"I may have lacked gym skills, but these hand skills didn't have any issues," I joked before explaining. "Our dad used to be an amateur boxer back in his heyday, and since he didn't have any boys, he showed us girls a little technique to defend ourselves or, you know, back down a bully."

"Such a shame you used that good training for a clown."

I whipped around to face him with a giggle. "I know, right? If I had known then he'd be a trash human, I would've let Tristan loose on his little awkward ass. Instead, I turned my pet project into a boyfriend and, even worse, a fiancé."

He chuckled. "At least tell me, y'all tag-teamed Tristan or something." When I gave him the "now you know" look, he slid his hand down his face. "Aww, man. How do you let a female come to your defense, and you don't protect yourself or her? Bro been trash since the womb."

I pointed at him. "And probably will be to the tomb. I wish I'd seen that then."

Kinston grabbed the bowl of oatmeal, alternating between giving me a scoop and feeding himself. "So, I take it from your description that he wasn't the fittest child," he said once he'd swallowed his mouthful.

"No." I shook my head. "By the time we were adults, he was three hundred pounds. Of course, I wanted both of us to be healthy, but his weight was never a problem for me. To me, he was my teddy bear. He'd often express his disdain for his body weight and image, and ironically, it was me who encouraged him to make a change. My point was that he should make a change if he were unhappy with himself, and I wanted that for him. Not that I couldn't stand to lose some pounds now."

Unhurriedly stirring the oatmeal, Kinston nodded with something obviously on his mind, but it didn't take long for him to reveal his thoughts to me. "Is that when he also expressed his disdain for *your* body image?" he asked cautiously, trying to pepper his question with ease and comfort.

"Not at first. It was solely about his mission. Eventually, he began to mention that I should go with him. I did a few times because I assumed his request was because he wanted me to see him in action, so to speak. Encourage his process. Then he began making snide remarks about how an article of clothing fit me and questioning why I ate certain foods. Gradually, the suggestions of my attendance switched to tirades of what I should be doing, and not long after, the downright insults started. I should've left then, but I assumed it was just him being enthusiastic about his new weight loss journey. I thought he would calm down until the insults became unbearable, and then the disrespect in his words and actions moldered our relationship."

"You didn't speak up or confront him about his behavior?"

"At first, I didn't. I believe I was so caught off guard by his new persona that I didn't know how to broach it. I excused it, thinking it was a phase until I couldn't ignore it. When I finally did catch a context clue that I couldn't tolerate his antics, it only resulted in worse arguments and even more disrespect. For the longest time, I believed that's when the cheating happened, but in hindsight, I realized the cheating happened with his 'suggestions.' It may not have been physical then, but it was emotional until it was more. Sadly, I knew I should've left. It shouldn't have taken for him to pull a Charles on me to leave."

"A Charles?"

"From Tyler Perry's *Diary of a Mad Black Woman* when that fool burst into the house with his mistress and kicked Gloria out with the U-Haul guy," I scoffed. "If we're going to be together, you gotta keep up with the references, man."

He burst into laughter, nearly spewing the last of the oatmeal out of his mouth. "Woman! I see right now eating and drinking when you're in story mode is detrimental to my health. And I'll remember to stay updated on my movie references."

"Songs and TikTok references too," I cackled with a shrug. "*So take me as I am—*"

"*Or have nothing at all*," he interrupted, finishing the Mary J. Blige song lyric.

"Yasss! You got it, bae!"

"See, *we gon' be a'ight*," he sang in his best Kendrick Lamar voice, making my heart swoon.

Leaning into each other, we kissed, surrounding our giggles. He leaned his forehead into me as a quiet resolve blanketed our playful reverie. His deep breath foreshadowed his next question, and I felt the uneasiness settling into the pit of my stomach as I braced for what I knew would be the most challenging piece of this story. However, I trusted Kinston more than anybody outside of Nia and my immediate family since Nigel. His was a judgment-free safe haven, and I found respite in his care and concern for me.

"So why did you? Stay, I mean."

And there it was. As I went to answer, emotions that I thought had long since passed bubbled to the surface in a rushing tide. My lips twitched, and I bit them, struggling to quell the thunderous storm within. Yet, I was determined to share with Kinston no matter how difficult. I'd already hit the tipping point. Now, I needed to clutch the turning point to fully embrace this next chapter of my life. My chapter with Kinston.

"For the same reason that I didn't have an issue with my body weight at the time," I lifted my eyelids to meet his gaze as droplets pebbled in the corners. "Because that's what happens when you're pregnant."

His eyes ballooned at my admission, and his hand instinctively moved to my belly. "You . . . You were pregnant with his baby?" Unable to speak, I nodded my answer. He thumbed away my tears and caressed my face. "Damn." It was his only response as he cradled me in his arms. "I'm so sorry, Beautiful. I'm sorry I even brought this up. Let's take a beat."

"No," I interrupted, my eyes flickering to meet his. "I need to talk about it. With you, I want to talk about it."

He pinched my chin between his fingers and planted the gentlest kiss on my lips. "I'm listening."

I wonder if he understood the power in the magnitude of his simple gestures. Those two words were medicine to my soul and gave me the courage to release the encumbrance of my past hurts.

"I lost the baby, Kinston. When I was planning to tell Nigel, he announced he was leaving me for his side chick and moved out . . . all on my birthday. A couple of days after he moved, I miscarried, so I never told him. The only person who knew I was pregnant and miscarried was Nia because she was the one who nursed me through it, both physically and emotionally. I didn't even tell my sisters, and I could never tell my parents. And now, you're the only other person who knows. I stayed to make my family work, but I lost him, and then I lost our only connection to each other, my would-be firstborn child."

We were quiet for an extended time as Kinston held me closely. Being nestled in the confines of his arms melted away years of disappointment, regret, and sorrow for the marriage and the child that never came to fruition. Oddly, this was my first time feeling a sense of peace with everything that had transpired.

And it felt good, a renewing. I'd been with Nigel for years and never had the covering and protection of a man. This had been Kinston's way since we began dating. It was only now, as his woman, I wholly accepted it and could see what a difference a real man made.

When I mustered adequate energy to pull away, I noticed Kinston seemed to be in deep contemplation. "What's on your mind, baby?"

My voice must've brought him out of his reverie because he seemed to snap out of it and back into the present. "Just thinking of you, honestly. I appreciate that you were so open and forthcoming with me. And I want you to know I'll do the same with you, but tonight is about you. I know you say you only told Nia and now me, but have you ever considered speaking with someone professionally? I won't pretend to understand the depths of what you went through. What you still must be going through. I'm here for you for anything, but I also understand that sometimes, there may be a need for a little extra help to cope and heal."

In the past, I'd considered visiting a psychologist, but I'd never followed through. Ultimately, I did like most people and decided to deal with it alone. Except, sitting here now, with the aftermath of tears and stewing in the depths of my painful past, I realized that his concerns held validity. I'd nearly lost this marvelous man behind my hang-ups with Nigel. It was that realization that made me reevaluate my decision to seek counseling. If that situation still impacted me all these years later, then perhaps I should, not because Kinston suggested it or I was scared to lose him, but instead, so I could make sure I didn't lose myself. I had to take care of Angela for Angela. Healing and loving myself first was the only way to pour positive nourishment into this relationship. We both deserved that.

"I wasn't open to it in the past, but I believe it's worth a shot. But I must say you talk as if you speak from experience." I patted his hand. "Now, *you* talk to *me*."

Kinston tapped his chest with the palm of his hand. "Like you, the only people who know this are my pops and my brother, but losing my mother at the cusp of adulthood was tough for me. I was so angry. Angry with God. Angry with my dad for not being my mom. Angry with the world. Angry with my mom for leaving us. Angry with myself. Angry for all the times I took her for granted, but mostly because I couldn't do anything to stop the inevitable. So much was happening in my life when she passed away, and I felt like a ticking time bomb. It was Roman who suggested I get some help."

The surprise on my face caused him to grin. "I know he can be a bit wild, but there's always been a calm and mature side of him that he reserves for those closest to him. At first, I thought he was crazy, but after a few incidents of losing my temper, I knew it was time to seek some therapy before I lost everything, so I did. And it was a tremendous help. It's why I know that it could help you too. Listen, I'm here for you for anything, whether to guide you, to listen, to hold you, or even if you ever want to hit the gym." He raised my hand to his lips and kissed my fingers. "If there was one thing losing my mother did teach me, it was the importance of protecting and caring for those who are most important to you."

This time, it was me who kissed his cheek. "I should thank you."

"For what?" he asked, genuinely perplexed.

"For encouraging me to talk this through. For not allowing me to cower in my past hurts. For listening earnestly without judgment. For not giving up on what we could be. For being you. It took me a while to reach this point, but I love it here."

He moved all the food platters back to the carrying table, placed them on the nightstand, took my hands in his, and kissed them. "You never have to thank me for that. I'm your man, and that's what this is like all the time between us. I promise you that."

Blushing, I quipped, "I know, but I still want to thank you."

Slipping down underneath the sheets, I eased his boxer briefs down, and his man below sprang forth. Gripping his girth in my hands, I massaged up and down, admiring its thickness and length. Even limber, it was a beautiful sight to behold.

"Beautiful, what you are . . . What are you doing?" he asked between bated breaths.

"Thanking you," I said before performing a disappearing act with my mouth.

With a sharp hiss, he entangled his fingers into my long ponytail. "Say fucking less," he groaned, his head falling back in sheer ecstasy.

Chapter Twenty

ANGELA

SINCE KINSTON AND I made our relationship official, I had only occupied my time with work and him. I felt and acted like a teenage schoolgirl crushing on her first love. He'd often spend the night with me, even when I insisted we spend more time at his house because he had an expansive bed to support his huge frame. He always declined, not wanting to inconvenience me when I had to go into the office. According to his reasoning, I was the one with the nine-to-five with a supervisor to report to. He only had to answer to himself. It made sense and was a huge benefit because breaking away from bed with Kinston was a feat in and of itself. Indeed, if I had to leave his place and return to mine before work, I'd likely have been terminated for tardiness by now.

When we weren't joined together at the hem, we Facetimed each other in the morning and at night before bed. We'd text check-ins and nasty gifs and messages to each other throughout the day. His "order ahead" Starbucks game was strong, always making sure I had the Cinnamon Dolce Latte Grande with an extra expresso shot, cinnamon sprinkles, and blueberry muffin ready for my pickup. And the sex had me damn near certifiably insane. It was like I didn't even remember what life was like pre-Kinston. Nor did I desire to. He had me out here in these Miami streets stomping hard on some my man, my man, my man tip.

Our days were consumed with each other, which was why I was currently fielding teasing remarks from my sisters.

"I almost forgot I had another sister. I hadn't talked to you in so long," Aquila laughed.

"I know, right? She hooked up with Kinston on that yacht and has been ghost ever since. I would've thought they were lost at sea if I hadn't seen them exit the boat with my own eyes," Nissi chimed in, adding to the tomfoolery.

"First off, we've only been together a couple of months. You all act as if it's been years. Second, since the yacht party, I've talked to both of you, so stop the cap. Besides, you both rooted for this, so zip it and let me enjoy my man."

"Oooh . . . Okay, my bro-in-love has finally tapped that act right into you!" Nissi howled. "And don't even deny it. I'm married to a Jordan man. I know how it is. Just one question, sis."

Feigning exasperation, I asked, "And what's that?"

"Do you need that flashlight now or nah?" Nissi burst into laughter almost before she could finish the question, which caused me to squeal in hysterics.

My mind instantly shuffled to the time I first met Kinston and my conversation with Nissi about why I denied being his plus one at Cami's wedding because I didn't want him to have me looking like Dora Explorer and seeking him out over the "D."

"*Backpack, backpack. Backpack, backpack.*" My eyes rolled with tears as I lightheartedly sampled a snippet from one of the Dora Explorer songs.

"I don't think I even want to know," Aquila said, shaking her head at our hilarity.

"Trust me. You don't." I patted my reddened and inflamed cheeks to quell the ache. "I swear I can't stand you, Nissi. You two almost made me forget the reason I made this call."

"Don't blame me. That's on you, Ms. Backpack," Aquila smarted. "But I do need to finish making the boys' snacks before they wake up from their nap time, so I'm all ears."

"Yeah, my lunch break is almost over, and I have an afternoon full of appointments," Nissi added, calming down her banter.

Taking that as my cue, I settled my nerves before I made my revelation to them. "I don't want you all to freak out on me when I tell you, but rather, simply support me. I'll start by telling you I won't give specifics, but I will explain it in a way that hopefully will shed some light."

As I spoke, I saw Nissi sit in her office chair, and Aquila leaned forward on her sofa. Clear indicators that I not only had their undivided attention but also that my plea for them not to make a huge fuss over what I was about to say probably wouldn't be honored.

"You're going to have to let us judge our reaction, depending on what you're about to say," Aquila flat-out dictated in her most "Aquila-esque" voice.

"That part because you know we don't play about one another," Nissi added.

Le Sigh. I brought my fingertips to my temples and massaged them. "And that is exactly why I started this conversation so that you two would know there was nothing to get out of pocket about. I only want to share some news with you."

"We're listening," they said in unison with tones that clearly made me aware that they were standing firm in their stance to be the determinators based on said news.

"In doing some self-reflection, I came to grips with the fact that I am still wrestling with some trauma behind my relationship and split with Nigel. In hindsight, I've realized how badly it impacted how I dealt with Kinston, but it has also skewed how I view others and how I carry myself. Therefore, I've decided to see a therapist to come to terms with my underlying issues and regain my power."

With exuberance written all over her, Nissi air high-fived me three times. "Sis, I am so proud of you. Anything you need from me to assist you on this path, you've got it. It's high time you stopped torturing yourself behind the ghost of Nigel's past."

Her enthusiasm after hearing my news was just the confidence boost I needed. Of course, I hadn't revealed the part about miscarrying my first child, but being able to admit that I needed help and confiding in them about it was a major step in the right direction for me. Perhaps in time, I'd come to a place where I could divulge the remainder. That thought was short-lived because, in the midst of my air high-fiving Nissi in return, Aquila put her palm up, halting our celebration.

"Wait. I'm a believer in the therapeutics of counseling, but why, after all this time?"

"Because of what I just stated. I've silently blamed myself for years and secretly made comparisons that I shouldn't have all because I haven't dealt with the trauma of that relationship. Sure, I've moved forward, but I haven't moved on."

"And if you're doing this for you, I support you—one thousand percent. But I heard you mention Kinston, and I don't want this to be about him," Aquila levied as if she were confident this was a charge led by Kinston rather than a decision I'd made for myself.

"And it's not. If anything, he's helped me understand the power of therapy. It's not because I want to change for him, or he's forcing me to go based on some warped power trip. Did we discuss it? Yes. But that's irrelevant to the reason I'm seeking help. It's about me. It's for me."

Aquila raised her hand in surrender. "If you say so. Like I said, I'm all for it. I just don't want it to be because another man in your life is dictating your life."

I'm sure my brows were bent into a screw face when I stared at my phone at her unmitigated gall. This testament coming from the woman married to the man of master manipulations had me ready to hit a home run of insinuations on her. Nissi stepped in right on time before I could part my lips to take this conversation to the precipice of no recovery.

"Now, Aquila, lighten up a bit," Nissi said, jumping to my defense. "You know Kinston is not that type of man."

"No, I don't, and you don't either, Nissi. All we know of him is what we get as his friend, me as a trainer, and you as his sister-in-law. We don't know how he is in a relationship, and, might I add, Angela doesn't either since they've only been together a month."

The following words were out of my mouth faster than reason could enter my mind. "It's been *two* months, actually, and dating for several. From what I *do* know about him, he wants the best for me . . . *for me*. Not for him, nor to stroke his ego, and especially not for his own benefit."

Silence. Not a peep could be heard across any of our phone lines. My words were as scathing as I'd intended them to be. We all knew my slight was about her marriage to Joel. Aquila had such keen advice for everyone else but couldn't tell the difference between apples and tomatoes if she grew them herself. As my sister, I comprehended and valued her concern, but not to the point where it became disrespectful.

Once the stun lifted, Aquila said, "My bad. You made yourself clear. I'm sorry." The words flowed out in one swoop after she recovered from my backlash.

Since I was still a bit heated about her off-color comments about Kinston, I didn't readily respond. Instead, Nissi spoke up, trying to move the conversation past our tiff.

"Anyway, you said there were two things you wanted to share with us. What's the second one?"

"The second was that Kinston's birthday is in December. I wanted to throw him a surprise party on the second Saturday, so please make sure your calendars are clear. That's *if* you would like to be a guest."

My sneer was toward Aquila, and they both knew it, but I didn't care. Honestly, her issue was with whatever was happening in the Oliver household, and until she could be truthful about that, I wasn't about to entertain her theatrics. For the life of me, I couldn't fathom how she managed to turn any sliver of positivity into a negative. But then again, we all knew that company was misery's best friend.

"Of course, we'd like to be guests. And if you need help planning it, just say the word," Nissi answered for both of them.

Aquila shrugged, throwing her hand in the air. "Excuse me for being concerned. I'll be at the party."

"Oh, you're excused," I scoffed.

"On that note, I have to get back to work, and you all have to get back to what you all were doing. Let's talk later," Nissi said, no doubt trying to quell the searing inferno simmering between Aquila and me.

"Sure, let me get the boys together. I love y'all," Aquila said and disconnected without waiting for a response.

"Nissi—"

She placed her hand up to stop me. "I know, girl. I'll talk to her. Don't let that deter you, though. We are both proud of you, and you know this. I really have to go now. Love you, roundtrip."

"Back at you."

We disconnected the line, and while I didn't feel as excited as I'd hoped when we hung up, knowing that Nissi and Kinston's support was behind me lifted my spirits, especially after this battle with Aquila. Exiting my car, I made my way into the building.

"Welcome to Better You Counseling. May I help you?" an older Hispanic woman asked, addressing me.

"I have a two o'clock appointment with Dr. Abrams."

Chapter Twenty-One

KINSTON

IF ANYONE HAD told me at Kannon and Nissi's wedding that by November, I'd be in a happy and thriving three-month-long relationship with Angela, I would have recommended they be deemed mentally insane. But we were. I'd never known what bliss felt like until her. I'd always been attracted to her nurturing spirit and larger-than-life personality, but I didn't realize I could fall so fast. I know Roman called me out for loving her, but what I felt for her wasn't solely love. I loved my brother, my pops, my friends, heck, even my career, and yes, I loved Angela, but that love was far deeper than what I had for anyone else. With her, she made me hope again, believe again, live again. I hadn't known how preoccupied I'd been with my career until we began dating.

Now that she was my lady, she had me considering the family life. Frequently, I flipped through houses for sale online and pondered over engagement rings. My imagination and dreams ran wild with thoughts of Angela possibly becoming my wife one day. Sometimes, I thought I had to be losing my mind because it all seemed to be moving too swiftly. But in speaking to my father about it, his advice was a familiar ideology, one that I'd referred to a time or two, especially when I was trying to explain my feelings for Angela to my boys: *when you know, you know.* It was confirmation that I needed to take my own advice. And regardless of whether I chose to acknowledge it, something in my gut ... knew.

"I take it you didn't hear me." Cami, one of my top trainers, pulled me out of my conclave of thoughts.

"My bad. I'm sorry. I didn't." I offered her a sheepish grin, sliding my hand over my beard.

She wagged a teasing finger at me. "I know that starry-eyed, far-off gaze. I've had it a time or two over Travis. You were over there daydreaming about Angela."

As soon as her name graced Cami's lips, I was all cheeses and blushes. My queen had me gone for real over her. Cami couldn't help the laugh she released as she launched into a litany of jokes at my sprung expense. I took no offense because it was all facts, and I'd never deny anything about our relationship. If I were simping, then I'd be that for her.

"Whatever, man." I waved off her comments. "What did you come in here to tell me?"

"Brook and I finished our last classes. Roman and Tyrod should be done at the other facility soon." I went to stand, but she gestured her hands for me to sit back down. "You don't have to walk us to our cars. Marvin is meeting us at the front," she informed me, referring to the complex's security guard.

Slowly, I eased back down, returning to my seat. "All right. Be sure you and Brook text me when you ladies make it home."

"Will do. Tell Angela I said hello." Cami wriggled her fingers as she turned to leave.

"I wasn't even talking to her when you came in." I shrugged, trying to downplay my infatuation.

Cami halted and tossed her head backward with an eye roll. "Like you won't call your woman as soon as that door clicks behind me. You're completely gone over her, and that's good for you. *She's* good for you. It beats these little thotianas vying for your attention, that's for sure."

Pure facts. I'd had to fend off my fair share of women who graced KinRo's doors before, but since I began dating Angela, it's almost as if I'd become a magnet. Most of the women respected the boundaries when I explained that I had a girlfriend. A few tried to test how sound that relationship was, to which I promptly and sternly shut them down. There was only one incident that ended with me revoking the woman's membership for breaking the rules of the contract, which were to respect everyone who comes through the doors.

One day, Angela and I stopped by on our way out so I could drop off a shipment of cleaning supplies for our cleanup crew when one of the women who tried to approach me saw us. I heard her make a snide remark about Angela and her weight to my trainer Tyrod, who reprimanded her, but I'd heard it. Thankfully, Angela hadn't. I asked Angela to wait in the car while I spoke with Tyrod, and she did.

When I approached Tyrod, he knew from my incensed expression and terse body language that I had heard the client. When I pulled him to the side to confirm what I knew I'd heard, he did, so I stopped their session and asked the receptionist and Tyrod to step into our conference room with the client and me, where I immediately ended her contract. Of course, she was upset, especially since she'd be charged the remainder of her balance. She went into a slew of insults about Angela and threatened to sue. Since I'd recorded the conversation on my phone and the gym had cameras with signs posted that active surveillance was in place, I informed her of that and the fact that she violated the contract, then told her to bring it to court, and I would as well with all my evidence. Needless to say, she left, and we never heard from her again. And thankfully, Angela was none the wiser about the incident, which I was eternally grateful for. There was no telling if that would have sent her into a downward spiral, and I was not about to lose my irreplaceable woman over a replaceable client.

By now, anybody who was a regular or semiregular knew that Kinston Jordan was off the bachelor's list.

"Yeah, she is." I stroked my beard in a horrible attempt to hide my blush.

"Oooh yeah, I'll be looking forward to my wedding invitation next, minus the drama," she snickered, and I winced thinking about the verbal altercation that Kannon and I had gotten into with Dr. Benji Eloi over Nissi at Cami's reception. I went to apologize again, and Cami fanned away my words. "I've told you, it's water under the bridge. Nothing serious happened, nor did it ruin my day. Listen, I'm out. Brook looks irritated."

I chuckled because, knowing Brook, she was. "All right. Get out of here. Text me!" I called out to her retreating back. She threw up a thumbs-up, and I tried to focus on the paperwork ahead of me.

After about fifteen minutes of reading and rereading the same paragraph, I decided to do what was on my mind . . . call Angela. Tapping my AirPod, I instructed Siri to dial her number. When she answered on the third ring, my entire world lit up.

"Hey, Beautiful. How was your day?"

"Long, as usual, but such is life. And how was yours, baby?"

"Uneventful. Same ole same. I'm trying to focus on this paperwork, but I can't get a certain someone off my brain long enough to concentrate."

She giggled. "Umm, I wonder who that someone could be? She must be a baddie."

"Oh yeah," I drawled out, leaning back into my leather chair. "She's a beautiful chocolate sister about five foot five with thicker than a snicker thighs, and that ass . . . shhh. Makes me want to spend all day worshipping it and the God that created it."

"Ooh, tell me more," she whispered salaciously.

"Not to mention her inside matches her outside. She has a sense of humor and is sweet, but she can be a little sassy. But I don't worry about that because I got that act right for her to calm that feistiness down."

"Oh, you think, huh?"

"Shidd, I know. In fact, I'm about to wrap this up and head over to her place to put some of it in her right now."

"Oh, a little birdie told me you can't do that."

Her denial had me sitting straight up in my seat. "Why not?"

"Because she isn't at home."

My eyes darted to the time on my cell phone sitting on my desk. It read 9:40 p.m. Not that I wanted to control her life. I mean, she was a grown woman, after all. But none of that stopped me from being concerned over my lady's whereabouts at this time of night.

"Beautiful, where are you? It's late."

"Why don't you come and unlock the front door?"

I smiled, and my head fell back. "I'm not at home."

"I'm not at your home either."

Curiosity got the better of me, and I stood up, intrigued as I stalked to the front of the gym. When I saw Angela waving at the front door in her winter coat at me, I couldn't help the feeling that overcame me to see her. Giddiness. Yes, as my girlfriend says, at my big ole manly age of thirty-three, my six-foot-three burly frame was grinning like a schoolgirl with butterflies in my belly. Rushing to unlock the door, I swiftly swung the door open and ushered her inside. No sooner had she entered than I swept her into my arms and kissed her as if it were our first time.

"Whew. Remind me always to surprise you at work," she said breathlessly when we finally relinquished each other's tongues and lips.

Locking the door and easing us farther inside, away from the unusual chill of the 40-degree weather, I asked, "How did you know I was still at the gym, and why didn't you tell me you were heading over here?"

"Then it wouldn't have been a surprise." She patted my chest. "I just left from Nissi and Kannon's, and he told me that you would be here late, so I chanced it. I promise I didn't exit my vehicle until I saw your SUV out front."

She knew my overprotective nature. "Well, at least you did that. I know we have security, and this is a posh area of the city, but I still don't like you roaming around at night without letting me know where you are. Miami is nice, but it's that Dade County side that bothers me."

She heaved a sigh. "Normally, I'd get irritated that at my big ole age of thirty, you'd be checking for me, but I appreciate your genuine concern, so I'll just say thank you."

"But," I added because I knew it was hanging off her lips.

"But . . . I'm a grown woman, so ease up, chief." She cupped my chin, gazing into my eyes. "Besides, it's been a week since we've seen each other. I don't want to discuss that kind of safety."

The way my man below jumped at her insinuation, I loved it when she talked dirty to me. I even loved her independent and slightly rebellious nature, especially when she was right. It had been a week, and we had other ways to occupy our time.

Last weekend, I'd been out of town in Orlando, hosting a bodybuilding competition. I'd asked her to come with me, but she had to stay to prep for a case her boss had upcoming in Tampa. When I arrived in town, she departed with the attorneys to Tampa. She'd arrived back in town late last night, but since she had to be at work this morning, I didn't bother her other than to talk briefly on the phone. So, we had lost time to make up.

I licked my lips before parting them to plant an openmouthed kiss on the side of her neck. "No worries, Beautiful. I always have a safety net ready and waiting for you."

"You know just how to make me wet," she murmured, her breath kissing my lips.

I lifted her. She wrapped her legs around my waist, and we began kissing. It was soft and supple pecks at first, but when her mouth parted, giving me access to her tongue, I devoured her. She placed her hands on either side of my face and moaned into my mouth as I carried her over to one of the bench press benches. I hovered over her as we nipped and suckled on each other's hot spots. When I unbuttoned her peacoat, I noticed the workout attire and sat up, straddling the bench.

"Umm, what's this?" I assumed she was going to reveal some type of fetish that I fully planned on taking advantage of.

She sat up, penning her coils behind her ears, and then took my hands. "I had a whole speech planned for when I came to visit you, but, as usual, we can't ever seem to keep our greedy paws off each other."

We laughed, and I raised my hand, caressing her cheek. "You know you can tell me anything."

She cradled her hand around my wrist and bent her face down, brushing the palm of my hand with her pouty lips. "I do. It's nothing bad, but we didn't have time to talk before you were off to Orlando, and then I was off to Tampa. But I wanted you to know that I thought it over and took the step. I'm in therapy with Dr. Abrams at Better You."

"That's great news." Excitedly, I embraced her tightly. "I'm proud of you."

"Thank you." She peeled back and nodded. "And it felt right. Our first session was easy. There weren't any major breakthroughs, but for the first time, I felt lighter afterward."

"You've already had your first session?"

"Yes, last week. I didn't want to say anything in case I hated it and decided not to return."

I cracked a smile, shaking my head at her. "That sounds like you," I teased, playfully gripping her waist as she swatted at me. "I'm familiar with Better You. I've done a few health fairs with them."

"Oh, I know. Dr. Abrams suggested different self-care strategies. One was exercise, and she recommended KinRo Fitness, which she learned about from the health fairs."

"So, does that explain this sexy workout outfit?" My eyes roamed her full body in the one-piece yoga short unitard that appeared painted on her bodacious curves.

She marched her fingers down my chest until she reached the hem of my T-shirt and pulled me close. "I figured since I'm making these life changes, I'd let someone assist me with this new exercise self-care." Wrapping one arm around my neck at a time, she leaned until our mouths lightly brushed together as she gazed at me under low-hanging lids. "Do you happen to know someone who could assist me?"

With my hands grazing between her waistline and her butt, I gripped her fleshy mounds tighter and quickly slid her into me with her yelping out at the sudden movement. "I know a guy."

With us sitting so close, she interlocked her fingers around my neck, and I returned the gesture around her waist. Slowly, our blithesome banter morphed into mischievous teasing, nipping at each other's erogenous spots. Our foreheads met as we basked in the intimacy of our shared time. There was nowhere else in the world that I'd rather be than nestled in her arms and she in mine.

If I could remain in this exact spot for the remainder of my life, I'd die as a man with my life fulfilled. But then Angela peeled away from me, disrupting my forever fantasy.

Easing to a standing position, she slid her fingers along my jawline and cupped my beard. "So, why don't you assist me with my exercise regimen? We can call it 'workouts after dark.'"

Both me and my throbbing member were on point with this plan. "I can do that." I stood, taking her by the hand and leading her into one of the training session rooms.

As long as I'd been in the business, I'd never experienced a more erotic session in my life. Between the stretches and warm-ups, I could barely keep focus. There was no way to describe how I felt pushing one of Angela's legs up, toes pointed to the heavens, and not being buried between her thunderous thighs. There was something excruciatingly magical about it. Afterward, she wasn't the only one who needed a thirty-second break. Starting her with a light total-body routine, I chose two upper-body, two lower-body, and two core exercises to work the muscles and build her endurance before enhancing her regimen. Before she realized it, forty-five minutes had flown by, and we were finished with her first workout session.

When Angela stood up from her cool-down stretches, I high-fived her. "Great job, Beautiful. If we keep up the routine, you'll see a difference in your endurance, energy, stress levels, sleeping habits, and mental clarity."

"And my fupa!" she sassed. "Don't forget *that*."

I placed my hand on her hips, bringing her close to me. "But I love your fupa," I whined like a begging toddler.

Her grin was infectious. "I know you do, baby. You always show me, but I could stand to get rid of your little buddy."

I slapped her ass and gripped it. "As long as you don't get rid of this, we cool."

"Then you better give me an exercise to keep it."

"And why do you think I had you doing squats? Yes, it's healthy, but it was damn sure for my benefit."

She shook her head at my revelation. "So, put me on a schedule, Coach Kinston. After hours, I'm all yours."

My eyebrow lifted at her choice of words. "Is that right?"

She caught my drift without me having to say a word. Stepping back, she released her coils from the ponytail holder she'd secured her hair with and slid her yoga suit down until it dropped to her ankles, exposing a black thong and bare breasts. Kicking out of her shoes, she discarded the suit and then the thong. Prancing over to her purse hanging on a hook behind the door, she produced a layer of protection between her index and middle fingers. She knew what I needed: that Trojan man lambskin packet. I sat on the bench press and used the crook of my forefinger to beckon her to me. As she sashayed over, thoughts of the dream I'd had months before invaded my memory. The realization that the dream was a premonition made me ache with excited anticipation. Workout sweat be damned. When she straddled me, I kissed her neck and told her about my unspoken fantasy.

"I had a dream that we had sex in my gym."

"Well," she drew out between moans, "you know your dreams are your reality in subconscious form. So let's bring it to the physical."

Before I could respond, she slipped her hand inside my basketball shorts and compression tights and then stroked my already-rising member. The way her hands felt on me drove me insane every time. My head fell back as a deep moan reverberated up my throat through my parted lips. She kissed my bobbing Adam's apple with her pouty lips, and I knew if we didn't get to the point, I'd get to my happy ending.

Since she wasn't playing fair, I didn't either and slipped two of my lengthy fingers inside her core, strumming her insides while circling her love button with my thumb.

"Aah, Kinston."

"Mm-hmm," I moaned in her ear before sucking in my bottom lip from the feel of her moistened warmth gliding over my digits. "Let me prime this pretty pussy."

My words made her wetter instantly. Removing my fingers, I inserted them into my mouth to taste her essence. Better than any nectar ever created. Once I had my fill, I slipped the same fingers into her mouth and watched intently as she slurped the remaining juices as if she were partaking of her last meal. That made me say, "Forget this foreplay." She must've had the same thought because as I lifted, we both went straight for the band of my shorts, playing tug-of-war to bring them down. I didn't even take them off entirely as they hung midthigh before she slid on the protection to cover me and eased down on my hardened shaft. We both wailed out at the reunited connection we'd missed all week. Seven days without her felt like seven years. I knew then she could never take this away from me.

I smacked her roughly on her cheeks. "Ride it like you want it," I demanded.

She bucked and began jockeying on me, taming the stallion underneath her, and I was caged in her utter control. The way she rolled back and forth and forth and back in a unified cadence almost lulled me into a completion that I was not ready to release. When I was sure I was about to burst, I yanked her into my chest, almost melding us together, and began pounding upward to meet her thrusts. The jolt caused her to claw at my back, and she tossed her head between the crook of my shoulder.

"Mm-hmm. Give it to me," I panted, knowing the sign that my queen was nearing her end as well.

"Kinston," she wailed, extending my name as euphoria overcame her.

"I know, Beautiful. I know."

She splashed all over me, covering my manhood and my shorts with her sticky goodness. It was so much that I immediately came right behind her, filling the protection to the brim.

"Angela, I've missed you, baby," I moaned out as the last remnants secreted from my body.

She lifted her head, resting her sweat-drenched forehead against mine, twirling my locs in her fingers. "I missed you, too, Papí Chulo."

"Damn, I got you speaking in foreign languages now?"

"Baby," she hissed sexily. "The way you lay pipe, you have me speaking in tongues." She threw her hand up in pretend praise. "Shondo! He's-coming-with-a-long-stroke or whatever the phrase said," she strung together, causing me to burst out in teary-eyed hysterics.

"Nope, I am not playing with you."

"Shit, neither was I." She fanned herself before planting a sweet kiss on me. "Neither was I."

Holding her close, we hugged and savored the aftertaste of our blissful tryst. Internally, I chuckled to myself. Fantasy, dream, premonition ... fulfilled.

Chapter Twenty-Two

ANGELA

IT SEEMED LIKE the calendar used the turbo fuel from the *Fast and Furious* franchise because we'd flown through November up to December 9th in a nanosecond. Between work, therapy, working out, and putting up a ruse to orchestrate a surprise party for Kinston, I was nearly worn to the bone. The only relief I received was Thanksgiving. Nissi and Kannon hosted their first Thanksgiving dinner at their home, and it was a lovely time. Kinston made it through the crash course of my parents, Nisante and Abigail Richards. Kannon teased that he'd softened the landing pad for Kinston since he was the one who unofficially introduced them to the Richards's parents from his relationship and subsequent engagement and marriage to Nissi. While there was truth to that because my parents already loved Kinston as a bonus son, that was "predating-their-daughter." However, I must admit the interrogation was less strained and a bit lighter. By the end of dinner, Kinston had sealed the gold star of approval, so we had to concede that Kannon had a point. What could we say? Kannon ran so Kinston could walk.

We even got a chance to enjoy my nephews, Nisante and Joel Jr., or as we lovingly called them, "Sante and Junior," without any debauchery from their annoying father. For whatever reason, God decided to bless our family gathering by allowing Joel to be on his best behavior. He didn't even try to commandeer the dinner with his five-star bourgeois advice. He sat back and chilled with my father, Papa Kain, and Kinston in the man cave. The most adorable gesture was having Kannon ask our mother for permission to cook the meal with her. She was so honored and enthused by his request that she even deemed him head chef and followed his lead. We all insisted that Nissi be their sous-chef so she could learn her way around the kitchen aside from the microwave. It was a beautiful bonding moment between the loving couple and our mother. And I unequivocally praised the fact that we weren't the type to conform to the ideologies that only females were the cooks because my brother-in-love was not to be messed with in the kitchen. Even had Mr. Iron Chef Joel licking his damned fingers! When our mother ate the first bite of Kannon's peach cobbler, she officially handed him the holiday chef hat and deemed him the certified and unanimous family holiday meal cook. No one dared say it, not even my mother, but that peach cobbler was better than hers. Besides, her passing of the torch was a testament to those unspoken words. Bro earned that slot, and I planned to be a partaker for many years to come.

Once Thanksgiving was over, I was thrust back into shaking and dodging Kinston to plan this surprise party. Now that the day was finally here, I prayed it went off without a hitch. I'd fooled Kinston into believing that I was going to treat him out to an elegant dinner for two, so I'd made the arrangements with his hairstylist to get his locs retouched, and I'd reached out to the fashion stylist who'd styled him for the grand opening party to style him for tonight's "dinner." He would be none the wiser when I pulled up at his house on a party bus. We'd all agreed to meet at my house and ride the bus to Kinston's. This way, I'd ensure no one had idle time to blabber mouth the plans to him, and no one would be late. As far as the party, it was simply the usual crew invited. My sisters and their spouses, Cami and her husband, Travis, Jovan and his girlfriend, Jasmine, and Nia and Roman, whom no one knew precisely what the existing tea was. Other than a few dates and tapping the goods, Nia hadn't eluded to anything of significance with Roman. I'd been so consumed with my own relationship that I hadn't bothered to snoop, but I had time while she, my sisters, and I enjoyed this spa treatment that Aquila treated us to as a truce to me over how she'd acted when I told her about my therapy, which I was happy to say was going relatively well.

"Aquila, you've outdone yourself with this new spa. I've never been to a salt cave, and the way that man massaged my feet, I almost asked him to marry me," Nia said as we sat, enjoying our cucumber facials and sipping white wine.

"Uh-oh, I need to tell Roman he ain't on his job then," I kidded.

She pointed a lazy finger in my direction. "You're not slick with that Roman comment."

Leaning forward, I turned to my side, gawking at her. "Well, save us all the trouble and spill the tea."

"Now, *that's* how you can thank me," Aquila joined in.

"And you know I'm on the bandwagon with my sisters," Nissi added, lazing back in her seat to prepare for the gossip.

Flipping her hand up in the air in a blasé motion, she quipped, "Then you all are about to be sorely disappointed because there's nothing to tell."

"Nothing?" Aquila asked, disbelief shrouding her one-word question.

"Nothing." Nia deadpanned.

I shook my hand because I knew much more than nothing had happened between the two. "Now, I know you test-drove the whip, so don't even play."

Nia sat up. "Girl, yes, and I drove the hell out of it too, but it's no haps. When that man said he was not looking to be locked down, he meant it. We went out on a couple of dates and had sex, but . . ." she dragged with a casual shrug. "That's it. We haven't seen each other in over a month. The last time we went out, he stated he'd get up with me later, and later has turned into never, it seems."

All our faces were upturned at this news, which made Nia quickly pipe up.

"Don't do that. Roman and I established from the beginning that this was only a beneficial hookup, so I'm not pressed over the fact that it has run its course. Besides, I do not want to be strung along or hold on to strings that will not serve me in the long run. It was what it was, and now it isn't. We are still cool, trust."

"Dang, I thought it was going to be an all-family and friends affair for us," Nissi smacked her lips.

"Ugh, no. Only you and Kannon can have that fairy-tale ending," Nia chirped.

"Nah, my big sis and bro-in-law are working on theirs," Nissi countered to my blush.

"And are," I added with a snap of my fingers. "But, girl, at least tell us the drive was worth it," I said, turning my attention back toward Nia.

Nia giggled, pumping her hands in the air. "Now, I ain't say nothing about it not being worth it or never doing *that* again. I may not own the car, but I'd absolutely let my boi spin the block for a lease option any time."

Our thunderous elation had us quickly trying to tamp down before they threw us out of the facility. Although Nia and Roman weren't the next hot couple on the block, I couldn't argue with her about allowing him to spin it. He may not have been a Jordan man, but Mr. Patterson assuredly held his own amongst his friends. All of the men did, actually, except for nerdy and narcissistic Joel. He was cute in a desired taste sort of way. Let's just say my nephews inherited their good-looking genes from my sister. The only thing Joel truly had going for him was his culinary skills, and even that was questionable to me. Truth be told, Aquila could run circles around Joel in the kitchen, in my humble opinion. Then again, in my humble opinion, so could my mama, Kannon, and Kinston. Rather than voice that thought, I kept it to myself since Aquila and I had just gotten back on good terms, and today was not the day to muck up our energy.

"But enough about me and my drive time. Ang, are you ready for tonight? Do you think he's going to like his surprise?" Nia asked.

"Yes, I am. He's always giving to me and others. It feels good to surprise him on his special day. I hope he loves it. I had to do a ton of back-door prowling, investigating, and interrogating to make this day happen."

"Y'all are so stinking cute. He's going to love it, I'm sure." Nissi patted my hand to reassure me.

"I know that's right. He loves anything from Angela," Nia dragged my name out with my sisters cackling at her.

I threw a hand towel that appropriately hit all three of them for teasing me. That only caused them to go up with the antics even more as they all chorused together, "He loves anything from Angelas." Adding an "*s*" at the end of my name to mimic the way the actor said Selena's name in the movie, *Selena*.

After applying my final coat of lipstick, I gave myself the once-over in the mirror. The reflection staring back at me gave off vixen vibes, and I hoped I wasn't the only one to notice. Burgundy was my man's favorite color, so I'd had the stylist pick out a few burgundy-tailored two-piece suits with matching loafers for Kinston. As for me, I'd searched and found an exquisite floor-length, long-sleeved, burgundy ruched dress with a high slit up the front. The fabric cinched my waistline perfectly and clung to my hips and rear end to accentuate my curves. The slit highlighted my thick thighs that Kinston couldn't get enough of, and the low-cut neckline showcased a beautiful silhouette of my cleavage. The teardrop necklace added a sensual view of my breasts. To top it off, I'd paired the dress with my sky-high, glitter-gold Jimmy Choo platform shoes. With extra-volumized curls to my bob cut hair, my face beat to the goddess of Oshun herself, and a lip pop of my favorite matte burgundy lipstick from Beat by London, if my plans didn't make his day, I hoped that my ubersexy appearance would.

If I needed confirmation about it, I received it wholeheartedly when I entered my living room from the hoots and hollers from the ladies and protruding eyes and gaped mouths of the men.

Nia took my hand and twirled me around. "Sissss, I think you might've wasted our time tonight. One glance at you and Kinston will turn this night out into a night in." She topped it with a little shimmy shake, which made me blush.

"Right!" Nissi added. "I need to exchange my gift from this cologne for some baby clothes because y'all are definitely going half tonight."

Aquila moved both Nia and Nissi out of the way and grabbed my hands, swinging my arms out to catch the full view. "You look fabulous. Kinston is a lucky man," she fussed over me as Cami and Jasmine nodded approvingly.

Kannon waved his hands to stop their fawning. "Y'all are all smiles and giggles, and I'm over here trying to figure out how to keep my brother from knocking out every dude who gawks at you, sis-in-love. I'm really trying not to catch a charge tonight."

A collective "yeah" went up between Roman and Jovan, which caused everyone to chuckle at their shared concern.

Patting Kannon's shoulder, I sassed, "No worries, bro-in-love. I have ways to keep him distracted from that all night long."

"I could've lived a lifetime without that thought in my mind," Joel huffed, soliciting scathing stares in his direction.

"And I could've lived a lifetime without you as my miserable-ass brother-in-law, but we can't always get what we want, can we?" I popped off before I could halt the comment.

Joel stood as if he were going to say something to me when Kannon turned completely to face him, daring him to open his mouth by the way his shoulders squared up. Roman, Jovan, and Travis also shared the stance. One point about standing in the presence of real men is that they would never let a clown like Joel disrespect a woman—theirs or any other. Before a misunderstanding could occur amongst the men, Aquila walked over to Joel.

"This night is about Kinston and Angela. That was unnecessary. We rarely have a fun time together. Let's enjoy this night, please?" she all but begged him to act as if he had some couth and common sense.

With a huff and a pinch of the bridge of his nose, he conceded. "I'm sorry, Angela. Let's just celebrate tonight so we can go about our regularly scheduled program," he said, stalking out the front door.

With a slow turn, Aquila walked back to me, pulling me into a hug as she whispered into my ear. "Sorry, Ang. He's under a lot of pressure right now. It's no excuse, but he needs this tonight. *We* need it."

Releasing a deep breath, I reined in my attitude. "Okay, Lah. For you."

That I meant. It was only for her. When Aquila called to smooth out our issues, she'd confided in me that Joel's restaurant was having some financial troubles and that his private catering sales had been unseasonably low this year, contributing to his less-than-personable demeanor. I could understand his frustration with that uncertainty, given that he had a whole wife and kids who depended on him, but Joel had always been an arrogant prick. This life change made him insufferable, which had begun to filter through my sister. However, I appreciated that she'd trusted me with that rare glimpse into their life to help me better understand so our dynamic wouldn't suffer. Therefore, if she requested grace for her husband, I'd grant it, but I only had two cheeks to offer. He'd slapped one. One more offense, and he'd be begging for the grace I was willingly offering, so he'd better tread light, especially tonight.

She mouthed "Thank you" to me and turned to face everyone else. "Sorry, you guys. He'll be on his best behavior from now on tonight."

The doubtful expressions and side-eyes clearly indicated that no one believed that, but before anyone had a notion to express it, Joel opened the door and announced, "The party bus is here."

The black Sprinter party bus had all of a club's atmospheric amenities. Multicolored lights danced around the interior, with Kinston's favorite hip-hop and club mixes blaring throughout. Two poles were planted in the center for simulated dancing, and confetti and balloons topped off the décor. Bottles of champagne and D'ussé were spread throughout, and trays of charcuterie boards were also in place for our pregame party. When we arrived at Kinston's house, I had the driver stop the music so he wouldn't be alerted. We all exited, but the crew remained outside by the bus while I rang his doorbell.

"Hey, Beautiful, I could've picked . . ." His words trailed when he took one glance at me. Without hesitation, he gripped me about the waist and pulled me into him, planting a succulent kiss on my lips. His hand instinctively slipped to my thigh and lifted it to wrap around him as his fingertips grazed my exposed skin. I ended our kiss to see him biting his bottom lip, his eyes twinkling in lust. "Damn, Beautiful. We got time for a little—"

"Surprise!" We heard our crew yell from behind me.

Stunned, with his brows lifted, he peered behind me for the first time to see our family and friends waiting on us and the party bus before glancing back at me.

"Surprise?" I said timidly with a shrug.

"We thought we'd let you know it was a group party before we were privy to something we didn't need to see," Nissi shouted.

I slid my leg back down, standing in front of him with my hand on his shoulders. "Umm, do you like it?"

Brushing the tip of his thumb across his bottom lip, he eyed me up and down sexily. "I more than like it."

Giggling, I swatted him on the shoulder. "I mean the surprise party."

"Oh yeah, I like that too." He lifted my hand and pulled me close to him again. "But I do hope our night ends with some alone time with you," he whispered.

"Oh, absolutely, Mr. Jordan."

We wrapped our arms around each other and sealed our promise with another sensual kiss. Before we could release each other, we heard the catcalls of our family and friends behind us.

"We would tell y'all to get a room, but you two might just do that and leave us with this party bus for the night," Roman chided amongst the billowing laughter.

Kinston reared back, rumbling and pointing at his friend. "And you already know!"

We made our way over to the group as Kinston greeted everyone, slapping hands and giving hugs before we all entered the party bus. The D'ussé and champagne flowed as we rode around Miami, eating and drinking while enjoying one another's company. After a few shots, we really turned up. We all began dancing as Kinston's favorite artists blared across the speakers. When the tunes started to mix in old-school Miami bass music, the bus turned up an extra level. Kinston gripped my waist, and we grinded and dirty-winded on each other as our crew was on their feet dancing on each other or on the poles.

"Get it, Nissi!" The ladies shouted as she used the pole to balance as she twerked on Kannon.

She pointed at me, and I grabbed the other pole and balanced my back against it as Kinston gripped the pole above my head and slowly rolled his body against me as if he were my own private dancer. And everyone went up about our sensual dance.

That's when Nia bellowed, "Your turn, Aquila!"

Aquila, who was in rare form from the multiple glasses of champagne, turned to the pole closest to Nissi and sexily waltzed around it until she was in front of Joel, then swayed her hips, beckoning him to come to her with the crook of her finger. Joel stood with flames in his eyes, gripping Aquila about the wrist and pulling her to sit down. By the time it registered on us that he was fussing at her, the driver announced that we'd arrived at our next destination, the Cigar Bar, that I'd rented out for the finale.

"Wait a minute. Hold on." I began to make my way to where Aquila and Joel were. "I know good and damn well you didn't snatch my sister. How dare you embarrass her like that?"

Joel stood, audaciously glaring at me as if he were prepared to take this conversation wherever I dared to go. "I will if she is embarrassing herself. She's a wife and a mother. She shouldn't be out here gyrating like some ho from the hood," Joel spewed, casting a backward glare at Aquila, who sat mortified.

His words landed with the abrupt callousness intended and momentarily stunned me into silence because neither I nor any of us were used to this brand of his personality. Sure, he was curt, egotistical, and blunt, but he'd never outright insulted our sister to this degree, at least not in our presence. So, his brashness had taken me for a loop. However, where I couldn't recover as quickly from his adolescent tirade, Nissi picked up and hurled her own insults at him.

"And she was gyrating for and with her husband, so zip it, Joel!" Nissi roared. "It's called having fun. You should try it sometime." Nissi inched a bit closer to austerely deliver her following words. "And if you disrespect our sister again, I'm going to forget you're my brother-in-law."

Not to be deterred, Joel fired back at Nissi, proving he was truly on one tonight. "And I don't give a damn what it's called. She may be y'all's sister, but she's *my* wife, and *I* won't have her acting so unbecoming. I couldn't care less what *your* husband allows, but *my* wife has standards."

"*Excuse* me!" Nissi and I barked in unison.

In my determination to set Joel straight, I'd nearly forgotten our closest friends and our men surrounded us. Nissi and I were expeditiously reminded of that fact when I felt my body being gently pushed backward along with my sister's with Kinston and Kannon replacing us in front of Joel. Their body language alerted everyone that the two lovable brothers we knew had gone rogue, replaced by two vicious villains. Leave it to Joel to activate two Mr. Dade Counties.

"Listen here, man. I've tolerated you for the sake of the Richards family, but if you fix your mouth to disrespect my wife *or* her sisters again, I'ma turn this party bus into a jail transfer bus because that's exactly where I'll be headed," Kannon boomed, his face inches from Joel's.

"And trust me, bruh, we'll both be some fighting motherfuckers because I damn sure don't play about mine," Kinston added.

Joel scoffed, throwing his hands in the air. "Oh, that's just rich coming from a TikTok boy toy and his meathead trainer brother."

Kinston's booming "Fuck you say?" was just enough to snap all of us into action to attempt to come between the men before all hell broke loose. Immediately, Nissi and I tried to hold on to Kannon and Kinston while Aquila pounced to her feet to pull Joel out of harm's way. In the mix, I could see additional male bodies trying to break between us to separate them amid deafening yelps and screams. Just before the chaos was broken up, I saw Joel get shoved backward by Roman, which caused him to slam back and butt-plant into the seat he once occupied. By then, the driver called for us to exit the bus as Roman, Jovan, and Travis controlled the scene and helped cool the temperatures.

Kinston, Kannon, Nissi, and I were the first to exit the bus to get them away from the vicinity of Joel. The remainder of the occupants filed out one by one but allowed us four the space needed to de-escalate and decompress from the pandemonium on the bus. After a few minutes, Kannon had calmed, and he and Nissi trekked to where Kinston and I were standing as Kinston paced back and forth, still in fight mode.

Typically, I was the one out of my sisters with the hothead, so in circumstances like this, I usually wasn't the sensible one. Knowing that Kinston used to suffer from anger management issues after the death of his mother sobered me quickly. It was quite clear that his level of rage was eerily dangerous, and I wanted to be his peace to quiet the internal storm brewing within. This was also his special night, and I would not allow the likes of Joel Oliver to ruin it for him.

"Baby, it's going to be all right. We'll handle this," I coaxed, rubbing his back as he paced back and forth.

Kannon walked over to us and placed a hand on his brother's shoulder. "Aye, bro. You're good. Calm down for your lady, please."

"That motherfucker there," Kinston spewed through gritted teeth. He turned away and punched his palm so hard that it startled Nissi and me. Pinching the bridge of his nose, he exhaled. "Give me a minute."

When I went to touch him, Kannon placed a hand on me. "Let him process, sis. He'll be fine, but he needs to decompress in his way. Give him a little space."

I stepped back with Kannon and Nissi, and Nissi hugged me. That's when it dawned on me that I needed to check with the party bus driver to ensure there were no damages and see if we needed to find an Uber ride for everyone.

"I need to talk to the driver," I told Nissi and Kannon.

"I'll come with you," Nissi agreed. "Kannon—"

"I've got my brother," he circumvented Nissi's question, knowing exactly what she would ask.

We made our way back over to the driver who was on the bus. We surveyed the bus with him and found only a few broken bottles of liquor, but there was no damage to the bus. I'd have to pay a clean-up fee, but that was to be expected. After we offered our sincerest apologies, the driver stated he heard how it all went down and agreed he wouldn't report it and leave us stranded, but that either Kannon and Kinston must leave the bus or Joel must since they were the offenders.

Just then, Aquila approached us with tears in her eyes.

"I'm sorry, Angela. I don't know what else to say except I'm sorry," she said as all three of us hugged one another.

After our group hug, I held Aquila's hands to tell her how I felt. Enough was enough. "Sis, I know he's your husband, but this is too much. I can't have him around us constantly picking fights with you or anybody else. But my concern is for you. I don't trust him around you."

"We're both concerned, Lah," Nissi chimed in. "I don't know what's going on, but you didn't deserve this, and neither did Kinston."

As if he heard his name, Kinston entered the bus and apologized to the driver first before heading my way and embracing me.

"I'm sorry, Beautiful. You planned this night for me, and I'm ruining it."

"No, you're not," my sisters and I told him.

Aquila placed a hand on Kinston's shoulder. "Thank you for coming to my sisters' defenses and mine. I'm sorry to have ruined your night, Kinston."

They exchanged a hug before he said, "Nah, it's not you who is the problem. I want to continue the night if we can, but I can't spend it with your husband. In fact, it'll be a good minute before I can be around that man."

Kannon entered the bus, clearly hearing his brother and piggybacking his sentiments. "Yeah, me too. I love you, sis, but your man is bad business."

"I know. I know." Aquila nodded as we handed her napkins to dab her face of the unrelenting tears.

"Sis, to keep the party bus, either Kannon and Kinston must leave, or Joel has to leave," I said somberly.

She nodded and turned to exit the bus as we all followed behind her.

"So, you're going to be huddled with your sisters and their men instead of checking on me, *your husband*," Joel barked as soon as we stepped off the bus.

Aquila rolled her eyes with a huff, then turned to me. "Angela, I'm going to pay for any fees you incurred. I promise. Just send me the bill."

"Why are we—"

Before Joel could formulate his question, Aquila spun around and shrieked, "Christ! Could you shut the hell up, Joel? You've already almost ruined Kinston's birthday, and you're still going when you should thank your lucky stars that you've come out of this unscathed. Now, thanks to your actions, you're being kicked off the party bus."

All of us eyed each other at her last statement. Of course, I was going to do the honor of tossing Joel off the bus because I knew I wasn't going to kick off the birthday boy or the brother-in-law I did love, but seeing Aquila take the initiative was shocking and high-key gratifying. However, that meant my sister would forfeit a much-needed evening out for herself.

"Whatever. I don't want to be here celebrating with people I dislike or don't care for me, either. I'll call us an Uber," Joel touted, slipping his cell phone out of his pants pocket.

"Call yourself an Uber. *I'm* staying," Aquila said defiantly.

Joel slowly raised his head, confusion and annoyance marring his features. "What?"

Surprisingly, Aquila stood her ground. With folded arms, she boldly declared, "You heard what I said. Call *yourself* an Uber. I'm staying to party with my sisters and celebrate with my almost brother-in-law."

Joel appeared as if he was about to fix his lips to sign a check that his ass couldn't cash but thought better of it when Nissi and me, followed by our men and the remaining guests, rallied around Aquila in a show of solidarity.

Fanning his hand away at her, Joel grumbled, "Fine with me."

Nissi and I turned to Aquila, and I asked, "Are you okay, sis?"

She nodded. "I meant what I said. I'm staying, and I'm just fine. I promise."

We all took turns hugging her, but Aquila saved the last hug for Kinston.

"I'm sorry, Kinston. I still want you to turn up and enjoy your night," she told him.

His smile beamed down at her. "I am, and I want the same for you, almost sister-in-law."

We shared a bit of laughter as I led the charge to head inside the Cigar Bar to enjoy food, drinks, and cigars. The remainder of our night went seamlessly as if we hadn't almost gotten locked up. Spending time with my man and seeing him truly let the foolishness go to have a good time was the highlight of it all. The entire night, we couldn't keep our hands off each other, and when he pulled me on the makeshift dance floor to slow dance with me, he made his thanks and intentions known.

"My Queen," he whispered against the nape of my neck, "you have made this night unforgettable. I appreciate you to the fullest, and when I get your sexy ass home, I'm going to spend the rest of the night and morning showing you just how much."

Placing my hands on the sides of his face, I stared deep into his auburn orbs and professed, "Well, I'm ready to get our private party started whenever you are."

His dimpled grin ran deep before he growled, "Say fucking less."

Chapter Twenty-Three

KINSTON

Although I'd been slightly disappointed when I found out my birthday dinner for two turned into a party night of twelve, then eleven when that clown Joel exited, I had to admit that I sincerely relished my night despite the hiccup. Our time at the Cigar Bar was filled with toking premium cigars and drinking premium liquor with our family and friends while I received premium kisses and dances from my lady. Being back at her house and bidding our siblings—the last of our guests—good night, I could barely keep my hands off her before she could close the front door.

"Kinston, wait, baby," Angela pleaded as she attempted to back away from my fondling hands and roaming pecks.

"I've been waiting all night." I continued placing open-mouthed kisses behind her lobe, down her neck, and between her cleavage. "I'm ready for our private party, Beautiful," I whined, crushing her lips with mine.

Again, she pulled away, stilling my hands into hers. "I still have one more birthday present to give you."

I lifted my head, staring at her quizzically. "You mean this pussy ain't the gift?" My question set off a barrage of giggles.

"Now, I didn't say that because *that* is always a gift."

"Hell yeah. I know that, Beautiful."

"And don't you forget it." With a deep rumble, I tried to dive in again, but she placed a finger to my lips. "But this gift is also special."

By her relentlessness, I knew she wasn't going to give up this attempt to ensure I received the present before gifting me with the treasure nestled between her thighs, so with a frustrated exhale, I entertained her notion. "All right. I give in." I sat on the sofa and unbuttoned my suit jacket. "Lay it on me."

She leaned on the sofa and cupped my chin. "Don't look so disappointed. You'll love your present."

With her bent before me, it gave me a clear visual between her luscious breasts, and my hungry eyes devoured them before my tongue took a long swipe up the center strip. "Beautiful, I'm a patient man, but between the bottles of D'ussé and fighting the urge to take you all night, there's only so much virtue a man can possess." I trailed the curve of her breasts with my forefinger.

Before I could press her into me to feel my hardening core, she stood and straightened her clothing. "Duly noted. Sit here, and I'll be right back."

With that, she turned to walk upstairs, much to the groans of my dismay. As she began to walk away, I slapped her rear and was rewarded with the soft jiggle of her juicy mounds. Turning to walk backward, she rewarded me with a sexy wink and blush before shuffling up the stairs. I had half a mind to trot behind her and take her right there on the landing of the staircase, but instead, I resisted, then removed my jacket and draped it across the back of her sofa. The removal left only my bare chest with dress pants, loafers, and two gold rope chains draped around my neck. I sat back on the couch, my legs gapped with both arms spread across the top. I tossed my head back from the effects of the alcohol. Just when my eyelids began to grow heavy, I heard Angela clear her throat.

I lifted my head to see her lustful gaze consuming my body, and a smirk crossed my face. "I told you to come unwrap *this* gift, but you're playing."

Her brow lifted as she pursed her lips before saying, "Oh, I'm *definitely* getting to that, but first this." She patted a large square wrapping in her hands, and it was the first time I paid attention to what she held.

Intrigued, I sat up and leaned forward with my forearms resting on my thighs. "What's that?"

She walked it over and sat down beside me. "Open it."

Following her directions, I ripped the brown paper from the front of the gift. Confusion filled me as I partially saw my college graduation picture taken in the yard of the university. When I peeled back more of the covering, I gasped. My heart nearly stopped beating as emotions flooded my entire being. Somehow, Angela had gotten a picture of my mother and had it superimposed with me as if she were standing there with me on graduation day.

Marie Jordan never got to see me walk across the college stage. One of my biggest regrets was that I never had the chance to share that moment with her. My pops was the one who introduced me to football, but it was my mother who cleaned my smelly gear, purchased my equipment and apparel when it needed to be replaced, and made sure I made every practice and every game from Pop Warner through high school. With my pops' work schedule, he was there as much as he could be, but my mother was there every step of the way. No doubt, her dedication, along with my determination, landed me a full-ride football scholarship. Without my football scholarship, I might not have gone to college.

It was college where I embraced her speeches about excelling in my studies and earning my degree rather than having a tutor help push me through. Having lost my chances to be in the NFL made earning my degree that much more special, so not having my mother to witness the completion was devastating. It made the achievement of the day bittersweet—more bitter than sweet. But this photo suddenly brought beauty to the memory of that moment. The endearment gave me the feeling for the first time as if my mother were right there with me the entire time, and that made my chest go tender.

With tears pooled in my lids, I glanced at Angela and broke down. She held me close as the waterfalls dripped freely. A cleansing I never knew I needed washed over me, and I'd never felt so safe and valued by a woman since, well, my mother.

"Oh, baby," Angela whispered, holding me tightly. "I'm sorry. I didn't mean to upset you. I asked Kannon for a picture because I knew how much her being there would have meant to you, and I thought it'd be nice to show you that she's always here with you."

Gripping her hand, I lifted my head. "No, Angela. I'm not upset. I'm so ... so ... damn ... happy," I wailed, a smile breaking across my lips. "You'll never know how much this means to me. And you did this for me."

My emotions overcame her as droplets careened down her cheeks. We bent our heads, and our foreheads touched as she took her thumbs and wiped my face. "Happy thirty-fourth birthday, baby."

Slightly nodding, I opened my eyes to take her in. My reverie of her traversed every facet of her face before staring into the depths of her heart through her watery eyes. If she never told me how she felt about me verbally, she didn't have to. It poured out through every crevice of her being into this heartfelt gift she'd blessed me with. It was that notion that left me unable to contain the inner thoughts of my own heart. Clearing my throat, I confessed, "I love you, Angela. So much."

Her hands flew to her face, covering her mouth with a gasp, causing more tears to cascade. My admission took her by surprise. Standing, I placed the portrait on the love seat. Then I gently pulled her hand into mine and lifted her to her feet.

"No one has ever done anything so special for me." I peered into her dampened orbs. "I thank you, my Queen, and I love you," I reiterated because I knew deep down she was struggling to accept my confession.

I'd accepted that I was in love with Angela for a while but never expressed it. Truth be told, I'd fallen for her from the first day I met her. Having her give me this extraordinary one-of-a-kind gift only solidified what I'd known. I was in love with her, and she was the only woman for me. I wasn't worried if she did or didn't feel the same, but this moment was for her to know how I felt about her. As long as I lived, there'd never be another woman for me.

"You do? You love me, Kinston?" she asked timidly, struggling to speak around the thick emotion stealing her voice.

"I do, and I'm pretty sure I started falling the day you first walked into KinRo Fitness, and it has done nothing but magnify ever since. Not only do I love you, but I'm also so *in love* with you. Only you."

It was as if every apprehension she'd ever held released from her as she threw her arms around my neck. "I love you too, baby. So, so much. I never thought it'd be possible again, but I am so in love with you too."

A shriek bellowed from her as I lifted her into my arms as if I were carrying her over the threshold. We stared lovingly at each other as if our souls connected and aligned, establishing an unbreakable bond. Our heads leaned forward, and as if it were magical, we sealed how we felt with a passionate mingling, our tongues dancing in sensual tandem. We never relinquished each other as we continued exploring our mouths. At the same time,

I carried her upstairs to her bedroom, where I kept my earlier promise and made passionate love to my woman all night into the wee hours of the morning. No frenzied pace. No regrets about the confessions we'd uttered earlier. Just sweet and unadulterated love. Nothing in life felt better than this. After our lovemaking sessions, when I finally drifted off to sleep, I could see a vision of my mother smiling and uttering to me: *she's the one.*

Chapter Twenty-Four

KINSTON

THE LAST THING I wanted Angela to do was to drop me off at my house on Sunday afternoon but after spending all night Saturday and the wee hours this morning partying, drinking, and making love, Angela needed rest and recovery, and so did I. Hand to God, if my woman stepped foot inside my home, neither one of us would get either one. It was bad enough that I couldn't get enough of her regularly, but after last night and the profession of our love for each other, I was a whole new animal. Therefore, a little time apart would do us both some good.

Before I did anything, I quickly hung the portrait of my mother and me in the living room. I hadn't stopped cheesing yet behind the sentiment. I missed my mother tremendously, but that gift soothed a gaping hole that I'd never truly been able to repair. The fact that Angela knew exactly what I needed and provided it earnestly without question made me want to hop in my Range and go thank her all over again.

That thought brought me to one I pondered over a bit, but now, I was confident about my decision to move forward and ask Angela. I'd grown tired of our commuting back and forth. I wanted twenty-four-seven access to my woman, so I intended to ask her to consider moving in with me. Going to bed and waking up beside her in the mornings felt natural and right, and I hoped she felt that same feeling and desired the same as me. Of course, if she said no, I'd understand, but I prayed and hoped she'd say yes.

Exiting the shower, I wrapped a towel around my waist, feeling refreshed. I was eager to get some sleep as I applied my lotion and threw on some basketball shorts before plopping on my bed. I noticed a few missed calls and texts when I grabbed my cell phone to set my alarm. Most were happy birthday messages, which I vowed to respond to later tonight. It was the voice message from a familiar number that gave me pause. My attorney. His message began simply enough with birthday well wishes, but then he explained that I should've received an email with passcode protection and should call him on Monday. With that news, both sleep and rest immediately took a backseat priority. Sliding over to my personal inbox, I swiped until I saw the email I'd been waiting on for the past two weeks. Once I opened it, I followed the directions to download the information via the passcode instructions.

When the document was downloaded, I took a deep breath, reading the letter that might change my life forever. I skipped over the header, scientific lab test, and numbers, and my scan landed at the bottom paragraph, the most crucial portion of the letter.

The alleged father is not excluded as the biological father of the tested child. Based on testing results obtained from analyses of the DNA loci listed, the probability of paternity is **99.999999%**.

The moment I read the percentage numbers, my throat felt like it was closing. Everything else I read became a blur. The phone felt hot as it slipped from my sweaty palms. A gamut of mixed emotions coursed through me as I tried my best to process the one-eighty my life had just taken—a baby. *I have a freaking baby.*

Suddenly, my body weight became too much to hold upright, and I fell backward on my bed in a heap.

As I tried to pull my bearings together, my cell phone began to ring. I had the mind-set to let it ring, but the ringtone was one I'd dedicated to my brother, whom I desperately needed to talk with, so I forced myself to get up and retrieve my fallen device.

"Hey, bro!" Kannon greeted me once I answered. "I hoped this was a safe time to call and check on you. I knew you'd have Angela hemmed up for a minute, especially after she gave you the gift."

"I need to meet with you and Roman." The words came out so choked that I barely recognized my own voice.

Kannon paused and then dropped his voice to a barely audible whisper, "Did the results come back?"

Dropping my head into my hands, I croaked, "Yeah."

"Name the place and time, and I'm there."

Chapter Twenty-Five

KINSTON

Sitting at a private table away from the sparse crowd, I aimlessly stared into space. It had been five days since the bombshell email was dropped in my lap, and aside from speaking to my attorney, I hadn't been able to process much more outside of dealing with the paternity results. After he reassured me that the test results were valid, the realization sank in. I was a father. So lost was I in that singular thought that I didn't even notice when Kannon and Roman approached the booth.

"Hey, bro. Are you all right, man?" Kannon asked, snapping me out of my trance.

"Nah, man. I'm not." I slapped hands with them both as they sat on the opposite bench.

"Well, that's the truth because you look like shit," Roman added the obvious.

Usually, I was well groomed, but I hadn't slept in days, so I was sure my face reflected the lack of rest. My locs were wild and loose, and my beard was unkempt. I'd canceled all my appointments for the week to stay at home and try to get my life in order—whatever that may be.

"Have you spoken with your child's mother?" Kannon's voice permeated the air with a question that brought dread and years of headache and heartache to mind.

"Yeah, we had a Zoom call with our attorneys, and I requested her to bring her daughter . . . *our* daughter . . . to my house tomorrow." I shook my head at the notion that I now had a child—a daughter.

"Man, I can't believe this. I'm upset for you. You asked that chick if you were the daddy, and she claimed you weren't. This is some bull. After all this time?" Roman ranted.

"Man, I can't even do nothing about that. I was blowed about it initially, but I'm beyond that. I have a whole kid who doesn't know me, and I don't know her. I can only move forward with doing the right thing, and that's to be the best father to her now that I didn't get the opportunity to be in the past."

Kannon and Roman nodded in agreement. The waitress came over, and they ordered beers and appetizers for themselves as I sat there with the weight of the world on my shoulders, staring at my untouched glass of beer.

"So what's on your mind, bro?"

Looking up, I rubbed my forehead against the palm of my hand. "Hell, what ain't on my mind?" I scratched my beard. "But at the present moment, I'm wondering how am I going to tell Angela that I have a kid?"

Roman nearly spit out the beer the waitress had just left on the table. "Wait. You never told Angela about the petition for paternity?" Kannon and I glanced at him with sullen expressions. "Man, I thought you said you would tell her?"

Kannon sat back and threw his hand up. "I told him he needed to tell her just in case. He was holding out hope that the child wasn't his. Why? I don't know."

They didn't know, but I did. Knowing that Angela had lost a child from that bum Nigel and then hearing that her new man potentially fathered one was not news that I wanted to break to Angela without being a thousand percent certain. In hindsight,

I wished I had because this was now an unavoidable topic. I loved Angela and didn't know how she'd take this news, but I couldn't avoid being a father to my child. I'm positive that Angela would never ask me to abandon my seed, but remaining with me through it was the question that presented the elephant in the room. Would this be too much to bear? Would she leave me?

"I think you should just come out with it straight up. The sooner, the better," Roman proclaimed, being the consistent straight shooter he always was.

"I haven't even told her about Lilah. Now, I have to tell her about Lilah *and* a baby. Man, this cannot be life."

Kannon leaned forward, his expression one of bewilderment. "Bro, you and Angela have dated for a while. You've been together a few months. What do you mean you never told her about Lilah? How?"

Shaking my head, I confessed, "She knows about her in a roundabout way. I never fully went into detail about her. Considering Angela's and my relationship, I didn't feel it was quite necessary."

Roman let out a scoff. "Well, now, it's necessary *and* urgent."

"Bro, I hate to agree, but Roman is right. You're going to have to tell her the full story at one time, let those chips fall, and pray they fall in your favor," Kannon advised before taking a long swig of his beer.

Just then, the waitress walked over, placing the wings and potato skins Roman and Kannon had ordered on the table. After ensuring they wanted nothing more, she turned her attention to me.

"You sure I can't get you anything?" she inquired.

"Nah, I'm good." I placed a polite hand up to halt the questioning.

With a sheepish grin, she placed one hand on her hip before saying, "Well, maybe I can get you my number instead?"

Roman put his hand out and snapped his fingers to get her attention. "Aye, Miss Lady. No offense, but move around. My boi has enough issues to contend with. He can't add no more drama to it."

She reared back, the offense pinging off her like darts at Roman. "He's a grown man. I'm pretty sure he can speak for himself."

"And as his boi, I'm pretty sure I can speak up for him in this situation," Roman came back.

Kannon stood and interrupted the back-and-forth. "I'm sorry. Tracy, is it? I apologize if our friend seems abrupt, but we're trying to have an important and private conversation. My brother here is accounted for. So, please, let this one go."

She swallowed a lump in her throat and bowed her head. "My apologies. If you all need anything more, please let me know," she said before scurrying away.

Kannon and I shared a "what the hell" glance at Roman as Kannon returned to his seat.

"What?" Roman asked, looking at us as if he didn't see the issue. "That's why y'all lover boy asses be ending up in predicaments. Well, not anymore for you, Kannon. But that smooth and caring stuff is what has those women losing it for y'all."

"So that's why you had a gym stalker?" I shot back.

"One time." Roman held up his finger. "But she knew the deal. Besides, she was just crazy, and it doesn't matter how you handle crazy. Crazy is just crazy. Matter of fact, don't even breathe her name into the atmosphere. Worry about how you will salvage your relationship once Angela catches this news."

"It's all I'm worried about."

I'd been able to avoid Angela this week because of a major case her firm had been working on. Our lives had been reduced to quick phone calls and texts. It was my saving grace because any type of prolonged conversation would have surely given my mood away. But Kannon and Roman were right. My parents didn't raise me to be a coward. I would have to face my music with Angela as a man. I was just about to call it and do precisely that when I heard a voice I hadn't heard in over thirteen years.

"Well, well, well. If it isn't my old buddies, Kinston Jordan and Roman Patterson." The annoying rumble of Jah Michaels's voice invaded my eardrums. "And look at li'l brother, Kannon."

When we looked up, we saw Jah standing among a few other football league players from the Miami Sharks. He was the last person I wanted to see for the rest of my life. Although I knew I'd possibly come face-to-face with him again, I wasn't expecting that interaction to happen this soon. I would've preferred to prepare myself, but life just couldn't help but toss me another curveball.

"Jah," Roman seethed through gritted teeth. "What are you doing here?"

In response, he fanned his arms outward to the men beside him. "Hanging out with my new teammates for a team building day."

Team building day. That was a certified joke. He wouldn't know how to build with a team if it was built and created specifically for him. Besides the paternity suit, the next blowback was finding out that Jah Michaels had been traded to our hometown franchise football team from L.A. It was the fifth trade of his diminishing career. He was drafted into the league by Philly, where he was cut due to failing a drug screening test after two years. He'd finally landed in Tampa Bay, then Carolina, and from there in L.A., which was his longest stint. He was one of the bona fide "bad boys" of the league. Due to his hothead, he was traded frequently. He was a superior talent, but his on-field and off-field issues tarnished his legacy. By the time he settled himself, he'd landed in L.A., but that was nearing the tail end of his career. L.A. confirmed that when they traded him for younger, better goods because, at thirty-four years of age, his only option left was to serve in a veteran leadership role. Someone a team hires when they need the wisdom of an old head to lead them to the Super Bowl but whose time was fleeting. That was Jah Michaels.

Jah tilted his head to stare at me while hunching his shoulders. "What? You can't speak to an old friend, Kinston?"

His comment caused me to shift my entire body in my seat to face him. "*Ex*-friend is more like it," I muttered. "Better yet, never was a friend." This was the arrogant Jah Michaels, I knew . . . my ex-best friend from college.

Jah clapped his hands with a sinister laugh. "You're still holding on to the past? I figured you'd let that go, seeing how you've broken up *my* family. Funny how you can come down off your high horse to screw my wife." His heated words seethed out through gritted teeth.

Puzzled, I stood. "What the hell are you talking about?"

He eased into my personal space with a menacing scowl on his face. "I'm talking about Lilah telling me y'all are fucking . . . again."

"Nah, that's a whole lie." I waved my hands. "But if I did, you deserve it. So back up out of my face."

"So that's why you convinced her to all of a sudden pursue this whole paternity situation involving *my* daughter? You still big mad? You want what's mine? My woman and my kid?"

He inched closer, and by now, Kannon and Roman were on their feet as his teammates also stepped in to attempt to de-escalate the situation.

"Listen." I huffed, flicking the tip of my nose. "I don't know what lie Lilah cooked up for you, but your grimy ass slid behind my back and took her years ago, and you can keep her." I leaned in so he could hear my next words loud and clear. "But that little girl—she's mine, boss. I don't need Lilah to prove I'm a stronger soldier than you."

Before I knew it, Jah stole a punch on me, and I saw red. Staggering backward, I caught my balance and slammed my fist back into his jaw before he could advance on me. Pandemonium broke out as we began a slugfest of blows that sent us careening over tables. Plates filled with food and drinking glasses filled with alcohol flew everywhere. The screams of other patrons and our boys trying to break us up did nothing to control our two giant frames from attacking each other. Lick after thunderous lick was thrown, sounding like it was a clash of the Titans' war unleashing in the small pub.

Finally, I got the best of Jah when I body-slammed him into a surrounding booth. He gripped his back, rolling and groaning. Before I could snatch him and pummel him to pieces, I felt tons of arms from all over, gripping and trying to detain me. Hearing the Dade County Police Department issue a warning was enough for the realization of what was happening to sink in, especially when I felt cold steel wrap around my wrists.

I felt Kannon touch my arm. He was on his cell phone. "I'm calling your contact down at the station," Kannon said as I saw Roman and the other players speaking to another cop.

I looked over just in time to see a third cop handcuffing Jah, and my eyes peered around at the pub manager speaking to another cop while the employees tried to clean up our disastrous mess and calm down the other patrons. The wake of the catastrophe hit me like a barrel of bricks. This. Was. Bad.

"Call my attorney too, bro." I managed to say to Kannon before the cops began to whisk me away.

"Okay. I'll be right behind you heading to the station." I heard Kannon say to my back.

My head fell forward against the partition in the back of the squad car. Jah Michaels ruined my life thirteen years ago. I'd be damned if I let him bombard his way into my life and destroy it again.

Chapter Twenty-Six

ANGELA

THE SUNLIGHT FILTERING through the blinds rudely awakened my tired soul. Groaning, I placed a palm on my forehead to shield the invading light. I outstretched my other arm to feel around before turning my body to see that I had made it to the bed. By my posture, I realized that somewhere along the way, I'd passed out. Hence, why I was on top of my comforter with my feet freezing, the bathroom en suite light still glaring, and my cell phone at the foot of my bed instead of plugged into the charger on my nightstand.

Sitting up, I stretched and hurriedly hopped up to close my curtains before I schlepped over to my dresser to fish out my plush socks to slip on my icy feet. Warmth spread through my core once I placed them on as I wiggled the numbness out of my toes. My next mission was to go to the bathroom to relieve myself, wash my face, and brush my teeth. It had been a strenuous week with the case, but it was worth it to finish prepping for the trial after the new year. With my hectic schedule, I hadn't seen my man all week. Our communication had been phone calls and texts, and even that was accomplished sparingly. Since we rarely spent a day apart these days, I'd gotten acclimated to his presence, which made me miss him that much more. Whoever said absence makes the heart grow fonder was a wise person. I always looked forward to my Christmas vacation, but this year, I was like a kid waiting for Santa. My vacation officially began when I left work last night. That meant two entire weeks to spend quality time with my baby.

The day after Thanksgiving, he'd taken me tree shopping. My lumberjack chopped down the tree and helped me get it put up. Usually, my sisters would come over to help me decorate, but this year, Kinston and I did it, creating our own Christmas memories. He even endured my endless Hallmark channel Christmas movies in exchange for my spiced hot chocolate and sticky buns for both of our official cheat days. He wasn't much for decorating, but I'd convinced him to at least put a wreath on his door and purchase a prelit and predecorated Christmas tree to add some holiday cheer. He had only agreed because he stated whenever I came over, he wanted me to be comfortable and feel at home. Just the thought of having him over to lounge around in our pajamas, watch movies, and wrap gifts had me barreling to my phone to see if I'd missed his call.

"Dang it!"

My cell phone was dead to the world since I'd forgotten to charge it. I plugged it in and decided to spruce up my house while waiting for it to juice up. When I finally came up for air, the clock on my microwave indicated that I had been at it for nearly four hours. It was to be expected after the week I had. Let's just say during times like this, my usual meticulous pad became a pigsty. Heading back to my bedroom, I lifted my cell phone to see that I had no missed calls from anyone except Aquila. That was weird because I'd left Kinston about three different voicemails yesterday. I even shot him a flirty text last night, and even that had gone unanswered. That was not like him. Typically, he would beat me to the punch, and when he didn't, he would quickly return my calls and messages.

I tapped his number, and it went straight to voicemail.

"Hey, baby, I'm just checking on you. I've tried to call and text a few times since yesterday, but you haven't contacted me. Please call or text me to let me know everything is all right. I . . . I love you."

I hung up and tossed my phone back on my nightstand. I blushed because of my stumble while saying I loved him. Ever since we confessed those feelings, we'd ended every phone call and text with the sentiment. I was still getting used to the fact that I was in love with a man whose name wasn't Nigel. Although it felt refreshing and exhilarating, I still struggled with the anxiety of it being too fast, too soon, and honestly, wondering if it was real.

According to Dr. Abrams, even though my fears were understandable, they weren't justifiable. Kinston has constantly shown me that what we have is special and genuine. He's never faltered in his actions, which always aligned with his words. Dr. Abrams helped me understand that it would take more than a few months into my new relationship to unpack fifteen years of my old one. The fact that I don't have any personal barometers of measurement aside from the one relationship with Nigel also adds to my sense of fear.

The only tangible proof of a sustainable relationship was my parents' marriage, and while that was an excellent example, I was an outsider to their union. Not only was their marriage solely between the two of them, but also, my parents never argued or fought in front of my sisters and me, so I hadn't been privy to how they dealt with relational disappointments and adversities. To me, they never had any. I'm grown and intelligent enough to know that isn't the truth, but I can't glean on what I never witnessed. I could only pull from the well of my past experiences. That boiled down to a fifteen-year stint with Nigel. This is why even though Kinston and I were solid, I still struggled.

At least now, I recognize it for what it is and work tirelessly to prevent it from hindering what we are building. And in Kinston's words, that's all he asks of me.

After I unloaded my dishwasher, I went back to retrieve my cell. I became worried when I noticed that Kinston had not called or texted me yet. I was just about to dial Nissi but remembered she was out of town until Wednesday at a dentist association conference that had been rescheduled from November to this week in December. Instead, I tried Kinston again, but it went straight to voicemail. Rather than try another time to reach him, I decided I'd call Kannon to find out what was happening, but I remembered I had never returned Aquila's call. So, I called her first.

"Angela!" she practically screamed into the line, causing me to turn down the volume before she burst my speakerphone.

"Hey, sis. I passed out last night once I got in, and my phone was dead this morning. My bad for just now returning your call. Is everything all right?"

"Umm, so," she dragged the word "so" longer than necessary. "Have you spoken with Kinston?"

All my internal alarms went off. I could tell by the sound of her voice that something was amidst. I inhaled a gulp of air to settle my nerves. "No, I haven't been able to reach him since early yesterday morning."

"So . . . You don't know." Her words came out so cautiously that I couldn't gauge if she were asking or telling me.

My breath hitched, and I sat on my bed to brace myself. "Aquila, what is going on? What aren't you saying?"

"I know what I said before about us really not knowing Kinston, and to be honest, I said that because I believed you were trying to change yourself for him and not for you. It's not that I meant that about him per se. I think he's a great guy. I'm just not sure—"

"Aquila! What the hell is going on?"

I hadn't meant to yell, but her rambling had triggered me to hit the panic button.

"Sis, Kinston got into some sort of an altercation. It's all over the local and national news and blog sites—"

"Wait a minute! Kinston is on national news and blog sites?" The explanation confused me even more. "That doesn't make any sense. Yes, he's well-known and has some celebrity clientele, but he's not famous. Why in the world would he be a hot topic for national news and gossip blogs?"

"Because of whom he got into the altercation with," Aquila answered. "Listen, Ang—"

"Aquila, I need to call Kannon and find out what's happening. Let me call you back."

Before she could respond, I'd hung up on her. I was just about to scroll to my brother-in-love's number when I changed course and decided to pull up the first app I could get to... Instagram. Instead of going to his IG page, I went to my search bar and typed his name in the hashtag locator, and tons of posts populated from our local news station, even down to blog pages like Page Seven and Player Alert. Since I followed Player Alert, I clicked on their post. There was a picture of Kinston and another man, and the picture caption read: "**Miami Sharks Star Cornerback Jah Michaels involved in an altercation.**" The word "what" slipped through my lips as I hurriedly pressed the link in the bio, scrolled to the post, and pressed it to read the complete article.

According to eyewitness information obtained by Player Alert, Kinston and this Jah Michaels guy got into a heated argument at a sports pub, which led to a brawl. The article also states the eyewitness overheard that the man, identified as

Kinston Jordan, a local celebrity fitness guru, was accused by Jah Michaels of having an affair and a baby with his wife.

I had to clutch the edge of the bed to keep from tumbling over. This had to be an egregious lie. At best, a misunderstanding. My breathing turned rapid as I returned to the IG post and scrolled the comments. There was one woman whose comment was pinned. She went by MUA305Boss. Her comment said: No shock there. Kinston tried to hit on me last month at his gym. When I asked him about his little girlfriend that he had waltzed in there with, he had the nerve to cancel my membership. These (ninja emoji) really ain't ish, ladies, especially these trainers in Dade County. Her comment had already amassed over two thousand likes and four hundred replies.

Rather than read the replies, I clicked on her profile name. According to her IG bio, her name was Gianna G. Apparently, little Miss Gianna was a popular makeup artist in Miami with just over twelve thousand followers. As much as I wanted to claim she wasn't attractive, I couldn't. She was gorgeous. Her cinnamon-toasted features boasted light brown eyes set against a beautiful face and a body that appeared as if she had trained for the Olympic decathlon.

A few swipes down her page set my soul on fire. It was a picture of her in KinRo Fitness posing with Tyrod and Kinston, boasting about her one-year gym member anniversary. In the photo, which had been taken three months ago, she was leaning in toward Kinston further than she was to Tyrod, and all three of them flexed their biceps. Her caption read: *Crushed my anniversary session with my trainer Tyrod. Big flex with @tyrodkinro and the man, the myth, the legend @kinstonkinro.*

The hair on the back of my neck stood at attention because not only did she know Kinston, but she was also a member of his gym. That alone added validity to her post on Player Alert. Her comment on the post stated that she asked Kinston about me, which meant she saw him and me together. There had only been a select few times that I'd been at his gym during business hours, making it easy to recall one time that stood out to me. We'd stopped by so Kinston could drop off a package, and out of the blue, he asked me to wait in the car. That had to be the time she was referring to. It hadn't struck me as out of the ordinary then, but now, with a whole post of this Gianna lady snuggled up to my man, a controversial news article all over the internet waves about Kinston fighting a man over having an affair with his wife and fathering a child with her, not to mention, his lack of response to any of my phone calls and texts, it became a glaring red flag.

Hot tears brimmed my eyes as I fought not to cry. *How could he do this to me?* He couldn't. He wouldn't. But the facts began to swirl in my mind and mix with an old, familiar feeling of dread. I stood up from the bed as I fought to maintain my temper and my sanity.

"Not again, not again . . ." I repeated.

I needed answers, and I needed them expeditiously. Flying through my master closet at the speed of The Flash, I threw on my clothes and snatched my phone to head to his house. He may not be ready to see me, but I was *definitely* about to see him.

Chapter Twenty-Seven

KINSTON

I WAS EXHAUSTED AS I walked in the door at six o'clock in the morning. It took all day and night to get my attorney and my contact on the police force to get me out of holding without being processed, and there was no way I was about to spend the weekend in jail. Kannon had dropped me off since Roman and Jovan had gotten together to bring my SUV back to my house. The first thing I did was head straight to the shower to cleanse myself of the last twenty-four hours. Aside from a cut under my eye, a cut on my lip, and my busted and bruised knuckles, I bore no evidence of the squabble I'd been involved with. I was happy about that because, at nine o'clock, Lilah was supposed to bring my baby girl over to meet me. I didn't want our first meeting marred because I resembled some street thug. As soon as I showered, I pinned my unkempt locs in a high bun and placed a turban over my hair. Next, I threw on a T-shirt and sweats, set my alarm, and passed out on my bed.

It felt that only five minutes had passed when my alarm went off at eight thirty, even though I'd been asleep for two hours. Still, I forced myself up to drain and ensure my living room was tidy. By the time I had, I heard my doorbell ring. I grabbed my cell phone to check the camera and saw Lilah standing at my front door.

With every step I took toward the door, my heart galloped in my chest. In addition to the scope of emotions I was experiencing and still trying to process, I also had to contend with Lilah's lies and my altercation with her husband, Jah. I was clueless about how I would approach that part, but I decided that the initial portion of this meeting had to be focused on my child. With my hand on the doorknob, I released a calming breath, sent up a quick prayer, and opened the door . . . only to be greeted by Lilah with no sight of a child. I searched the porch before finally settling my sight back on her.

"Where is she?"

Lilah fidgeted with her fingers and quietly said, "She's in the car. I wanted to talk to you first, and then I'd bring her in."

After the fiasco I'd been thrust into, there was no way she could enter my house without a witness. With a nod, I permitted her to proceed while blocking the entryway into my home. Whatever she had to say would be at the threshold.

"I can't come in?"

"When you have my child with you, you can."

"Kinston—"

"Lilah." Her name vibrated with authority off my lips. "Enough time has been wasted. Don't waste any more of mine."

With a huff, she relented. "Fine. I wanted to check on you first. Jah was pretty beaten and banged up after the tussle, and I wanted to be sure you were good. I don't want my daughter meeting you for the first time with war wounds."

"That's ironic. From what I was told, I wouldn't have war wounds if it weren't for you. What kind of games are you playing, Lilah? Telling your man that we were screwing. I haven't seen you in thirteen years."

She put her hands up to stop my rant. "Can you lower your voice? I don't want her to hear us." She looked back to see if anyone had heard our exchange. "I apologize about that, but Jah is just mad because we're divorcing."

"I couldn't care less what you two are doing. Leave me out of whatever it is. That goes for both of you. Right now, I have bigger concerns, such as why didn't you tell me for all these years there was a possibility when I flat-out asked you when you first found out?"

"At first, I thought it wasn't. I honestly thought she was Jah's. It wasn't until she was born early that I had my suspicions. But by then, Jah and I were married, and you wanted nothing to do with me. I thought it was best for everyone involved."

"Nah, you thought it was best for *you*. You cheated on me with a man who was supposed to be one of my best friends, popped up pregnant, and then married him because he could provide the life of the Football League Wag you so desired after my dreams were crushed. Now that you and Jah are on the outs, you want to disrupt my life again. My feelings, Jah's feelings, and most of all, our daughter's feelings be damned." I stepped closer into her space to emphasize my point. "You were foul then, and you are foul now. The only thing you can do is introduce me to my child so that we can finally establish a relationship."

Tears trickled down her face as she nodded and wiped them with the back of her hand. "I deserved that." She turned sad eyes to me. Acceptance at the finality of the conversation shone in her gaze. "Regardless of what you think of me, I am trying to do what's right by our daughter. I'll . . . uh . . . I'll go get her out of the car."

When she turned to walk away, I thought I would regurgitate. As I leaned against the doorjamb, my nerves got the best of me, and I dry heaved in anticipation. It all seemed like too much, too fast. But as I heard two sets of footsteps against the pavement making their way to me, I knew that any adjustments needed had to be immediate. This was happening.

When the footsteps stopped, I lifted my head to find the most beautiful young lady standing before me and instantly fell in love. She stood at about five-foot-three to my six-foot-three frame with long, wavy hair, skin the color of hazelnut, and big round eyes that reflected the same auburn hue as mine. She looked just as timid and nervous as I was, but when the corners of my mouth raised into a bright smile, hers did the same, revealing deep dimples that parroted my own. She'd taken her nose, mouth, and hair color and texture from her mother. She was the perfect blend of Lilah and me, and there was no denying that we had truly gone half on a baby.

Lilah placed her hands on our daughter's shoulders and slightly shifted her forward as she introduced us. "Fawn, this is your father, Kinston Jordan." Lilah looked into my eyes and said, "Kinston, this is your daughter, Fawn Marie."

I gasped, hearing her name. Back in the day, when Lilah used to talk to me about having a family, she said that she always wanted to name her baby girl Fawn. She had an infatuation with it since her childhood. When I saw the name on the papers, that was not a surprise, but hearing that she gave Fawn my mother's name as her middle name swelled my chest with pride and filled my heart with immeasurable joy.

She nodded her head to answer my unasked question. "Just in case," Lilah said.

Fawn extended her hand to me. "Hi."

Gently taking her hand, I shook it and said, "Hi."

Overwhelmed with fatherly love, I pulled her into my chest for a doting hug and wailed like a newborn baby as I kissed the top of her head.

"Fawn Marie. It's so good to meet you, baby girl. My baby girl."

Fawn gazed up at me with matching watery eyes. "I'm sorry I don't know you. I can't believe this." Her voice cracked, and she couldn't continue. Instead, she buried her face in my chest as I continued to hold her.

I understood her feelings. She'd also just learned over the past couple of months that Jah may not be her birth father, only to find out now that he wasn't. The man who'd raised her, whom she'd called "daddy" all this time, was fraudulently holding the title. Here, we were confronted with each other and had to accept this new bond and, hopefully, kindle some type of relationship. Although I was livid with Lilah for this unjust and unnecessary pain, I was more grateful for the opportunity to be a father.

"It's okay, Fawn. We'll get through this and figure it out together."

Even though Lilah was a teary emotional wreck herself, she didn't interfere in the moment Fawn and I shared. I was thankful for that. I had no extra coddling to issue to her because it all belonged to Fawn. Her mental and emotional well-being was my primary concern.

"Let's go in the house, shall we?" I asked as we all moved inside.

I was grateful that Fawn kept her arms wrapped around me as we entered because I wasn't ready to disconnect from her either. I didn't even know her, but she already had me wrapped around her fingers. Anything she wanted from me was a given. If she asked me for the moon, I'd buy a rope and try my best to yank the motherfucker from the sky.

Once inside, I brought us all some bottled water and asked Fawn if she wanted to get to know me, and I also asked for permission to get to know her. Surprisingly, she was willing to do both. In the few conversations Lilah and I had previously, she revealed that Fawn was more upset with her for keeping the possibility of her father's identity away from her. According to Lilah, she was eager to meet me. If she was anything like me, she had to see it to believe it. Actions spoke volumes to me. Not words. Seeing me made the reality of this situation real to her, the same as it did to me.

Unlike me, Fawn wasn't shy and reserved. She inherited that trait from her mother. She asked me all types of questions, from my full name to what I did for a living. She even asked about my childhood and even about my parents and siblings. She asked everything she could think of, and I answered it all, even showing her pictures of my mother, Pops, and Kannon. Likewise, she returned the favor. She answered anything I wanted to know, from her favorite subject in school to her hobbies, her goals, her friends, and even if she'd ever had a boyfriend. Sadly, she bounced around with Jah and his career hopping so frequently that she never had a chance to establish any roots. Her closest friend was in L.A., and so was her old crush. I wanted to box that little boy immediately. She hadn't been in my presence twenty-four hours, and I already wanted to shield her from all the evils in the world, especially boys. The subject made me realize that Lilah and I would have to figure out how to coparent while I even figured out how to parent. We'd been assigned a family counselor, which would be helpful and much needed as we all tried to figure out how to navigate our new normal.

"Oh, I forgot to ask. When's your birthday?" Fawn tossed out as we mulled over food menus to have lunch delivered.

We'd been talking nonstop for hours, neither of us eager to stop. However, we were all starving, so we opted to have lunch at my house rather than go out. Besides, after the incident with Jah, the last thing I needed was to be seen in public with his wife and the child, whom everyone thought was his.

"I just celebrated a birthday. I was born on December 9th. I turned thirty-four, and your birthday is April 13th, right?"

"Yep. I turned thirteen on the thirteenth, so cool." She beamed an infectious grin at the correlation. "Ooh, that means you're a fire sign like me," she said excitedly, ensuing laughter from her mom and me.

"This girl loves to study the zodiac," Lilah chimed in.

"I sure do. What sign is your girlfriend, Mr. Kinston?"

Her question made me choke on the last bit of water I'd just drunk from the bottle.

Lilah scoffed. "*Girlfriend?* Girl, why on earth would you think such a thing?"

I'd given Fawn my cell phone to search the food menus, and she turned it to face Lilah. "Because his screensaver is a picture of them. Duh, Mom." She rolled her eyes, turned the phone back, and returned to Google. "Besides, he doesn't have a ring on his finger, and I'm pretty sure if he had a wife, she'd be here too."

"Stop making assumptions, Fawn Marie. She could be a friend," Lilah warned with a little bit more sass than she needed to have about my love life.

Fawn lifted her head with bunched brows. "Mom, I'm thirteen, not three. No dude will have to a girl, besides his mom, as a screensaver." Pointing to my phone, she added, "She's too young to be his mother, which, remember, I just saw a picture of her, and the way they are hugged together is giving major bae vibes." Fawn turned to me. "Mr. Kinston, she's your girlfriend, right? Is she a fire sign too? I bet she is. Or a water sign."

Two daggers at once. Whenever she called me "Mr. Kinston," I got irritated with Lilah all over again, but I wouldn't push Fawn for more. To her, Jah was her dad. It would take time to sync her heart and mind that the title belonged to me. That's *if* it ever did.

The second dagger was the mention of Angela, which made me wince for more reasons than one. With Fawn's question, I realized I hadn't spoken to Angela this entire time. I'm sure the multiple missed calls I'd seen when I gave Fawn my phone were from her. My next source of contention was that I still had to somehow explain to Angela how I now had a daughter. Honestly, I was more terrified of that outcome than when I met Fawn. While Fawn held my heart as my daughter, that was a lifetime bond bound by blood. Angela held my heart as my woman, and I couldn't force that bond to last.

A demure smile spread across my face as thoughts of Angela entered my mind. "Uh, yeah. That's my girlfriend, Angela, and she's a fire sign too. Her birthday is April 1st."

Before I could change the topic, we were all startled when Angela appeared in my living room holding the hidden spare key to my house in her hand. Her quick survey of the people in the living room showed all the inferno of my fiery Aries woman flickering in her eyes. The key slipped from her fingers and pinged on my hardwood floor.

"And I'm the biggest April fool ever created," she whispered, droplets falling freely from her face.

"Shit, Angela!" I made a mad dash toward her from across the room as she turned to hightail it back down my foyer.

To see me sprinting across the room and hurdling my coffee table, you'd never believe that I missed my Football League chances. My explosive take-off and agility allowed me to catch up with her before she could reach the front door. Quickly clasping her elbow, I halted her departure, but she snatched away from me.

"Don't," she seethed. "Don't you *dare* touch me."

"Beautiful, just hear me out. I can explain."

"There's nothing for you to explain to me, Kinston. I have two competent eyes, and they just confirmed all I needed to know." She stepped into my face. "You're out here with a whole daughter and screwing your baby's mother. *Lying to me.*"

"Angela, if you'll just let me explain. You have it all wrong."

"Oh, so that isn't your child and your baby mama in that living room?" She pointed in the opposite direction, spewing the accusatory question like bullets.

I had to take a beat because the simple yet not-so-simple answer to that question would only give her more ammunition she needed to reload her accusations. There was so much to unpack, but sadly, now was not the time or the place for this discussion.

"Well?" she pressed.

"Angela, I need a little time to explain, and now isn't the time. If you could—"

She threw her hands up and backed away from me. "You don't have to explain your *family* to me." She shrugged. "Apparently, I'm just the idiotic side chick."

Suddenly, Lilah appeared and stood beside me with her arms crossed. Her attitude was on full display as she scanned Angela up and down with disgust. "I can't believe you're really doing this with the likes of her." Lilah waved Angela up and down with her hand as if she were showcasing her before addressing Angela. "Are you done with your little temper tantrum? Right now, he's trying to spend time with his family, and this *scene* is upsetting our daughter."

I spun on Lilah with quickness. "Yo, what the hell? You're way out of line, Lilah."

"Wow," Angela dragged out the word, commanding my attention back to her. "Everything that chick on Player Alert said about you was true. You didn't even have the decency to tell me yourself. I had to find out from the blogs." I stood there stunned with my fingers interlaced atop my head because I had no clue what she was even talking about, and I was still stuck on the fact that Lilah had further blown up my spot. My brain was overloaded between needing to salvage my relationship, check on my daughter, and cursing Lilah out about her interference. When Angela turned and left, it was as if my senses energized my reaction.

"Lilah, go back into the living room with Fawn. I'll deal with you in a minute." Without giving her a chance to respond, I went out the front door behind Angela and closed the door. "Beautiful, hold up, *please*. We need to talk."

She stopped short and turned to face me. Despite her reddened eyes, swollen nose, and pouring tears, she held the most staid gaze. "No. You know what? We don't. I'm madder at myself than you, Kinston. I *knew* you weren't serious about me, but I let you play in my face. But no more. Save whatever you have to say for your little Barbie inside and your daughter. *They're* the ones you owe because whatever this was between us is finished."

"Angela! No!"

I attempted to approach her, but she was faster as she hopped inside her car. I ran to the vehicle, banging on the window with my palms and pleading with her to stop.

"Angela, please. No. Beautiful. Baby. *Please!*"

None of it was to any avail. She backed out of my driveway as quickly as she'd blown into it. I watched as she sped down the road, away from my house and out of my life. Everything inside wanted to get in my SUV, track her down, and make her listen. But I also had to field my daughter's feelings and check Lilah for her actions. My heart split in half because my head told me to do what my heart didn't want: deal with the situation at hand and let Angela go. At the moment, I had no choice but to follow my head.

Chapter Twenty-Eight

ANGELA

When I left Kinston's house, I drove mindlessly behind a blanket of blurry-eyed tears directly to my house. I couldn't remember if I locked my car or my front door. All I remembered was turning off all the lights in my home, placing my phone on DND, turning on my Christmas playlist on Spotify, and falling into my bed with the comforter pulled over my head. I had no sense of time. All I knew was that everything hurt from my head to my heart. I couldn't move, and I could barely breathe without feeling excruciating pain.

As I lay there listening to "What Do the Lonely Do at Christmas" on repeat, my mind kept replaying all the times I questioned Kinston's motives and blamed myself for allowing him to chip away at the iceberg around my heart. My anger bounced from me to him as I also thought about how low he had been to approach me. I didn't pursue him. Of course, he's a fine specimen of a man. Still, I never tried to catch him, especially feeling as though I wasn't his type, which he proved to be correct between his baby mama, the BBL Barbie at the yacht party, and his former client, Gianna G. All of them looked like the next Instagram model, and here I was ... his pet project.

The thing that baffled me the most was the fact that I assumed this "baby" allegation was on a newborn. The young lady sitting in the living room was not a baby. So, he was really playing me the entire time with a hidden family or, rather, a hidden daughter and screwing her married mother. Trifling.

My mind floated to my sister. Surely, Kannon had to know about this. I understood him not betraying his brother, but to allow me, his sister-in-law, to be caught up in this mess was reprehensible and unforgivable. He could have at least warned me not to go down the rabbit hole, even if he had to confess to his wife. What if Kannon was just as grimy as Kinston, but his skeletons hadn't been shaken from the closet yet? If Kinston could do this to me, I shuddered to think how Kannon could treat Nissi. Roman and Jovan weren't to be trusted either. If Kannon knew, then there was no doubt those two also knew.

Men weren't worth the ink printed on their birth certificates. I'd had these lying and conniving men in my space and my home. They all broke bread with me, laughed with me, partied with me, and talked with me, and no one told me the truth. What kind of breed of men had we been exposed to?

I never thought I'd say that Nigel was a better man than Kinston, but it was panning out to be true. At least with Nigel, he showed his hand. I didn't have to wonder if he no longer cared or if he had cheated. His disrespect showed me that in his words and actions, and even threw a lifeline and phone a friend if I needed any more proof. It made me realize I didn't need therapy because of Nigel. Instead, I'd need it because of Kinston. I'd much rather prefer a hurtful truth over a deceiving lie. That reality detonated in the pit of my belly, and the spigot of waterworks turned into a dam break because my worst fear had come true. Kinston Jordan broke me beyond repair.

I nearly jumped out of my skin when I felt a pair of arms encircle my body. Somewhere between my warring contemplations and depressing music, I'd fallen asleep. Believing that the arms were Kinston's, my initial reaction was to headbutt him for coming to my house and attempting to canoodle with me after his indiscretions. That was... until I heard a light voice.

"We were so worried about you, Ang," Aquila's voice softly pierced my ears.

"Aqui..." I struggled to say. My voice came out hoarse from being dry and scratchy. "Aquila." I finally managed, using all my strength to turn and face her. "What are you doing here?"

Aquila adjusted her body and lay down on the pillow beside me, stroking my arm. "Do you even know what time or day it is?"

Furrowing my brows, I squinted. My head immediately throbbed with pain. "No." I placed my hand on my forehead to quell the thump.

"I've been calling you since yesterday. It goes straight to voicemail. You missed Sunday dinner at Mom and Dad's. It's Sunday evening."

The pain surged through me so cripplingly that the surprise couldn't register. "What? Are you serious?" There's no way I'd missed an entire day.

"Seriously. When I told Mom and Dad what was happening, they told me to use the spare key you'd given them to do a wellness check. They wanted to come, but I convinced them to allow me to come over first just in case you and Kinston were making up. So they are keeping the boys for me."

She let out a short sniggle, but her attempt at the joke only made me groan. "That is something you don't have to worry about. We are over."

That admission jolted Aquila upright. She turned on my bedside lamp and faced me.

"Turn the light off," I shrieked, scrambling to cover my head with the comforter.

"Sis, I'll cut it off only if you agree to talk to me. I need to know what happened."

As much as I didn't want to admit this, I had to so she would know the severity of the situation and not think I was throwing a pity party.

"I will, but please, turn off the light. I have a migraine." When I heard her gasp, I exhaled and provided further instructions. "Look inside the top drawer of my nightstand and pass me the sleep mask. Then you can leave the light on. I have medicine in the middle drawer in my bathroom called Ubrelvy."

Aquila searched the drawer and passed me the mask. Braving the light, I sat up with my back against the headboard and slipped it over my eyes. That's when it dawned on me that my somber music had ceased. That more than likely meant my phone had died rather than the music being stopped by Aquila, which made sense about why I never heard the vibration of my phone. My parents and sisters were the only ones who could reach me despite an activated do not disturb. The sound of Aquila trotting through the house and the crepitation of the fireplace were the only sounds I heard before the bed dipped again.

"I'm going to cut off the light so you can lift the mask," Aquila informed me just before I heard the lamp click.

When I lifted the mask, I tilted my head back because it was still throbbing profusely. "Did you find the medicine?"

"Yes, but first, I will turn on the bathroom light and leave the door cracked to have a little glow in the room. You have to drink some water and eat this blueberry muffin. You need to rehydrate and get some sustenance."

Once I drank and ate half the muffin, I took the migraine medicine and lay down again in the bed with the mask over my face. "Thank you." The words were barely above a whisper.

"Sis, you know that migraine medicine isn't the only prescription I found." I felt her hand grasp my hand gently before she continued. "Do you want to tell me why you have antidepressants and if that has anything to do with why you are now suffering from migraines?"

The cat was entirely out of the bag now. I'd forgotten that medicine was also in the drawer. After the loss of the baby, the doctor prescribed the medication to help balance my mental and emotional states. I wasn't ready to reveal my miscarriage, so I chose the safer option regarding my relationship with Nigel.

"There were many traumatizing emotions that I dealt with behind Nigel's treatment of me and our subsequent breakup. I never told you all that once he began losing weight, he began to belittle me about mine, and before long, the disrespect spoke louder than any love he ever had for me, *if* he ever had any. It took such a huge toll on my mind that the doctor thought it was best. Currently, I am not taking them, but I never threw the bottle away. I may need a refill anyway after this foolishness with Kinston. My migraines began with the split from Nigel. This is the first one I've had in a while."

Aquila scooted close to me and brought my head into her lap as she stroked my hair. "Oh, Angela. Why didn't you tell us? You didn't have to go through it alone."

"To be honest, I was afraid of y'all's reaction. And no offense, sis, but you can be a bit judgmental. It's not as if you were exactly encouraging when I told you about going to therapy."

I felt Aquila steel beneath me as her strokes momentarily halted. After the briefest of seconds, she began stroking my hair again. "You have a point. My apologies, Ang. Sometimes, I can be a bit overbearing in my quest to protect my sisters. I know it comes off rude, but I mean well. And I never want you to think you can't come to me. I'm your big sister."

The care and concern in her admission triggered a fresh onslaught of the sobbing from earlier, and I couldn't stop the flow as I squeezed her legs, trying fruitlessly to stop the ache from swelling in my chest again.

"Oh my God, sis. I've never seen you like this. What in the world happened between you and Kinston?" Panic heightened her already concerned demeanor.

It felt like hours had passed, but it had only been a few minutes before I could relate the horrid chain of events. "Everything you heard is true. He has a child and has been sleeping with his married baby's mother." She listened intently as I explained what I'd read on Player Alert and what happened when I showed up at his house. "This entire time, he's been toying with my heart. You were right."

Aquila didn't readily respond. She sat there and continued to caress my face and run her fingertips through my hair as I lay like a baby in her lap.

"I can only imagine how much this hurts, sis. He was wrong, dead wrong." The inflection in her tone, paired with her briefly suspended words, told me there was a strong "but" lingering. And she didn't disappoint. "But you haven't had a chance to hash it out with him. I know anything is possible, but Kinston's actions and this situation don't align. I can't believe I'm playing devil's advocate here, but something feels off about this."

Appalled... I was simply appalled at her introspection, and I couldn't help but feel somewhat slighted. "And somewhere in this, he still lied to me!"

"And that's the part he's dead wrong about," she agreed. "But just hear me out. You owe it to yourself to know exactly how this all came into fruition."

"He screwed a woman, and procreation happened."

Aquila snickered, and I huffed. "It's not funny, Lah." My voice sounded nasally and whiny.

"I apologize because it's not. You know how you are." She took a beat, then drove her point home. "Listen, I didn't make that previous assumption about Kinston because he gave me a reason. It was purely because I didn't want you to feel you had to change for him to prevent him from leaving you as Nigel did. We may not have known about the disrespect, but we saw how you felt the need to be someone different when Nigel shed the pounds. Kinston has always been a stand-up man whose words and actions have been proven in a positive light. Besides, the child isn't an infant, so it's not recent. I just think you should hear him out first before you throw in the towel."

"To listen to him confirm that he slept with his baby mama and hid his family from me?"

She lifted the mask slightly from my eyes and peered at me with all seriousness. "And if he does, then we'll sit around and whip his natural ass along with Kannon too."

That made me crack my first smile in twenty-four hours. And we shared the moment. "I love you, Lah, but you know you can't fight."

"I mean facts, but I'll still throw these hands for my little sisters even if I get beat down."

"And that's why we love you with your saddity ass."

"Saddity and oh, so pretty." She wagged her finger at me. "Don't forget *that* part."

We laughed heartily at the fact that she was the only one who didn't grasp the relevance of our father's fighter lessons because she was the prissy one. Sitting up in bed, I propped my head on her shoulder. "I love you. Thank you for checking on me."

Aquila shrugged, picking up my hands and holding them in hers. "And I always will. I love you, roundtrip."

"Stay with me?" I chanced a glance up at her. Weariness weighed on me, and I needed the comfort.

She wrapped her arm around my shoulders and pulled me closer. "For as long as you need."

Chapter Twenty-Nine

ANGELA

A WEEK. ONE FULL week had crept by since that fateful day at Kinston's, and I hadn't spoken to or seen him since. It wasn't for his lack of trying. Since I'd promised Aquila I would humor him, I didn't delete his contact information. However, I ignored every phone call, text message, and voicemail. Petty me would have everyone believe that I was icing him the same way he iced me out, but the truth of the matter was I wasn't ready to confront Kinston. I dreaded the regurgitation of what I already believed to be the truth. There was no need to rush to reaffirm that. Instead, I took the time to settle my mind and my spirit. To assist with that, Aquila helped me pack some items on Monday, and I opted to stay at my parents' house for the week. Being around my family always anchored my soul, and I'd learned to value them at my big age of thirty. And yes, part of me wanted to be away from my house in case Kinston got the wild-haired idea to pop up unannounced.

For most of the week, I busied myself by working on case files and helping my mother prepare for Christmas dinner at the house, which, unfortunately, was the host house this year. That meant Kannon would be present. Nissi had arrived home from her dental conference this past Wednesday to a pure shitshow. After learning about Kinston, she was livid with Kannon, but apparently, Kannon fed her with some preposterous explanation because she offered me the same conclusion and advice that Aquila had given me . . . talk to Kinston.

Even though today was the day before Christmas Eve, and I had nothing but idle time to finally have said talk, I tried to block my situation with Kinston mentally. Yet, the more I tried, the more it penetrated my mind. Rather than sit in the house and pine away over him or, worse, contact him, I wanted to go out to clear my mind, but the issue was Nia was on a date with her flavor of the month, Aquila was attending Joel's celebrity Christmas family feast, and Nissi and Kannon were on a double date with Jovan and Jasmine to hear Black Violin at the Indie Lovers Club. Not only did I not have a date, but I also still wasn't vibing with Kannon or Jovan. Even my parents were ditching me tonight. My mother and father were about to head out to a Christmas party, which I asked to attend, and those old heads had the gall to tell me that it was their date night, so I wasn't allowed. I was in crisis, and they were worried about a date? How do empty nesters not have all the time in the world to date?

Since I couldn't find anyone to hang out with, I threw on my pajamas, made a bowl of popcorn, and decided to watch scary Christmas movies because Lifetime and Hallmark were too much to bear. Still, I put on my usual trained brave front to make everyone feel I was doing better when I honestly just wanted to fall apart.

"Knock, knock," my mom said as she opened the door to the guest bedroom dressed to the gods with sexiness oozing from her.

Admiration spread across my face as I eyed her up and down in the resplendent winter-green sequined cocktail dress. "I see why I'm not invited to the *partay*. Don't hurt my daddy. You know he has a bad back."

Her lips pursed cunningly. "Nothing a little Aleve can't alleviate with twelve hours of strength." She snapped her fingers, leaning inside with one hand on the doorsill.

"Look at you now," I cackled. "Don't bring me back a little brother or sister."

Grinning, she dismissed my jest with a wave. "The only kids coming in here are grandbabies." She placed a hand on her hip. "Anyway, see us to the door so you can lock up."

Even though I was comfy in my bed with my popcorn, I scooted out of the confines because my very grown self still knew better than to challenge my parents, especially my mother. Not in Abigail Richards's lifetime and definitely not in Nisante Richards's. Respectfully, I rose and followed her from the back of the house through the living room to head to the foyer. However, my steps were stopped short when I nearly stumbled over my feet at the sight of Kinston sitting on the sofa beside my father. When they saw my mother and me, they both rose.

My dad buttoned his suit jacket. "Are you ready, Abi? You're radiant, darling."

Walking to him, she straightened his lapels and cooed, "Thank you, sweetheart. And aren't you debonair?"

As they shared pleasantries, Kinston and I held each other's regard in a silent and unreadable exchange. The will it took not to react to him could rival that of Job. Even with sadness etched in his auburn orbs, the man dripped sex appeal. His locs were wrapped in a high bun atop his head and covered by a black turban. How he managed to make a dark blue hoodie with matching sweatpants and some J's appear as if he'd stepped off the cover of *GQ*, I do not know. That only enhanced my self-consciousness. He was *GQ* modeling, and I was a bargain basement Walmart shopper in my red and white candy cane Christmas jammies with hunter-green Merry Grinchmas socks.

"Angela," he breathed out warily.

"Kinston." I swallowed the poignant emotion building inside.

Still wrapping my mom in an embrace, my father briefly relinquished his eyes from my mother and turned them toward Kinston. "Respect my daughter. Respect my house. Understood?"

"Understood, sir," Kinston agreed with certainty, eyeing him man-to-man.

"Good," my dad said, satisfied with his agreement. Then refocusing on my mom, he said, "Let's go before we're late." With that, he clasped her hand as they sauntered to the front door.

I followed them, and as they stepped over the threshold, I opened my mouth to express my disdain at this blatant setup, but my mother interrupted me, palming my cheek with a gentle hand.

"Talk to him for *your* peace of mind."

"And if he disrupts your peace, you can use *the piece*," my father solemnly expressed. My daddy played not one game about his daughters—period.

Mom turned Dad away. "Okay, that's enough. Call us if you need us," she said before they walked away, and I closed and locked the door.

With my back pressed flush against the door, I used the time to tuck my feelings and gather my thoughts. Even if I wanted to remain stationary and stall, eventually, Kinston would come searching for me. Though upset at the trickery of forcing me to communicate with him, I had no choice except to grapple with this one day. Today may as well be the day to relieve us from this limbo. Thrusting myself off the door, I let out a swoosh of air and stalked into the living room.

When I entered, Kinston stopped pacing and turned to me. Sorrow shone in his melancholy eyes, his handsome features marred from the remnants of stress. That might have broken me down if I didn't feel this sadness was from the repercussions of him being caught in his lies.

With my hip poked to one side and arms folded, I asked, "What are you doing here?"

Somberly, he flicked the tip of his nose and slowly raised the sleeves of his hoodie up his arms. Walking to the coffee table, he picked up the small golden vase with one bright red Amaryllis flower and handed it to me. "To talk face-to-face since you won't answer my calls or texts."

Accepting the flower, I admired it. I applauded Kinston for the thoughtful gesture. This flower in this particular color meant to sparkle with pride, determination, beauty, and love. Turning, I placed it on the nearby bookshelf. With my back still to him, I scoffed. "Funny, I remember calling and texting you too. Only when I went to talk face-to-face, I was faced with your ready-made family."

I turned just in time to see his hand slide down his face to tug at his beard. "Angela, that's not what that was or even is. I would've explained it to you . . . *wanted* to explain it at the time, but it wasn't the right time. I hate that because not for one second do I ever want you to believe that you aren't important in my life."

"Just as important to you as the baby mama you're sleeping with and the child that you hid from me, right?"

"No, you're important because you're the *only* woman in my life—"

"Was I not clear that I am no longer your woman?" My declaration thwarted his next sentiments.

"Abundantly."

"Good. So again, why are you here?" My hand gestured between him and me.

Eradicating the space between us, Kinston crowded me with his stratospheric frame. "Because I owe you an explanation, and regardless of whether you walk away from me, you deserve the truth, and I deserve the opportunity to tell it."

My body went into sensory overload. His cinnamon breath wisped against my skin, evidence of his favorite Big Red chewing gum. At the same time, his Sauvage cologne tickled my nostrils, stirring a heated rumble in my belly. Being this close to him, feeling the warmth of his stature and the determination exuding from his presence was doomed to be my downfall. Pressing my hand against his chest, I pushed away to give my senses and my kitty breathing room.

"State your piece so we can both go about our night."

He placed his hands up in the surrender pose. "Okay. I hate that you had to hear the disparaging news about Jah and me fighting through internet bloggers who don't know any of us, the history, or the current situation. Remember when I discussed the ex-friend that I had the altercation with while in college that caused me to lose my chances in the Football League?" I considered his words for a moment, and when I remembered, I nodded, and he continued. "That was Jah Michaels, the guy I squabbled with at the pub. Back in college, he and my girlfriend at the time were cheating with each other behind my back. That woman was Lilah, whom you saw at my house that day. Our fight back then was because I'd found out that my so-called best friend betrayed me by sleeping with my girl and also for getting her pregnant."

A soft "oh" fell from my lips, with him tying the two together. Still, it didn't explain why he had the woman who betrayed him in his home and the fact that he'd been accused of sleeping with her now, and I let him know just that.

Swallowing, I said, "I see. And as foul as that was, what does that have to do with the present day? If she threw dirt on you all those years ago, how could you allow her to come into your life now and do the same?"

"That's what I'm saying to you. Beautiful, no one could ever take your place in my life or in my heart. I haven't touched that girl in over thirteen years, and I won't ever touch her again for the rest of my life. Jah recently got traded to the Miami Sharks. When he came into the pub and saw Kannon, Roman, and me, he confronted me and accused me of sleeping with Lilah."

The disbelief immediately clouded my features. "Kinston, why would that man randomly accuse you of something so damning if you haven't seen either of them in years?"

"Because that's the lie Lilah told him since they're in the middle of a divorce," he boomed, his words cloaked in frustration.

"That makes *zero* sense, Kinston."

"Neither does snow in June, but it happens, Angela." Backpedaling, he took a beat before he calmed. "I can't explain that phenomenon any more than I can explain why she told that man that bald-faced lie. All I know is that it is one."

"Let's say I believe all of what you're saying about Lilah lying about you to Jah; Gianna G sure had a scathing report about your antics on Player Alert." My attitude was on full go with that piece of information.

"Humph," he said with a scowl before pulling out his cell phone. "Player Alert," he scoffed as he tapped on his phone.

He turned his phone so that we both could see it, and a video populated. When he pressed play, I saw Kinston, Tyrod, and Gianna enter Kinston's office. The next few minutes were Kinston confronting Gianna about overhearing her disrespect me to Tyrod. Then he explained how that went against the gym membership rules. I watched as he canceled her membership, and Gianna had a complete meltdown about it before being reminded she was being recorded and leaving.

"The truth is, you were with me in the gym that day. I asked you to wait in the car because I heard the disrespect and refused to let it slide. I would've done the same if it had been anyone in my gym, but I would especially lay the smackdown over you. No one can come into my home or my establishments and think they can offend what's mine, and I stand on that."

I was speechless. How could I debate the cold, hard facts?

Kinston patted his chest. "As your man, it's my duty to shield you from anyone and anything that harms you. You want the truth? I'm a single, attractive, heterosexual man with businesses and assets that ain't about no bullshit and treat women with the utmost respect. And I am yours. There's a line a mile long to have a fraction of that from any man. And guess what? I'm on that mile-long list. So, you have to know that some women are willing to sell their souls and orchestrate lies because they are jealous of you for having that with me."

He approached me, cupping my face in the palms of his hands. "When you ask me about the Giannas and the Lilahs of the world, all I can tell you is that their lies and delusions happen." He tenderly stroked my cheeks with his thumbs and peered into my eyes. "But that's when we have to lean on and trust each other. Trust that what we have—what we've built—is real and that it's enough."

Be still my heart. Under his intense gaze and his infectious words, I was mush. My resolve faltered faster than an avalanche. Droplets pooled at my lids, and my lips quivered as I tried to withhold from caving into his arms. But how I wanted to. There's nothing more that I desired than to wrap myself in his warm and awaiting embrace, forgive him, and rekindle our love. In the same breath, that's what halted me. If he loved me, if he genuinely wanted to protect me, then why did he hide his child from me? It was that notion that powered me to push away from him.

"What does that have to do with you hiding a child from me?" I inquired, waving my hands in the air to dismiss this portion of the conversation and move on.

"I didn't hide my daughter because I didn't know I had one." My brows furrowed as he continued. "The child Lilah was pregnant with all those years ago was not Jah's. She was or rather *is* mine."

"Wh . . . What?"

"When Lilah told me that the baby she was carrying was Jah's, she was wrong. After Fawn was born early, she had her suspicions but never addressed them. All this time, Jah believed Fawn was his daughter, and she believed Jah was her dad. So did I. It wasn't until I received the notice about paternity that I thought twice about there being a possibility."

Fawn. His daughter's name was Fawn. This revelation was astonishing. I couldn't imagine not knowing my child until they were a teenager. I couldn't imagine how upset, disrespected, and robbed he must've felt. It was so egregious of an act that it still felt unbelievable to me. "All this time, you haven't known you have a child?"

Kinston shrugged. "No, I haven't. I just found out she was mine a couple of weeks ago."

To say I was shocked was an understatement. Kinston had piled so much information on me that I had to sit down to process everything he'd said, so I went to the sofa to sit and reflect. Kinston followed suit, taking a seat beside me. He didn't speak but rather gave me time to absorb it.

Kinston gently picked up my hand and held it. But it was as if a lightbulb went off in my mind, and I turned to face him slightly and tossed a finger up at him. "Wait a minute. You just learned a few weeks ago that you fathered a child with Lilah. So, that means paternity has been established. Kinston, when the hell did you find out that you may have a child?"

His head tilted forward as he released a deep sigh. "That's the part that I'm not proud of myself about. I found out about two months ago and—"

I bounced off the sofa as if flames stroked my rear end. "Two *months* ago?"

He stood and tried to approach me, but I signaled for him to back up. "Beautiful..."

"No." I shook my head. "Don't you dare gaslight me."

He apologized with his hands in a prayer pose. "I'm sorry. I wasn't trying to do that. If there was one thing I was wrong about, it was not telling you about this."

"So you mean to tell me that you had me confessing like Usher about my entire past with Nigel, confiding in you with secrets that I haven't even told my sisters... *my parents*, and you hid the fact that you may have fathered a child from me?"

"I know. I know, and it was wrong—"

"Oh, did you figure out it was wrong when you got caught or when I ended things?" My soul was vexed because he'd hidden this from me all this time. "You stood here and preached an entire sermon on trusting each other and believing in what we built, and the one thing—*the one thing*—that you needed to give me that same benefit, you hid from me. I trusted you with a past that doesn't affect you, and you couldn't trust me with information that impacts me. Because it's *me* who has to consider having to interact with your daughter and deal with your baby mama if we were to continue dating."

With his eyes closed, he nodded. "I have no excuse. I was being a coward, and by the time I decided to own up to it, I guess you'd heard about the fight with Jah on Player Alert and came to confront me. All I can give you are my deepest apologies. If I could redo it, I would've told you the moment I received the first notice about it."

There it was. The entire story. Did I believe him? Yes. Was I swayed? In some ways, yes. Was it enough for me to be able to drop my reservations and continue our relationship? No.

Wholeheartedly, I felt in my heart of hearts that Kinston was sincere. Sadly, that wasn't my grouse. Yes, I may have felt less than compared to Gianna and Lilah because of my own esteem issues, and that was my cross to bear. His cross to bear was questioning the validity of his love for me and the strength and realness of our relationship when it came to them. Then on top of that, he hid his child. I'm positive all of this was difficult and life-altering for him, but my feelings were mutually inclusive, not exclusive.

 This time, it was me who cradled his face. "Kinston, I hear you, and I understand everything with better clarity, so thank you." Hope danced in his eyes, and a slow, kidlike grin emerged on his face. "But you allowed your fears to leave me vulnerable to the shots from Gianna and Lilah. You were the one who said it was your job to protect me, and you fell short, not because of anyone else but because of your lack of action . . . your cowardness. Had you practiced all that you preach, all that you asked of me, Player Alert never would have happened. Lilah's slick dissing me and making me appear like the side chick and the afterthought never would've happened. Finding out about your daughter because I'm coming to confront you about a fight, and a so-called cheating scandal never would have happened." His once hopeful glints quickly turned into a downtrodden muse. "And because that happened, we can't. I have to protect myself, Kinston. I allowed Nigel to strip me of protecting my heart. I won't let that happen to me again. Please leave."

 We stood there suspended in time with my hands cradled around his face, and my waist softly captured in his hands, gripping the hem of my shirt, desperate to hold on. His long lashes blinked at the saddened tears puddled in his lids. He tipped his temple to nestle against mine, and his head slowly turned back and forth in defiance of my request.

"No," he whimpered, his voice strained with unshed tears. "I love you."

I didn't have the heart to tell him to leave again. Instead, I stood on my tiptoes and kissed his cheek as his tears spilled over. Without hesitation, I pulled out of his hold and walked to the back of the house to my bedroom. After a few minutes, I heard the front door open and close. When I walked to the front, I peered out of the blinds to see Kinston's truck easing out of the driveway. Just like that, he was gone. I locked the door and slid down to the floor, releasing a gut-wrenching wail.

Chapter Thirty

KINSTON

"Merry Christmas, old man!" Kannon and I announced as we entered our pops' house.

He stood from the new recliner we gifted him to hug us. "Merry Christmas, knuckleheads."

Kannon and I settled on the sofa beside each other as our pops nestled back into his new favorite chair.

"I see you're enjoying that new gift, Pops," I chuckled, watching him get comfortable as he picked up the remote to mute the Christmas movie *Miracle on 34th Street*.

He patted the armrest. "Yes, indeed I am. And these heated massages, my God in heaven, are a blessing straight from Jesus and my sweet Marie. I knew having you two boys would come in handy one day."

"*Really*, Pops?" Kannon said, all of us enjoying the hearty laughter.

"What brings you boys by this morning? I wasn't expecting y'all until later on tonight," Pops asked.

"I have the family dinner at Nissi's parents' house, so I wanted to stop by early to spend some time with you. You sure you don't want to go with us? We'd all love to have you," Kannon asked.

Pops waved his hand. "Nah. These old bones just wanna rest today. Long as I got my new chair, the remote, and a cup of sweet tea, I'm all right. And I got some leftover fried chicken and macaroni cheese you made me the other night."

Kannon shrugged, conceding. "A'ight, Pops. If you change your mind, let me know. Nissi and I will drop by later to bring you a plate from the Christmas dinner."

"Shiidd, that's good enough for me right there. That woman knows she can cook," Kain belted to our amusement before he turned his attention to me. "You and Angela gonna be there today too?" I stroked my beard, and my Pops squinted his eyes. "Ah hell, Kin. What you done do to that woman now?"

"How you figure that, Pops?"

"Boy, I've known you since you dropped from my ball sack. Anytime you get to scrubbing yo' face and all that fidgeting mess, you done messed up. So, instead of playing dumb, why don't you answer my question."

He already knew something was wrong, so I didn't waste time beating around the bush. "Angela and I aren't together anymore, Pops." My shoulders scrunched. "She left me."

His brows bunched in a stupefied expression. "She left you? Over that baby situation?"

I flittered my hand side-to-side. "Yes and no," I said before providing the full explanation of what happened.

"You mean to tell me, when you were going through all that jazz with that girl, you ain't tell her nothing?"

Kannon tossed his hands in the air. "Same thing I said, Pops. Had my sister-in-love mad with me and the whole crew thinking we were out here on some foul womanizing games."

I shot my middle finger up at him. "Nobody asked you."

"Don't be mad at him. Be mad at yourself. It was you who wasn't forthright and had that young lady thinking you were out here cheating and having babies. Marie and I taught you better than that. I know she's rolling in her resting place."

"Don't you think I realize that, Pops?" Even though it was deserved, I still didn't want to hear it. Angela's brutal breakup was enough for one week. He didn't have to add Mama to the mix.

Pops put up his hands. "You grown, so you don't need my help."

"It's not that. I've done all I can do. I tried, Pops."

Pops scoffed. "Do you want to be with the young lady or not?"

Without hesitation, I nodded. "Hell yeah. I love that woman, Pops."

"Then you show up for her regardless of whether she likes it," he advised. "Let her be free out of here if you want to. You think she acted stupid over them little hot-to-trot gals? You wait 'til a musty Negro get to sniffing in behind her tail. You gon' act a plum damn fool. Ya ass really be on the news for squabbling then."

My temper inflamed at the mere thought of another man being with Angela. I'd burn the entire city down—everything be damned. That's when I knew my Pops was right.

Pops pointed at me. "Look at him, Kann. He mad just thinking about it."

Kannon peered at me. "Bro, you tight."

I pushed his shoulder. "Yeah, that got me tight. You already know. Tight as you were when Nissi was with Benji."

A scowl immediately graced his face. "Don't even mention that mutha—I'm so glad he moved his practice to another city. I swear Miami wasn't big enough for both of us."

We slapped hands together. "Bro, what? Let a dude push up on Angela. Damn Miami. Florida won't be big enough to keep me off his ass."

Pops nodded. "So, do what you gotta do to get yo' woman back. 'Sides, I like ole Angela. She funny as hell. Sweet young lady. We can talk for hours."

I stretched my arm to stop him from talking. "Aye, calm down, old man. You're over there sounding like a dude I need to check about my woman."

He hushed me with a wave of his hand. "Stop worrying about me and worry about her."

"Duly noted." I stood up and touched knuckles with him. "But I do have one more reason that I had us all meet here today."

"Oh yeah? What's that?" Pops asked after taking a swig of his sweet tea.

Just then, the doorbell rang, and I stood and walked to answer it. When I returned, Kinston and Pops gasped before smiling brightly at my surprise guest.

"Pops, Kann, this is my daughter, Fawn Marie," I introduced her to them. "Fawn, this is my brother, your Uncle Kannon, and this is your grandpop, Kain."

Demurely, she waved. "Hi."

My pops sat forward in his recliner and pulled a handkerchief from the front pocket of his button-down shirt. "Hi, little lady. Is it too much to ask for a hug?"

Fawn smiled brightly as she sprinted to him and wrapped her arms tightly around his neck. "Hey, Grandpop."

Three grown men dropped tears as my pops embraced her tightly. Wiping his eyes with the handkerchief, he stared up toward heaven. "We got us a grand girl, Marie. Named after you. You heard that?"

As Kannon stood up to hug Fawn, my pops glanced at me, placing his hand over his heart. "Thank you, son," he mouthed.

Nodding, I mouthed, "You're welcome, Pops." Then I lifted praying hands to my lips as I looked toward the sky and mouthed, "I know you're here, Mama."

Chapter Thirty-One

ANGELA

CHRISTMAS DAY. MY most favorite day of the year was here. Though this year was met with challenges and heartache, I vowed that today would be a good day. I would honor the birth of Jesus and celebrate the season with my family. I was happy to be in better spirits because I was a wreck just two days ago. When my parents came home and found me bawling my eyes out, my mother called an emergency intervention with my sisters to keep my daddy from hunting down Kinston. Surrounded by my mother and sisters, I told them the story of everything that had transpired when Kinston visited me to hash things out.

"Sis, I know that you stated you went to therapy to deal with issues stemming from Nigel, but it still feels like you're allowing that situation to impede on this one," Nissi said as we all held hands in a semicircle on the bed.

My mother reached out and stroked my hair. "Baby girl, what are you not telling us about Nigel?"

Aquila darted her eyes at me, then between Nissi and our mother. "I'm sorry, Ang. I have to tell them." I didn't even have the energy to protest, so Aquila continued. "When Nigel lost his weight, he started belittling Angela about hers. It caused her so much stress that she was diagnosed with depression and started suffering migraines. She was on antidepressants for a while afterward."

"What!" my mother and Nissi whisper-screamed.

"I'll kill his ass my damn self," my mother declared, jumping off the bed and pacing a hole in the floor.

"After all you've done for him and your history as friends? He's all the way foul. He better pray he never runs into me," Nissi added before looking at Aquila. "And you knew she was going through this and didn't tell us?"

Aquila shook her head immediately, explaining her knowledge. "No, I didn't. I only found out this week when I went to Angela's house to check on her after she learned about Kinston's fight with that guy from the Miami Sharks."

I nodded. "It's true," I said, trying fruitlessly to wipe the never-ending tears from my face. "But the only thing that she doesn't have entirely correct is the reason I was depressed."

They all looked at me intently, and I knew it was time. Dr. Abrams had advised me that my spirit would know when I was ready to share my journey with those closest to me, and I should embrace the opportunity. I knew they'd be upset and maybe even somewhat disappointed, but I also knew my mother and sisters would do as they'd always done and show up for me.

"The reason that I was depressed and the reason that I am so hurt over Kinston's decision not to tell me about his child is that when Nigel was belittling me about my weight, I'd just found out I was pregnant with his child. Soon after, he left me for Leticia, and the next day, I miscarried. I'd never told anyone except Nia about it. She helped me get through it because I had an anxiety attack surrounding the miscarriage and called her since she's a nurse. She helped me get to the hospital and nursed me through the entire ordeal. The only other people I confided in about that dark time in my life were my therapist . . . and Kinston."

In my entire thirty years of living, I'd never seen a time where all of us Richards ladies were in a room, and it was silent.

It happened that night. A pin dropped would've been the loudest noise. When I glanced around the bedroom, their faces matched mine, marred with saddened tears. Simultaneously, they gathered around me, and we hugged and let our emotions flow as I expelled all my hurt and pain to the women I loved the most in the world.

That was how our Christmas Eve morning went. While they agreed that I was correct in forgiving Kinston, they now understood why it pained me so much and why I chose not to rekindle our relationship. Though yesterday, and honestly, the entire week, had been emotionally tumultuous, it was also cleansing. This morning, I woke up feeling as if the weight of the world had finally been lifted from my shoulders, and regardless of the circumstances surrounding the failure of my past relationship with Nigel and the heartache of my relationship with Kinston, I was okay. I survived. And I knew then that everything would be all right. That was more than enough for me.

After I said my prayers and showered, I helped my mother prepare for our guests today, which I was looking forward to, even Joel and my brother-in-love, Kannon. Yeah, I'd forgiven him and the other crew too since I was confident, they learned about all of this the same time that Kinston did, which was recently. Jesus was proud of his child this good Christmas Day.

Nissi and Aquila came by early to help Mama and me finish the pies and cakes. We were all in the kitchen talking, laughing, and baking when my dad's voice bellowed for us to come into the living room where he was watching the sports channel, of course. Even on Christmas, my father didn't take a break from his sports. We all filtered into the living room when he turned the volume up on the television.

"Listen." It was his one-word response to our questioning stares.

The sports news reported Jah's three-game suspension stemming from the brawl he instigated with Kinston. The news went on to state that the fight began over a rumor of infidelity, which was denied by Lilah Michaels, Jah's soon-to-be ex-wife. It also revealed that Lilah was in custody negotiations with Kinston after it was determined that the child she shared with Jah was actually Kinston's from their past relationship over thirteen years ago. Though the charges were dropped by the pub owner and the police department, the question of the damages still remained unsettled.

My dad glanced over at me. "You know I put my baby girls before any man, and whatever you decide with Kinston is your choice. I'm just letting you know that if you have a change of heart, I won't object."

I turned surprised eyes to my father. When he came home and saw me in a ball of tears, I just knew he was going to prison that night, so his change of heart threw me for a loop. The joy of Christmas must be infecting everyone. Before I could respond to him, my mother placed her hands on my shoulders and squeeze-hugged me from behind.

"Sometimes, the best intentions go awry. If it's right, your heart and your mind will align. Trust that."

Aquila and Nissi giggled at our parents, trying to make a love connection for me. When our mother waltzed back into the kitchen, my sisters walked up beside me. Nissi playfully knocked my hip with hers.

"You heard Mama. He's a good man, Savannah," she cackled slyly, much to my chagrin, quoting the famous line from the movie *Waiting to Exhale*.

"If you don't get your TikToking self away from me," I chided with a stubborn grin.

Aquila patted Nissi's hand. "Come on, sis, before Angela lights up on you." As they passed by me going into the kitchen, Aquila leaned into my ear and teased, "A *good* man."

I turned around and popped them with my hand towel as they scurried away. Shaking my head, I walked over to my dad and hugged him. "That news report may not have changed my mind, but it piqued my curiosity. Still, it's good to know that you trust my decisions."

"Plus, I know their father. Those Jordan boys come from good stock. Better stock than that punk Nigel."

"Ooh, just when I thought the season's good tidings and cheer had overcome you."

"Yeah, well, baby Jesus, Jesus on the cross, and resurrected Jesus would all have to descend from heaven to change my mind about that punk."

Falling into him in a fit of laughter, I hugged him tightly. "OMGeee, Daddy . . . Let me finish helping Mama because you're a whole mess."

"All right. Love you, baby girl."

With that, I trudged back to finish helping with the dessert portion of Christmas dinner. We continued our gleeful baking and Christmas carol-singing until everyone began to arrive. Besides Aquila's family and Kannon, a couple of my parents' friends were set to arrive. Nia was coming since her parents opted to take a cruise, and Ciara and Zach, Nissi's best friend and husband, were coming over since they didn't want to go out of town to visit their families due to their work schedules.

As they rolled in, I went to change into my Christmas outfit, a red, form-fitted, off-the-shoulder sweater dress with cream knee-high boots. I pulled my curly tresses up into a cute, messy bun and even added a small face beat with sexy lashes because . .

. Why the hell not? After feeling down this week, I embraced my lifted spirit with a pick-me-up.

Before I left to mingle with the guests, I pulled out my laptop and did a little research because that's what I mastered personally and professionally . . . finding out the truth. Before I realized it, forty minutes had passed, so I closed the laptop and hurried to where the festivities were taking place.

"I thought we had to come to rescue you," my mother said curtly before kissing my cheek. "But don't you look cute."

"Yasss, sis!" Nia approached with a hug. "You didn't have to flex so hard on the girls," she bantered. "Got me over here ready to go home and rethink my life."

"Girl, stop. You look gorgeous." I admired her ensemble of black leather pants and a cream-colored crop sweater.

I greeted my parents' friends, Kannon, and then played with my nephews while Aquila changed her clothing. It didn't slide past any of us that Joel had dropped the children off and left. I guess the Grinch in him was still disgruntled with the family—which received no objection from us. We weren't particularly enthusiastic to spend time with him either, especially Kannon. Once Ciara and Zach arrived, we were already heavily involved with our Christmas charades game. They came in, grabbed a mug of Nissi's specialty eggnog, and joined in the fun.

"Ooh, Santa coming down the chimney!" Nia yelled.

Kannon circled his arms for her to continue as she and Nissi pondered what else it could be.

"Up on the rooftop!" Ciara shouted.

"That's it!" my mother yelled.

Kannon tossed his head back in defeat. "Babe, come on. How did you *not* get that?"

"Well, nobody told my bestie to come through shooting Steph Curry threes out the gate," Nissi joked as Ciara held up three fingers in the universal "okay" symbol and blew on them.

The entire room roared, and then the doorbell rang. My father stood to answer it, but I shooed him back to his seat since I was closer. "I've got it. It's probably Joel anyway," I leaned close to his ear to murmur.

My dad rolled his eyes. "Then you *definitely* can answer it."

I quickly trotted to the door as they started the next round of charades. When I opened it, instead of it being Joel, I was shocked to find Kinston standing at the door looking extra scrumptious. *Geezus.* His fitted, cream-colored turtleneck shirt adorned with his signature gold chain links paired with fitted black pants, a single-breasted red wool trench coat, and red and white high-top Air Force Ones made him appear as Father Christmas coming to deliver all the holiday cheer I needed. The same way I was eye-fucking him, he was eye-fucking me, evidenced by his low-hanging lids and his famous lip bite at the corner of his mouth.

"Kinston, what are you doing here?"

He licked his lips and then wiped a hand down his face as if to wash away the longing etched in his gaze. "Before you broke up with me, I had an invitation for Christmas dinner, and I was hoping that since we are kind of like family, it would still stand." When I didn't readily answer, he fanned out his arms. "Please don't make me be subjected to watching *Miracle on 34th Street* for the millionth time at my pops' house."

I attempted to hide my giggle behind my fingers.

"That's funny to you?" he said with a dazzling smile.

Stepping back, I waved him inside. "Come on in because that would be a travesty." I was well aware of his father's infatuation with the local news, westerns, and the only Christmas movie he ever watched. That was Papa Kain for you.

Dipping his head to enter, he glided inside past me, and the whiff of his cologne almost took me to glory. *God, give me strength.* When I closed the door and turned around, he was still standing in the foyer instead of heading farther into the house to join the others.

"Do you mind if we talk?"

"Kinston," I whined, exasperated by the discussion of our woes.

He placed a hand up to stop my protests. "I'm not going to discuss anything about our breakup. I just wanted to give you something away from the group."

Gesturing for him to proceed, I waved my hand for him to go ahead.

He placed his hand inside the pocket of his trench coat and retrieved a blue box. His solemn eyes found mine as he gently tossed the box in his hand. "I got this for you when I thought we'd spend the holiday together as a couple. I only say that because if you feel this is inappropriate and want me to return it, I will, but if you would accept it, I still very much want you to have it. It's . . . umm . . . It's from my heart to yours."

Outstretching my hand, he placed the box inside of it. Slowly, I lifted the lid of the box, and as soon as I examined the contents, I covered my mouth with a gasp. Tears instantly flowed as I softly wailed. It was a silver necklace with a pair of rose gold baby footprints with a diamond at the heel of the feet encased in a circle with the words "Mommy of an angel" engraved on it. The card the necklace was attached to read: *I carried you every second of your life, and I will love you every second of mine.*

Fanning my face, I gazed up at Kinston, who appeared so scared that he might've bolted out of the door if it were still open.

"It's too much, isn't it? I'm so sorry, Angela—"

Before he could finish his sentence, I rushed into his arms and kissed him as if my life depended on his lips for my next breath. At first, I caught him off guard as he stood there, but it didn't take him long to pull me into his broad form and return the lip-lock with heated fervor. He had one hand holding my neck and the other wrapped around my waist as I wrapped my arms around his neck, burrowing deeper into our affection.

"Angela, are you—"

My dad's words stopped short at the sight before him. It wasn't until he cleared his throat that it dawned on either of us that someone else was present in the foyer. When we disconnected, I peeked over Kinston's shoulder to see the shocked faces of my parents staring at us.

"Sorry," I apologized to them before hiding my face in Kinston's chest in embarrassment.

Kinston thought it was humorous as he kissed the top of my head and then turned, shielding me from my parents. "Evening, Mr. and Mrs. Richards. I apologize for disrupting your dinner, but would you mind if I had a few moments with Angela? And, umm, when we're done speaking, I hope that dinner invitation still stands for me."

My parents blinked rapidly, staring back and forth from us to each other, baffled as to how to respond to his question.

"Umm, I guess. Sure, it's fine with us . . . right?" my mother stumbled.

"Yeah, if it's okay with Angela, I mean," my dad added.

"Thank you," he said to them and turned back to me. He took off his coat and placed it around my shoulders. "Let's sit in my car and talk for a minute." He moved to the door and opened it. "You ready, Beautiful?"

Staring at him like a starstruck teenager, I exhaled. "Yeah," I purred airily.

With that, he motioned me outside and followed me. Once on the porch, he placed the necklace around my neck. I picked up the charm, caressing it between my fingertips in admiration. This was the most thoughtful gift anyone had ever given me. Kinston took my other hand and led me to his SUV. Once he opened the passenger door and I climbed inside, he hopped into the driver's side. Before he could speak, I asked him if I could. He motioned his hand, granting me the floor.

"First, I want to thank you for this gift. You don't know how much this means to me. How healing this is to my mind and soul." I clutched the charm. "I feel as though my little one is right here with me." My eyes fluttered closed as I placed my other hand on my belly.

Kinston softly swiped away the lone tear I didn't notice was careening down my cheek. "But I do, Beautiful," he interjected. "It's how I felt when you gifted me that portrait."

With a soft coo, I kissed the inside of his palm. "Can I make a confession?"

"Absolutely. No judgment."

Collapsing against the seat, I shifted so I could face him head-on. "The reason I pushed you away was because it hurt me to my core that I trusted you with such precious information about the loss of my child, and you didn't trust me in that same way. It felt like a betrayal."

Kinston's face fell with understanding. Likewise, he turned his body to face me. "I'm sorry I made you feel that way. You're my Queen. Please know I never meant to hurt you. Angela, I didn't readily tell you, not just because I was trying to deal with the news myself but also because I felt I had to protect you. I recently learned that you lost your child. It felt cruel to turn around and tell you that I found out I had one. I only wanted to figure out a way to tell you without hurting you. That's all."

The rose-colored lens in which I'd viewed the situation fell off. With this gift and a new outlook, I could view the entire situation and Kinston with a fresh new sight. For me, he wore his feelings on his sleeve, and I could sense his love and truth seeping through his soul's fabric.

Exhaling, I held out my hand with my pinky finger crooked up. "Let's promise to always go to each other first, no matter how difficult or hurtful it will be. Like you said, we have to lean on us."

With a gleaming smile, he looped his pinky finger with mine and said, "I promise." When I locked mine to seal it, he yelled, "CMB!"

"We all we got!" We yelled together in hysterics.

"I knew you were my person!" I pumped my fist in the air, amped at his quick-witted usage of the quote from the movie *New Jack City*.

He licked his lips, and his once good-natured gaze turned mischievous. "Oh yeah, I'm your person, huh?"

Curling my forefinger for him to come to me, I nodded. "My *only* person."

He leaned over and captured my lips before muttering against them. "And you're my one and only person, Beautiful."

Our kiss turned passionate, and when his lips touched the spot on my neck, I hurriedly pulled back. "Wait, baby, we can't."

He fell back, kicking like a kid. "We may have to ditch this motherfuckering dinner because your man's about to catch the blue balls for real. I *need* you."

Feigning nonchalance, I piped. "We worked too hard on that meal not to partake." He groaned at my stance. "But before we do, I also have a gift for you. Not the gift I purchased for you because that's under the tree at my house, but another one."

He eyed me curiously. "What's that?"

"Well, I was going to reach out to you tomorrow when I could give you my other gift, but since you're here now, I have some information to pass along." That made him sit up straight and tune in. "When I saw the news today, it mentioned that Lilah debunked the rumor that she had an affair with you, but I remember you said she told you that's the lie that she told Jah. That made me wonder why a married woman would tell her husband that she was having an affair. The first thought was that it gave her a reason to bring up the paternity of her daughter, but the second was if she were upset about something else. It sounded like it could've been a revenge lie. So, I used my little paralegal research fingers to investigate a little further.

"Come to find out, they are getting a divorce because Jah fathered a baby last year by a seventeen-year-old girl. The parents of the girl accepted hush money to keep him out of prison because, apparently, he didn't know she was underage and also to keep the secret from Lilah, who found out anyway. Next thing you know, she files for divorce and makes up a lie to bring up the paternity of Fawn. Now, that last part is pure speculation, but I bet every dollar in my bank account that's how dragging you into this got started. Anyway, I felt the information would serve you well regarding some of this legal bartering you need about the fight with Jah."

The way his eyes ballooned let me know this was news to him. He banged on his steering wheel. "I *knew* there was a reason. That's what being foul gets you. Damn, and you found all that out for me?"

I dusted my shoulder. "I *am* the best researcher and paralegal in this city, baby. All I have to do is mention Pearson. My access is limitless. One text to him to ask for the lawyer to give me a peek at some sealed documents, and it's done." I snapped my fingers. "Merry Christmas, baby."

"Merry Christmas, indeed. Damn, my Queen is a boss!" We high-fived. "Come here, girl, and give me some."

We leaned into each other for a few pecks.

Finally, he opened his car door. "Now that we've talked and blessed each other with gifts, we better head inside."

I halted him, my mind on more erotic thoughts. "Wait a minute. I thought my man said he was getting the blue balls."

He closed the door. "I did."

I leaned over and unzipped his pants. Then I slipped my hand inside the opening of his boxers and pulled out a familiar friend. "Then as your woman, it's my duty to handle that."

He pressed the side button to lean his seat back and made room for me. "Shidd, you can handle anything you want, Beautiful."

My head tilted over, and his semierect girth disappeared into my hungry mouth. Humming, I caught my rhythm quickly as I bobbed up and down until he was standing in full salute.

"Shidd, Angelaaa," Kinston stretched my name.

"Mmm," I groaned my pleasure of his taste and thickness.

Wetness poured from the corners of my mouth and droplets from the corners of my eyes as I forced myself to continue suctioning him deeper and deeper into my cavernous gorge. His pants grew heavier and louder as I continued my pursuit. When I began two-hand fisting him, I felt him lifting out of the seat from the indulgence as his hands gripped my hair, moving my head with the cadence.

"Oh, shidd, Beautiful. I ain't never had my . . . mmm," he grunted. "My toes. Oh, shidd. Oh, shidd. Queen, I'm fucking . . . coming," he bellowed with the roar of a lion.

The gush of his volcanic eruption flowed into my mouth, and I sucked and swallowed it all until the very last drop. When I felt his sack release the tension, I released him and licked my tongue up his shaft to clean up any remaining remnants as he stared at me with lazy and satisfied eyes.

Once I'd tucked him back inside his boxers, I sat back and smiled at him, my face a beautiful mess. "Better?"

His hungry stare told me he was better but not finished. "We're going in here to eat this meal, and as soon as your plate touches the sink, we're leaving. Your house. My house. I don't give a damn if it's your parents' house. I am burying my dick inside you tonight. Understood?"

"Understood," I quickly agreed, his authoritativeness turning me on.

He kissed my swollen lips, and then his lowered lids focused only on me. "I love you."

Licking the tip of my tongue up his lips, I parroted, "And I love you. Now, give me some napkins before I go back in there to face my daddy."

Chapter Thirty-Two

KINSTON

ONE MONTH LATER

Even though it was a cold and cloudy day, I felt like the sun beamed brightly on me as I buttoned up my suit jacket and exited my attorney's office. Today was filled with one legal meeting after another, but all of them were victorious for me. The pep in my step was lighter as I strode to my Range Rover and climbed inside.

As soon as I closed my door, I bowed my head. "Thank you, God. Thank you, Mama," I praised before yelling out in exuberance. There was only one person I wanted to contact immediately, and as I pulled out of the parking lot, my phone connected to my Bluetooth. I asked Siri to call the only person on my mind.

"Hey, baby. How did everything go?" Angela's sweet voice floated through the airwaves of my speaker.

"Baby, thank you. You were absolutely correct. I presented my lawyer with the information you provided me, and Jah and his attorney were so flabbergasted. I wish you could've seen their faces."

"If your excitement is any indication, I can imagine. But go on," she urged, just as giddy as I was.

"Jah is going to pay for all the damages at the pub, which amounted to twelve thousand dollars, my attorney's fees, and

I'm getting ten stacks for intentional infliction of physical and emotional distress and defamation of character. He's looking at upward of forty grand because these attorney fees ain't cheap. On top of that, I'll be getting a public apology."

"I told you."

"You did. Thank you for proposing I pursue damages. My attorney was like . . . Does she want to come work for me?" We laughed together. "When that meeting ended, Jah looked sick. I never desired revenge for anything that he did other than to beat him senseless, but this was Karma's payback tenfold."

"Exactly. Karma beat him senseless for you and then paid you to witness it."

I couldn't help but smile. I wasn't even petty in real life, but Angela had enough in her for both of us, and I wasn't mad at it. The most gratifying part was that I never had to cross paths with Jah again. And I let all my ill will toward him go. Life was doing a decent job of repaying him far better than I ever could, but I was collecting my ten stacks before I fully turned his ass over to life.

"I'm going to put five stacks of that into savings for Fawn, and the other five stacks are going toward a nice vacation for you and me."

"Aww, baby, you don't have to do that."

"Yes, I do, and moreover, I *want* to do that. Either that or take you on a shopping spree. It's whatever you want to do with *your* five stacks. I got you."

"If you want me to give you some head tonight, just say that," she joshed, sexily moaning into the phone.

"Oh yeah, I *definitely* want that tonight." I paused before I uttered, "Every night if I can."

My mind drifted to my previous thoughts about the direction of our relationship prior to our brief breakup. With everything that had transpired, I decided not to ask Angela to move in with me. I'd just gotten back into her good graces and with the new dynamic with Fawn, it just didn't feel like the right time. Best believe, when the time *was* right, nothing would stop me from having an all-access pass to twenty-four-seven Angela Richards.

"Silly man," she howled. "What about your other meeting?"

"You're the one that sidetracked me with that nasty talk. No complaints," I chortled. "Anyway, my knowledge of that information worked out for me with Lilah. She also doesn't want Jah's secret exposed because she feels it would sully her name and ruin her settlement. So, she agreed to all my terms. Jah will have no more contact with my child, especially given his indiscretions. I now have joint custody of Fawn with alternating holidays. We're splitting her expenses fifty-fifty, and last but not least, Fawn's name change must be completed in thirty days. Fawn Marie Michaels will rightfully be changed to Fawn Marie Jordan."

"Yes," Angela shouted, the joy pinging through every decibel of the surround sound in my vehicle. "We have to celebrate."

"You read my mind, Beautiful. Tonight, I'm going to have Fawn. She wants to go see the Christmas light show before it leaves. I want you to come. It's time the two loves of my life meet each other."

She paused briefly before asking me, "Kinston, are you sure?"

"I've never been more sure of anything in my life."

I paced around the house, trying to busy myself to keep my nerves at bay, but it wasn't working. You'd think I was preparing to meet Angela's father instead of her meeting my daughter. I wasn't even this uptight then. Granted, I already knew her father, but the point was I couldn't believe I was fearful of this introduction. But the more I considered it, I understood why. What if Fawn hated

Angela? What if Angela decided she didn't want to be with a man who had a child? So many negative "what-ifs" were running through my mind that my worries were about to aggravate my always carefree daughter.

"Dad!" she shrieked, stopping me in my tracks. "It's going to be fine. Can you please sit down? You're about to give me a headache just watching you."

I would've sat down, but I couldn't. Not because I was worried about the introduction any longer but because this was the first time Fawn had called me dad. I stood stoic in disbelief of what I'd heard. The thump in my chest filled with unfathomable joy. Slowly, I moved to the sofa, where she sat listening to music on her iPhone.

"Kiddo," I called out to her, garnering her attention. "You . . . You called me Dad."

She shrugged. "Because that's who you are," she surmised and returned to her phone.

It's just that simple. I think that's what makes children the realest humans ever. They don't make a big deal out of things that could be much better if we kept it simple. Even with that, I couldn't help but wrap my arm around her shoulder and hug her.

She looked up at me, giving me a very teenage side-eye. "Now, *you're* making it weird."

Just as quickly, I relinquished her. "Okay, my bad. I'll be cool."

When the doorbell rang, I almost floated on cloud nine to answer it. I kept calm long enough to do a celebration dance away from her so I could keep my cool status intact. When I opened the door, Angela stood looking every bit as nervous as I had just minutes ago. When I ushered her inside, we kissed each other.

"Just a word of advice. Leave your nerves at the door. You'll make it weird," I advised, using Fawn's words to offer Angela.

"Got it. No weirdness."

Fawn stood and smiled at Angela when we walked into the living room. Before I could get a word in edgewise, Fawn took charge by extending her hand. "Hi, I'm Fawn Jordan, and you must be Angela."

Angela blinked with shock before taking her hand and shaking it. "Why, yes, I am. Angela Richards. It's nice to meet you, Fawn."

"You too. I figured I'd do the honors because Dad has been so nervous about our meeting. He acts as if he doesn't talk about you all the time. 'Angela this' and 'Angela that.' I feel like I already know you."

Angela burst into laughter. "Same."

Fawn's eyes bucked. "He talks about me?"

Angela leaned forward. "All the time. I think he really loves you."

She giggled. "Then he big loves you because he *never* stops yapping about you. Yeah, you got him down bad."

I stood back with my arms folded across my chest at this little tag-team duo. "Hmm, I *am* right here. And ain't nobody down bad. Furthermore, what do you know about down bad?"

They looked at each other and fell into a barrage of giggles. Then Angela leaned into her and whisper-yelled, "No worries. We'll talk later." They gave each other exaggerated winks.

"You two little comedians should take this show on the road," I quipped as we gathered our things. "Let's head out to avoid some of this traffic."

My two girls bounded out ahead of me, and as I was locking up, the most beautiful incident unfolded before me.

"Miss Angela," Fawn called out, looking back at Angela. "Do you like Sia?"

"OMG, I *love* her music," Angela answered, awe dancing in her eyes.

"Because I'm unstoppable." They sang loudly in excited unison and gave each other girly high-fives.

The remainder of their conversation was lost on me as they entered my SUV as if they were long-lost bosom buddies. This entire time, I had been so worried about the negative "what-ifs" that I hadn't allowed myself to consider the positives. What if they adored each other and formed a bond? Just as they were doing right now. I should've known those two kindred spirits would connect. And as I walked to my car, watching my two leading ladies sing their hearts out, I knew.

Epilogue

ANGELA

As I swayed back and forth, I couldn't help but reminisce about this day a year ago . . . club-hopping from venue to venue all night, drinking, and enjoying my girls. I was still in the club now. However, this year, I was celebrating with my girls *and* my man. Our usual crew was out together in full force, partying and enjoying life as I brought in my thirty-first birthday.

"Are you having fun tonight?" Kinston asked as I rocked in his arms to Musiq Soulchild's "So Beautiful."

"Yes, baby. Whenever I'm with you, it's always a great time." I hugged him closer. "The shopping spree, the spa day, the dinner, and tonight with our family and friends, you've outdone yourself."

"And I say I haven't done enough, but we'll get there in due time." He kissed the top of my head.

This year, this particular club of choice was more our speed. The thriving Indie Lovers Club. Though they didn't have a live event, they often hosted smooth R&B nights, which was what we were attending. The only alcohol served was beer, wine, and cocktails. Classy and sophisticated.

Perhaps I'd spoken too soon on the classy and sophisticated thought because we heard a commotion, which caused everyone in the club to turn their attention to what was happening. At the sight, my mouth dropped before a smirk crossed my face.

Security was in the process of kicking out of the club none other than Nigel, his wife, and some other man. From my ear hustling, the tea was that Nigel's wife had gotten caught cheating on Nigel again—emphasis on the *again*. And Nigel was there to confront the pair. It was so ironic that this birthday had similarities to my last one yet was so different.

It didn't take long for everyone in the club to turn their attention to the commotion. I wasn't surprised when my sisters and Nia walked up beside Kinston and me while we were wrapped in each other's arms also watching the scene unfold.

"Did you hear what I heard?" Nia asked aloud.

A collective "Mmm Hmm" filtered through the rest of us before we said in unison, "*Again.*"

Just as the police and bouncers were clearing Nigel, Leticia, and her most recent fling out of the door, Nigel's eyes somehow found and landed on me. He scanned me up and down in stunned approval, before embarrassment clouded his features as he passed a glance between Leticia and me. In the past, I would've activated my petty, but tonight, and for the first time, quite frankly, I didn't give a damn. Kinston, however, initiated all the petty by offering a quick wave with a smirk to Nigel, before bending over and planting a succulent kiss on my lips. Although it wasn't necessary, my man put a smile on my face and a fire in my crotch with that move. I won't lie, though. Seeing Nigel's countenance fall after witnessing said kiss as he stormed out of the doors made up for the past two hellish birthdays. Year thirty-one was already treating me right. Oh well. He received the exact type of wife he deserved, and I couldn't be happier for both of them.

After Dade County's Finest safely escorted out the rowdy crew, Kinston looked down at me and smiled.

"Seems Karma has struck again."

"And I got the pleasure to watch for free."

Kinston turned serious. "Did it bother you? Seeing him."

As I gazed at my wonderful man who had done nothing but shower me with all his heart had to offer, a man who loved me senselessly sometimes, relentlessly all the time, and would love me boundlessly for a lifetime, I was able to say unequivocally, "Not in the slightest."

It had been three months, and everything was going strong. Kinston had picked up more celebrity clientele behind the whole scandal with Jah. I'd gotten a hefty raise to stay with Pearson since a few attorneys tried to poach me, and I'd made significant strides with my mental health with the help of Dr. Abrams. Kinston and Fawn's relationship had flourished beautifully and continued to do so daily, and she was my best buddy. I loved that little girl with my entire heart to the point that I'd even go head-to-head with Kinston about her. Yeah, she was his daughter or whatever, but she was mine too. Even Lilah and I had come to a mutual understanding, and she agreed not to disrespect me or my relationship with Kinston. I wish Kinston or I could take credit for that, but it was courtesy of Fawn. My best buddy let her mama know under no uncertain terms was she to come between her dad and Ms. Angela. She was our number one fan. For the first time, I could honestly say I was at my best mentally, emotionally, and even physically since I'd hit my goal of losing fifty pounds. I was still thick as a Snickers, but not thicker than one. And as happy as I was for Nigel's fated marriage with Leticia, I was truly the happiest for me, and in addition, I had a man who complemented me in every way.

When Kinston guided me off the floor back to our VIP section, our crew was waiting with wineglasses in their hands. Kinston picked up two and handed me one as the bottle girls came out with champagne bottle sparklers. Then a waiter rolled out a birthday cake.

"Glasses up, everyone," he announced as we raised them. "On the count of three, everyone give it up for my Queen. One, two, three..."

"Happy Birthday, Angela!" they said in unison as we clinked glasses and drank up.

I placed my glass down and began to thank everyone when I noticed everyone gasping and getting hyped. When I turned around, Kinston was down on one knee with an open box holding an engagement ring, and the artist Vedo's hit song, "Forever," serenaded us in the background.

"Kinston!" I bellowed. "What is this?" My voice was shaky as I processed what he was doing.

"This is due time."

As it came to the chorus, Kinston mimicked the words, the most important ones landing straight in my heart.

"Let's make it forever, girl. All you gotta do is say... Yeah, yeah, yeah," Kinston sang. "Angela, I knew that you were it for me the moment I saw you. And you didn't make it easy for me. Then when I had my opportunity, I almost fumbled the pass, but the woman you are gave me one more chance. I'm not perfect. I won't always get it right. But I promise you that for you, I'll always try. I'll never stop showing up for you. And I'll love you... forever. Will you do me the honor of becoming Mrs. Kinston Jordan?"

"Yes!" I screamed. Tears crowded my eyes, and our crew and the entire club cheered.

The DJ gave us a shout-out as Kinston slid the ring on my finger, and we sealed our pending nuptials with a kiss. When I turned around, I stuck my hand out to my girls as we all hopped up and down, admiring the ring.

Starting from Nissi, Aquila, and Nia, I warned. "You all know you better get fit for those dresses!"

Nissi and Kannon glanced at each other. Then Kannon asked, "Bro and sis, how soon do you all plan on having the wedding?"

We looked at him, confused, until Nissi placed a hand on her belly and rubbed it. Aquila and I looked at each other and then at Nissi.

"Sis, are you . . . ?"

Nissi nodded. "Yep. Two months pregnant today."

We hugged her, gushing over our soon-to-be newest edition to the family as Kinston gave Kannon a brotherly hug, and the other guys dapped him and offered congratulations. We should've known when she only drank water, claiming to have an upset stomach.

"It's all kinds of celebrations tonight!" Nia shouted. "Birthdays, engagements, pregnancies—"

Aquila tilted her wineglass in the air. "Divorces."

Collectively, we turned to her. As usual, Joel was absent, but we assumed it was because he no longer participated in group outings with us.

"Oh, sis," Nissi and I said, rushing to her side.

She shook her head. "No, I'm not upset. I'm . . ." she contemplated for a second and then let out a small chortle. "Relieved," she shouted happily. "Oh God, I'm *so* relieved." Her outburst was so comical we couldn't help but join in.

"Are you sure you're all right?" I probed further to be sure.

She picked up a spoon and yelled, "How did Taye Diggs say it in that movie?" She clinked the glass with the spoon and said, "*We're celebrating . . . my divorce!*"

Nia shook her head. "Like I said, a night of celebrations."

Our crew continued talking about Nissi's pregnancy and Aquila planning a divorce party when Kinston pulled me aside.

"We sure know how to party, don't we?"

"Facts!" I pointed at him. "And honestly, I'm happy for all of us."

"So, are you ready to do this, Future Mrs. Jordan?"

Cupping his chin in my hand, I pecked his lips. "Forever."

THE END

Please stay tuned for Aquila's story: *Love on Board*. As my gift to you, enjoy the following snippet from my upcoming book.

DEDICATION

This is dedicated to the Black girls who do not feel seen and the Black men who do not feel heard. I see you. I hear you. I love you because I am you.

ACKNOWLEDGMENTS

My Forever Thank Yous

To my God, the creator and blesser of this precious gift of writing. Without you, there is no Aries Skye, but with you, I can touch the skies.

To my backbone, greatest supporter, and number one fan, and my forever... my husband. You inspire me to write these whimsical fairy tales because you ensure I live it every day. I love you.

To my precious womb fruits, you are my reasons, and I pray I continue to inspire you to follow your dreams the same way you encourage me to follow mine.

To Black Odyssey Media, I may have given these characters a voice, but you gave them a home.

To Black, BlackEncryption Designs—my friend, my brother, you are a phenom. You produce legendary covers through your extraordinary vision.

To model Tina Rich thank you for gracing my cover and being my muse for Angela Richards.

To Black Queens Who Write, you ladies propel me to give my best. Your sisterhood is everything to me.

To my Skye's Sweeties: Crystal, Isatta, Queen Jefe, Tameka, Jaleesa, Shar, Robyn, Megan, and Kita, you ladies are my MVPs. I cannot say thank you enough for all that you selflessly do.

To my Sweethearts: the readers, bloggers, friends, and family who tirelessly support all things Aries Skye, I am grateful to you all. You opened your readers' space for my words, and that is more than I could've ever dreamed of.

To Kinston and Angela, your story will forever resonate within my heart. Thank you for allowing me to be the vessel.

OTHER BOOKS BY ARIES SKYE

Love on the Ninth Floor—Available Now
Love on Board—Coming Soon

Follow me on social media @ariesskye_ on Instagram
and @AuthorAriesSkye on Facebook and TikTok
Visit my website: https://www.authorariesskye.carrd.co

PLEASE ENJOY THIS PREVIEW OF LOVE ON BOARD.

Prologue

AQUILA

*P*ULL YOURSELF TOGETHER. Internally, I coached myself.

I parked my G-Wagon in the empty church parking lot, flipped down my visor, and peered into the mirror. Inhaling, I breathed deeply in and out as I closed my eyes and tried to center myself. I couldn't fathom how I practiced thirty minutes of yoga every day and went to the gym four days a week to *still* be this stressed out.

I'd left the house twenty minutes ago, determined to do as I had planned and have a girls' night out with my sisters. A night that I'd advised my husband of for the past month. He knew that our sisters' quality time had been limited since Nissi got married and Angela solidified her relationship with Kinston. Having been in their position, I understood. All they wanted to do was have couple time with their significant others, and I couldn't blame them. Once upon a time, I'd been in their shoes with Joel. Back when it was Joel and Aquila Oliver forever. Those days now seemed to be a far distant memory. It made me feel reduced to a group member in the Oliver clan instead of his wife and life partner, as if he were David Ruffin, and I was the Temptations. But he forgot the main rule: no one was bigger than the group. Everything, and I do mean *everything*, was centered, focused, surrounded, and concentrated on Joel and his needs and desires over anything and everyone else.

Just like tonight. He waited until he came home to announce that he was invited to some function supporting one of his mentors, and I needed to be available to attend. I was taken aback for a few reasons: his lack of asking but rather demanding, his lack of concern for who would babysit our children, and his lack of thoughtfulness over my previously discussed plans. Thank goodness our kids were already at my parents' house. After reminding him that I had planned an evening with my sisters, I slipped on my celadon, sleeveless, ankle-length bodycon dress that paired perfectly with my gold YSLs.

Rather than concede and attend the function unaccompanied or stay at home for all I cared, he began ranting about my attitude and absences of late . . . as if he had any room on his moral barometer to chastise me on one's attitude and absences. The same man that not one of my family members or friends wanted to endure. The same man who made me feel as though I were a single parent in my marriage. The same man who made me feel as though I were a single woman masquerading as a married one. I'd become accustomed to biting my tongue over the years, so much so that I had lost who I was aside from being Joel Oliver's wife-turned-handmaid. Lately, though, I'd been finding my voice more and more, and tonight had been no exception. A full-out argument ensued, with me leaving the house and heading for Angela's place—Joel and his demands be damned.

However, halfway there, I reverted to the doting wife, and guilt began to gnaw at me, not necessarily for Joel but for the guest of honor. Jansen Carlyle had helped us bail out financially when Joel's restaurants had taken an unexpected hit. Being among the elite with friends in high and well-off places fared well in dire circumstances. Jansen had been our ram in the bush, and I'd always be eternally grateful for that. Had my husband taken the liberty to notify me ahead of time, I would've gladly been present. And that's what chipped away at me now. As much as I loved my sisters, it would have felt disrespectful not to attend Jansen's soiree, given the measures he'd taken to support my family. It was for that reason that I sat in this empty lot coaxing myself into a façade so that I could support Jansen as the dutiful wife of Joel Oliver.

"You've got this, Lah. Just head home, apologize, slip into a little black dress, and do what needs to be done."

Smoothing the edges of my hair, which was perfectly pulled into a slick ponytail meeting at the nape of my neck, I cast away the negative vibes of earlier and pulled out of the lot, heading back to my house. Thankfully, my phone call to Angela went unanswered so I could disappoint her and Nissi via voicemail. As I drove, my eyes kept bouncing to the three-carat princess-cut diamond on my hand. *Be his wife.* If Joel did nothing else, he afforded our babies and me a lifestyle that most longed for, so I couldn't be upset that he wanted to honor the man who helped continue making that American Dream a reality for us. With that, I resolved to make this right with my husband.

Easing into the house, I expected Joel to be in our bedroom getting dressed for the event. When I didn't find him in our bedroom or bathroom, I went on a search for him throughout the rest of the house.

"Joel?" I called out, checking in our family room. "Humph."

Then it dawned on me. His man cave.

Schlepping toward his private mantuary, I opened the door when I heard a sound resonating from the television. "Joel, baby, I'm sor—"

The words were lodged in my throat as the entire scene unfolded in my view as if it were in slow motion. There sat my husband on the couch, jerking off to the sight of two men on the screen, straight barebacking. Tears filled my eyes as my hand flew over my mouth, trapping the wail that could barely squeak past my closing esophagus.

"Shit! Aquila!" Joel scrambled, trying to cover himself and turn off the television simultaneously. "I thought you were with your sisters."

Hot droplets fell from my rapidly blinking eyes as I tried my best to gather my bearings before I fainted. Joel had somehow managed to turn off the porn and reclothed by the time I found my voice.

"Aquila . . ."

"So, *this* is what you do while I'm not at home? Get your rocks off on gay porn?" Joel moved to touch my arms, and I swatted him away. "Don't you dare," I hissed.

His face fell as worry lines spread all over it. "Baby . . ."

"*Baby? Baby?*" The audacity of his words displayed in mine. "You're standing here with precum leaking through your slacks from watching men . . . *men* . . . have sex, and now, you want to call *me* baby?"

"Just let me explain, please. It's not like I was cheating on you."

The rage of every disrespected married woman in the history of marriage set my soul ablaze, and I reached back to the depths of before Christ and smacked the hell and probably the rest of the ejaculation out of him. His head snapped so far to the right it appeared as if I'd sprained his neck. I could only hope.

"You sorry sack of shit. When I accepted your hand in marriage, you promised this would never be an issue. You told me—*swore* to me—that you loved me and only me and that I'd never have to worry about your infatuation with men."

There it was. Our closeted bones laid bare.

Joel and I had met when we were in college through mutual friends. We'd become fast friends and eventually decided to explore being lovers. I'd broken it off with him because while I loved and cared for him, something didn't seem quite right between us. Joel had pleaded with me to give him another chance, but I didn't. We agreed to remain friends, and we did. We became the best of them, in fact. We were so close that one night, in a drunken binge in my apartment, he confessed his greatest secret. He was bisexual. Before we could delve into his admittance, we passed out in my living room, senselessly inebriated, and the next day, the encumbrance of his confession came down like the weight of the world. He tried to backpedal, but after reassuring him that our friendship was a safe space, he admitted that his confession was the truth. Though he stated he'd never cheated on me, and I'd believed him, he said that he still had urges from time to time. According to him, it wasn't every man he was attracted to, just whoever caught his eye. As far as women, he was definitely attracted to them, and he was still head over heels for me. He'd even confessed to having slept with two men in his past. One guy was during his senior year in high school during a band competition. The other guy came during the summer of his freshman year in college during a summer internship. He claimed neither was a relationship, just mutual sexual attraction and intimacy.

While I had been devastated because he didn't disclose this information before we dated and slept together, I put our friendship above my angst and disappointment. Besides, we'd both been tested and yielded negative results, so I could at least be thankful for that. But in that moment, it became painfully obvious why he insisted that we test before we had sex. He claimed that I'd been the only woman, hell, the only person he'd ever been in love with, and he wanted to ensure our safety. He'd only been the second man that I'd slept with besides my high school boyfriend after our senior prom, but I went along with it because I'd never tested after intercourse with my old boyfriend, so I could see the benefit. It only took one time to contract a disease, just as easily as it was to get pregnant after one time. Now, here we were, back here again.

"And I've kept that promise to you, Aquila." Frustration oozed from him as he scrubbed his bald head. "I've never cheated on you with a man or a woman."

"No, you just jack off to men when I'm not around!" I paced the floor. "So now, I know why our sex life has been nonexistent."

His hand flailed up as he held up his index finger to cut me off. "Don't. Don't do that. You know I've been stressed. The financial struggles we had to power through with the businesses left me drained and depressed. You know that. My focus was on securing a future for my family, and I'm sorry if intercourse and intimacy were not on my menu."

"But clearly, men and pornos *are* on your plate right now." My eyes squinted as I stalked up to him and poked him in the chest. "We haven't had any type of relations in a year, but instead of arranging quality time with me and showboating this farce of a marriage in front of your power elite friends, you'd rather bust quickies from porn hub."

"Like your rose doesn't get overtime," he seethed. "I've come home plenty of nights to hear that thump-thump buzz setting getting more action than me."

The incredulous scoff that I released echoed throughout his den of lies. "*Excuse* me for creating time to nurture *my* needs that you hadn't bothered to take care of. At least my rose time was spent thinking of you, Joel, instead of thinking of John and James, like *you*."

The reality of what was transpiring suddenly tumbled down on me, and I couldn't stop the sting of fresh, hot tears from clouding my eyes. I swallowed and blinked to no avail. A guttural wail emanated through my body as I began to shake uncontrollably. My marriage and my life had fallen apart. Only it'd been falling for a few years now. The friendship we'd built had long since withered away, and the vows we'd recited were nothing more than devalued words on paper devoid of any truth it once held. We had officially become two people joined by babies and business. This was not what he promised me; he owed me that and so much more.

His eyes and demeanor softened when I glanced at him as I leaned on the bar to keep myself supported. He looked genuinely concerned about me, an emotion I hadn't witnessed or felt from him in so long that it had appeared foreign on his features. It dawned on me how asinine it was that concern from my husband felt unnatural. He was the one person that I should be able to lean on for love, care, concern, and comfort, yet he wasn't. My parents, my sisters, my babies, and my friends had filled that void for so long that I hadn't realized that he'd vacated the spot that only he was supposed to fill. They were supposed to be the supporters. He was supposed to be my one. My person. My husband. I'd been his wife a million times over without reciprocation. And that thought shifted my heartbreak into rage.

Swiping my hand down my face to wipe away my tears, I turned unemotional and hardened eyes to him. "I stood by your side as your friend even after you weren't forthcoming about your attraction and intercourse with men before we dated and slept together. I stood by your side as your woman even after that when you begged me to give you another chance because you stated that I was the only one for you. I swallowed all your deceit and secrets because I loved you when any other woman would have left, leaving you to pray she kept your hidden desires to herself.

But I stayed. I forgave. I supported. I trusted you. I loved ... you a hell of a lot more than you were ever capable of loving me."

Droplets fell from his eyes as he sniffed and cupped his hand over his face, sliding them away. "But I do love you so much. Baby, I realize how this may seem, but you must believe it's still you for me. I still—"

I rolled my eyes, and a knowing smirk crept onto my face. I peered into his deep-set, russet eyes that once held the charm to convince me of anything short of disavowing my faith and separating from my family . . . only to feel emptiness coursing through my veins. Nothing about him could sway me. Not his dazzling Colgate smile, his creamy beige, bald head that I used to caress, or his plush beard that used to tickle places on my body that used to have me submitting to his every will. Nothing.

"Not this time, Joel. What is it that you need me for now? To ensure you're included in more of your family's business ventures? Or are you just holding on so you won't get cut from your father's will?" I exhaled. "What type of sacrificial savior must I be for your gain?"

He was stuck on stun because he knew I was correct. When Joel first asked me to marry him, I knew we weren't ready despite how much we loved each other. Initially, I'd asked to wait, but he kept pressing, so I figured that perhaps my insecurities about his past were holding me back. I loved him, and he loved me, so marriage seemed to be the next progressive move. It wasn't until the night of our wedding rehearsal dinner that another hurtful truth was revealed.

Our wedding rehearsal dinner had been one for the history books. It was filled with delicious food, beautiful family, and entertaining music. The DJ had the atmosphere poppin', and I found myself dancing from my future husband to my sisters to my entire wedding party. I was sweaty and exhausted when we finished every Black person's slide dance imaginable. Earlier, my future father-in-law had wrangled my future husband off the floor from me to talk, so I decided to grab some fresh air and locate my man.

When I languidly waltzed out on the patio and into the plush green gardens outside the restaurant, I heard Joel and his father before I saw them. I almost called out to them when I heard Mr. Oliver express his pride in Joel. I didn't want to interrupt such a precious moment, so I waited in the background for him to finish.

"Son, you don't know how proud it makes me that you've chosen Aquila to be your wife. She is a marvelous young woman and will be a wonderful and doting wife."

"Thank you, Father."

"And I'm so glad you let that other lifestyle go. I knew it was only a fad. I couldn't have my only son out here ruining the Oliver legacy. We're thoroughbreds. Now, with Aquila by your side, you'll bless your mother and me with the grandchildren we deserve."

"Can you not bring that up? I love Aquila, but it's not like you gave me much choice but to rush into marriage."

"You love her. She loves you. Where's the rush? Marriage is the natural progression of love for two young people in a relationship." He cleared his throat. "And we both know there was no way I'd pass the restaurant on to you if you continued sowing the wrong oats. There's no place for that sassiness in our family or our family business. Besides, your mother wanted me to retire early so we can travel the world." He patted him on the shoulder. "I only guided you to do the naturally right thing."

At those words, I bolted from around the corner as if someone had lit a torch on me. "Joel!" I cried out. "Is that the only reason you wanted to marry me? To obtain your father's restaurant?"

Mr. Oliver and Joel spun around at my words. He looked mortified, but not more so than me. Running over to me, Joel grabbed my hands and pleaded. "No, baby. Not at all. It's just that my father, he—"

"He wouldn't turn over his business to you until he felt secure that you'd be with a woman and not a man." The words came out softly as realization poured over me.

Mr. Oliver walked over to me, gently turning me to face him. Cupping my face, he peered into my teary eyes. "Aquila, my son loves you. So, for that, I owe you a debt of gratitude. You're the only woman he's ever loved, and quite frankly, you saved him. You shouldn't look at this as him settling but rather as him setting you up in life. As his wife, you'll have total access to all things Oliver."

"I don't care about all things Oliver. I care about Joel. I love him, and up until this moment, I thought he loved me. How can I go through with a wedding with a man who's unsure of this union because of his sexuality?" I tossed a glance at Joel, who appeared outright terrified.

"Oh no, darling," Mr. Oliver coaxed me. "He's not confused at all." He turned a stern glare at his son. "Don't you see your future wife needs you? Get over here and settle her."

Joel walked over to me, taking my hand and guiding me away from his dad. "I love you, Aquila, and yes, Father wants me to take over his business. But that doesn't negate how I feel about you. I love you. I'm sure we both would've been right where we're at sooner or later, but my father wants to retire."

"And he's going to need a wife to assist," Mr. Oliver cut in.

"Father," Joel said, exasperation lacing his tone. "Can you let me talk to my fiancée?"

"Sure, son." He came to me, attempting to comfort me by touching my arm. "Don't walk away from this opportunity. My son can and will provide a wonderful life for you." With that, he made his way back into the restaurant.

I slapped Joel before the door could close. "You used me."

"No, I did not. I love you, Aquila, but is it so bad if that comes with perks?"

"If it comes at the price of not living your truth—yes."

"My truth?" he whispered, caressing my face and leveling me with his mesmerizing aura. "My truth is that I'm completely in love with you. I have been since the moment I laid eyes on you. Have I dabbled in the past? Yes. But I only have eyes for you. I only love and am in love with you. If you take my hand in marriage, I promise you'll never have to worry about me with any other person, woman or man. I'm committed to you and the life that we're building. I'm dedicating my life to us, Qui. Please. Just trust me."

I loved that man so much he could've told me he walked on water, and I would've believed him.

"I trust you."

Joel and I stood there in a test of wills. However, I refused to be the one to give in this time. Not this time. This time, I was putting Aquila first.

"Baby, I don't know what to say. I . . . I love you," he stammered.

I closed my eyes as a solitary tear streaked down my face. "Say your truth. Not for me. For you. You love me, but you're no longer *in love* with me, Joel, and you haven't been for a long time. Free us both."

When I opened my eyes, he stared at me with a gamut of disappointment, confusion, and regret stirring in his orbs. "I . . . uh . . . I think . . . I think I want to explore . . . men."

He'd said it. Spoken his truth. Now, it was time for me to speak mine.

"And I want a divorce. Get out of my house."

WWW.BLACKODYSSEY.NET

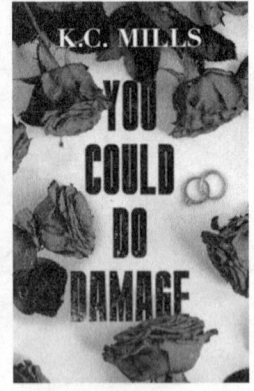